Praise for
the GOWN

"Jennifer Robson embroiders life, friendship, and hope into the somber gray world of postwar London every bit as skillfully as her seamstress heroines embroider crystal flowers into the folds of a royal wedding dress. Marvelous and moving, a vivid portrait of female self-reliance in a world racked by the cost of war."

—**KATE QUINN**, *New York Times* bestselling author of *The Alice Network*

"An unforgettable story of friendship, hardship, and hope. Robson has managed to craft a story that is personal and universal, timely and timeless. *The Gown* soars!"

—**PAM JENOFF**, *New York Times* bestselling author of *The Orphan's Tale*

"A moving story about the power of female friendship and renewal in the face of adversity. Like the good-luck sprig of heather hidden amid the embroidery on Princess Elizabeth's wedding dress, this story promises secrets and lives that bloom in unlikely ways. Perfect for fans of *The Crown*!"

—**LAUREN WILLIG**, *New York Times* bestselling author of *The English Wife*

"Once again, with an impressive depth of research, Jennifer Robson provides an enchanting glimpse into the past, each word and detail a carefully placed stitch. Told through the eyes of three compelling women, *The Gown* is a heartwarming story of friendship, resilience, and the power of heirlooms to connect people through generations, sometimes in the most unexpected ways."

—**KRISTINA McMORRIS**, *New York Times* bestselling author of *The Edge of Lost* and *Sold on a Monday*

Praise for *The Gown*

"Jennifer Robson embroiders life, friendship, and hope into the somber gray world of postwar London every bit as skillfully as her seamstress heroines embroider crystal flowers into the folds of a royal wedding dress. *The Gown* is marvelous and moving, a vivid portrait of female self-reliance in a world racked by the cost of war."

—Kate Quinn, *New York Times* bestselling author of *The Alice Network*

"In *The Gown*, Jennifer Robson illuminates with her signature meticulous historical detail and sure voice the story behind Queen Elizabeth's wedding dress. . . . An unforgettable story of friendship, hardship, and hope. Robson has managed to craft a story that is personal and universal, timely and timeless. *The Gown* soars!"

—Pam Jenoff, *New York Times* bestselling author of *The Orphan's Tale*

"A moving story about the power of female friendship and renewal in the face of adversity. Like the good-luck sprig of heather hidden amid the embroidery on Princess Elizabeth's wedding dress, this story promises secrets and lives that bloom in unlikely ways. Perfect for fans of *The Crown*!"

—Lauren Willig, *New York Times* bestselling author of *The English Wife*

"Once again, with an impressive depth of research, Jennifer Robson provides an enchanting glimpse into the past, each word and detail a carefully placed stitch. Told through the eyes of three compelling women, *The Gown* is a heartwarming story of friendship, resilience, and the power of heirlooms to connect people through generations, sometimes in the most unexpected ways."

—Kristina McMorris, *New York Times* bestselling author of *The Edge of Lost* and *Sold on a Monday*

"Embroidering a magical moment in royal history, Robson tells a heartrending story of friendship, loss, love, and redemption."

—Leslie Carroll, author of *American Princess: The Love Story of Meghan Markle and Prince Harry*

"A story of friendship, family bonds, and courage, *The Gown* is the ideal read for fans of historical fiction and royal watchers alike!"

—Brenda Janowitz, author of *The Dinner Party*

"Jennifer Robson delivers a satisfying multigenerational epic linked by the intricate embroidery used on Princess Elizabeth's wedding gown. Robson's meticulous attention to historical details—notably the intricacies of the embroidery work—is a wonderful complement to the memorable stories of Ann and Miriam, making for a winning, heartwarming tale."

—*Publishers Weekly* (starred review)

"Robson vividly brings to life these three women's struggles. Historical details about fabric, embroidery, and the royal family are well incorporated into their stories, with light romance rounding out this charming work of historical fiction."

—*Library Journal*

"A fascinating glimpse into the world of design, the healing power of art, and the importance of women's friendships."

—*Kirkus Reviews*

The Gown

Also by Jennifer Robson

Goodnight from London

Moonlight Over Paris

After the War is Over

Somewhere in France

Fall of Poppies

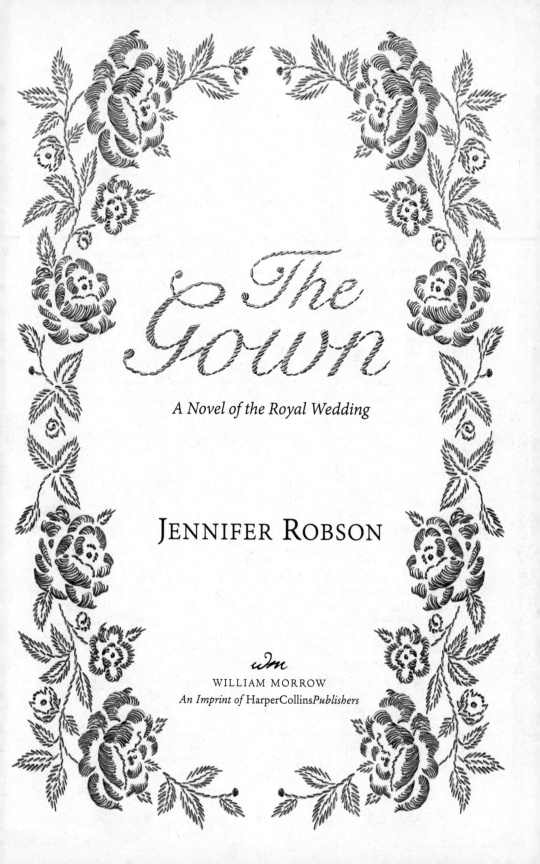

The Gown

A Novel of the Royal Wedding

JENNIFER ROBSON

WILLIAM MORROW
An Imprint of HarperCollinsPublishers

With grateful thanks and credit to the estate of Louis MacNeice for an excerpt from *Autumn Journal* (Faber & Faber).

P.S.™ is a trademark of HarperCollins Publishers.

HarperCollins books may be purchased for educational, business, or sales promotional use. For information, please email the Special Markets Department at SPsales@harpercollins.com.

FIRST EDITION

Designed by Diahann Sturge

Title page and chapter opener art © Rodica Prato

Library of Congress Cataloging-in-Publication Data

Names: Robson, Jennifer, 1970- author.
Title: The gown / Jennifer Robson.
Description: First Edition. | New York : William Morrow Paperbacks, an
    Imprint of HarperCollinsPublishers, [2019]
Identifiers: LCCN 2018060274 (print) | LCCN 2018061621 (ebook) | ISBN
    9780062674968 (E-book) | ISBN 9780062674951 (paperback)
Subjects: | BISAC: FICTION / Historical. | FICTION / Sagas.
Classification: LCC PR9199.4.R634 (ebook) | LCC PR9199.4.R634 G68 2019
    (print) | DDC 813/.6--dc23
LC record available at https://lccn.loc.gov/2018060274

ISBN 978-0-06-267495-1
ISBN 978-0-06-288427-5 (library edition)

20 21 22 23   LSC   11

In memory of
Regina Antonia Maria Crespi
1933–2017
an immigrant, a seamstress,
and a most beloved grandmother

Sleep serene, avoid the backward
Glance; go forward, dreams, and do not halt
(Behind you in the desert stands a token
Of doubt—a pillar of salt).
Sleep, the past, and wake, the future,
And walk out promptly through the open door;
But you, my coward doubts, may go on sleeping,
You need not wake again—not any more.
The New Year comes with bombs, it is too late
To dose the dead with honourable intentions:
If you have honour to spare, employ it on the living;
The dead are dead as Nineteen-Thirty-Eight.
Sleep to the noise of running water
To-morrow to be crossed, however deep;
This is no river of the dead or Lethe,
To-night we sleep
On the banks of Rubicon—the die is cast;
There will be time to audit
The accounts later, there will be sunlight later
And the equation will come out at last.

—Louis MacNeice, *Autumn Journal,* Part XXIV

The Gown

Chapter One

Ann

Barking, Essex
England
January 31, 1947

*I*t was dark when Ann left work at a quarter to six, and darker still when she reached home. Normally she didn't mind the walk from the station. It was only half a mile, and gave her a chance to clear her head at the end of the day. Tonight, though, the journey was a cheerless one, for the midwinter cold had burrowed through her coat, setting her shivering, and the soles of her shoes were so worn that she might as well have been barefoot.

But tomorrow was Saturday. If she had any time after queuing up at the butcher, she would visit the cobbler and see what he had to say. She didn't have enough coupons for anything new, and these had been resoled twice already. Perhaps she might be able to find a half-decent used pair at the next WI swap meet.

She turned onto Morley Road, the memory of countless home-comings leading her surely through the night; it would be another few days before there was any moonlight to guide her way. A yard or two more and she was at her front door. Pushing past the curtain they used to keep out drafts, she switched on the wall sconce and was relieved when light filled the vestibule. Last night the power had gone off at eight o'clock and hadn't come on again until the morning.

"Milly? It's me," she called to her sister-in-law. The sitting room was cold and dark, but appetizing smells were coming from the kitchen.

"You're late!"

"I think they were running fewer trains than usual. One way to save on fuel, I suppose. And the ones coming through were all jam-packed. I had to wait for an age before I could squeeze on."

"Did you hear it's supposed to snow again tomorrow? Imagine what that'll do to the trains."

"Don't make me think about it. At least not until I've thawed out." Ann hung her coat and hat on the wobbly rack behind the door and pulled off her shoes. "Have you seen my slippers?"

"I brought them in here with me to warm."

She switched off the light and, bringing her bag along, crossed through the sitting room and into the kitchen. Milly was at the cooker, her attention fixed on the contents of a small saucepan. "I'm just heating up the potatoes and veg from yesterday, along with the last bit of the gammon." She turned her head to offer a quick smile, then bent to open the door of the oven. "Here they are," she said, and handed over Ann's slippers. "Warmed through and not a scorch mark in sight."

"You are a dear. Ooh—that feels lovely."

"I knew it would. What's that you've got there?"

Ann was at the sink, gently unwrapping a small clay pot from a twist of newspaper. Brushing off some loose soil that was clinging to its rim, she lifted the pot so Milly might see the plant within. "It's heather. From the queen."

"The queen gave *you* a pot of heather?"

"Not just me. We all got one. Well, all of us who worked on those last set of gowns. The ones she and the princesses are taking to South Africa. There was ever so much beadwork, and one of them—she's wearing it to a ball for Princess Elizabeth's twenty-first birthday—was nothing but sequins. Millions of them, it felt like. So she had these sent down from Scotland to thank us."

"It doesn't look like much," Milly said, wrinkling her nose.

"Haven't you seen heather in bloom? It's ever so pretty. And this is white heather. For good luck, one of the girls said."

Milly returned to the cooker and resumed stirring. "I think this is warmed through. Can you set the table while I dish up?"

"I will, and I'll switch on the wireless, too. We can listen to the seven o'clock news on the Light Programme."

The royal family had left for South Africa earlier in the day, and their leave-taking would certainly be at the top of the news. No hopping into a cab with a pair of suitcases for the king and queen. Instead, according to the papers, the royal tour would begin with a carriage procession from Buckingham Palace to Waterloo Station, where the king, queen, princesses, and dozens of retainers and servants would be given a formal farewell by a host of dignitaries before boarding a train to Portsmouth. And the dresses, suits, and gowns that Ann had helped to make would be part of that historic journey.

She had worked for Mr. Hartnell for eleven years. There was no reason for her to still find her heart racing when she thought of her handiwork being worn by the queen. Her family and friends had stopped being impressed by it long ago. Some, like Milly, all but groaned when she came home with stars in her eyes.

She couldn't help it, though. It *was* exciting. She was an ordinary girl from Barking, the sort of girl who usually ended up working in a factory or shop for a few years before getting married and settling into life as a wife and mum. Yet by some twist of fate she had ended up working for the most famous dress designer in Britain, had risen to one of the most senior positions in his embroidery workroom, and had helped to create gowns that millions of people admired and coveted.

It had been a near thing, too. When she'd finished school at fourteen, there'd been no money for anything like secretarial college. So she'd gone to the labor exchange, and a gray-faced woman had set a list of jobs in front of her. They'd all sounded awful. Trainee shirt machinist, assistant nursemaid, restaurant cashier. She'd turned the page, ready to give up, and that's when she'd seen it:

Apprentice embroiderer, central London, training
given.

"This one," she'd said shyly, pointing to the listing. "'Apprentice embroiderer.' What does that mean?"

"Exactly what it says. Let me see the reference number. Right . . . it's at Hartnell, where the queen has all her clothes made."

"The *queen*?"

"Yes," the woman said, her voice sharpening. "Are you interested or not?"

"I am. Only . . . I don't know how to sew very well."

"Can't you read? 'Training given,' it says."

The woman wrote down an address and shoved it across the desk.

"I'll ring them up to say you're coming. Be there tomorrow at half-past eight. Don't be late. Make sure your hands are clean."

She'd all but waltzed home, eager to share her momentous news—London! the queen!—but her mother had only sighed. "You, an embroiderer? You can barely thread a needle. They'll see the dog's breakfast you make of whatever they put in front of you, and then you'll be out the door. Mark my words."

"But they're expecting me. The woman at the exchange won't send me out for another job if I don't go. *Please*, Mum. I'll get in trouble."

"Suit yourself. But straight there and back, mind you. Can't have you traipsing around London all day when there are chores to be done."

The next morning she'd left at dawn, since the early trains cost sixpence less, and had perched on a bench in Berkeley Square Gardens until Big Ben in Westminster chimed the quarter hour after eight o'clock. Then she'd finished her journey, which ended in a quiet back mews in Mayfair, and had rung the bell with a trembling hand.

A girl about her age had answered the door. "Good morning."

"Good morning. I'm here for the job. Apprentice embroiderer?"

The girl had smiled, and nodded, and told her she was at the right place, and then she'd taken Ann upstairs to meet the head of the embroidery workrooms.

Miss Duley had looked her over, had asked if she had any experience with embroidery, and Ann had answered fearfully, but honestly, that she did not. For some reason that had pleased Miss Duley, who nodded and smiled just a little, and said to Ann that she would do, and that her pay would be seven-and-six a week, and she would begin on Monday next.

"Seven-and-six?" her mother had scoffed, even though it was more than any of Ann's school friends were making in their new jobs as shop assistants or trainee stenographers. "You'll spend all of it on the train."

Ann had started work at Hartnell the next Monday, and those first few months had been a blur. She had learned later that Miss Duley had chosen her because she knew nothing, so there was nothing for her to unlearn. Things were done a certain way at Hartnell, which is to say they were done to the highest conceivable standard, and anything less than perfection was unacceptable.

Miss Duley's eye was infallible: if a bead sat in the wrong direction, or one strand of satin stitch sat proud of the rest, or even one sequin was duller than its neighbors, she would notice. She would notice, and her left eyebrow would arch just so, and she would smile in that confiding way she had. As if to say she, too, had once been an apprentice and had made her share of mistakes.

It was hard to imagine Miss Duley as a girl of fourteen, or indeed as anything other than the diminutive yet somehow towering figure who dominated the embroidery workrooms. She had bright blue eyes that noticed everything, the faintest echo of the West Country in her speech, and a calmly certain demeanor that Ann found immensely soothing.

"Attend to the work in front of you, and the rest will take care of itself," Miss Duley was fond of saying. "Leave your cares at the door, and think only of Mr. Hartnell's design."

The years since had brought no end of cares to her door, and some days—some years—it had been almost impossible to follow Miss Duley's advice. Her mother had died suddenly in the summer of '39. Her heart, the doctor had said. Then the war, and the Blitz, and the horror of the night when her brother had been killed. Burned beyond recognition, they'd been told, with even his wedding ring melted away.

Then the spun-out wretchedness of the years that followed, and all the while her certainty had grown that *this* was all she would ever know. The house on Morley Road and the workrooms at Hartnell, and the anonymous spaces in between. *This* life, this succession of gray days and cold nights and loved ones forever lost, was the furthest her dreams would ever stretch.

The sitting room clock chimed seven, startling Ann from her reverie. Standing by the table, a bundle of cutlery clutched in her hand, she tried hard to summon up an appetite for the supper Milly had prepared. It was a struggle, for the gammon was little more than gristle and fat, and the vegetables had collapsed into a grayish sort of paste. Even the school dinners of her childhood had been more appealing.

"Weren't you going to turn on the wireless?" Milly reminded her.

The wireless, a big old-fashioned model in a walnut-veneered case, sat in the sitting room to the right of the fire. Ann switched it on and quickly set the table, having left the door between the two rooms ajar. By the time they'd eaten and washed up, it might even be warm enough to spend an hour there before bed.

No sooner were they seated than the blandly inoffensive music of the BBC's Light Programme gave way to the news.

"On the last day of the coldest January London has experienced for years, Their Majesties the king and queen and the two princesses set off for the first stage of their tour of South Afri—"

"I can hardly hear," Milly said abruptly. "Let me turn up the volume."

"Yes, yes. Shh . . ."

"—have gathered along the route to wave the royal family an affectionate farewell, every single member of those half-frozen crowds wishing that they, too, could be transported from the bitter January afternoon to the fabulous sunshine of South Africa—"

"You wouldn't catch me lining up to wave at them," Milly muttered. "Not in weather like this."

As if responding to Milly's complaint, the newsreader turned to that frosty subject.

"Temperatures in London at midnight last night had risen to twenty-seven degrees, more than ten degrees warmer than earlier in the week. By the middle of the night, when snow was falling on parts of the capital, the temperature had scarcely dropped. But the winter has yet another blow for British housewives: a mass shuttering of laundries across the nation is expected unless coal supplies are increased."

The kettle had boiled, so Ann went to the cooker and busied herself with making tea for them both. Only a scant spoonful of tea leaves for the pot, as the tin was almost empty. And no sugar, for she and Milly had both learned how to do without that small luxury long ago.

"I wonder if those girls know how lucky they are," Milly said.

"The princesses? You always say that. Whenever they're in the news."

"But they are. Just look at how they live. All those clothes and jewels, and never having to lift a finger to do anything. I should be so lucky."

"They work. No—don't make that face. They do. Just think what it'll be like for them on that tour. Day after day of the same boring conversations with strangers. Being stared at wherever they go. People being struck dumb at the sight of them. I doubt they'll even see a beach, let alone have a chance to go for a swim."

"Yes, but—"

"And no matter how hot it is, or how much their feet hurt, or how bored stiff they are, they have to keep smiling and pretend there's nothing they'd rather do than cut a ribbon and declare that some

little town in the middle of nowhere has a bridge or park named after their father. If that isn't work, I don't know what is. I do know I
wouldn't trade places with them for all the . . . well, for all the coal
and tea and electricity in the world."

"Of course you would, silly. You'd be mad not to want to be rich
like them."

"I wouldn't mind being rich. But for everyone to know my name
and expect something from me? Watch every move I make? That'd
be *awful.*"

"I suppose."

"I've heard stories from the saleswomen and fitters at work. Some
of our wealthiest clients are the rudest ones. Ever so demanding, and
they never bother to say thank you, let alone smile, and they definitely never send gifts to the girls in the workrooms. Compared to
the princesses, or the queen? Those are the people who have it easy."

"Fair enough," Milly acknowledged. "So let's be millionaires, and
we'll winter in the south of France, or down in the toe of Italy, and
get suntans and be mistaken for American film stars."

Ann had to smile at the notion of her or Milly ever being mistaken
for a film star. "Wouldn't that be lovely? To just hop on a ship or a
train and go somewhere exotic." To see something beyond gray skies
and soot-dulled bricks and the backs of winter-dead gardens from
the window of a train.

"Not so far as that. A few days at the seaside would be enough
for me."

Conversation faded as they set to work on the washing up, with
Milly doing the washing to save Ann's hands from chapping. It was
scarcely half-past seven when they finished.

"Do you think we can light a fire in the sitting room? Just for an
hour?" Milly asked.

"All right. But only a small one. I checked the coal store this morning and it's almost empty. Goodness knows if the coalman will even come by this week."

"A very small fire, then, and we'll sit close, and I'll read to you. I stopped at the newsagent's on the way home and got the new *People's Friend*."

The fire Milly made was very modest indeed, but it warmed the sitting room by a degree or two. It was a pleasant way to end the week: sitting in her comfortable chair, her eyes closed, her feet warm at last, listening to one of the romantic short stories her sister-in-law loved so much.

Milly was too young for a life like this. She and Frank had only been married a matter of months before he'd been killed, one of those awful, senseless Blitz deaths that still upset Ann if she allowed herself to think about it. Her brother had been a fire-watcher, not a firefighter, but when the factory down the road had been hit, he hadn't hesitated. He'd gone in, looking for survivors, and had never come out.

But Milly was still young, twenty-six to Ann's twenty-five, and before she and Frank had married she'd been the sort of girl who loved to go to the pictures on a Friday night, or out dancing with friends, and would have turned up her nose at an evening spent reading aloud in front of the fire.

When was the last time Ann herself had gone out, for that matter? It wasn't for lack of opportunity, for hardly a Friday went by that a group of girls from work didn't go to one of the West End dance palaces. They always invited her, and she always said no, thanks, perhaps another time. It was a habit, one she'd acquired when her mother had been alive and would respond to her rare requests for an evening out with variations of the same reproachful lecture.

"Might as well throw the money away. Clothes, shoes, paint for your face, food and drink that'll turn your stomach and your head, not to mention a shilling or more to get in," she would say, counting off on the work-roughened fingers of an outstretched hand. "And for what? So you can hold up the wall with the rest of the plain girls?"

Her mum hadn't said such things to hurt her, of course. She'd only meant to toughen her up. Make her aware of how pitiless the world could be, especially for plain girls. And she had been right, of course. There was little chance of anyone taking an honest interest in Ann, and it would be silly and self-indulgent to insist otherwise.

The same could not be said of Milly, however, who was young and pretty and never in her life had been described as plain. There was no reason Milly couldn't go out and have some fun. All she needed was something to wear and a little encouragement from Ann.

The women who worked at Hartnell were allowed to borrow patterns for their own use, and even to use such scraps of fabric and trim that the workroom heads let them have, and from time to time Ann had gleaned enough material to reface the lapels on a blouse, or cover a set of buttons.

That's what she would do. She would go to the next WI swap meet and find a frock for Milly that she could freshen up with some scavenged trim from work, and then she'd persuade her to go out dancing with some friends. Perhaps Milly might find a new beau. Perhaps she might aspire to a future that was a degree or two warmer and wider than a wanly flickering fire and the pages of *People's Friend*.

The mantel clock sounded the hour. It was nine o'clock, the fire had faded to a few glowing crumbs, and suddenly Ann felt so tired she wasn't certain how she'd manage to climb the stairs to her bedroom. At least she didn't have to get up at the crack of dawn the next morning.

"You go on up to your room," she told Milly. "I'll bring you a hot-water bottle to take the chill off the sheets."

Alone in the kitchen, waiting for the kettle to sing, Ann admired the pot of heather she'd brought home. In the spring she would plant it outside, for their house had a tiny back garden that had just enough room for one flower bed, tucked between the shed and the coal store. For most of the war it had been filled up with practical things like beans, carrots, marrows, and potatoes. The June after VE Day, though, she'd planted a handful of marigold seeds that Mr. Tilley down the street had given her, and they'd popped up again the next spring, and bit by bit she'd squeezed in more and more flowers, until she'd covered every square inch of soil with plants that did nothing more to earn their keep than give her pleasure.

Milly might scoff, but the heather was something to treasure. A gift from the queen herself, given in recognition of the work she had done. She'd baby it for the rest of the winter and then, if spring ever did come, she'd find a spot for the heather in her own garden. It was a long way from Balmoral to Barking, but her garden was a fine place for it to end up.

"You'll be happy here," she told the plant, letting her fingertips brush against its downy stems. And then, feeling a little silly at her flight of fancy, she filled her and Milly's hot-water bottles, switched off the kitchen light, and went up to bed.

Chapter Two

Miriam

London
England
March 3, 1947

*H*er first impression would forever be the grayness of it all. It was late in the day, the half-seen sun withering by degrees as it sank in the western sky, and arrows of sleet were beating against the windows of the train. Outside she could make out a dull, leaden sort of countryside, its winter-bare fields and lonely cottages giving way slowly, almost mournfully, to the huddled buildings and tangled streets of a city. The city. London itself.

The train shunted from one track to another, then another, steadily losing speed, its engine groaning in a deeper, gloomier cadence. Soot-stained brick walls were her view now, relieved by the briefest glimpse of rushing water as they crossed a river. The Thames, she supposed. Slower and slower they moved, the train lumbering forward, until with one last, shuddering lurch it reached the end of the platform and halted, belching out its ire in great huffs of smoke and steam.

The people around her were gathering their cases, pulling on gloves, wrapping scarves tightly around their necks. She followed in their wake, hurrying along the platform, matching her stride to theirs. Her bags were light; it was easy to do.

They reached the barrier, and she saw the people before her were showing their tickets to the inspector, or guard, or whatever he was called in England. She watched his expression as he punched their tickets, and felt an easing sort of relief when he smiled at those who seemed unsure or anxious.

She already had her ticket in hand, having anticipated she might need it again, but all the same she hung back until everyone else had passed. No sense in calling attention to herself by holding up the queue. She had heard stories about English people and queues.

"Good evening," she said to the man.

"Good evening, miss." He took her ticket, punched a little hole in one corner, and handed it back to her. As if it were a memento she would want to keep. The journey that took her away from France, from everything she knew, and deposited her in this strange, cold, and desperately shabby place.

"I beg your pardon, but would you be so kind as to direct me to the Wilton Hotel? I believe it is near the station." A few weeks ago, she'd combed through the racks of the *bouquinistes* along the Seine until she'd found a guide to London. From its description the Wilton had seemed like a safe and economical choice.

"It's not far at all, miss. Go out those doors straight ahead, then turn to your right. That takes you to Wilton Road. The hotel's just past the Victoria Theatre on the far side of the street. If you cross

Gillingham Street you've gone too far. D'you need any help with your cases? I can find a porter who'll—"

"No, thank you. I can manage. Thank you very much for your help."

It was just as he had said, and in only a few minutes she was at the door of the hotel. Its grubby exterior, illuminated by a single dim bulb above the front entrance, had certainly seen better days, and the air inside smelled of damp, cabbage, and cigarette smoke.

A man sat behind the desk, his chin in his hand, his eyes closed. The lapels of his jacket had begun to fray, and a faint dusting of dandruff adorned his shoulders. As she watched, the corner of his mouth began to twitch, as if something amused him, then stilled just as quickly. Perhaps he was dreaming of happier times.

"Ahem," she said, and waited for him to stir. Nothing. "Excuse me," she said a bit more forcefully.

He sat up with a gasp. "I do beg your pardon. I was, uh, resting my eyes."

"It is no trouble at all. I wonder if you have available a single room?"

He frowned down at the ledger before him. "For how many nights, miss?"

"I am not certain. Two or three to begin. May I ask what it is, the rate, for each night?"

"Ten and six including breakfast, or fifteen bob for full board. Bath and WC at the end of the hall, room made up once a day, linens changed weekly on account of the coal shortage."

Her guide to London had provided a brief explanation of the strange British currency, but even so she was having trouble wrapping her brain around it. Presumably a bob was a shilling? And there were twenty shillings to the pound, which meant one night at this surprisingly expensive hotel would cost her something like two hundred and fifty francs. Too expensive to remain for long, but the thought of finding somewhere else to stay was more, in that moment, than she could bear to contemplate.

"Very well. I shall take one room with breakfast for three nights to begin."

"Right you are. I'll need your passport." She handed it over, squelching a thrum of panic when he held it up and compared her face to the photograph. He had no power over her. He was not the police, or the Milice, or the Gestapo. He would write down her passport number and proceed to do nothing with it. That was all.

"Here on holiday, Miss . . . Dassin?"

"No. I have moved here. From France."

"Hate to say it, but you couldn't have picked a worse time. Coldest winter in living memory, not enough coal to go round, and rationing worse than ever. Potatoes are on the ration now, if you can believe it. *Potatoes*."

She forced herself to smile. "We both survived the war, did we not? And it will be spring very soon."

"I hope you're right," he said, and the thought of it, or perhaps the memory of past springs, made him smile, too. "We could all do with a bit of sunshine."

He finished scribbling in another of his ledgers and handed back her passport. "If you're staying longer than a week or two—I mean in England, not here necessarily—you'll need a ration book. But you can eat in restaurants off-ration without any trouble. Breakfast is served from half seven to half nine, just so's you know. Oh, and here's your key," he added. "Third floor, end of the corridor. We've a lift but it's out of service, so you'll have to take the stairs. Hot water's shut off until morning. That includes the central heating. Sorry about that."

"It is of no matter. I am used to the cold. May I ask . . . might it be possible to borrow an iron and a board from your laundry?"

This simple question seemed to confound him. "I don't know. I . . . well, I *suppose* so. Usually guests send things down that need pressing."

"I am certain they do, but this garment is precious to me. I feel . . ."— she had to reach for the word—"*uneasy* entrusting it to anyone else. I do hope you understand," she said, softening her voice so it was little more than a whisper, and she aimed her most convincing smile at him, the one that was ever so slightly tremulous, with just a touch of diffidence. Such a smile had served her well over the past seven years.

"I'm sure I can sort something out for you, Miss Dassin." Dass'n, he said, swallowing half her name. She suppressed an instinctive shudder and renewed her smile.

"May I have the use of them this evening? I have an important appointment tomorrow, you see, and I will not sleep well if I am not ready."

"Of course," he said, his face flushing a little. "I'll bring them to your room. Do you need me to carry up your bags?"

"Oh, no—they are not heavy at all. Simply the iron and the board. Thank you so much. You are very kind."

She rather missed having the lift, for her cases, light as they were, weighed heavily on her arms by the time she reached the hotel's top floor. Her room was at the end of the hallway, as he had said, and she hoped it would be quiet. If it were quiet enough she might be able to sleep.

She unlocked the door, switched on the light, and set her cases down where she stood. And then she waited, her eyes shut tight, letting herself rest. Catching her breath and letting the pain fade from her arms. It had been almost two years since her liberation, and still she was weak. What had the American doctor said? Good food and rest and careful exercise, and above all patience, and she would one day be herself again.

He had been a kind man, shaken to his core by the suffering he had seen, and he had done his best to help. But he had been wrong, for no amount of fresh air or nourishing food or pleasant walks in the sunshine could ever restore what had been taken from her.

The day she had made her decision, she had written to the one friend who knew her well enough to understand. Catherine had sent a reply the next day.

20 February 1947

My dear Miriam,

Can you spare the time to see me before you leave? Not because I hope to change your mind—I assure you I understand your reasons—but only so we may say a proper farewell. Shall we say Thursday evening at six o'clock? I am staying with Tian at his new premises. I will tell the staff to expect you. If this time does not suit, do let me know.

With my warm regards,
Catherine

Tian was none other than Christian Dior, *the* Christian Dior whose first collection had astonished the world only weeks before. She had embroidered some of those gowns, for Maison Rébé was Monsieur Dior's preferred *atelier de broderie,* but she had never met the man, nor would she have ever presumed upon her friendship with Catherine to try to engineer such a meeting.

It had felt very strange to walk through the front door of Maison Dior, as if she were a great lady arriving to be fitted for a gown, but Catherine would have known had she tried to creep in through the staff entrance. Miriam was escorted to an exquisitely furnished room, shown every courtesy, offered any refreshment she desired, and after protesting she was in need of nothing, she had been left alone. Only for a moment, though, before the door had opened and Catherine had rushed in.

"My dear, my dear—such a joy to see you again. Come and let us sit together. Would you like anything? Some coffee? A tisane?"

"No, thank you, Mademoiselle Dior," Miriam said, suddenly cowed. Friend or not, she was the sister of the greatest couturier in the world.

But her friend shook her head and took hold of Miriam's hands. "To you I am Catherine. I insist. Now, tell me—what has happened?"

"The trial began last week. I am sure I told you about it."

"Your parents' neighbor? The gendarme?"

Miriam nodded. She had gone to the courthouse on the first day of the trial, believing it would mean something if she were present to see justice done. Adolphe Leblanc had lived down the street from her parents for as long as she could remember, the local policeman with his big, tight-knit, and devoutly Catholic family, and in all those years he'd never once said hello, never once asked after their health, never once allowed Miriam to play with his children. "Dirty Jew," they had called her, and she had learned to fear them and their red-faced, loudmouthed father.

He had helped to round up her family, an eager cog in a human machinery of death that had spread over nearly an entire continent. Yet he had been acquitted before the trial had even properly begun.

"They set him free, along with half of the other men who were on trial," she now told Catherine. "The judges said they had atoned for their crimes by helping the resistance."

"The wretch. He probably didn't lift a finger until the writing was on the wall," Catherine huffed.

"He brushed past me when he left. He was so close our sleeves were touching. I know he recognized me."

"He wasn't so foolish as to say anything to you, was he?"

"No."

She had hoped to discern some slight evidence of guilt, of shame, in his gaze. What she had seen instead was hatred. Corrosive, incendiary hatred, and she had looked around the courtroom and recognized it in the eyes of others there, too.

"He did something to upset you. I can see that he did."

Miriam shut tight her eyes, trying to wipe the memory from her mind. "He smiled. He smiled, and he nodded, and I knew that if it were in his power he would do it again. Maman, Papa, Grand-Père. He would send them to their deaths a second time if he could."

"Not all of us hate," Catherine whispered, her voice pleading.

"I know. But now I am afraid. He has reminded me of my fear."

"I understand. I do."

"I wanted to say good-bye, and to thank you for helping me. I would not have survived without you."

"Nor I without you," her friend said, and it was enough, then, that they both knew and remembered. "Will you wait here for a moment? I wish for you to meet someone."

Before she could react, her friend had left the room. Catherine wanted her to meet someone? But surely she did not mean—

Catherine returned, and with her was a tall, balding, and instantly recognizable figure. "Monsieur Dior," Miriam said, leaping to her feet.

He shook her hand, just as if she were his social equal, and his shy smile lent warmth to his earnest features. "Mademoiselle Dassin. It is an honor to make your acquaintance. My dear sister has told me of your many kindnesses to her, and to others, when you were imprisoned. I do hope you will allow me to express my gratitude."

"She was, ah . . . was kind to me as well," Miriam stammered. "We helped one another survive."

It was true that Miriam had helped Catherine, but only in the small ways that prisoners often helped one another. She had scavenged a few morsels of impossible-to-find bread when the other woman hadn't been able to keep down the rancid soup that passed for rations. She had used scraps of cloth, wheedled from another prisoner, to bind Catherine's feet when they'd become infected. At night, when her friend had been close to despair, Miriam had reminded her of beautiful things. Gowns of silk, flowers in bloom, memories of comfort and love.

After their liberation, they had returned home to France on the same refugee train, and Catherine had paid for Miriam to attend a convalescent clinic to regain her health. She had known that Miriam had no family left to care for her.

"Catherine told me yesterday that you are emigrating to England, and she asked me if I would compose a letter of reference for you. Naturally I was delighted to do so, for I believe your work graces some of my newest creations. At least that is what Monsieur Rébé tells me."

"It does, Monsieur Dior, but I would never presume—"

"I have also written out a list of names where you might apply for work. There are but a few embroidery ateliers in London, so I suggest you look to the designers themselves. Of these I especially recommend Monsieur Norman Hartnell. To my mind, his embroiderers produce particularly exquisite work. Please accept this, together with my sincere good wishes." With that he handed her an envelope, shook her hand once more, and retreated back through the still-open door.

As soon as he had gone Miriam turned to her friend. "You did not have to do this for me. I would never have asked it of you."

"I know that. I do. But I want to help you, and we both know that Tian's name can open a great many doors. Promise me that if you do encounter any difficulties you will let me know."

"I promise."

Miriam had not noticed, then, that the envelope was heavier than two sheets of paper would normally warrant. Only later, after they had embraced and said their good-byes, and she had returned to her lodgings to pack the last of her things, had she discovered the English money, five twenty-pound notes, which Monsieur Dior had tucked inside the envelope. They were with her now, sewn inside the lining of her coat, an insurance policy against darker days.

She opened her eyes and looked around her hotel room, though she remained where she stood. It was cleaner than she'd expected, though it was hard to see very much in the dim light of the single bulb hanging from the ceiling. There was one window, rather small, with a view of next door's fire escape. A narrow bed was set against the right-facing wall, its counterpane darned in several places, its pillow worn thin. Beside the bed was a wardrobe with a mirror on its door. In the far corner was a sink, a single towel folded over its edge. To her left, a small desk and chair. A lamp sat on the desk, and she stepped forward and switched it on. Nothing. The bulb was burned out.

A knock sounded behind her. "Hello? Miss Dass'n?"

"Yes. Please do come in."

Having set the iron on the desk, the clerk attempted to unfold the board, but its mechanism was evidently a mystery to him.

"Please do not trouble yourself," she said. "I can manage it."

"Sorry 'bout that. There's only the one power point in the room, here by the desk. You'll need to unplug the lamp first."

She nodded. She would wait until tomorrow to ask about the burned-out bulb. It would be foolish to make any more demands of him tonight. "Thank you very much. Shall I bring the board and iron back to you when I am finished?"

"No need. I'll tell the maid when she makes up your room in a day or two. If the laundry needs them back any sooner they'll come by earlier."

"You are very kind," she said, wishing she could spare the money for a tip. Instead she shook his hand and smiled into his eyes, hoping that he understood.

"It's no trouble at all," he said, his tone genial, and she guessed that he did understand. Or perhaps it was the case that tips were not generally expected here in England. She would have to consult her guide to make sure. "Good night, then."

The door clicked shut behind him. She locked it, paused until his footsteps faded away, and then took her first easy breath of the day. *Alone.* Free of strangers hemming her in, free of half-remembered words and phrases that tugged at her brain like fishhooks. Free of the ingrained need to smooth her every expression into a neutral and unthreatening blank.

First things first. She unfolded the board, setting it close to the desk, and plugged in the iron. While she waited for it to heat, she set the larger of her two cases on the bed and extracted her best suit and blouse. Though she'd packed them meticulously, with tissue guarding every fold, they had still become creased. The iron was a rather ancient and unreliable-looking device, but a few hesitant passes on the inside hem of her skirt revealed no scorch marks, so she set about erasing the worst of the wrinkles from her garments.

She was too tired and cold to bother with any sort of nighttime toilette. After changing into her nightgown and hanging up the clothes she'd been wearing, she switched off the light and got into bed. Though the sheets were faintly damp, it wasn't long before she stopped shivering and began to relax into the comforting embrace of the bed.

It was there, waiting for her, as soon as she closed her eyes: a panel of ivory silk, luminous in the late afternoon sun, stretched tight over a frame. Her embroidery frame, right by the window in the atelier at Maison Rébé, just where she had left it.

She considered her progress. The design, a wreath of flowers, was nearly done; it had occupied her mind's eye for many nights now. Already she'd finished the bourbon roses, their blossoms pale and tender, and the nodding tendrils of honeysuckle winding between their stems. Tonight she would begin the first of the peonies.

There had been an old peony in her parents' garden, planted long before they had moved into the house, and every May it had produced armfuls of blooms, some of them as wide as a dinner plate, their petals deepening from palest pink to the cerise of the ripest cherries. It had been Maman's favorite, and hers, too.

Last year she had forced herself to go. To discover if any trace of her family, of their lives, still remained. The people who had taken over her parents' house had said they knew nothing. They would not let her enter, so she had begged to see the garden. Five minutes in the garden, and then she would leave.

They had killed the peony. They had dug up her mother's flowers and put in a vegetable garden. They had destroyed every beautiful living thing her mother had planted. They had—

The peony lived on in her memory. She could see it so clearly, its petals glowing and bright and perfect. Unchanged. Whole and alive.

She blinked back her tears. She threaded her needle. She touched her fingertips to the ghostly fabric. And she began again.

Chapter Three

Heather

Toronto, Ontario
Canada
March 5, 2016

*H*eather? It's Mom. I've been calling and calling."

"Sorry. Didn't hear it ringing. What's up?"

"Where are you?"

"I'm just finishing up with my groceries. It's a zoo. Typical Saturday morning in Toronto. Why?"

"It's Nan."

The clamor of the busy store, the chatter and complaints of those hemmed in around her, the clang of carts being marshaled outside, the too-loud din of oldies played on crackling speakers—all withered away. In their place rose a drumbeat, dull and steady, pounding insistently against her breastbone. The sound of her own heart.

"Heather?"

"What about Nan?" she asked, though she already knew the answer.

"Oh, honey. I'm so sorry to tell you like this. She died this morning."

The line was moving forward, so Heather pushed her cart ahead, obedient to the dictates of the queue. It was hard to steer with only one hand. She wrenched the cart in the right direction, her fingers throbbing where they clutched at the handle.

"But . . ." she started. Her mouth had gone dry. She swallowed, licked her lips, tried again. "But Nan was fine the last time I talked to her."

How long had it been? She usually called on Sundays, but things had been busy at work. Not good busy, just mindless-crap sort of busy, and by the end of the week she was always so tired, and—

"Heather? Are you still there?"

She pushed the cart forward again. "I don't understand. You didn't tell me she was sick."

"I saw her on Wednesday, and she seemed fine enough then. But you know how she hated to admit she was under the weather."

"I guess," Heather whispered.

Something was tickling her cheek. She brushed at her face, her fingertips coming away damp with silent, stealthy tears. She rubbed at them with the woolly cuff of her coat, the same stupid coat that didn't have any pockets. Maybe she had a tissue in her bag.

"What happened?"

"When she didn't show up for dinner, one of her friends at the Manor checked on her. She was asleep in her chair—the one by the window in her room—and her friend had a hard time waking her up. So they called 911, and then they called us. The doctor said it was pneumonia, the kind that starts as a cold and sneaks up on you. At her age, you know, there isn't a lot they can do. And we'd talked about it before with her, you know, so we knew she didn't want it. Any fuss, I mean. So Dad and I stayed with her until . . ."

All last night Nan had been dying, and she hadn't even *known*. "Why didn't you call me?"

"Heather. *Honey*. You know she wouldn't have wanted you to see her like that. You know that. She was asleep when we got there, so—"

A sob erupted from Heather's throat, noisy and mortifying. The placid shoppers around her looked alarmed for a moment, then studiously turned their heads or bent over their phones. Was it kindness or indifference that made them look away?

Another sob, even louder, as if a dam were bursting.

"Heather? Listen to me. Forget the groceries. I want you to take your cart over to the help desk, or whatever they call it, and tell them you need to go. Tell them you have an emergency. Are you listening?"

"Yeah, Mom. I'm listening." She pulled her cart to the side, steering it carefully so she didn't bump into anyone. The help desk wasn't all that far.

"Can Sunita or Michelle come back and get the groceries?"

"I guess."

"Okay. Then tell whoever's there that you need to go but your friend will come back for the groceries. Give them your name and number."

The woman behind the help desk was busy inserting lottery tickets into a countertop display. She glanced up, her smile thinning as she took in Heather's tearstained face.

"Can I help you?"

"I, uh—"

"Heather. Pass the phone over. I'll talk to them."

The woman took the phone when Heather offered it, her questioning frown melting into an expression of sympathy as she listened.

"Hello? Yes? Oh, no. I'm so sorry. Yeah, sure—I can do that. No problem. Okay. No, I won't hang up." She handed the phone back. "You're all set. Your mom explained everything. I'm so sorry about your grandma."

Heather tried to smile, but even without a mirror she could tell the result was unconvincing. "Thanks. My friend will be along soon."

She turned herself in the direction of the doors, her phone still tucked against her ear. A minute or two later and she was at her little car. Nan's old car.

It was an ancient Nissan hatchback, already used when her grandmother had bought it a decade earlier, and entirely lacking in "mod cons," as Nan liked to say. No air conditioning, no stereo beyond an AM/FM radio, no power steering, and a crank instead of a button to roll down the windows. But it still felt like Nan's car, and for that reason she would keep it until the wheels fell off.

Collapsing into the driver's seat, Heather switched her phone to speaker, dumped it onto the dash, and rested her head on the steering wheel.

"Are you still there?"

"Yeah, Mom. Still here."

"I don't want you to drive anywhere just yet. You're too upset."

Deep breath in. Steady breath out. She'd give it another minute, and maybe her hands would stop shaking, and she'd be able to breathe without that awful choking kind of feeling that clawed at her throat.

"I'll be okay," she said after a while. "I just need to get home."

"Sure. Take a couple of deep breaths. And roll down the window for some air. Can you see okay? Wipe your eyes. Love you, sweetie."

"Love you, too."

"Call me when you get home?"

"Promise."

A fizzing instant of static replaced her mother's voice, then silence.

She swiped at her eyes again, then put the car in gear and pointed it in the direction of home.

Nan was gone.

Nan was dead.

How could it be?

Nan had never seemed that old. She hadn't even retired until she was eighty. She'd sold the little shop on Lakeshore Avenue that she'd opened fifty years before, and then, five years later, she'd sold her bungalow and moved into Elm Tree Manor, one of those apartment buildings for seniors that had a nurse on call and a dining room for people who didn't feel like cooking, and so many activities and clubs and outings that she was busier than Heather most weekends.

Heather could admit that Nan had been slowing down a bit. She had stopped driving and cut back on her volunteer work, and when she picked up a cold she hadn't been able to shake it off in a day or two like she always used to do. Until now, though, she'd always got better. Always.

A staccato beep startled her into awareness. The light had changed without her noticing. She waved in apology to the driver behind, her eyes on the road ahead, her thoughts tangled up in memories of Nan.

She turned left and parked in front of the house, but rather than go straight inside she stayed put, her hands resting on the wheel, and let her gaze drift to the gardens across the street, the sunny side where the ground was warmer and the bulbs had begun to bloom. There were snowdrops and crocuses and even some early daffodils, and she couldn't be sure if the sight of them made her happy or sad.

Nan had been looking forward to spring. As president of the gardening committee for the Manor, she'd been in charge of the planters on the patio outside the dining room. The last time Heather had visited, Nan had shown her the annuals she'd been growing from seed. Marigolds, sweet alyssum, cosmos, and petunias, arranged in neat banks of rinsed-out yogurt pots on her living room windowsill.

What would happen to Nan's plants? She had to make sure that someone remembered to water them.

Heather switched off the ignition, took a few deep breaths to steady herself, then braved the short walk to her front door. She only just made it to the bench in the hall before her knees gave out, her purse slipping down her arm to land on the tiled floor.

The hall was a small space, hemmed in by two doors: one to her little apartment upstairs, and the other to the main-floor apartment where Sunita and Michelle lived. The house had been divided up when her friends had first bought it, and one day they would likely want the top floor back, but for now they were happy to rent it to her for almost nothing.

"Sunita?" she called out. "Michelle?"

"Suni's out," came a voice from the back. "You're stuck with me. What's up?"

"I got a call from my mom when I was at the store."

"And what's up with Liz and Jim this week? Are they going on another trip?"

"No. It's Nan. She called about Nan."

"Is she all right? Did she have another fall?"

One deep breath. Another. "No," Heather heard herself say. "No. She died. She's dead."

There was a metallic clatter, as if something had been dumped in the sink, then footsteps hastening to the front. An instant later, she was enveloped in a warm, vanilla-scented embrace. Of course. It was Saturday morning, so Michelle was baking.

"Oh, sweetie, *no*. Oh, that's just *awful* news. Come into the kitchen. You need a cup of tea."

"Y-you sound like Nan," was all Heather could manage, and then she was blinded by another rush of tears.

She sat there and let Michelle peel off her coat and unlace her boots, and then, with only a little urging, lead her to the kitchen.

"Sit down. I'll get the kettle going. Do you want a muffin?"

"No, thanks. I don't think I can eat anything just yet." She rested her head on the kitchen table, its vintage Formica wonderfully cool against her brow. "Where's Sunita?" she asked without looking up.

"She went for a run in High Park. Should be back any minute."

"I left all my groceries at the store. I couldn't think straight, so Mom talked me through it. I said I'd send someone back for them."

"I'll go. Or Suni when she gets home."

Heather closed her eyes and tried not to think, not about anything at all. The kettle began to whistle, and Michelle busied herself with fixing up the teapot just so. She was always so particular about tea.

"Sit up, now. Here it is. I made it with lemon and honey. Just how Nan used to fix it for you."

Heather straightened herself. Let the homely pottery mug warm her hands. "I can't believe it. I can't."

"Did your mom say what happened?"

"It wasn't anything dramatic. Just a cold that turned into something worse. And I know she was almost ninety-four, and people don't live forever. Except she was the sort of person who seemed like she might live forever."

"I know what you mean. All those people who lived through the war. You'd think they were made out of cast iron."

The oven timer sounded. Michelle switched it off, pulled out a tray of muffins, and set them on a nearby cooling rack. "Okay. That's the last batch. I'll head to the store now. The Loblaw's on Dundas?"

"Yeah. Thanks so much. Oh—do you want my debit card?"

"I'm good. We can sort it out later. You just stay here and drink your tea. And I'll call Suni and tell her. That way you won't have to explain all over again."

The front door shut behind her friend, and Heather was alone in the house. She should go upstairs to her own apartment, call her mother, lie down for a while. Let Seymour curl up beside her and soothe her to sleep with his purr. But inertia bound her to the kitchen, to the hard wooden chair, to the scents of citrus and spice that perfumed the air.

It had been two weeks since she'd last gone to visit Nan. She'd meant to go the other weekend, but she'd been getting over a cold herself and hadn't wanted to pass on her germs, and she'd been so tired, besides, that she'd barely made it out of bed all day Sunday.

Two weeks ago she'd gone to visit Nan and they'd had tea and some scones from the Scottish bakery that her grandmother loved, and they'd talked about the queen's ninetieth birthday and the fuss people were making over it. Then the phone had started ringing, and it had been Nan's friend Margie giving her the ten-minute warning for tai chi class in the recreation room.

"I'm sorry, my dear," Nan had said. "I feel as if you only just got here."

"I've been here for ages. It's only that we've been having such a good time. How about I call you in a few days?"

She'd given her grandmother a big hug, and even though Nan wasn't a demonstrative person she had hugged Heather in return. She always hugged her back. Heather had walked down the hall, and Nan had waited outside her door as she always did, just until the elevator came and Heather could blow her a kiss.

She had got on the elevator and blown a kiss to Nan, and then the doors had shut and Heather had filled the rest of her Sunday with errands that had already vanished from her memory. She had said good-bye to her Nan, without really knowing what she was doing, for there was so much to tell her, still, and now she would never get the chance.

She had never once imagined it would be good-bye.

Chapter Four

Ann

March 10, 1947

*A*nn was already awake when her alarm went off at six o'clock. She nearly always opened her eyes a few minutes before it began to trill. Before she could think twice, she threw back the mountain of blankets and sat up, swinging her feet over the side of the bed. Only then did she reach out to silence the bell.

Her slippers, she realized, were on the floor next to her bed; usually she remembered to tuck them under the covers before falling asleep. She gasped as she slid her feet inside, though the worst of the chill was absorbed by her socks. She was further disheartened by the telling plumes of vapor that rushed from her mouth and nose.

She slipped on her robe and made her way downstairs, stopping to collect a pint of slushy milk from the front step. In the kitchen, she stood at the sink for a long minute before trying the tap. Holding her breath, she opened it all the way. Nothing. The pipes were frozen again.

She and Milly had learned to keep the kettle full, for the only thing worse than frozen pipes in the morning was no water for tea. She set it to boiling, first filling a small bowl so she might wash her face and brush her teeth, and then hurried out to the WC. After the pipes had frozen for the first time, back in January, Milly had brought home an old-fashioned chamber pot from the shop where she worked. "Mr. Joliffe had been using it as a pot for his ostrich fern, but it died months ago and he said I could have it. The pot, not the dead fern." It felt awfully undignified, having to use such a thing instead of a proper toilet, but it was better than enduring a full bladder all the way into London.

Back in the kitchen, Ann washed her hands with some of the water she'd set aside, then considered the matter of breakfast. There was a heel of stale bread, but it was only enough for two thin slices of toast; she'd leave it for Milly. Leftover porridge it was. It took only a minute or two to heat through, and was ready before the kettle had begun to boil. She added some cream from the top of the milk and, not bothering to sit, ate it up in a half-dozen bites.

The kettle was singing. She made up a pot of tea, using leaves she'd saved and reused twice before, and added an inch of water to the saucepan and bowl from her porridge. They could soak in the sink until she got home from work. The tea was a pallid shade of beige, and likely would get no browner. A splash of milk did little to improve the flavor, but it was hot, at least, and the mug took some of the awful chill from her hands.

Back upstairs she went, feeling her way quietly through the dark, for Milly didn't have to be up for another half hour and it was unfair to wake her. She dressed quickly, her bedroom having grown no warmer, choosing the nicest of her work frocks and cardigans. Normally she wore a white coverall at work, but it was in the bag of things she and Milly sent out for laundering at Mrs. Cole's every Monday. It was a luxury, paying for someone else to wash their clothes and linens, but with both of them working there was nothing else for it. Her small things she kept back, of course, as well as anything that was delicate or precious—Mrs. Cole did a fine job with sturdier items, but buttons and trim tended to vanish after a trip through her mangle.

There was a mirror on the wall, next to the electric sconce, and she stood before it now, hairbrush in hand. Last year she'd made the mistake of having a fringe cut into her hair. It hadn't suited her one bit, and nearly ten months later it still wasn't quite grown out. She clipped it back from her forehead, making sure the kirby grips crossed properly, and brushed out the rest of her hair until it was smooth and shining.

Her skin was too pale, and last summer's freckles, which she rather liked, were all but gone. Against the pallor of her complexion, the gray-green of her eyes was all the more startling, and the color of her hair didn't help at all. It was just a fraction too alarming to be a proper strawberry blond. Ginger—that's what it was. Her mum had always said it looked like dried-out marmalade.

When she'd been young, her hair and too-bright eyes and even her freckles had made her miserable. The boys at school had never failed to tease her, and some of the girls had been even more unkind. Even her friends had suggested she try a fading cream on her skin, or consider bleaching her hair.

One boy had thought Ann was pretty, and had told her so. It had been the summer before the war, not long after her mum had died, and she'd been miserable, feeling out of place and out of sorts. Probably she ought to have stayed home from the dance. Even Frank and Milly, newly engaged and annoyingly happy in spite of the war, had given her a wide berth. But Jimmy had stayed at her side all evening, and the last time they'd danced together he'd bent his head and whispered into her ear.

"I think you're lovely. I hope you don't mind me saying so."

Just thinking about that moment had been enough to make her smile for months, but after he'd been killed at Dunkirk, the memory had grown bittersweet. She'd barely known him—hadn't known enough of the poor boy to properly mourn him—and yet his kind words had sung to her for years. Someone, once, had thought her lovely. Not pretty, but *lovely,* which had seemed somehow better. Deeper and truer, a compliment born of honesty rather than obligation.

For a short while, she'd fancied she was falling in love with him. They'd written to one another, after he'd joined up and been sent to France, but the letters had never plunged past rote formalities of weather and food. And then he'd been killed. At his memorial service, when Ann had introduced herself, his parents hadn't known who she was.

She turned away from the mirror. What was the point in thinking about such things? She wasn't the sort of woman to make anyone's knees go weak, she never had been, and fretting about it would get her nowhere besides late for work.

At Milly's door, she paused and knocked lightly. "Are you up?"

"Yes. Almost," came the muffled reply.

"Sit up now, or else you'll fall asleep again. Don't forget to take the laundry to Mrs. Cole."

"I won't. What are you thinking for supper?"

"We've a few potatoes. Let's make a cottage pie from the leftover stew."

"Right, then. Have a good day."

"You too. Oh—I forgot to tell you. The pipes are frozen again."

"Wonderful. That really does make me want to get out of bed."

"Sorry. I'm sure they'll thaw once the sun is up. Right—I'd best be off."

She hurried out the door, not bothering to pack her dinner, as it was easier, and cheaper, to eat at the canteen in the basement at work. A biting sort of sleet had begun to fall, and she had no umbrella, hers having collapsed in tatters the week before. By the time she reached the station, her wool hat, already on its last legs, was a sodden and shapeless ruin.

The trains were running, at least, and she was even able to get a seat in her usual carriage. A man across from her was reading the *Daily Mail,* his attention fixed on the football results. She could see the front page from where she sat, and the headlines were a variation on a familiar theme: more bad weather expected, food shortages increasing, dire predictions of economic collapse, further unrest in India.

At Mile End she switched to the Central line, but two trains came and went before she could squeeze on. Nine stops to go, penned in on every side, the smell of damp wool and unwashed bodies almost unendurable. That's what happened when the soap ration was slashed to nearly nothing.

She all but leaped from the carriage when it pulled into Bond Street station. Up the steps she ran—the escalator was still under repair, or perhaps they simply didn't want to waste the electricity on running the thing—and out into the street, head down against the needling rain, her feet leading her to Hartnell's as surely as they'd send her home come evening.

The grand entrance on Bruton Street was reserved for Mr. Hartnell, his clients, and senior staff such as Mademoiselle Davide. Everyone else came and went through the mews entrance on Bruton Place, chanting a string of hellos and good mornings to one another as they streamed up the stairs to the cloakrooms.

Ann hung up her coat and scarf and set her wretched excuse for a hat on one of the radiators, though she held out little hope of its drying. Then down a flight of stairs and along a warren of corridors to her second home, the main embroidery workroom, where she'd spent nearly every weekday of the past eleven years. She knew every inch of it by heart.

The heavy fire door and the short run of steps with its rickety hand-rail. The rows of embroidery frames, their plain wooden stretchers filled with panes of fabric. The bank of windows that stretched to the ceiling, and the hanging electric lights, their cords bunched and tied so they shone just so. The scores of drawings and samples and photographs pinned to the whitewashed walls, with one entire section given over to the women of the royal family and their Hartnell gowns. The low tables along the perimeter of the workroom, their tops messily shingled with trays of beads and sequins, boxes of buttons, and skeins of embroidery silk.

Every blue moon Miss Duley would ask the assistants and juniors to sort everything out, but the return to order never lasted more than a week or two. Soon enough they'd be onto the next big push—a state dinner, a set of theater costumes, an export order for American clients—and the workroom would revert to its usual state of artfully disordered chaos.

It didn't bother Ann. She knew where to find whatever she needed, and it wasn't as if Mr. Hartnell's own office was shipshape—far from it. The few times Ann had been to that part of the premises, usually to deliver a finished sample, his desk had been awash in books, correspondence, and art supplies, with one end entirely given over to bolts of fabric and lace so fine and precious that a single yard easily cost more than she earned in a year.

A gaggle of the younger girls burst through the door and clattered down the steps, their excited voices shattering the comfortable silence.

"Look, Ann! Look!" cried Ruthie. "Go on, Doris, *show* her."

"Yes, show her," squealed Ethel. "Just stick out your hand so she can see."

Ann moved closer, still unsure as to why they were so excited. "I don't—"

"Don't you see? Doris got engaged!"

"That's wonderful news," Ann said. "And your ring is very pretty," she added, though she'd only caught a glimpse of it before everyone else had crowded round.

"He asked me yesterday, right after Sunday lunch with my mum and dad. I'd been helping with the washing up, and in he came and got down on one knee. I still had soapsuds all over my hands!"

"That's ever so romantic," cooed Ruthie. "What did your mum say?"

"She had a good cry, of course. And Dad was happy, too. He liked that Joe had asked his permission first. That's what they were doing when me and Mum were in the kitchen."

"When are you thinking? A summer wedding?" someone asked.

"I think so. Joe's mum is all on her own, so she's happy to have us stay with her."

"Will you be leaving work, then?" Ann asked, though she already knew the answer.

"Not until after the wedding. Joe wants to start a family straightaway, so there isn't much point in staying on."

Ann disagreed, but there was no point in making a pill of herself by saying so. The point of working was to earn her way, spend her days in an interesting occupation, and retain some measure of independence for herself. Once children arrived, Doris would be tied to home and hearth for years, so why not make the most of her freedom while she could?

"I suppose not," she said instead. "We had better—"

"Good morning, ladies! I'm surprised to find you still standing about."

"Sorry, Miss Duley," said Edith. "It's only that Doris got engaged and—"

"Splendid news. I'm very happy for you, my dear. Perhaps we could all continue the conversation at break? In the meantime we have quite a lot of work to get through."

"Yes, Miss Duley," came the chorus of voices.

On Friday afternoon Ann, Doris, and Ethel had begun work on a gown for a client who was moving abroad—apparently her husband had been named to a very important diplomatic post and she required a wardrobe to match. While Doris and Ethel worked on the skirt, Ann occupied herself with the bodice. She had Mr. Hartnell's design at her elbow, as well as a sample of the motif that she'd worked up herself, and she was confident in her ability to translate his vision from paper to silk. Swirls of tiny gold beads, translucent crystals, and matte copper sequins would cover nearly all the bodice by the time she was finished, the design continuing onto the skirt in irregular waves. It was straightforward work, and relatively fast, too, since she could use a tambour hook for most of it.

She enjoyed the rhythm of such work, for it left no room in her head for anything beyond pushing the hook through the fabric in just the right spot, setting the bead or sequin, pulling the hook back, repeating the same, repeating and repeating, pausing only to check the design and sample to ensure she was copying them exactly.

At their morning break for tea, predictably enough, they all sat together in the basement canteen and discussed Doris's plans for her wedding.

"I don't want to waste coupons on a dress. I was thinking I could make over my mum's."

"When was she married?" asked Ruthie, one of the assistants. Only seventeen and as starry-eyed as they came. A good worker, though, and she would settle down in time.

"In 1914. White cotton and inset lace down to the ground. And a high neck. It looks like something Queen Mary would wear to a picnic."

"Does your mum mind if you change it?" Ann asked.

"She said she doesn't. I'm not sure where I'd even start."

"Don't worry about that now," Edith broke in. "Tell us again how he proposed. Did he give you any hint ahead of time?"

Morning continued in the same vein as before, the workroom hushed and nearly still as the women bent over their frames. Once or twice the flash of a reflected thimble, caught in a rare beam of brighter sunshine, made Ann look up from her work, and then she would remind herself to stretch her neck and arms, rub her hands and wrists to get the blood flowing again, and close her eyes for a long, soothing minute.

When dinner began at half-past twelve, Ann stayed behind, promising the others she'd catch up. Working quickly, as they only stopped for half an hour, she unearthed a piece of tracing paper and a pencil, then set to work. Five minutes later she was joining Doris and the others in the canteen for a sandwich and cup of tea.

"What's that you've got there?" Ruthie asked, her attention drawn to the sketch in Ann's hand.

"I had a few ideas for Doris's dress. They aren't—"

"Don't keep us waiting! Give it over here."

Ann set the drawing in front of Doris, now wishing she had chosen a quieter and more private moment to share her ideas. "Here, on the bodice, it's probably a bit drapey, so you'll need to add some darts under the bust, and then, if you're feeling brave, you can recut the neckline so it's lower and a bit curved, just here—"

"Heart-shaped," Doris sighed.

"Yes. And you'll need to take it in at the waist, or make a sash that will cinch it in tight."

"It looks a bit like something Mr. Hartnell would design," said Ruthie, and everyone gasped.

"Of course it doesn't," Ann said, her voice sounding a little sharper than she meant. "It's only because I used one of his drawings as a template—I traced the outline of the figure. Otherwise I'd never have got the proportions right."

At school she'd never been very good at art, but during the war she'd started carrying an old exercise book with her, along with a few pencils, and had taught herself to draw. It was cheaper than buying books or magazines, and easier on her eyes, besides. Some things, like people's faces or hands, would forever be beyond her capabilities, but it was a nice way to pass the time, and a means of remembering some of the really fine work she'd done over the years.

Last year, for Christmas, Milly had given her a beautiful sketchbook from the shop where she worked, the sort of thing a real artist would use, with thick paper and a lovely pale blue binding. It had taken Ann a week or two to work up the nerve to draw in it the first time, and even now she preferred to save it, like Sunday best, for her favorite ideas. She'd add Doris's dress to the book as soon as she had a bit of spare time. Maybe on Sunday afternoon, when she'd finished her mending and other small chores.

"It's perfect," Doris said. "Isn't it?" she asked the others, and they all agreed that Ann's ideas were perfect and Doris would look a dream on her wedding day.

Ann was still basking in the remembered glow of their praise when she arrived home that evening, and even the prospect of a cold house and near-empty larder weren't able to dim her spirits.

"It's me," she called out as she came in. "Are you there?"

"I'm in the kitchen," Milly responded, and there was something about her voice that put Ann's nerves on edge. She hastened through the darkened sitting room and found her sister-in-law sitting at the kitchen table, still dressed in her work uniform, an untouched cup of tea at her elbow.

"What's wrong? Something's wrong."

"I've had a letter from my brothers," Milly said. "They want me to come and live with them in Canada." Only then did Ann notice the airmail envelope left open on the table.

She sank into the chair opposite Milly. "You haven't seen them for ages. For *years.*"

"The businesses they've opened are doing well, and . . . and there'd be work for me. They say that life is better in Canada. No rationing, no shortages. They—"

"Better? What about the winters? They get feet and feet of snow. You hate the cold."

"They say it isn't all that bad. Once you get used to it."

"How would you get there? It can't be cheap to—"

"They'll send me a ticket."

"Oh. So you're thinking about it."

Milly looked up, and only then did Ann see that she'd been crying. "I have, but I don't know . . . I'd be leaving this house, and my life with Frank, too. And you. I'd be leaving you, and you're my best friend in the world. What will happen if I go? How will you keep the house?"

Ann knew what she must do. "You can't make such a big decision based on what'll happen to me. I'll be fine. I will. This is a nice place, and I'm sure I can find a lodger without any trouble."

"What if the council gets wind of it? If anyone notices there's only two women living in a house that's meant for a whole family, you'll be—"

"*Milly.*" Ann took her friend's hands in hers and squeezed them tight. "As long as I pay the rent on time I doubt they'll care. And what's the worst that can happen? They give me notice and I find somewhere else to live."

"But you'd have to leave your garden behind, and you love that garden."

"I do. But the plants aren't chained down, are they? I can bring some of them along with me if ever I do move."

Milly was shaking her head. "It doesn't feel right. It doesn't."

"Now you're being silly. Let me ask you something: If it wasn't for me, would you go?"

"I don't know. I suppose I would . . ."

"Then you should go. Of course I'll miss you, but that's what letters are for. And maybe I can save up and visit you one day. I've always wanted to see Niagara Falls and, well . . . there's sure to be other lovely places to see."

"I'm scared," Milly whispered.

"I know. But it will be a fresh start for you. I really think you should do it."

They sat there for a few minutes, silently regarding one another, and at last Milly nodded.

"When are you thinking, then?" Ann asked.

"Dan and Des said it's best to wait for summer. It won't be such a shock that way, they said. Will that give you enough time?"

"Loads. Now, what do you say to a spot of supper?"

"I didn't get started yet. Sorry about that. I opened the letter, and then . . ."

"Not a bother. You sit there and drink your tea, if it hasn't gone completely cold, and I'll sort it out. Why don't you turn on the wireless? That way we can hear the news when it comes on."

All through supper and afterward, listening to the Light Programme as they sat by the fire, Ann maintained a veneer of resolute good cheer. What else could she do? If she fell to pieces, Milly would change her mind and insist on staying. So she kept the conversation light and bright, in the process nearly boring them both to death with descriptions of Doris's wedding plans, and never once did she let on that a part of her felt like weeping.

Once Milly was gone, she would be alone, with no one to notice if she was sad, or sick, or struggling. She'd be on her own, with nothing but her own strength of will to sustain her. Never mind that it was already worn thin from nearly a decade of grief and strain and hunger and war.

She would manage. She'd find a lodger and continue to pay the rent on time. She would manage, somehow, and spring would come, and her garden would grow green and bright. And she would survive.

Chapter Five

𝓜iriam

May 2, 1947

Ｓhe was ready.

Her suit was perfection, its precisely fitted jacket and volumi-nous, calf-grazing skirt bringing to mind Monsieur Dior's sensa-tional new designs, but in a gentler, less aggressively chic way. Here in England, she knew, they were wary of the New Look, constrained as they were by their rationing and coupons, and she had no wish to antagonize anyone by reminding them of things they could not yet have.

Her gloves were white, her shoes were shining, and her hat, an elegant oval of finely woven black straw, sat on her head just so. Her portfolio was filled with samples of her work, a reference from Mai-son Rébé, and, most precious of all, the letter of recommendation from Christian Dior.

The morning after her arrival, exactly nine weeks ago, she had compiled a list of the best fashion designers in London. For this she had relied on Monsieur Dior's suggestions, which she had supplemented with addresses from a copy of British *Vogue*. She had eaten a fortifying and quite disgusting breakfast of porridge and weak tea, had dressed in the garments she had prepared the night before, and had set out to conquer London.

The first name on her list had been Lachasse. She'd been certain they would offer her a position on the spot, for her credentials were impeccable, her samples proved that she was capable of working at the highest level, and she had that coveted letter from Monsieur Dior.

It had all counted for nothing.

The woman who had answered the door, wearing a frock that any self-respecting Frenchwoman would have instantly consigned to the rubbish bin, had been impatient and irritable, and twice she'd asked Miriam to repeat herself. "I can't understand what you're saying. This is England, you know. You need to learn proper English."

Miriam's nerves had got the better of her. She'd lost words that she ought to have known, she had begun to stammer, and altogether she had sounded like an utter fool.

"We're not looking for embroiderers," the woman had finally said. "Best try your luck elsewhere."

Undeterred, she had proceeded to Hardy Amies on Savile Row, the second establishment on Monsieur Dior's list. Miriam had gone to the staff entrance and asked to see the head of embroidery. The man at the door had told her they weren't hiring.

Her next stop had been at Charles Creed in Knightsbridge. This time she'd been ushered inside and instructed to wait for someone from the embroidery workroom. A woman had appeared after nearly a half hour, and it was evident, from her pinched expression and clipped words, that she was annoyed by the interruption. Before Miriam had finished introducing herself, the woman had cut her off.

"Do you have any English training or experience? No? Then we're not interested."

By the end of the day she had also been turned away from the workrooms of Victor Stiebel, Digby Morton, Peter Russell, Michael Sherard, and Bianca Mosca. No one had wanted an embroiderer. No one had cared to hear of her training and experience. No one had given her the chance to so much as mention her letter of reference from Monsieur Christian Dior.

Miriam had scuttled back to her hotel room and had perched on the edge of her bed and had stared at nothing for hours. When the worst of her panic had subsided she had opened her little notebook, the one into which she had copied the list of designers Monsieur Dior had given her, together with addresses for their London workrooms. Only then had she noticed that two of its pages had been stuck together, and she had somehow managed to skip over the first name on the list.

Norman Hartnell. The designer who, according to Monsieur Dior, had the best embroidery workroom in England.

She had seen pictures of the gowns Monsieur Hartnell made for the English queen, the grand crinolines and softly serene day dresses that weren't especially chic but suited her so well. Surely his premières would appreciate someone with her training and experience.

It had been stupid and foolhardy to persevere after that deplorable woman at Lachasse had rejected her, and she had only compounded her stupidity by working her way through every name on her list but one. It had left her teetering at the edge of a precipice, and if she were to stumble . . .

She would take a step back. Take the time to polish up her English, immerse herself in its awkward idioms and ridiculous grammar, and sand away the veneer of desperation that had tainted her brief conversations at every workroom she had visited that day.

She would take some of the money Monsieur Dior had given her, and she would buy herself some time.

Two days later she had moved to cheaper lodgings, a dismal little *pension* in Ealing that charged the same for a week as did the hotel for a single night, and then she had set about practicing her English. After breakfast each day she had gone to the Italian café near the Underground entrance, had bought a coffee—it was far nicer there than at the Lyons and A.B.C. cafés that seemed to be on every corner—and had eavesdropped on the other customers, writing down words she didn't understand so she might look them up later. Most afternoons she had gone to the cinema, silently parroting the actors' words under the cover of darkness, trying to make sense of the strange idioms they used.

And everywhere she had gone, though it grated at her solitary soul, she had engaged people in conversation: the other women in the breakfast room at her *pension,* the man who sold newspapers on the corner, even the sweetly flirtatious waiter at the Italian café, though his English was worse than hers.

It had taken her more than two months, but now she was ready. Today she would try again.

Checking her *A to Z* to ensure she was heading in the right direction, Miriam set off for Mayfair, alighting at Bond Street station. Ten minutes later she turned onto Bruton Place, her heart pounding, her hands clammy beneath her gloves.

It was easy to find the staff entrance to Hartnell, for a gleaming delivery lorry was parked about halfway along the mews, and a series of enormous white boxes were being loaded into its open back doors. A man in a white coat was checking the boxes off against a list, his expression so serious he might have been in charge of delivering chests of gold bullion. Rather than interrupt, Miriam hung back and waited for him to finish.

"That's everything, then," he said to the waiting driver a good fifteen minutes later, once the last of the boxes had been placed in the lorry. "Off you go."

Before the man could vanish inside, Miriam came forward. "Excuse me."

"Yes? What do you want?" He looked her up and down, a puzzled frown furrowing his brow. "The salesroom entrance is on Bruton Street," he offered in a marginally more courteous tone.

"I would like to see your head of embroidery."

The frown returned. "For what reason?"

"I wish to seek employment. I have with me a reference from Monsieur Christian—"

"You'll have to go through the usual channels."

"Very well," she said, her patience fraying. "What are they?"

"Buggered if I know, but they don't involve letting in strangers off the street." With that he darted through the door and pulled it shut behind him.

Panic bloomed in her throat, her heart, her mind. *What to do, what to do, what to do?* She had come to the end of Monsieur Dior's list. There was nowhere else to go. She was trained for nothing else.

She spun around, ready to flee, and caught sight of her reflection in a window. The man in the white coat had thought she was one of Monsieur Hartnell's customers. Only for a moment, but it might be enough.

She walked to the end of Bruton Place, turned the corner, then doubled back along Bruton Street itself. She held her head high. Straightened her spine. Remembered how she had managed such moments before. If she could keep her cool when presenting false identification to the Milice, she could maintain a veneer of serenity when entering the front door of a London dress designer. This she could do.

The entrance was a grand affair of green malachite and sparkling glass, the equal to anything one might see on the rue du Faubourg Saint-Honoré. A footman appeared silently, ushering her inside, and she paused, forcing herself to stand very still as she took the measure of the space. Modern, she thought. Cool and elegant and masterfully restrained. Nearly every vertical plane was mirrored; the few bare walls were painted in the cool gray-green of young lavender leaves.

A woman came forward, beautifully dressed, her welcoming smile radiating sincerity. "Good morning. How may I help you?"

"Good morning. I am here to see Monsieur Hartnell."

The woman's eyes widened fractionally, but her smile did not waver. "Of course. If I might first—"

"I am Mademoiselle Dassin. My friend, Monsieur Christian Dior, told me I must pay Monsieur Hartnell a visit upon my arrival in England." Not quite the truth, but not precisely a lie.

"Ah. I see." The woman's eyes darted toward the stairs.

"Shall we?" Miriam asked, and without waiting for an answer, she set off across the foyer.

"Ah, yes, of course. Miss, ah . . ."

"Dassin."

"Yes. Miss Dassin. If you could perhaps wait while I speak to his secretary, then I—"

Miriam began to ascend the stairs. "I do not mind waiting."

"If I could perhaps trouble you to take a seat down—"

"It is quite all right. I am certain he will wish to see me."

As they reached the first floor, the woman slipped past Miriam, walking as quickly as her high heels would allow. "I really do need to speak with Mrs. Price and let her— Oh, my goodness."

They stood at the door of an office. One glance told Miriam it was empty. "Madame Price does not appear to be at her desk."

"No, she isn't. If you could please wait here while I find her?"

"Of course."

On the far side of Mrs. Price's office, which was actually an ante-room, a door stood open. A man was speaking on the telephone, and though she knew it would be best to stay where she was, Miriam found herself inching toward the door.

A sign hung on the wall nearby: NO ADMITTANCE BEYOND THIS DOOR EXCEPT BY EXPRESS PERMISSION OF MRS. PRICE.

She was certain, now, that Monsieur Hartnell was on the other side of that door. He had finished his telephone call; it would not be entirely beyond the pale to knock and ask for admittance. If she waited for permission, Mrs. Price might decide to let her in. Or she might just as easily have Miriam escorted out.

This was her chance. Her *only* chance. She knocked on the door.

A man was sitting at an enormous desk, a smoldering cigarette in his left hand, a pencil in the other. He was in his late forties, she supposed, with reddish hair that had gone white at his temples, and his suit was beautifully tailored.

"Hello? Monsieur Hartnell?" she asked.

"Hello," he said, and he smiled when he saw her at the door. "What a lovely ensemble."

"Thank you. I beg your pardon, but your Mrs. Price is not at her desk."

"I see. Will you come in? Do sit down."

She advanced into the room, which was every bit as elegant as the rest of the premises, and perched on the edge of the chair he indicated. "My name is Miriam Dassin and I am an embroiderer, most recently at Maison Rébé. I also have a letter of recommendation from Monsieur Christian Dior."

She opened her portfolio, relieved that her hands were steady, and handed him the letter. Only after he had accepted it did she realize he might not understand French. But as she watched him read, marking the changes of expression on his face, she felt certain that he was able to make out the general tenor of its words.

"A warm introduction indeed."

"I also have some examples of my work, if you . . . ?"

"I should be delighted to see them."

She had bound them into a folder, the edges of each piece carefully whipstitched, and as he looked through the samples, his cigarette held well clear, inspecting the front and back of each, she found herself holding her breath. So close, so close. He seemed to understand and appreciate what she had done, but was it enough?

"You are an exceptionally talented embroiderer, Miss Dassin. This is marvelous work. I'd be a fool to send you away."

The vise of fear around her chest, so omnipresent she'd almost forgotten it, loosened a fraction.

"Thank you, Monsieur Hartnell. I—"

"Mrs. Price!" he called.

A middle-aged woman, short and stoutly corseted, came to the door.

"Yes, Mr. Hartnell?"

"Could you ring down to Miss Duley? Ask her to come up? I have someone new for her."

Miriam very badly wanted to say something, but what if she stumbled over her English? Said something that made him reconsider? So she sat where she was, her back ramrod straight, and watched as he looked through her samples again, nodding his head from time to time, all the while puffing on his cigarette.

Mrs. Price had returned. "I just spoke with her. Says she can't come up just yet. Something to do with a pair of scissors left on a frame?"

"Oh, very well. We'll just have to beard the dragon in her den." He handed the samples back to Miriam, then stood, stubbed out his cigarette in a heavy crystal ashtray, and came around the desk. "If you don't mind bringing along your things, Miss Dassin, I'll lead the way."

The Hartnell premises were a series of buildings that had been joined together in an almost haphazard fashion, and after going along several corridors, then up and down at least three sets of stairs, Miriam was completely turned around. At last they came to a heavy metal door, its paint flaking away in spots. Monsieur Hartnell hauled it open and waved her through.

They stood at the top of yet another flight of steps. Beyond was a large, brightly lit workroom, the late morning sun from its bank of windows generously supplemented by hanging electric lights. Two rows of embroidery frames on trestles ran the length of the room, though most of the occupants were standing around a single frame in the far corner. One woman, very young, was crying softly into a balled-up handkerchief while another rubbed her back, consoling her with soft words. Most of the embroiderers seemed to be in their early twenties, more or less the same age as Miriam; a few were younger, and a very few were conspicuously older.

Although those still seated got to their feet as soon as Monsieur Hartnell entered the workroom, and everyone waited patiently for him to explain his arrival, Miriam could discern no change in the temperature of the room. No current of anxiety rising to the surface.

"As you were, as you were. I just came to have a quick word with Miss Duley."

A woman in her early fifties broke away from the group in the corner and approached, a look of bemusement on her face. Her hair was pulled back tightly, unforgivingly, and the black of her severely tailored frock was relieved only by a simple white collar.

"So sorry to drag you down here, sir," she said, speaking with the ease of long acquaintance. "We've had a tempest in a teapot. Pair of scissors left on a frame. Nicked one of the designs, but it's easy enough to repair. The young lady responsible has assured me she won't be so careless again."

"Good, good. Mistakes happen, of course. Not to worry."

"Who is this we have here?" Miss Duley asked.

"Oh, yes. This is Miss Miriam Dassin, lately of Paris. She showed me some of her work just now, and it is very good. Very good indeed."

Miss Duley looked to Miriam, her gaze assessing but not in the least hostile, then back to Monsieur Hartnell. "We do have a few girls leaving to get married this summer, and I've been worrying as to how we'd replace them. How soon might you be able to start, Miss Dassin?"

Was that it? Could it truly be that easy? "Perhaps Monday?" she ventured. "I have missed my work, you see, and—"

"Monday it is. Come for half eight and we'll get you set up with the girls in accounts. Just go to the staff entrance on Bruton Place and tell them you're starting. Someone there will point you in the right direction."

"Monday morning at half-past eight, yes. Thank you." She turned to Monsieur Hartnell, who now bore an expression of extreme satisfaction. "I thank you as well. Most sincerely. I hope you can forgive me for—"

Shaking his head, he waved her apology away. "I was, and am, delighted to make your acquaintance. Welcome to Hartnell. Miss Duley, I'll leave you to make the arrangements."

"Of course, sir." They waited in silence for the few seconds it took for him to retreat through the fire door, and then Miss Duley turned her attention to her staff, none of whom had returned to their frames. "We're only a few minutes shy of half twelve. Why don't you go on and have your dinner now? Ann—if I could ask you to stay for a minute?"

The same woman who had been consoling the younger girl earlier now came over. Her pretty red-gold hair was pinned back severely, and like Miss Duley she wore a well-tailored frock. Its dark brown color did nothing for her, however, deadening her complexion and making her fading freckles rather too noticeable.

"Miss Dassin, this is Miss Hughes. Ann Hughes. One of my senior hands. I think we'll have you work with her to begin."

Ann's smile was wide and unaffected. "Welcome to Hartnell, Miss Dassin."

"Thank you. I wonder, Miss Duley, if perhaps you would like to see my samples?"

"I don't see why not. Although you must be good if Mr. Hartnell is keen." Taking the bound samples from Miriam, she set them on the edge of the nearest embroidery frame. "Ann. Come and look," she said only a few seconds later, her voice almost reverent. "Look at these designs."

"These are beautiful. Really, they are. Where did you do your training?" Ann asked.

"At Maison Lesage."

Miss Duley nodded, her attention still fixed on the samples. "And, ah, during the war . . . ?"

"I was at Maison Rébé. The atelier stayed open. It was a difficult time," she said, hoping against hope that Miss Duley would not question her further. It was hard enough to merely think of those years, let alone speak of them. Hiding in plain sight, lying to everyone she knew, holding her breath whenever she had to cross a checkpoint or queue up for bread.

She was holding her breath now.

"I'm sure it was terribly difficult," Miss Duley agreed. "We like to go on about how bad things were during the war, but we never had to live with Nazis lording it over us. Such a relief that it's all over now."

Miriam nodded. Swallowed. Tried to think of how to respond in a fashion that wouldn't provoke further questions.

"Now, wages. Most girls come in as assistants, but your skills are well above that level. I think . . . well, why don't we start you as a junior hand? Pay is thirty-five shillings per week."

"Thank you. That is most generous."

"We start at half eight each day, Monday to Friday, and finish at five. From time to time we might ask you to work longer hours, say if we've a last-minute commission and are hard put to finish on time. We've a canteen in the cellar, and we break for tea midmorning, for dinner at half twelve, and again for tea in the afternoon. No smoking in the workrooms, no lipstick or rouge, fingernails kept short. You can wear a coverall if you have one, but street clothes are fine. I'd tell you to keep a smart appearance, but"—and here she waved a hand at Miriam—"just look at you. If I didn't know better I'd think you were here to be fitted for a gown."

"You are very kind."

"It was smart, you know. Going to see Mr. Hartnell straight off. Mrs. Price told me when she called down."

"I assure you, I meant no offense by it." She waited for the woman to remonstrate with her, or tell her she would be sacked for further acts of insubordination. Instead Miss Duley smiled, a true smile that went all the way to her bright blue eyes.

"None taken. Now I'd best get my dinner in before the girls come back. Ann, can you show Miss Dassin the way out?"

"Of course."

Back they went through the warren of corridors, finally emerging onto the mews at the back of the premises. "Here we are," Ann said. "Where are you heading?"

"I am returning to Ealing. On the Central line."

"Not so far, then. I'll see you on Monday."

They shook hands, and then Miriam was walking away, through the warm midday sun, her eyes stinging in the light, her every limb shaking from relief and an unexpected and unfamiliar surge of joy. The clouds had cleared, the sky was the most beautiful shade of *bleu azur,* and spring was in the air.

At long last, and against all hope, spring had come again.

Chapter Six

Heather

May 14, 2016

$\mathcal{T}$o the consternation of their friends and neighbors, Heather's parents had shunned tradition when planning a memorial service for Nan. There'd been no visitation, no wake, and no funeral.

"She said she couldn't stand the idea of me and Jim spending a penny more than we had to on seeing her off," her mom explained when people asked. "When I asked her what she wanted, she told me to toss her on the compost heap."

Since the authorities frowned on such unorthodox burial practices, they'd chosen the simplest and cheapest option: a straightforward cremation, with the ashes returned in a plain wooden box. "She'd have preferred a cardboard one, but when I asked the undertaker if that was possible he looked like he was going to pass out."

So a pine box it was, and they'd set it on the fireplace mantel for the time being. "As soon as the peonies are in bloom, we'll scatter her ashes in the garden."

Instead of a funeral, Heather's parents had hosted a gathering at their house. There'd been a bakery's worth of scones and squares and cookies on the dining room table, and pots of tea and coffee besides. Heather's mom had thanked everyone for coming, and her dad had recited that poem about the dead person simply being in the next room, and though people had smiled and wiped away tears and nodded their approval, Heather had been strangely unmoved. She suspected her grandmother would have reacted the same way.

The best part of the gathering had been the stories people told about Nan, who'd always been the first to come by with food and flowers from her garden when a baby was born or a loved one died. She'd been an ESL tutor, a Meals on Wheels driver, a hospital visitor, a volunteer at the food bank, and back in the late 1970s she'd quietly taken in an entire family of Vietnamese refugees.

The Nguyens had moved on before Heather was even born, but she knew Nan had kept in touch with them over the years. Their youngest son, a doctor, had driven all the way from Montreal to pay his respects.

"Whenever we tried to thank her," he told Heather and her parents, "she said she knew what it was like to move to a new country and start over."

Dr. Nguyen's words had come back to her later, when she was washing the dishes, for the idea of Nan having to start over had given her pause. Of course they all knew that Nan was English, from somewhere near London, and had moved to Canada after the war. Even if she'd never told them, her accent would have given her away.

Growing up, living just around the corner from Nan, she'd never seen a photograph of her grandfather, nor any other pictures of her grandmother's life in England. She'd asked a few times, when she was little, but Nan had always changed the subject.

Her mother hadn't been able to answer any of her questions either. "They're all like that, you know. The ones who lived through the war."

"Because things were so awful?" Heather had been in high school, and they'd been talking about the world wars in history class.

"I suppose. And because they came here to make a fresh start. Away from the memories of everything they'd lost. So you can't blame them for not wanting to talk about it."

As she dried the last of the good china, Heather stole a glance at her mother. She seemed to be holding up well in spite of everything, but her mom had always been good at putting on a brave face.

"Are you sure you're okay? I can finish this off on my own. You should sit down for a bit."

"I'm fine, honey. I'd known it was coming for a while. And you know, part of me is grateful—not that she's gone, of course. Only that she stayed herself right to the end. She'd seen so many of her friends fade away, and I know she dreaded it."

"Like Mrs. Jackson from across the street."

"Yes, exactly. After that funeral, you know, Mum turned to me and made me promise to put a pillow over her face if she ever went dotty like poor Martha Jackson. Of course I'd never have done such a thing, but I knew what she meant. That's why we didn't have the doctors jump in when she got so sick. You seemed upset about it, when I talked to you the morning she died, but—"

"I understand, Mom. Honestly I do. You absolutely did the right thing."

"I'm glad you think so. Oh—I keep forgetting to tell you. I found something when I was going through Nan's things. All the overflow from her house that we'd been keeping in the basement."

"What kind of something?" Heather asked, her interest piqued.

"Please tell me it isn't another box of stuff from Nan's shop. Sunita's the only one of my friends who knits, and she's neck-deep in yarn already."

"No, nothing like that. Just some pieces of beaded fabric, but she'd written your name on the box, so she must have wanted you to have them. Hold on—they're in the spare room."

Heather sank into the nearest chair, her feet aching, and closed her eyes. She'd get up and wipe down the counters in a minute.

"Here we go," her mom said, depositing a large plastic box on the kitchen table. On its lid, in black Sharpie marker, were the words *For Heather* in Nan's handwriting. "I'll let you do the honors."

Heather pulled the box toward her and pried off the lid. Inside was a single, tissue-wrapped bundle. Suddenly tentative, she looked at her mother for reassurance, then folded back the top layer of fabric to reveal a rose.

Not a real rose, of course, but rather an embroidered rose, its petals made of stiff white satin, each attached separately to a backing of fine, nearly translucent fabric. Each petal was edged with tiny pearls and even tinier glass beads, all of them sparkling merrily under the harsh fluorescent lights of her mother's kitchen.

She wiped her trembling hands on the fabric of her yoga pants, suddenly remembering that Nan had always insisted on clean hands when handling precious things. The edge of the fabric had been rolled under, a bit like an expensive scarf, and the stitches were so fine she had to squint to see them. In the bottom corner was a monogram worked in thread that was only a shade darker than the fabric.

"*EP*," she whispered. "At least I think it says '*EP*.'"

Holding her breath, she lifted it up, really so she could look at the embroidery better, and saw there was something underneath. It was another layer of thin cotton fabric, the same as the wrapping. This she drew aside to reveal a second piece of embroidery: three star-shaped satin flowers, also decorated with pearls and crystals. Beneath that was a third design, this time of three curving ears of wheat, their grains made of rice-shaped seed pearls. And beneath that was a photograph.

"Hold on," her mom said. "I didn't notice that before."

"What is it?"

"I'm not sure. There's some writing here on the back. I think it might be Mum's handwriting. 'London. Oct. 1947. Waiting for HM.'"

It was of a group of women, most of them seated around one of four long, narrow tables in a large, bright, high-ceilinged room. Heather counted twenty-two women in total, most of them wearing white coats or aprons over vintage-style dresses. Not vintage when the photo was taken, she realized.

"Who are they?" she asked.

"I think they're seamstresses. Embroiderers, actually. Look at those tables. They're actually frames. Just like the ones we use at my quilting circle," her mother explained. "The fabric is stretched on the frames before they start adding the beads and sequins and what-have-you."

Heather examined the photograph minutely, searching for something familiar, something known, among the faces in the group. Her attention was caught by one woman, her fair hair clipped to the side, her expression solemn and unsmiling. She seemed wary, Heather thought, as if she was afraid of what the photographer might see.

"That woman by the window—" she began.

"I know. I think that's Mum. Younger than I remember her, but I think it's her. I just . . ."

"What is it?"

"It's just that it doesn't *fit*. I mean, Mum was good with her hands, and you know how she loved to knit, but she was never one for sewing or embroidery or anything like that. I don't think I ever saw her sew on so much as a button."

"Didn't everyone learn to sew in those days?"

"Yes, but even then it was pretty basic stuff. Mending and darning and how to knit a scarf. This kind of work," and here she nodded at the embroideries, "is another story. Embroidery like this takes *years* to learn."

"So you don't think Nan made these?"

"I honestly don't know. She definitely never said anything to me about it. On the other hand, there she is in the picture."

Heather couldn't tear her eyes away from the young Nan in the photograph. "So why did she stop? Why did she come here?"

"I always assumed it was sadness that sent her across the ocean. Grief over losing my dad, and before him her brother. And I think I remember her saying that both her parents had died before the war. That would have left her more or less alone in the world, apart from Milly, her sister-in-law. And she's the one who had already moved to Canada."

It made a strange sort of sense. Nan had decided to make a fresh start, away from the death and destruction of the war, and that's why she'd emigrated. That's why she hadn't ever talked about England—it had been too painful. And yet . . .

"If she wanted to leave everything behind, then why did she bring these embroideries with her?" Heather asked. "Why didn't she ever show them to us? And why did she put my name on the box?"

"I've no idea. Perhaps she meant to give them to you, one day, and then never got around to it."

"What do you think I should do with them?"

"I was hoping you could find out more. When you're not so busy at work. One rainy afternoon in front of your computer and you'll have it all figured out."

"I guess I could try."

And yet. For all that Nan had never shared the details of her life before she came to Canada, she hadn't seemed like the sort of person whose past was brimming over with secrets. She'd been Nan, honest and kind and generous, a good neighbor and friend. The sort of person you tended to take for granted until she was gone.

If Nan had kept secrets, it had been for a reason. What point was there in unearthing them now? What if, in searching for answers, she discovered something unsettling, even disturbing?

"I can see the wheels turning in your head," her mother said. "Let's put these away, now, and get to bed."

"Okay. It's just . . . what do you think she would want me to do?"

"Oh, honey. I wish I could say for sure. Maybe she did want you to know, and putting your name on the box was her way of telling. Of asking, in a way."

"Maybe."

Nan had never been one for answering questions; that was a given. But perhaps, just perhaps, she wouldn't mind if Heather went looking for answers.

Chapter Seven

Ann

July 10, 1947

Milly had left for Canada a month ago, but it had only taken a few days for Ann to decide she hated living alone. It wasn't as if she needed someone glued to her side every hour of the day, for she'd always been an independent sort of person. But this was different.

Without Milly, the house was empty. Hollowed out. Ann was lonely, with no one to share the little details of life, things that weren't important on their own but, added together, made up the warp and weft of her life: an interesting person she'd noticed on the Tube, a conversation she'd had with Mr. Booth about his prize sweet peas and how they were suffering in the near-tropical summer heat, a new song she'd heard on the wireless.

She was lonely and getting poorer by the day, because the rent on the house was more than she could manage without help. After Milly had fixed a departure date, Ann had asked around at work, but the few girls who were interested in lodging with her had balked at the commute out to Barking. Never mind that it might easily take just as long to travel from Mayfair to their current lodgings in London; it was the idea of living in the suburbs, far away from the lights and fun and glamour of the city, that put them off.

All she had to do was write up a notice and post it in the newsagent's.

Female lodger required. Rent 15/- p.w. Private
bedroom. Furnished. Friendly accommodations. Reply
to A. Hughes, 109 Morley Road, Barking.

Still she hesitated. Someone from the council might see the notice, or a busybody neighbor might report it, and then she'd be out on the street as soon as the council could issue an eviction notice.

Almost as bad: If she didn't get on with her lodger? What if coming home from work became something she dreaded? It wouldn't be fair to evict someone for being dull or silly, or for having tiresome habits. Eating with one's mouth open wasn't a hanging offense. There was no way she could really know until she'd lived with the lodger for a while, but no one she already knew was interested in her spare room.

Yet it had to be done.

Tonight, on her way home, she'd get off the train one stop farther, at Upney, and post her notice in the nearest newsagent's or post office. If that didn't work, she would look into the rates for the classified pages of the *Dagenham Post*. Then she might use their reply service to avoid unwanted scrutiny.

"'. . . and queen announce the betrothal of—'"

Ann dropped the teacup she was washing, ran into the sitting room, and turned up the volume on the wireless. Had she missed it?

"'—*Lieutenant Philip Mountbatten, Royal Navy, son of the late Prince Andrew of Greece and Princess Andrew, formerly Princess Alice of Battenberg, to which union the king has gladly given his consent.'*

The preceding was the official announcement from Buckingham Palace. No further information in regard to the betrothal has yet been announced. In other news . . ."

Thank goodness she'd turned on the wireless when she'd come down for breakfast. A royal engagement—a royal wedding. The last one had been . . . she couldn't be sure. Perhaps the Duke and Duchess of Gloucester? But that had been well before the war.

Milly would roll her eyes at the notion of getting excited over the wedding of a stranger. And it was true, for Ann had never met Princess Elizabeth. But she had met the queen, or rather curtsied to her when she and some of the other girls had been taken to Buckingham Palace as a treat just before the war. The queen had been ever so friendly, so gracious and kind to everyone, and they'd all felt bowled over afterward.

The royal family had made sacrifices, same as the rest of them. Bombed out more than once, and the king's own brother killed. The princess deserved a proper wedding in Westminster Abbey with beautiful music and flowers and decorations, a troop of bridesmaids, and a glorious gown. Surely the government would understand. Surely the gray-faced men in Whitehall wouldn't insist on some dreary affair that conformed to all their tiresome austerity directives.

And if that included a gown from Hartnell, so much the better.

Suddenly Ann was so excited she couldn't bear to sit in her lonely kitchen and eat her solitary piece of toast with margarine and a smear of watery jam. Today she would throw caution to the wind. She would take an early train, and stop off at the Corner House near Bond Street station, and have something delicious for breakfast. She would buy a newspaper, just in case it had more to say about the engagement, and she'd get to work early and be ready to hear the news when it came. If there was news of the gown, Miss Duley was sure to know.

She left for work a half hour early, so jubilant she all but ran up the road to the station, pausing only to buy a copy of the *Daily Mail*. On its front page was a picture of the princess from the evening before, a bit blurry, but Ann was almost sure she recognized the gown as one from the South Africa tour. One she had worked on herself.

Nearly the entire front page was taken up with news of the engagement—the betrothal, as they called it. Most was straightforward speculation, as there'd been no official announcement beyond the one she'd heard on the news earlier. There were a few more details about Lieutenant Mountbatten, who was a distant cousin of the princess, and had been decorated for his valor during the war.

She was famished by the time she walked into the Corner House, so she treated herself to a soft-boiled egg, a buttered crumpet, and a small pot of tea. It came to a shilling and tuppence, a shocking amount of money to spend on a single meal, but it had been months—no, years—since she'd done anything so frivolous and fun. If breakfast had been twice the price she still would have done it.

By a quarter past eight she was in the cloakroom at Hartnell, changing into her white coverall and smiling at the sight of her friends, all early for work, and all, like her, bouncing off the rafters with excitement. They were talking so quickly she could scarcely keep track of who said what.

"Remember back in the spring? When he gave up his foreign title and became British? The papers were saying there'd be an announcement any day."

"I read somewhere that the king didn't want her to get engaged before she turned twenty-one."

"Well, that was in April. Why've they waited so long?"

"He's in the navy. Maybe he had to ask for leave." This last suggestion was greeted with hoots of laughter.

"I doubt that. One word from the king would've solved *that* problem."

"I think they got engaged a while ago," Ann said. "I do. And they didn't say anything right away because they wanted to keep it to themselves for a while. Now that it's official, they have to share it with the whole world."

"I suppose that makes sense . . ."

"But we haven't talked about the most important part: Will they ask Mr. Hartnell to design her gown?"

"The queen loves him. We'll end up doing her gown at the very least."

"Who else can do the wedding gown? All the society brides come to Mr. Hartnell for their wedding. And he did Princess Alice's. That was the last royal wedding."

"Yes, but it was more than ten years ago. And Molyneux did make some of their clothes for South Africa."

"Only because so many were needed. For the important gowns it's always Mr. Hartnell."

"What if Princess Elizabeth wants a Dior gown?"

"No. She is an English princess. She will have an English dressmaker for her wedding gown." This last comment came from Miriam, herself a Frenchwoman. Although Ann had worked with her closely since May, she couldn't say she knew Miriam very well. But she was right: the queen and Princess Elizabeth would certainly choose an English dressmaker.

"The queen will want Mr. Hartnell. We'll be hearing the news any day now."

Ann looked at her watch; it was half-past eight. "Come on, every-one. Miss Duley will have a fit if she finds us gabbing away like this."

Still chattering gaily, they trooped into the workroom. Miss Duley was already waiting for them.

"Girls, girls. You're as noisy as a herd of elephants. I know it's ter-ribly exciting, but there's been no announcement yet. And you know what they say about counting your chickens."

"It's so romantic I could *die*," said one of the youngest girls. "Have you seen the photographs of him? He looks like a Greek god!"

"A Greek prince, at any rate," Miss Duley said dryly. "And if I can trouble you to set your dreams of royal romance aside, you all need to calm down. We've no shortage of work to get through."

Ann went straight to her frame, more than ready to begin her day. She and Miriam had been finishing off some fine beadwork on a gown for an American oil baron's wife, but today she had the straightforward task of adding sequins and seed pearls to a length of antique French lace; the client had asked Mr. Hartnell to incorporate the precious material into the bodice of a cocktail gown.

She set to work on stretching the lace, which had been given a back-ing of finely woven silk taffeta, onto her frame, then sorted the pearls and sequins into tiny piles on her bead tray, ready to be scooped up and threaded on her thinnest needle.

Ann worked for an hour or more, her thoughts never straying from the fabric before her and the delicate effect—dewdrops on flower petals, she liked to imagine—that she was creating. Only when her fingers began to cramp and her eyes were sandy and dry did she look up, stretch, and breathe in deeply.

"A good morning so far?" Miss Duley had been keeping an eye on the workroom, the apprentices and assistants in particular, making sure they were focused on their sewing and not the diverting news from Buckingham Palace. Now she came over to stand at Ann's side.

"Very good. Has he had a call?" In her mind, thinking of Mr. Hartnell, she all but put a capital *H* on "he." The man did have that sort of effect on the people who worked for him, as profane as that might seem.

"Not yet. Not as far as I know." Miss Duley pitched her voice low so as not to be overheard. "But I'm sure he'll hear from the palace in a day or two. He's working on some ideas now."

"Will they even bother to ask anyone else?"

"I'd be surprised if they did. I know for a fact that the queen was very pleased with our work on her gowns for South Africa. Once things are certain, he'll likely want us to do up some samples. Something to take along to the queen and Princess Elizabeth. Just to ensure they are completely happy with the design as executed. Naturally I'll want you to make them up."

Ann smiled and nodded, but otherwise gave no sign that Miss Duley had said anything. Never mind that she felt like jumping to her feet and doing cartwheels across the workroom. *She* would be given the task of making up the samples. *Her* work would be set before Princess Elizabeth. It was almost too much to take in.

"I gather you're pleased?"

"Very," she admitted. "Thank you. I won't let you down."

"Of course you won't. I also want to ask, while we have a quiet moment . . . what do you think of Miriam? Would you say she's getting on well?"

"She is. Very well. It's not often you see someone who can work to such a high standard who wasn't trained here."

"Oh, good. I've been thinking that if we are awarded the commission, I should like her to continue working as your junior. It may cause some bad feelings. Some of the others may feel jealous. I'll trust you to keep an eye on things, make sure there aren't any problems. That sort of thing."

"Of course."

"There will be plenty of work to go round. At least that's my guess. But everyone will be keen to work on the wedding gown itself."

Ann nodded. Of course they would.

"Does Miriam get on well with the other girls? She seems very quiet," Miss Duley asked.

"She is, but . . ."

"Is it a case of her not understanding? A problem with her English?"

"No, not at all. She's shy, I think. Reserved. And rather sad. She hasn't said anything, but I feel as if she must have had a hard time during the war."

"Didn't we all?"

Ann lowered her voice to the merest whisper. "Not like she did. I may be wrong, of course. It's just a feeling. Nothing she's said."

She wasn't wrong. If there was anything she had learned during the war, it was how to recognize the marks of grief on another.

"Well, keep an eye on her. Make sure she isn't left to herself when you're all sitting in the canteen. And if she's struggling, do let me know."

"I will."

"How long until you're finished with this lace, do you think?"

"Not long at all. By midday tomorrow at the latest."

"Good." Miss Duley nodded decisively, then moved on to the next frame to advise, to steady nerves, to caution anyone who was working too quickly or, conversely, was dawdling over a simple task.

Ann returned her attention to her own work, not pausing until it was time for their morning break. As she rose from her chair, already one of the last to head to the canteen, she noticed that Miriam was still intent on her work.

"You'll wear yourself out," she said. "Come on downstairs with me. I'm sure we can both use a few minutes away from our frames."

The other woman looked up and noticed the empty workroom. "Oh. Do excuse me. I had not realized—"

"That's a sign of a dedicated embroiderer. Come on, now, otherwise Miss Duley will be calling us back before we make it to the front of the queue."

Mugs of tea in hand, they found a quiet table in the corner. Ann was the first to speak. "When I first started here, we didn't have a canteen. I'd bring a flask of tea with me. It was fine in the morning but was always stone cold by the afternoon."

"Where did you have your break? Not in the workrooms?"

"Heavens, no. In the cloakroom, sitting in between everyone's raincoats and muddy boots. This is much nicer."

Miriam's smile was shy, a little hesitant, and Ann wished, now, that she had made more of an effort to get to know the other woman. This was the first time they'd talked about anything other than work, even though Miriam had been at Hartnell for more than two months.

Ann hadn't wanted to push her; had thought to give her a while to settle in. But she'd waited too long. Miss Duley had asked her to keep an eye on Miriam, but instead she'd been so wrapped up with her worries about Milly leaving that—

"How long have you worked here? At Hartnell, I mean to say."

Well, then. Perhaps Miriam wasn't all that shy. Perhaps she just needed a quiet corner and someone who was prepared to listen.

"Would you believe it's been eleven years? Feels like forever. I started as an apprentice, straight out of school. Could barely thread a needle. At first I swept the floor, fetched things for the junior and senior hands, things like that. Then they let me sort the beads and sequins, make sure they had what they needed. It was months before Miss Duley let me sew on so much as a spangle."

"But you learned."

"I did. Bit by bit, I learned."

"And you have been here all that time?"

Ann nodded. "All that time. Even during the war, when we weren't allowed to use embroidery on anything being sold here in England. Austerity regulations, you see. But we kept on making clothes for export, mostly to America, and quite often there were things to do up for the queen and other royals. And we did a lot of work for the London theaters. All in the interests of boosting morale, I suppose. Were you . . . were you able to keep working as an embroiderer during the war?"

The hovering smile faded from Miriam's face. Looking down, she focused her gaze on her untouched mug of tea. "Yes. During the Occupation there was talk of the Germans shutting the couture houses, or of moving them to Germany, but the couturiers convinced them, the Nazis, to keep things as they were."

"I remember reading about them. The Nazis at the fashion shows, with their wives and, well, their . . ."

"Mistresses."

"Yes. And how they wore the latest fashions while everyone else in France was starving."

"It is true. They did. Yet most of the women at the *défilés* were French. Can you believe it? Those with wealth kept their riches. They had little to fear as long as they behaved themselves."

"It must have been awful. Working on clothes for the enemy."

"It was, and yet I was grateful for it. For the work, I mean. It kept me alive."

"Of course," Ann hastened to agree. "I expect I would have done the same. It's not as if we were invaded. We never had to live under their thumb as you did."

"You had the bombing. That is something. Until I came here and saw the holes—I mean the open spaces where the bombs fell—I did not understand how bad it was. I had no notion of how much was destroyed."

"It was bad. Although I'm not sure I should complain after what you've been through."

Ann had meant only to commiserate. To show that she truly sympathized. But something in her words had struck at the other woman, as sharp and painful as a slap. Every vestige of color had faded from Miriam's face, and her hands, clasped tight around her mug of tea, had begun to tremble.

Ann reached across the table and touched her hands to Miriam's. Only for an instant. She didn't want to presume, or make the other woman feel worse. But how else to react in the face of such distress?

"I am so sorry," she said. "So sorry. I didn't mean to upset you."

Miriam shook her head and tried to smile. "It is . . ."

"I only meant to say that the worst never happened here, did it? I remember, that first year of the war, being so frightened I could hardly sleep at night. It was all people talked about. How France had fallen and we were next. How it was a matter of time. And then the Blitz . . ."

"There are times I wake," Miriam began, her voice so soft that Ann had to lean forward to hear her. The other girls were so awfully loud. "I wake, and there is that moment when everything is"—she twirled her hand to demonstrate—"not clear . . . ?"

"Fuzzy?"

"Yes. That is the perfect word. Fuzzy. And there are times, for a minute, my memories seem like a very bad dream, and I am slowly waking up. But I open my eyes, and I am truly awake, and then I know. I know in my heart it was not a dream."

"I am sorry," Ann said helplessly. What else was there to say? "Is it . . . is it better here? Do you like it in England?"

Miriam nodded. "I do. I was not sure, at first. The winter did not help, of course. But I do like it here."

"I remember, the day we met, you said you were living in Ealing. Are you still there?"

"Yes. At a small *pension*—a boardinghouse. But I am not very fond of it. The woman who is the concierge—"

"The landlady?"

"Yes. She is not a nice woman. Yesterday she complained that she could not understand me. She said she hadn't lived through the war just to listen to foreigners talking in . . . what did she call it? 'Mumbo jumbo.'" At this, Miriam made a face, as if she had smelled something unpleasant.

"Oh, Miriam. That is awful. I am sorry."

"You do not need to apologize. She is the one who is ignorant. Not you. Everyone here at Hartnell has been very pleasant to me."

"Well, you can't stay on there." And then an idea came to her. Why on earth hadn't she thought of it before? "I wonder," she began, her heart racing a little, "if you might be interested in lodging with me? For years I shared a house with my sister-in-law, but she emigrated to Canada last month."

Miriam seemed nonplussed. "You would wish for *me* to share with you?"

"I don't see why not." And then, to lighten the mood, "You don't have any strange habits, do you? Opera singing? Sleepwalking?"

"No," Miriam said, beginning to giggle. "I assure you I am very dull."

"It is rather a long trip on the Tube," Ann admitted. "But we have the whole house to ourselves, and a little garden, too. Do say you'll at least come and have a look. Do you have any plans for this evening? No? Then come and see the house with me. I'm sure you'll like it. And just think how lovely it will be to see the last of that awful landlady."

"Would it be, ah . . . is it very expensive?" Miriam asked uneasily.

"I was going to charge fifteen shillings a week. Half my rent. Would you be able to manage that?"

"I think so. Yes."

"Oh, good. I did ask some of the other girls when Milly first told me she was emigrating, but they all want to stay in London. And do you know, I was going to put a notice up tonight. This is *so* much better. I can't tell you how relieved I am."

The others were drifting back upstairs. "We had better go," she said, and waited as Miriam drank the last of her tea. Then, her heart light, she followed the other woman up the steps and back to the embroidery workroom.

Chapter Eight

Miriam

After hearing Ann's description of the length and tedium of the journey from Mayfair to Barking, Miriam had braced herself for a voyage of several hours' duration, with perhaps a long walk along dusty country roads at the very end. The reality was rather less daunting: first a ride of nine stops on the Tube, as she had learned to call it, and then a short walk through the station at Mile End for the District line trains heading east.

"Before last year, when they opened the Central line extension, I'd walk over to Oxford Circus and get on a Bakerloo train to Charing Cross," Ann said as they boarded. "But the District line platform was always packed out. Sometimes I'd wait half an hour or more until I could get on a train. This is ever so much easier."

"How far is it now?"

"From here, I'd say about twenty minutes. So, altogether, about an hour? I hope you don't mind."

"An hour does not bother me at all. The train to Ealing is very often delayed, or sometimes it stops for no reason. At least on this train we can look out the window."

It was nothing like the journey that had taken her to Ravensbrück. She'd had to stand the whole way, and she'd been half-dead from thirst and fright and exhaustion by the end, and then the woman next to her had fainted and an iron-faced guard had shot her in the head and warned the rest of them to give him no trouble.

She pushed away the memory. It was useless to think of such things, and Ann had begun to talk again. She really ought to be listening.

"—that there's much to look at. Back gardens and coal yards, and not much else. When I was a girl . . ."

"Yes?" Miriam prompted.

"Barking was a town proper, you see, and not wedged up against London like it is now. Sometimes, on a Sunday afternoon, we'd go for walks in the country, me and my mum and dad and Frank, and we'd go by farm after farm, and sometimes you could stop in and buy a pint of fresh milk, or they'd have jugs of cider later on in the year. I loved those walks. But now the farms are gone, most of them at least, and the rest of my family, too. Seems like forever since I've walked on a piece of ground that wasn't paved over."

"I understand. I feel that way as well. From time to time."

"Where did you grow up?" Ann asked. "Was it in Paris?"

This, she could answer. There was no harm in talking of her quite ordinary childhood. "No. Just outside the city. A place called Colombes. Once, I think, it must have seemed very far from Paris. Like your Barking. But the city grew, and the fields all have houses on them now."

"Are your people still there? In Col— I'm sorry, I don't think I can say it the way you did."

"No. They died during the war." This she could say without flinching. It was true, after all. "What of your family?"

"My parents both died before the war. My dad when I was young, and my mum when I was seventeen. And then my brother, Frank—it was his widow, Milly, who left for Canada—he was killed in the Blitz."

"I am very sorry to hear it."

"And I'm sorry about your family. I suppose that's why you came here? They do say a change can be good when you've lost people you love."

"Yes. In part." She turned her head, pretending to look out the window, and waited for her heart to stop racing. It was normal to speak of the war, of loved ones who had been lost, of the decisions made by those who were left. It was normal and expected and this was not the last time she would be asked about her family. "It is hard to talk of them," she admitted at last.

"I understand. I do. Just thinking about Frank gets me worked up. For him to die in that way seems so unfair. Forget what they say about valor and duty and sacrifice. But I don't have to tell you that. Your family didn't deserve what happened to them either."

A bubble of pain swelled in her throat, rising and rising, and Miriam knew that if she opened her mouth to say anything, even a simple thank-you, she would begin to scream. So she nodded and looked out the window again. Ann seemed to understand, which was a relief, and did not press her any further.

Instead she pulled some knitting from her bag, the wool a bilious shade of mustard yellow. Too late, Miriam realized she was letting her distaste show on her face. But Ann only laughed.

"I know. It's awful, isn't it? My nan always picked the worst colors. It used to be a jumper. Far too ugly to wear, but there's nothing wrong with the wool. Well, apart from the color."

"What are you making?"

"Liners for my boots. I didn't have any last winter, just a pair of worn-out shoes, and there were days I'd get home and my feet were like blocks of ice. I found some boots at the bring-and-buy a few weeks ago, but they aren't lined. So I thought I'd try this. Do you have warm things for the winter? I know it seems far off now, but it's worth thinking about. These eighty-five-degree days won't last for long."

"I have a coat, but it is not very warm."

"Then we'll have to find you a better one, or knit you a good warm cardigan to wear underneath. I've an extra scarf and gloves, and we can knit you a hat. Not out of this, though!" she said, gesturing to the sick-colored wool, and laughed again.

"Thank you," Miriam said, remembering to smile in return.

They were pulling into a station. "EAST HAM," the sign read. English place-names were so very odd. "Why is your town called Barking?" she asked, suddenly curious. "Is it for the sound the dog makes?"

Ann giggled, and the sound of it was so infectious that Miriam found herself laughing as well. "I don't think so. I feel as if it's from an old form of English, or at least that's what we learned in school. Of course now I can't remember what it means."

The train was moving again. Ann packed away her knitting and tucked her bag under her arm. "We're almost there. Our station is next."

It was a beautiful evening. As they emerged from the station and began their walk to Ann's house, the evening sun cast everything in the prettiest sort of rosy glow. Even a slum might look welcoming in such a light. But this was a good neighborhood, the houses neat, windows clean, front yards tidy. Here and there, people had planted out window boxes or left pots of flowers on their doorsteps.

"What are the names of the flowers? Those pink and white ones?" Miriam asked.

"Those? Petunias. What are they in French?"

"*Pétunias,*" Miriam answered, and they both smiled.

"I have some in my garden," Ann added. "It's very small, but I grow as much as I can. Probably more than I should, to be honest. It's very crowded."

They turned off the main road and onto a street of terraced houses. Every house was the same: liver-colored brick on the ground floor and whitewashed stucco on the first floor, with a tiled roof and white-trimmed windows.

"This stretch of road was built first," Ann said. "Before the rest of the estate. I grew up in the last house but one."

"The houses are very tidy," Miriam said, not wishing to lie by saying they were pretty or charming. Surely Ann could see that was not the case.

"They are. And it's quiet here, which is nice. People are friendly, but they keep to themselves, too, if that makes any sense."

There was such a relentless sameness to the houses on the street. One after the other they continued on, with little changing apart from the number on the door. Even the white lace curtains in the front windows looked identical. How would she ever find the correct house in the dark?

"Here we are," Ann said, and then, as if she'd read Miriam's thoughts, "the top of my gate is rounded, see? And the others nearby are all straight across or pointed. That's how I keep track when I come home in the evenings and it's black as pitch. Silly streetlights don't help either. They're so dim you can hardly see your hand in front of your face."

Beyond the gate, the front yard was covered with paving stones, with not a blade of grass peeping up between them. Ann unlocked the door and beckoned Miriam inside.

"Come on in, and don't mind your shoes." They stood in a tiny entranceway, with barely room enough for the two of them. "There's a coatrack behind the door, and in bad weather or winter you can leave your shoes on the mat here."

Moving into the front room, Ann pulled open the draperies, revealing a set of crisp net curtains beneath, their edges embroidered with a pretty design of marguerites. The room was furnished with a plump sofa and matching chair upholstered in brown horsehair, a small occasional table between them. On the opposite wall was the hearth, and it was flanked by a wireless in an enormous wooden cabinet. Near the window was an étagère crammed with little china figurines and other decorative items. Daintily crocheted lace doilies lined each shelf, as well as the top of the wireless cabinet, the mantel above the hearth, and the backs of the sofa and chair.

"This is the sitting room, and here's the kitchen," Ann said, continuing into the adjoining room. "I'll put on the kettle so we can have a cup of tea in a bit."

The kitchen was far more modern than Miriam's mother's had been. Instead of a coal range, the centerpiece of the room was a compact gas cooker adorned with white enamel and chrome trim. A sink was in front of the window, a draining board to its side, and on the far wall was an old dresser, its shelves laden with rose-patterned dishes. The remaining wall was taken up by a table with two chairs, and beyond, just past the dresser, was a sort of storage room with open shelves lined with jars and tins and boxes.

"If you go through that door you'll see the pantry, and beyond that is the washroom. There's a bath and sink and an inside WC, thank goodness. We're ever so lucky in that way."

Miriam edged forward, her attention caught by the door to the garden. "May I go outside?"

"Of course. I'll be there as soon as I've set the kettle to boil. Key's in the lock, so just give it a turn."

Miriam stepped into the garden and, for an instant, was stunned by the riot of color and scent that greeted her. It was, as Ann had said, quite small, with a modest patch of lawn in the center and a low shed in the far corner. Everything else was flowers.

An arching lilac, its plumy blossoms faded, dominated one corner. A climbing rose clambered across the fence, its sturdy canes intertwined with a tangle of clematis, its feet obscured by a shaggy mound of lavender. And in the middle of the main flower bed there was a peony, still flowering though it was well into July.

She reached out, her hand trembling, and let her fingertips brush against its petals. The scent was heavenly, like roses but even sweeter. It had been so long since she'd seen a peony in bloom.

Ann had come into the garden. "Can you believe it's still going? My neighbor gave it to me a few years ago. It was a division from one he's had for years. I can't remember the name."

"'Monsieur Jules Elie.' My mother had one." Her voice was calm, yet she had to blink back tears. How silly to cry over a flower.

"It sulked for ages. This is the first year it's agreed to put on a show. But then, everything is happy this summer. Endless heat and plenty of rain, too. And I was worried, I'll tell you, after the winter we had. I was sure I'd lose half— Oh, there's the kettle."

Miriam followed her inside, though she'd have given almost anything to remain in the garden, and watched as Ann filled a teapot with water from the kettle.

"There. Let's leave that to brew while I show you the upstairs."

The staircase was steep and narrow and led to a small landing with two doors. Ann opened one and beckoned for Miriam to follow. "Here we are. Milly left her furniture, since it was too dear to send it all the way to Canada. I hope you like it."

The bedroom was enormous, at least four meters square, and held a large double bed, a wardrobe, a chest of drawers, and a side table. There was even a small upholstered chair in the corner. The furniture, chair excepted, was a matching suite of veneered wood in a modern, streamlined shape. Not precisely to her taste, but what did it matter? It was a hundred times nicer than her horrid little room at the *pension*.

"What do you think?" Ann asked. "Nice, isn't it?"

"It is. You are certain you wish for *me* to have this room?"

"Of course. I like my view over the garden, and I'm used to my things being where they are. It would be ever such a fuss to switch things around."

She turned to Ann. "I would like to take the room."

"Oh, thank heavens. That is *such* a weight off my mind." The other woman's smile was wide and heartfelt, and it was hard not to feel her own spirits rise in accord. "Come on downstairs and we'll work everything out over a cup of tea."

Miriam sat at the kitchen table while Ann set out the tea things: a homely brown teapot, its spout chipped, a pair of rose-sprigged cups and saucers from the dresser, a little pitcher of milk, and two shining silver teaspoons.

"You take your tea with milk, right? I do have some sugar."

"Simply the milk. Thank you."

Ann fixed her own tea, drank deeply from her cup, and set it back on its saucer. "So. Like I said before, it'll be fifteen bob a week. Shillings, that is. And we can split the cost of food, if you like, and pool our rations."

"I think I would like that. Although I am not a very good cook," Miriam admitted.

"Really? A proper Frenchwoman like you?" Ann teased. "Never you mind. I'm not much of a cook either. We'll rub along somehow. As for the cleaning, I try to keep things neat during the week, then on Saturday, after I've done the marketing, I give everything a good going-over. It's a small house, so it only takes a few hours."

"Of course I will help you with that."

"Thanks. I will say I don't do the laundry, except for small things I can wash by hand. My undies and such. The rest I take to Mrs. Cole round the corner. She does a good job and never sends me home with someone else's sheets. Runs between one and two bob a week."

Miriam nodded, though she was still trying to add up the total in her head. There wouldn't be much left of her wages at the end of each week, true, but she would be living in great comfort, and Ann was pleasant and friendly.

"Is that all right? Honestly? Because . . ."

Miriam suddenly realized that Ann appeared nervous. Hesitant, somehow, as if she were struggling to find the right words. Of course. There was a catch. It was, as she had suspected, too good to be true.

"What is wrong?" she asked, her heart sinking.

"I, well . . . I need to be honest with you. This is a council house."

"I am not sure I understand."

"The town owns the house and I rent it from them. Or rather, my brother did. He and Milly were the original tenants. I moved in after he died, otherwise Milly wouldn't have been able to manage on her own. We've kept our heads down since then, done well not to attract anyone's attention. But if the council were to take notice, if they realized that two women are living here instead of a family, they might decide to, ah . . ."

Miriam's palms went clammy, and a swell of panic stole the breath from her lungs. It wasn't safe here. It wasn't—

"They might ask me to give notice. I do feel I must tell you. I will say that I don't think it's likely. The rent collector is friendly enough, and he's used to me handing over the rent each week. As long as we keep the place neat as a pin and pay him like clockwork we'll be fine."

"When you say 'give notice,' what does that mean?" she asked. "Would we be in trouble with the police?"

"Heavens, no. No, it's not the sort of thing you can get in trouble for. And I only mention it because there's a chance of having to move if someone at the council ever got wind of Milly going to Canada. I mean, we kept it as quiet as we could. But you know how people talk."

Miriam did know.

She would go to her grave without knowing the name of her betrayer. Had it been one of the other women in her lodgings? Someone at her work? Had Marie-Laure or Robert been tortured into giving them her name? She would never know for certain, never be able to look her enemy in the eye and force them to acknowledge what they had done. There would never be a trial to hold them accountable.

Ann was waiting for her to answer. "Yes," Miriam said. "People do talk," and she smiled as if she were thinking of a harmless neighborhood gossip.

"When would you like to move in? Milly's room only needs a good dusting. And of course I'll make up the bed with fresh sheets."

"I have already paid until the end of the week, and I do not think the *concierge* will give me back the money. So perhaps on Saturday I can bring my things?"

"That sounds perfect. I can meet you at the station if you like."

"I do not have many things. You do not need to trouble yourself."

"Well, then. I guess that's settled. Oh—I should have asked before.

Would you like to stay on for supper? I haven't much in the larder but I should be able to scrape together something edible."

"That is very kind, but I ought to return to my *pension*. There is a curfew and the concierge is diligent in enforcing it. But I will see you at work in the morning?"

"Yes, of course. Do you know your way back to the station?"

"I remember."

Miriam stood, ready to move to the front door, but Ann held out a staying hand. "Do you mind waiting for a moment? I forgot something outside. I won't be long."

Outside? Ann had only been in the garden for a minute or two, and she hadn't brought anything with—

"Here you go," Ann said. She held three of the peonies. "I'll just pop them in a tin for you, with an inch or two of water to stop them from drying out. Don't forget to top them up when you get home."

It was too much. "But those were the last of your peonies," Miriam protested as Ann arranged the flowers in their homely container.

"They're calling for rain tomorrow—they'll be flattened otherwise. And I'm glad for you to have them."

"They are beautiful," Miriam said, her throat still tight with emotion. "I thank you."

"You're very welcome. Until tomorrow?"

"Yes. Until then. *Bonsoir.*"

She stepped out the door, through the little gate, and began to walk down the street. She held the tin of peonies close to her chest and let the scent of them fill her nose. She walked through the gathering dusk, breathing in their magical scent, and with every step her heart grew lighter, gladder, more hopeful. She had made a new friend. She had found a new home.

And tomorrow would be better than today.

Chapter Nine

Heather

July 13, 2016

$\mathcal{I}$t had been an awful day at work, and now her friends in editorial were insisting that everyone meet up for drinks on the patio at the new bar down the street. They'd been bugging Heather about it all afternoon, and normally she'd have gone, but today she just needed to escape.

It wasn't often that a magazine's editor in chief canned a cover story, and though Richard kept insisting the piece was "stale-dated crap" and "not up to our editorial standards," Heather wasn't convinced. The story in question was a profile of the CEO of a controversial tech start-up; they'd hired a respected investigative reporter to write the thing, and at the time Heather had been annoyed that Richard hadn't assigned it to her. Now she was just relieved.

When word had leaked out that the piece made him look like a controlling, puerile, and misogynistic jerk, the CEO had freaked out. How he'd gained access to the story before publication was a problem—a big one, since *Bay Street* had always been known for its editorial independence in the face of corporate pressure.

Another problem was Richard's dissolving spine. He'd pushed for the profile, he'd approached the writer, and he'd been fine with the angle the story had taken. So why the change? Heather could only assume he'd run into some pushback from their publisher. Normally no one there seemed to care what went on at *Bay Street,* as long as they turned some kind of nominal profit. But this had all her spider senses tingling, and the last thing she felt like enduring after such a gross day was an evening of gossip, anxiety, and overpriced cocktails.

She told her friends she had a headache, and she waved off their pleas to join them, and in less than an hour she was on the couch at home, Seymour purring away at her side, with a bowl of leftover pad thai for dinner and the TV turned to a *House Hunters* marathon. It was just what she needed, and even after the show's ridiculously self-centered participants began to grate on her nerves she couldn't summon up the energy to find a more congenial activity. She was too tired to read, too tired to tackle the mountain of laundry on her closet floor, and too tired to head downstairs and see if Michelle and Sunita felt like going for a walk.

Only then did she remember the stack of mail sitting on the table by her door. There'd been an envelope from her mom, and she'd been about to open it when the cat had distracted her with his panicked pleas for dinner.

She heaved herself off the couch and grabbed the envelope. It held a commemorative guide to the queen's ninetieth birthday, the sort that was nothing but pictures and captions, and her mom had stuck a Post-it note on the front.

Bought this for you weeks ago but kept forgetting to pop in the mail. Enjoy!

Love from Mom

Her mom clung to the belief that Heather was interested in the royal family. And she was, but only in the most casual kind of way. She liked Princess Kate, as she persisted in calling the woman no matter how often her mom complained that it wasn't her real title. And of course she liked the queen. Who didn't like the queen?

But she didn't worship the royals the way her mom did, with the kind of devotion that involved getting up in the middle of the night for Will and Kate's wedding in 2011, and doing so while wearing a home-made fascinator and Union Jack slippers. Her mom had wanted her to come for a sleepover so as not to miss even a minute of the festivities, but Heather had wriggled out of the invitation by inventing an early meeting at work. Why get up so early when she could watch it later on DVR and skip all the commercials and boring in-between bits?

She flipped through the guide's glossy pages, her writer's eye tripping over the odd typo, and only began to pay attention when she came to an article on the queen's 1947 wedding. Heather hadn't realized how young she had been. Only twenty-one, and still a princess. She'd never noticed how handsome Prince Philip had been when he was young, nor could she remember ever having seen their wedding pictures before. The wedding gown didn't look familiar, at least not in the way she could close her eyes and instantly see Diana's dress in all its meringue-y glory. But there was something about it that captured her attention, something that made her look twice . . .

The star flowers.

The gown had swoops of embroidery on the skirt and its train, garlands of star-shaped flowers and roses and leafy things that had pearls and little diamonds sewn all over them, and they were exactly the same as the flowers on the squares of fabric that Nan had kept hidden away.

Hurrying into her bedroom, Heather began to rummage through the pile of things from Nan's house that her mom had insisted she bring home after the funeral. Framed photographs, a big white tablecloth she'd never use, some nice candlesticks that she remembered from every Christmas and Easter. And the white plastic box with her name on it that held the embroideries.

She sat on her bed, dumped Seymour on the floor when he bounced up to investigate, and opened the box. She was right. Nan's flowers were exactly the same as the ones on the gown.

Her laptop was sitting at the foot of the bed. She opened the browser, typed *Queen Elizabeth wedding dress embroidery* into the search bar, and hit return. Dozens of photographs filled the screen: stars edged with pearls, roses in full bloom, delicate ears of wheat, and interspersed between them were photographs of the queen on her wedding day almost seventy years before.

Nan's flowers couldn't possibly be from the gown itself, for it was in a museum somewhere, or in the attics at Buckingham Palace, and besides, no one was ever going to cut up the queen's wedding dress. Back and forth she looked, from the embroideries now arranged on her bed, to the images from her search, and back again.

She tried another search. *Princess Elizabeth wedding dress 1947*. A Wikipedia page popped up—the gown even had its own entry. November 1947, Norman Hartnell design, Botticelli inspiration, English silk, rationing, etc., etc.

Norman Hartnell. The name was kind of familiar, but she'd never been very interested in fashion or designers or anything like that. If he had designed the gown, and Nan had the embroideries, maybe she had worked for him in some way?

Yet a connection with Norman Hartnell raised more questions than it answered. Why wouldn't her grandmother have told them about something so important? Even if she'd only worked there for a month or two, it was *something*. It was making dresses for the royal family, and even though people Heather's age didn't get worked up about things like that—or at least she'd never found it very exciting—older people sure did.

She decided it was time to call her mother.

"Hi, Heather. What's up?"

"You know how you thought I should try to find out more about Nan's embroidered flowers? I finally got around to it."

"And? What did you find out so far?"

"I'm not sure, not yet, but I think she *might* have had something to do with Norman Hartnell." There was a weird kind of gasping noise at the other end of the line. "Mom? Are you okay?"

"Norman Hartnell? The queen's dressmaker?" her mother finally managed, her voice hushed and reverential and still a little wheezy.

"Yes. You know the embroidered flowers Nan left me? They're the same as the ones on the queen's wedding dress."

"Oh, my goodness. I don't know what to say. I thought they looked familiar, but . . ."

"And she never mentioned Hartnell or the queen or anything like that?"

"Never. I mean, she loved the queen, and she was so sad when the Queen Mum died. But she never *met* them. She'd have told me about that."

"Could she have worked for Norman Hartnell? Maybe as one of his seamstresses?"

"I suppose. Although I can't imagine why she'd never have told anyone. Why hide something like that?"

"I know. It doesn't make any sense. Oh—I just thought of something else. Do you have any more pictures from England? From before Nan came here?"

"I don't remember ever seeing any, but I'll have a look through her albums. Are you going to bed soon? It's almost eleven."

"Very soon," Heather promised. "Let me know if you come across any other pictures, okay?"

"Sure. Anything else?"

"Let me see . . . I've got her date of birth, the town where she lived . . . hmm. I don't have her maiden name. Hughes was her married name, right?"

"I suppose so." There was a long pause. "Isn't it silly that I wouldn't know?"

"She never said?" Heather pressed.

"She might have. But if she did, I don't remember. Still. It's probably written down somewhere. I'll have a look."

"Thanks, Mom. Love you guys."

"Love you, too."

Back to the search. Unless her mother came up with more photos, she had to assume the one in the studio, with Nan looking all serious, was all she had. The picture was at the bottom of the box, under the last layer of tissue paper, and she now set it on the bed next to her laptop.

Norman Hartnell embroidery studio, she typed, and row after row of images popped up, most of them pictures of 1950s-era dresses. She scrolled down, and there, at the very bottom of her screen, was a black-and-white photograph of a large, high-ceilinged room with hanging electric lights, big windows, and women bent over rows of embroidery frames.

Heather compared the two pictures. The perspective was different, but the room was similar. The light fixtures were a match, and the way the windowpanes were divided. It was the same room.

And suddenly it was too much to take in. She'd come back to it tomorrow, or on the weekend when she wasn't so tired, and maybe by then her mother would have more for her. Maybe then she'd understand why Nan had hidden so much.

THE EMAIL FROM her mom arrived the next morning, just as Heather was about to go into *Bay Street*'s weekly editorial meeting.

From: Mom & Dad
Subject: Some pix for you!

Dear Heather,

First things first. No birth certificate or marriage certificate. Not sure I ever saw either although she must have had copies at some point. I guess we could try to order a copy of her birth certificate from the English government. Let me know if you'd like to do that. It seems funny that I don't know her maiden name but I tended to just accept things as they were when I was growing up. I do have some good news about the pix. Dad and I stayed up late looking through old albums and some boxes of stuff from Nan and we found some photos we hadn't seen before. Only the three but I hope they will help. Dad scanned them. The first one is of Nan. It's hard to tell from the picture but she looks to be in her twenties. This is on the back: "109 Morley Rd, Barking, June 46." The second one, of her and the other woman, must have been taken at the same time. I'm not sure but I think it's my aunt Milly. She was married to Mum's brother, Frank, the one that was killed in the Blitz. From what I remember Milly came over to Canada first and my mum joined her in Toronto. She was still pretty young when she died in the 1950s but I can't remember from what. Mum and I moved out to Etobicoke after that. Again I never thought to ask more and as you know she wasn't one to volunteer information. The third picture has me stumped as I've no idea who this woman is with my mum or why they were all dressed up. From their hats and gloves and the whole shebang I'm thinking maybe they were going to a wedding or maybe it was just their Sunday best? Sorry we didn't unearth anything more.

Lots of love, Mom xoxo

There were three pictures attached to the email. The first was Nan, younger than Heather was now, dressed in the same sort of clothes she'd always worn: a knee-length skirt, plain white blouse, knitted cardigan, sensible shoes. Her hair came to her chin and was tucked neatly behind her ears. In the next photo, the one with Aunt Milly, she was smiling, her eyes squinting against the sunshine, and their happy expressions gave no hint of the war they'd just survived, let alone the sadness they must have felt when Uncle Frank was killed. They stood in a garden that was so small the neighbors' fences were visible on either side.

The third photograph had also been taken in the garden. Nan was about the same age as in the other pictures, but this time she was dressed up in a gorgeous dark coat, its wide collar wrapping around her shoulders like a shawl, and on her head was an elegant little hat.

The woman with her, the one her mom didn't recognize, was very beautiful, with dark hair and delicate, almost elfin features. She wore a tailored suit, its full skirt falling well below her knees, its fitted jacket flaring out sharply at the waist, and she looked, Heather decided, a little bit like Audrey Hepburn in that old movie where she was actually a princess and she escaped for a day or two.

Well, Nan hadn't been a princess. She knew that for sure. But what was her connection with Norman Hartnell? And who was the woman in the third photograph? If Nan had saved the photo, she must have cared about the woman. Have known her well. Might they even have worked together?

The night before, just before turning out the lights, she'd scanned the picture of Nan in the embroidery studio and emailed it to herself. She opened it now and began to study the features of the others in the photograph. Just to Nan's side, where she had been all along, was the mystery woman, her expression just as serious as Nan's.

Her phone rang; it was the boardroom extension. "Sorry, Richard—I got caught up in an email. I'm on my way."

She would have to leave off her search until after work.

THAT EVENING, AND at every lunch break for the rest of the week, Heather scrolled through online archives, searching for anything that even mentioned Norman Hartnell or the royal wedding of 1947 in passing. She began to haunt the downtown reference library after work, ordering up book after book from the stacks, and though she failed to learn anything more about Nan, she did acquire a working knowledge of midcentury fashion, postwar clothes rationing, and the history of royal wedding attire.

She even emailed the press office at Buckingham Palace, asking if they would connect her with the curator responsible for the queen's wedding gown and other Hartnell-designed garments, but they didn't respond, not even after she sent three separate inquiries.

Late one Saturday night, long after she ought to have gone to sleep, Heather decided to play around with variations on search terms she had already used. *Hartnell embroiderers royal wedding 1947* yielded nothing new, as did *Princess Elizabeth wedding dress embroiderers 1947*. Suppressing an enormous yawn, she forced herself to think. What hadn't she tried? What snippet of information had she overlooked?

There was a reason that Nan had left the embroideries to her. Nan hadn't wanted to talk about her life in England, or maybe she hadn't felt able to do so, but she had saved the flowers for more than sixty years, and she had put Heather's name on the box, and she had known that Heather would look for answers. She must have expected it—and that, in turn, meant she must have wanted Heather to know.

It was the only thing Nan had ever asked her to do, and she couldn't stand the idea of letting her down, and it was driving her nuts that she couldn't figure out how—

The pictures. Yes. She would do an image search on the pictures her mom had sent and see if anything similar popped up. She plugged in the photograph of Nan on her own; nothing. The same again for the one of Nan and Milly. But the results for the photo of Nan and the mystery woman instantly banished all thoughts of sleep from Heather's mind.

Miriam Dassin at the 1958 Venice Biennale. Miriam Dassin in her Hampstead studio. Miriam Dassin at Buckingham Palace after the queen had awarded her a damehood, which seemed, from what Heather could tell, to be the female version of a knighthood. Nan's mysterious friend was none other than Miriam Dassin.

In grade eleven, Heather had taken visual art as an elective; it had been that or drama. She'd been terrible at drawing and painting, really at anything that required she hold a pencil or brush, so her teacher had suggested she try collage work. He had given her a book on Miriam Dassin, who was best known for her large-scale embroideries, but had also experimented with mixed-media collage and sculpture.

"Here's an artist whose work is in every important museum collection in the world," he'd told her, "and none of it is painted or drawn."

She'd looked at the pictures in the book for hours, and she'd read everything she could find on Miriam Dassin, too, and yet she couldn't remember anything about the artist having ever worked for a fashion designer. Her heart in her throat, Heather began another search. *Miriam Dassin.*

The details were more or less as she recalled: French, active in the resistance during the war, imprisoned at Ravensbrück, emigrated to England, spent years working in obscurity. Then the sensational success of *Vél d'Hiv* at the 1958 Venice Biennale had propelled Dassin to fame in the art world and beyond.

But there was nothing about Norman Hartnell or the queen's wedding dress, and certainly nothing about her ever having been friends with a young woman from Essex called Ann Hughes.

Yet the proof was there, in the photographs, and unless Miriam Dassin had an unknown identical twin, she and Nan must have known one another. They had been colleagues at Hartnell, and possibly even friends. So why, then, had her grandmother never said a word?

"I wouldn't mind some help, you know," she said in the direction of the ceiling. "If you didn't want me to find out, why did you put my name on the box of embroideries? And what am I supposed to do next?"

All she needed was a nudge in the right direction. A hint to keep her going. But Nan had never been one for sharing secrets, and no answer came from the ether now.

Chapter Ten

Ann

August 8, 1947

I don't know why you're nervous," Doris said. "You look smashing. Really you do."

Ann forced herself to look at her reflection in the cloakroom mirror. At her mascaraed lashes, reddened lips, powder-burnished skin. At her new frock with its full, swirling skirt and plunging neckline. At her feet, so delicate in dainty new shoes.

She saw a stranger.

"'Mutton dressed as lamb,'" she whispered. "That's what my mum would say if she could see me in this."

"This idiom . . . what on earth does it mean?" Miriam asked. "You are speaking of sheep. It makes no sense." She stood at Ann's elbow and until a moment ago had been smiling in delight.

"Ann is trying to say that she isn't young enough to wear such a pretty frock," Ethel explained.

"Pfft," Miriam said. "That is not true. Perhaps it would be too young for my grandmother, but not for a pretty girl like you. Everything in your ensemble is perfect. I would not lie to you about this. You certainly bear no resemblance to a sheep."

"I still think we ought to have used the other fabric. Not this. This is too . . . too . . ."

It had been a moment of madness, agreeing to make a new frock from the material Milly had sent from Canada. There had been other fabric, practical fabric that would have seen her through the autumn and winter. A generous piece of woolen tartan, its colors nicely muted, that would have served for two skirts at least. But Miriam had been adamant.

"We will sew you these boring skirts later. When the weather is cold again and you need something warm. But now it is summer, and the weather is far too hot for such heavy fabric, and you deserve something pretty. We shall make you a frock from *this*."

This had been a length of pale blue rayon, gossamer thin, with a delicate tracery of ivory flowers that almost looked like lace. It had been one of countless treasures in the parcels Milly had sent from Canada and, even now, as she remembered it all, her heart still skipped a beat.

She and Miriam had only just got home from work. A knock had sounded, and Ann had answered to find Mr. Booth from next door, his face nearly hidden by a stack of five large parcels.

"Postman left these with me earlier. Complaining something fierce about how many there are and how lucky some folks are to have relations in Canada to send them anything they want."

"Thank you, Mr. Booth. I had no idea—I wasn't expecting . . ."

"I told him to mind his own business. If I had family overseas I'd ask for everything excepting a kitchen sink!"

She'd taken the parcels from him, one after the other, and had carried them into the kitchen. They were identical, each about a foot square and half as deep again, wrapped in brown paper and webbed round with string. One whole corner of each had been tiled with Canadian postage stamps. Miriam had helped her untie the knots in the string, and then they'd removed the paper and folded it neatly. Beneath was a layer of waxed muslin, still pristine; it would be perfect for storing things like cheese.

One of the boxes—actually metal tins, a bit like the ones biscuits came in, only without any lettering—had a letter on top.

June 17, 1947

Dearest Ann,

By now you'll have had airmail letters from me with news of Toronto, so I won't go on about that now. I'm sure I'll have told you all about the shops and how nothing is rationed and everything is so cheap compared to home—people here have no idea of what it's like in England right now. You can just go into any shop and buy what you want as long as you have the cash to pay for it.

So that's what I've done. My train from Halifax arrived on Sunday and on Monday morning—that's yesterday—I went out shopping. When I was on the ship and feeling bored to death I made up a list of everything you can't get at home right now. Things that are rationed or just aren't in the shops or are so dear only the queen herself can afford them. I found nearly everything and I bundled it all into these five tins and we weighed them to make sure they aren't more than five pounds each. The man at the post office here says you won't get points taken off your rations that way.

You must let me know if I've missed anything you want or need. There's nothing for winter in the shops yet but I'll send boots and woolies before it gets too cold.

It was such fun filling these tins. I felt like Father Christmas and I hope it feels like an early Christmas for you, too.

With much love from your friend and sister,
Milly

"I don't know how they got here so fast," Ann said. "It usually takes months for parcels to get here. That's what Mrs. Turner down the street always says. Her daughter lives in Vancouver."

"Yes, but is not Vancouver very much farther away than Toronto? And what does it matter? The parcels are here. Go on. Open them," Miriam urged.

Ann's hands were trembling by the time the last tin had been emptied and its contents arranged upon the table. Milly hadn't exaggerated when she'd compared herself to Father Christmas.

There were tins of corned beef, salmon, evaporated milk, and peaches in syrup. Dried apricots and raisins. A big jar of strawberry jam. Packets of powdered milk, cocoa, tea, sugar, and rice. Yards of heavy woolen suiting, finely woven tartan, and two bolts of silky printed rayon, one of pale blue and the other a smoky purple, all with thread and buttons to match. Half a dozen pairs of stockings, and, taking up almost one entire tin, a brand-new pair of high-heeled shoes.

"I thought Milly might send a few bits and pieces at Christmas. A plum pudding in a tin, or something like that. But not *this* . . ."

"She is a very kind person, your Milly."

"She is. There's just so *much* . . . I want you to have some of the fabric. You can have a new dress. And the shoes—"

"No," Miriam said. "Absolutely not. Those shoes are for you. Nothing could induce me to wear them. And you must make yourself a new dress. This blue, the color of the sky—this will be perfect for you."

"Then you must have the other length of rayon. I insist."

"Your Milly sent the fabric for you."

"Yes, but she seems to have forgotten that I have ginger hair. I look a fright in purple. If you don't use it, the fabric will just sit there."

Once Miriam had agreed to a dress, Ann borrowed a pattern from Miss Holliday in the sewing workroom, which Mr. Hartnell allowed as long as they were making garments for their own use. They'd worked on the dresses after hours, first sewing up the long seams with the help of Miss Ireland, one of the machinists. At home, they did the finer work of finishing and fitting in the sitting room, the wireless singing in the background. There was no mirror in the house, apart from a small one over the sink in the washroom, so she'd had to trust Miriam's assessment that the completed frock fit her perfectly.

They'd finished their frocks and then, a day or two later, Ethel had suggested a night out to say farewell to Doris, whose wedding was fast approaching.

"We'll have supper at the Corner House, and then we'll go dancing. At the Paramount, or maybe the Astoria. That's closer. Bring your best frocks and your dancing shoes in the morning, and we'll get gussied up in the cloakroom."

At first Miriam was the reluctant one. "I don't know how to dance," she'd protested.

"You must come," Ann had insisted. "Doris will be hurt if I don't go, but I'm nervous as it is. And we don't even have to dance. We can stand there and hold up the wall together."

There were nine of them all told: herself, Miriam, Doris, Ruthie and Ethel; Betty and Dorothy from sewing; Jessie from the millinery workroom; and Carmen, one of the Hartnell house models and so beautiful it was like having a film star in their midst. They'd shared round powder and lipstick, admired one another's frocks and hair-styles, and just like that another hour had passed and they still hadn't left the cloakroom.

So they said good night to Miss Duley, who warned them to be careful and for heaven's sake stay well clear of men in uniform, and they raced to the Corner House around the corner. While the others tucked into their suppers with gusto, Ann discovered her appetite had been replaced by a stomach full of butterflies. It wouldn't do to waste the perfectly good meal she'd been served, though, so she ate every scrap of her Welsh rarebit. It might as well have been sawdust.

Her apprehension finally began to melt away on their walk to the Astoria. The temperature had dropped a few degrees, a welcome re-lief after the late afternoon heat, and it was easy to imagine, as they strolled along Oxford Street, that life would always be this carefree and easy. That happiness might be found in a new frock and some pretty shoes and an evening out with friends.

She'd never been to the dance hall at the Astoria before, although she'd walked past it any number of times. There was already a queue to get in, snaking down the two flights of stairs to the basement ball-room, but it moved quickly enough. She handed over her admis-sion, a startling three-and-six for the evening, and followed along as Ethel and Doris debated where they ought to sit. Ethel wanted a table on the mezzanine that circled the dance floor, and thereby provided a better view of the proceedings, while Doris preferred a table on the main level, which had faster access to the dancing itself.

"The two of you can bicker all you like," Carmen declared after a few minutes, "but the place is filling up and I don't feel like standing. I'm getting a table. Come on, girls. Follow me." One of the large tables under the mezzanine was empty, and was just big enough for them all to squeeze round.

That settled, Doris and Ethel set off to fetch drinks for everyone. Another tuppence from Ann's pocket and, she hoped, the last she would spend that evening. It was a good thing she'd never made a habit of going out every weekend, otherwise she'd be living in the poorhouse by now.

Jessie and Carmen extracted packets of cigarettes from their handbags and offered them round, but only Miriam accepted.

"I didn't think you smoked," Ann said.

"Not anymore. Not since I moved here. These English cigarettes are awful." Miriam frowned as she exhaled a thin plume of smoke.

"Then why bother?"

"I am not sure," Miriam admitted with a smile. "Habit, I suppose. Why do you not smoke?"

"My mum didn't approve. And then . . . well, I never really liked the smell of it. I still don't. The air in here is like the top deck of a bus."

Ann looked around the ballroom, marveling at how quickly it had filled up. The dance floor was packed, with no shortage of uniformed men among the dancers. Some people were dressed in the same clothes they'd worn to work; some, like her, were wearing a variation of their Sunday best; and some were dressed to the nines.

The group at the next table fell into the latter category. The women wore gorgeously embellished cocktail dresses, one of which Ann was fairly certain had come from Hartnell, and jewels sparkled at their wrists, necks, and ears. One even had a pearl-and-diamond-studded comb tucked into her chignon. The lone man at their table wore a dinner jacket and reminded her of Clark Gable, only with rather less chin.

The woman closest to her was young, only just out of her teens, and had a mink-lined wrap around her shoulders in spite of the sweltering weather. As Ann watched, one end came loose and slithered down to droop on the floor, but the woman didn't seem to notice. It would be a shame for such a pretty garment to be ruined.

"Excuse me," she said, leaning forward. The woman didn't respond. "Excuse me," she said again, and this time she reached out to touch the woman's arm. "I beg your pardon, but your wrap has fallen."

The woman looked round, a vee of annoyance creasing her brow. "What?"

"Your wrap. It's on the floor."

"Oh, right." She yanked the wrap up and back across her lap. "Thanks." Almost as an afterthought, she offered a perfunctory smile before turning back to her friends.

Ethel and Doris returned just then with glasses of lemonade for everyone. "Barman says the licensing inspector has a beef with the owners. So this is the strongest the drinks will get tonight."

Their reassurances that they didn't mind at all, and in fact preferred lemonade to anything else, were interrupted by a squeal of protest from the next table.

"Really? *This* is the best you can do? I told you I didn't want to come to this grubby little place. Why don't you ever listen?" It was the girl with the fur wrap.

Another man had arrived at her table, his hands laden with glasses of lemonade, and she was making no secret of her disappointment. He bent his head low, said something that made her pout, then laugh, but rather than sit down he stood behind her, a hand on the back of her chair, and surveyed the ballroom. Perhaps he was looking for other people he knew. Perhaps he was feeling annoyed at her outburst and needed a moment to collect himself.

He really was terrifically handsome. Tall but not eye-wateringly so, he had a slim build and posture that hinted at time in the military. His fair hair was cut short and swept back from his brow, and his dinner jacket was tailored so perfectly it must have been made for him.

"Do you see that fellow at the next table?" Ruthie hissed in her ear. "Do you think that's the princess's fiancé? Lieutenant Mountbatten?"

"No," Ann whispered back, shaking her head. "There's a resemblance, but it's not him. The lieutenant is in his early twenties, but this man must be closer to thirty."

"Too bad. Imagine if we'd been able to say we saw him on our night out!"

Just then he turned and, as if he somehow knew she'd been talking about him, fixed his gaze on Ann. She shrank in her chair, although she knew there was no way he could have heard what she and Ruthie had been saying. And it wasn't as if being compared to Princess Elizabeth's fiancé was an insult, after all.

He smiled at her. He smiled until a dimple appeared in his cheek and his eyes crinkled at the corners, and all the time he never looked away.

She wanted so badly to check behind her, for surely he was looking at someone at the table beyond. Someone he knew and liked, and in a moment he would brush past her and she would know, definitively, that his smile had been too good to be true.

She must have had a questioning look on her face, because he nodded, just the once, and then he walked over to her. To her, not anyone else, and he held out his hand. To *her*.

"I beg your pardon if I'm intruding, but I should very much like the favor of a dance," he said, and his voice was as attractive as the rest of him.

"With *me*?" she asked, not even trying to hide her disbelief.

"Yes. With you. If your friends don't object."

"Go on," Ruthie said, nudging her sharply. "Don't make him wait."

"But—"

"Leave your bag. We'll keep an eye on it."

Ann looked to Miriam, but her friend only shrugged in that annoying French way of hers that never gave the slightest hint of what she really thought.

What else could she do but take his hand and let him lead her to the dance floor? It was a dream, a dream she'd never have conjured on her own, this moment when he set his hand at her back, his hand that was so wide she could feel the heat of it from her shoulders to her waist, and she let her hand rest on his shoulder as he pulled them into the mass of dancers, two more fish in a rushing stream, and he was still smiling at her, his teeth so white and straight, a film star come to life in her arms.

The band was playing a fox-trot, the melody unfamiliar, and she wasn't sure, at first, how she would manage to keep up. It had been so long since she danced. But he was a wonderful dancer, so assured in his movements that he could make even the clumsiest partner appear elegant, and after a few measures her fears melted away.

They danced across the floor and back again, and though she knew she ought to try to make conversation, even if only to talk about the infernally warm weather, her voice remained trapped in her throat. She felt the muscles of his shoulder flexing beneath her touch, marveled at the way her other hand was engulfed in his strong, warm grasp.

Their movements slowed, the music faded away, and she realized the dance had come to an end. It had been a lovely interlude, but—

"Surely you aren't going to abandon me now?" he asked, and before she could say anything they were moving again. It was "Fools Rush In," one of her favorites.

"I love this song," he said, bending his head to her ear. "It must have been early '41 when I first heard it. One of the chaps in my company unearthed a gramophone and a stack of records from God only knows where, and this was one of them. We'd sit in our smelly old tent in the middle of the desert and listen to the records, night after night after night. I remember how I wondered if I'd ever have the chance to dance with a pretty girl in a ballroom again. And here I am."

"You were in North Africa during the war?" she ventured.

"I was. Wounded at Tobruk, but they patched me up well enough. Sicily and Italy after that."

"Are you still in the army?"

"In a manner of speaking, though I'm not really supposed to talk about it. All rather hush-hush, I'm afraid."

"Of course," she agreed. "Loose lips and all that."

"See? I knew you'd understand."

She braced herself for him to ask her a question or two in return, but he seemed content to simply listen to the music and dance. When the band played the final bars of the song, she held her breath, hoping it would be another fox-trot, or even a waltz. She still remembered how to waltz.

But it was a jitterbug, a dance that half the ballrooms in London still banned, and even if she'd been completely certain of all the steps she wouldn't have dared to dance it with a stranger.

"Do you mind if we leave this to the younger crowd?" he asked. "I don't much relish making a fool out of myself in front of half of

London." Taking her near hand, he tucked it into the crook of his arm. "Why don't we get a drink before returning to our tables? In a quiet part of the room? Somewhere we can talk?" His expression, as he gazed down at her, implied that talking with her was likely to be the highlight of his evening.

He led her around the room, to the smaller of the bars under the mezzanine, and they joined the short queue. "Do you mind lemonade? I gather that's all they have on offer tonight."

"That's fine. I'm not really used to anything stronger," she admitted.

"My mother would approve. She's always twittering on about young women and their lack of decorum. Would you believe she insists that trousers are the real problem? That was the moment, she maintains, when our civilization turned toward disaster."

He paid for their lemonades with a five-pound note, told the barman to keep an entire shilling from the change as his tip, and carried their glasses to a small table in a relatively dark and quiet corner. He even pulled out her chair and waited for her to sit before joining her.

She took a sip of the lemonade and tried to think of something to say. "Thank you for the lemonade," was the best she could do. Even worse, she found herself softening her accent. Not much, not enough to sound as if she were aping her betters. But enough to shrink the distance between Mayfair and Barking by a few miles.

It was a stupid thing to do, for he'd heard her friends talking, and only Carmen, who was actually the daughter of a barrister in Cambridge, had an accent that would pass in polite society. The rest of them, Miriam excepted, spoke like ordinary people, with ordinary accents.

"Won't your friends mind?" she asked, and this time her voice was her own. But he didn't so much as raise an eyebrow.

"My friends? No, they won't be bothered. I'm here with my sister and some of her pals. She's the one who insisted on wearing a fur. Silly old thing."

Ann wasn't sure if he was referring to his sister or her fur. "She's very pretty."

"She is," he agreed, "and a handful. That's how I get myself dragged out to these places. Not," he added with another gleaming smile, "that I regret it in the slightest. You never know who you'll meet when you do something new."

It seemed like a compliment, but she couldn't be sure, and it wouldn't do to get too starry-eyed over the man. "It's been ages since I did anything like this. But Miriam, one of my friends here, she insisted. She said if I didn't go, she wouldn't either. So here I am," she said, cringing inwardly at how feeble that last statement sounded.

"And are you glad?" he asked, his eyes intent upon her.

"I am. I'm having such a lovely time."

"I should very much like to see you again," he said, and there was just a touch of diffidence in his tone. As if he felt uncertain of her answer. "I hope that doesn't seem too forward of me."

"No, it doesn't. That would be very nice."

Nice. Of course it would be nice, but was it sensible? Was it even sane? Surely he must be aware of the gulf between them. Surely he had to know.

"May I ask for your telephone number? I can give you mine. Let me find my card . . ."

"I don't have one," she said. She didn't know anyone with their own telephone. Well, apart from him. "I don't have a card either. I—"

"Well, I can't let you vanish into the night. If I give you my card, will you ring me up tomorrow? Promise you will."

This wasn't happening. This could not be happening. "I promise," she said, and took the card from his outstretched hand.

"Splendid. I suppose I'd better get back to my sister. I've a feeling she'll insist we go on to at least three more clubs before she's ready to call it a night. That girl will dance until dawn if I let her."

He drained the last of his lemonade, winced a little, and stood. "Oh—I almost forgot to ask. What's your name?"

"It's Ann. Ann Hughes."

"Delighted to make your acquaintance, Miss Hughes. Captain Jeremy Thickett-Milne, though I do hope you'll consent to calling me Jeremy."

And then he kissed her hand.

Ann had never expected to be the girl in the fairy tale. She didn't believe in them, for a start, and she wasn't certain she believed in *this*. She shouldn't allow herself to believe.

But did it matter? What was the harm in having supper with him? He did seem nice, and perhaps he was the sort of man who honestly wouldn't care that she was the daughter of a motor mechanic and lived in a council house in Essex. That she lived from pay packet to pay packet and spent her days making clothes for women like his sister. Perhaps he was simply a nice man who found her appealing and wanted to get to know her better.

Her free hand, the one that wasn't tucked against his elbow, clutched at the card he had given her, its corners digging into the perspiring skin of her palm. She had his telephone number. She would ring him up, and they would arrange to have supper together, and she would let herself believe for another day or two. And then, after he came to his senses and realized his mistake, she would set aside the memory of this lovely night, leave it by the wayside of her life, and continue on alone.

Chapter Eleven

Miriam

She wouldn't have admitted it to anyone at their table, with the possible exception of Ann, but tonight was the first time Miriam had ever been out dancing. She'd been so young when she had begun her apprenticeship at Lesage, and the curfew at her lodgings had always been so strict, that she'd never dared to stay out past supper. And then, once the Occupation had begun, her life had shrunk to secrets and shadows and the grim business of survival. Dancing had belonged to another world. Another, saner, universe.

Her colleagues at Hartnell, however, looked upon her as if she were the embodiment of sophisticated European glamour. As if she'd spent her youth gulping down tumblers of absinthe in dubious jazz bars in Pigalle and dancing alongside Josephine Baker at the Folies Bergère.

Not wishing to prove them wrong, she told herself that she belonged. That sitting at this table by the edge of a crowded dance floor, her ears assaulted by the thrum and thump of restless feet and raucous music, her lungs clogged by a fug of smoke and perspiration and cheap perfume, was second nature to her, and the sort of thing she'd done all the time when she had lived in Paris.

It had come as something of a relief, when they'd arrived at the Astoria, to see there were scores of tables around the edge of the ballroom and that she would not, as Ann had said, be called upon to hold up the wall with the other girls who weren't dancing. She'd accepted the vile English cigarette Jessie had offered her, although it had burned her throat and made her feel a little queasy, and the lemonade she'd sipped had been warm and unpleasantly tannic. Yet she was enjoying herself all the same.

It was interesting to sit with the others and try to make sense of this strange place where anyone might come and dance, as long as he or she had the money to pay the admission fee. Most were ordinary people like her friends from Hartnell, treating themselves to a night out and determined to make the most of their investment. A few, however, were like the people at the adjacent table. Wealthy and indolent and so convinced of their own superiority that their disdain for everyone else fairly dripped from the tips of their manicured fingers.

She'd noticed them straightaway. Their accents, all drawling vowels and clipped consonants, were so rarefied that even she could discern a difference in the way they spoke. And there was a languor in the way the women moved, as if dancing a waltz with an attractive man, or raising a glass of lemonade to their lips, were praiseworthy feats of endurance.

They seemed to complain about everything, too, their voices rising easily above the enveloping clamor of bystanders and dancers and music.

"What do you mean there's no champagne?" whined one of the

women. "You *know* I only drink champagne when I'm dancing. Gin goes straight to my head."

"There's no pleasing you, is there?" This from a dark-haired man at the far side of the table. He handed the girl a small metal flask, which she proceeded to empty into her glass of lemonade. Miriam's eyes fairly watered at the sight of it.

The other man in the group of aristocrats, the one who had just delivered the disappointing glasses of lemonade to his companions, was tall and fair and conventionally handsome in a very English way. He'd been standing next to the table, his gaze flickering around the ballroom, and she had seen him looking in their direction more than once.

All the same, it was a surprise when he approached their table and stopped in front of Ann. Earlier, her friend had been kind enough to let one of the women in his group know when her fur wrap had fallen on the floor. Presumably he had come over to offer his thanks. That was the only reason Miriam could imagine for him to speak with any of them.

He held out his hand. He said something in a low voice, and he smiled at Ann. He was asking her to dance. She hesitated; of course she did, for it was unimaginable that a man like him would ask one of them to dance. France or England, the gulf between classes was just as unbridgeable.

"Go on," Ruthie urged, and the other girls all nodded their agreement. Ann looked to Miriam, but what was she to do? Tell her to refuse? He was only asking for a dance, after all. So she shrugged, and Ann nodded, and she let the man, the stranger, lead her onto the dance floor and out of sight.

Miriam didn't see them again for that dance, nor for the one that followed, nor the one after that. There were hundreds of dancers, of course, so she wasn't worried. Not yet. And Ann had left her handbag behind. She would certainly never leave without retrieving it first.

The band began to play again, a softer, sweeter song, and Miriam swept her gaze over the dancers once more. There—there Ann was, coming toward them from the far end of the room, arm in arm with the charming aristocrat. She'd never looked prettier, her cheeks flushed, her eyes bright with happiness.

Close up, Miriam was struck again by how handsome he was. His manners could not be faulted either.

"I beg your pardon, ladies, for making off with Miss Hughes," he said, and bestowed an imploring smile on each of them. "Do forgive me." He released Ann's hand and took a step back. "Promise me you'll ring me up?"

"I promise," Ann echoed.

"I do hope you enjoy the rest of your evening. Thank you again." With that, he turned away and went to rejoin his friends.

While the others questioned Ann, their excitement fizzing over into giggles and squeals, Miriam angled her head so she might better eavesdrop on the discussion the stranger was having with his friends. One of them, the woman whose fur Ann had rescued, did not trouble to hide her annoyance.

"You just disappeared with her. It's like you forgot we were even *here*."

"I didn't forget, Tabby girl," he replied placidly. "And I'm back now. What say you to the 400 Club for a spell? The cocktails will be a far sight nicer than they are here."

"Fine. But I insist you stay with us from now on. Darling Caro had no one to dance with at *all* after you went off with that *shopgirl*."

"I'll stay. Promise I will."

Miriam stole a glance at Ann. Her friend's eyes were following the man as he departed, a wondering and faintly dreamy expression on her face. She hoped Ann hadn't heard the other woman's nasty comment.

"Good—now they're out of the way. Tell us *everything*," Ethel insisted.

"There isn't much to say. He asked me to dance, and after two songs they started up with the jitterbug, and neither of us knew the steps. So he bought us some lemonade and we sat and talked for a bit. He seemed very nice."

"Very *posh* is how he seemed," Doris said. "Did you see what those girls were wearing? And the jewelry they had on?"

"I know," Ann admitted. "I'm still not sure . . . I mean, why me?"

"Because you look very pretty tonight," Miriam said abruptly. The time for doubts was tomorrow, not now. "He saw you and said to himself, 'I want to dance with that pretty girl.' It is as simple as that."

"Are you going to see him again?" asked Doris.

"I don't know. He asked me to ring him up. He said he wanted to see me again." She set a business card upon the table, its corners bent from where it had been clutched in her hand. "But I don't know. I don't think I should go."

"Why ever not?" Carmen asked. "There's no harm in having supper with the man."

"I suppose not. Except I don't have anything to wear. This frock is the only really nice thing I have."

"Then you must wear my suit," Miriam said. "My good suit that I had made in Paris. We are much the same size."

"I couldn't. I—"

"Come on," Carmen said, her patience fraying. "It's a chance for you to kick up your heels and see how the other half lives. If he'd asked me I'd be off like a shot."

"But what if . . ."

"What if he's the sort that thinks a girl should pay for a night out one way or another?" Ruthie asked, oblivious to her friends' shared expression of dismay. "Oh, honestly. I know you're all thinking the same thing. And I'm only being practical."

"So? What should she do?" Ethel asked.

"If he pushes you to go anywhere with him after, you say you can't," Ruthie reasoned. "You have to be at work the next morning, or your mum and dad are waiting up for you—I know, I know, but how's *he* to know? And then you ask someone at the restaurant to call you a cab and you take it to the nearest Tube station. He won't know where you've gone, and that'll be an end of it."

Ann nodded, taking it all in, and then she turned to Miriam. "What do you think?"

"I think a restaurant is safe enough, but I agree with Ruthie. Do not agree to go anywhere else with this man. Even if he suggests something like a nightclub. Not until you know him better."

"Did he say what he does for a living?" Doris asked.

"He's a captain in the army, but he can't really talk about his work. He says it's all rather hush-hush."

"Hmm. I don't like the sound of that," Ethel said.

"Probably working in Whitehall. None of them are allowed to talk about it," Carmen speculated.

"See?" Doris asked, undeterred. "It's probably something very secret and important."

It was time for a change of subject. "What is the time?" Miriam asked the group. "Is it not the case that Ann and I must leave by ten o'clock so we do not miss our train?"

"Oh, yes. Yes, of course. I suppose we must be going." Ignoring the others' cries of disappointment, they said their farewells and made their way upstairs to street level.

"Do you mind that I suggested we leave?" Miriam asked as they stepped onto the sidewalk. It was so wonderfully cool outside, at least compared to the insufferably hot ballroom.

"Not at all. If we'd stayed they'd have kept badgering me all evening. And I was more than ready to go. The music was starting to give me a headache."

"Where shall we go now? Is there a Tube station nearby?"

"We passed one on the way—it's just at the corner. But would you mind walking for a while? If we go south it's about twenty minutes to Charing Cross. We can get on a District line train there."

It seemed that nearly every other building they passed was a theater, almost all of them disgorging hundreds of patrons, and before long it became an effort to stay together. Then it began to rain, albeit lightly, and the people around them became even more impatient to carve a path through the crowd, never mind how many others they had to shove or elbow out of the way.

They were crossing Shaftesbury Avenue, heads down against the rain, when a man bumped into Miriam, his shoulder catching hers and all but spinning her around. She stumbled, almost dropping to her knees, but managed to take an unsteady step forward. She was almost at the curb and out of harm's way, but with her next step she felt her heel sink into a hole of some sort. She looked down to discover that her shoe was stuck fast in a metal grate.

"Ann!" she cried out, and her friend, turning, crouched to help her. They tried to wrestle it loose, all the while enduring the complaints of passersby, but it was no use. The shoe would not come free.

"You'll have to undo the strap," Ann said. "Then we can at least stand on the curb. No sense in getting knocked down for the sake of a shoe."

"But these are my only good—"

"May I help you?" came an unfamiliar voice.

Miriam looked up, and then farther up again. A rather enormous man was standing next to them, his arms outstretched in an attempt to protect them from the passing crowds. "I saw you stumble," he explained. "Are you all right?"

"I think so. It is only my pride that is hurting me."

She'd managed to undo the buckle at her ankle, but she was reluctant to give up on her shoe.

"You ladies should stand on the curb," the stranger suggested. "I'll see if I can wriggle this loose. Any sane motorist would think twice before running me down."

"What about the mad ones?" she asked.

He grinned. "There's not a thing I can do about them," he admitted. Kneeling down, he took hold of her shoe and began to twist it back and forth, pushing it down and sliding the heel along the grate. "Almost there . . . *aha*. Here we go." He held up the freed shoe triumphantly.

"Thank you," Miriam said, taking it from him. "It was very kind of you to stop and help." She hopped to the corner and, after slipping on the shoe, crouched to fasten the buckle.

He was still there when she straightened. Not a handsome man, not compared to Ann's mysterious aristocrat, but there was something compelling about him all the same. His appearance was the furthest thing from chic she could imagine, for his clothes, though evidently of good quality, were ill-fitting and marked here and there with blotches of ink, and the knees of his trousers were stained with mud from where he'd knelt in the street. There was a button missing from his vest, which did not match his coat at all, and his bow tie was almost comically lopsided. If he were to tell her it was his habit to dress in the dark, and furthermore that he liked to choose his garments from the nearest pile of laundry, she would not have been surprised in the least.

He was very tall, for the top of her head only came to his shoulders, and his hands, as ink-stained as the rest of him, were similarly enormous. Yet he wasn't the least bit intimidating. Perhaps it was his pale eyes, much magnified by his spectacles, and the way they seemed to radiate kindness. Or perhaps it was the way his sandy hair, silvering at the temples and dampened by the rain, so badly needed a haircut. Whatever other failings might afflict this man, vanity was not among them.

As grateful as she was for his help, and as pleasant as he seemed at first glance, his failure to simply disappear into the crowds made her uneasy. Whatever did he have to gain from lingering?

"Thank you again for your help. I am certain you will wish to—"

"You're most welcome," he said, and held out his hand for her to shake. She did so, unable to ignore the way his hand enveloped hers so surely. "I'm Walter Kaczmarek."

"I am Miriam Dassin," she said. "This is my friend Miss Hughes. We are on our way home," she added pointedly. "Ann?"

"Oh, yes. Of course," Ann agreed. "On our way home. Shall we . . . ?"

They began to walk, side by side as the crowds were thinning, and Mr. Kaczmarek, moving to the curb side of the pavement, fell into step beside them. "Were you at the theater tonight?" he asked, as if it were the most normal thing in the world to make conversation with strangers. What sort of Englishman *was* he?

"No. We were out with friends. Dancing."

"I went to see *1066 and All That* at the Palace Theatre. Second time I've been. First time I was laughing so hard I missed half of it."

She smiled despite herself. "Ten sixty-six? What is it about, this play? I have not heard of it."

"It was the year of the Norman Conquest. The year a Frenchman, or something near enough to a Frenchman, conquered England. Of course it's all been downhill since then."

"Do you consider yourself an Englishman?" she asked, all too aware of how rude she must seem. But he didn't seem to mind.

"Despite my un-English name? I do. My parents were Poles but I've lived here since I was a boy. I'm not sure I'd feel at home anywhere else." He reached into his breast pocket and, after extracting a card, handed it to her. "Just in case you're worrying I'm waiting for the perfect moment to make off with your handbags."

PICTURE WEEKLY

WALTER KACZMAREK

EDITOR IN CHIEF

87 FLEET STREET • LONDON EC4

CENTRAL 7050

VERBA DOCENT, EXEMPLA TRAHUNT

"*Picture Weekly*," she read aloud. "You are the editor of this magazine? You are a journalist?"

"Yes. And I do realize that my profession might lead some to accuse me of criminality. I hope you believe me when I say I'm neither a confidence man nor an ambulance chaser."

"And this magazine? It is a successful one?"

"Miriam," Ann said, elbowing her gently. "It's on every newsstand. You must have seen it."

"Perhaps I have," she allowed. "What sort of magazine is your *Picture Weekly*? Is it full of scandal and film stars?"

"And scandals about film stars?" he offered. "No. They do grace our pages from time to time, but in the main I'm interested in more serious things."

"Such as?"

"The future of Britain in the postwar era. How the welfare state is changing the fabric of society. The dangers we face at the dawn of the nuclear age. Things like that. With a smattering of lighter fare to leaven the mix."

"I suppose I shall have to purchase a copy. Is it expensive?"

He grinned once more. "Fourpence an issue but worth every penny."

Ann nudged her again. "We need to cross the street. For the station."

"And I need to go the opposite way," he added. "It was a pleasure meeting both of you. Will you be all right from here?"

Miriam nodded, though she felt strangely reluctant to say goodbye. "We will. Thank you again."

"Think nothing of it. I do hope you'll ring me up. For lunch one day, if you like. My offices aren't far from here. Just so you know."

She searched his face, still uncertain as to what, precisely, would lead him to suggest such a thing. What did he know of her? What did he see in her that made him wish to learn more?

"Good night, Monsieur Kaczmarek," she said, not knowing what else to say.

"*Bonsoir,* Mademoiselle Dassin, Miss Hughes."

She watched until he was out of sight, and then she turned to Ann, wondering if her friend was as surprised as she. "Are all Englishmen so . . . so . . . ?"

"Practically *never,*" Ann admitted. "I'm starting to wonder if that fabric Milly sent along was sprinkled with stardust."

"Perhaps it was. It has been an unusual evening. Very much so."

"But a good one?" Ann asked, her voice threaded through with hope.

"The very best."

Chapter Twelve

Heather

August 12, 2016

The streetcar was only a block from Heather's stop when her phone buzzed. She dug it out of her pocket, hoping the driver wouldn't choose that instant to hit the brakes, and frowned when she saw the sender. Brett only texted in emergencies. Maybe the laser printer had run out of toner again.

> **BRETT**: where are you?
> **HEATHER**: on my way. what's up?
> **BRETT**: something's up. richard's here. looks like he never went home. in boardroom w guys in suits. they don't look happy.

It took her a few tries to type out her response.

> **HEATHER**: anyone else we know in there?
> **BRETT**: gregor and moira.

The magazine's publisher and the head of ad sales. At eight o'clock on a Friday morning.

HEATHER: be there in 5.

The streetcar lurched to a stop, bell clanging as some jerk in a Hummer tried to inch past the open doors. As soon as she found her feet again, Heather pushed her way through a sea of backpacks and down the steps to the street. The magazine's offices were on the south side of King Street, just at the end of the next block, and as she grew close, and then walked up the stairs to the second floor, she had to remind herself to breathe. Brett might have got things wrong. Gregor and Moira and Richard and a bunch of cranky-looking guys in suits didn't automatically equal a catastrophe.

Kim wasn't at her desk in reception. Not good. And the office was weirdly quiet. They all shared one big open-plan space, with shoulder-height cubicles that gave the illusion of privacy and towering plastic ficus trees that gave the illusion of a bright and healthy workplace, and most mornings everyone congregated in the break room for a solid quarter hour before drifting to their desks. Not today.

Heather made it to her cubicle, stowed her bag under her desk, and switched on her computer. Only then did she turn to face Brett, *Bay Street*'s other staff writer, whose desk faced the opposite wall of their three-sided pod.

"What's the deal?" she whispered.

"Check your email," he whispered back.

It took a minute or two to pull up her email, long enough for her heart to try to hammer its way out of her chest.

"The one from Richard?"

"Duh," Brett hissed.

Richard had sent it at 4:20 that morning. Brett had been right about the all-nighter.

Heather,

I need to speak with you this morning regarding some alteratlons In our corporate structure. Please remaln at your desk until I call, and refrain from unnecessary gossip and speculation with your colleagues until everyone has been briefed on the changes.

Richard
Editor in chief
Bay Street
Mitchell Media International

"And?" Brett prompted.

"I'm supposed to stay at my desk until he calls me in. Something about changes to the corporate structure. Does your email say that?"

"Yeah. But it also says I'm supposed to go to the boardroom at eight thirty."

"Have you talked to anyone else?" He didn't answer, so she swiveled to face him. "Brett?"

"I, uh . . . yeah. Most people are getting called into the boardroom. I'm sorry. This sucks."

It was as good as an actual pink slip.

She nodded, not trusting her voice, and turned away to stare sightlessly at her monitor. One by one her colleagues arrived and read their email from Richard, and most of them, Brett included, tiptoed to the boardroom.

The office grew quiet again, and when her phone finally rang Heather nearly jumped out of her skin.

"It's Richard. Could you come to my office?"

"Sure."

Her hands sweating like crazy, her mouth so dry she couldn't even swallow, she walked to his office on leaden feet. He'd left his door open, but she knocked on it anyway.

"Hi, Heather. Come on in. Take a seat."

She sat, and waited, and eventually he dragged his eyes from the sheets of paper spread out on his desk. As if he was dreading what came next. Or, rather, wanted her to think he was dreading it.

"So. Heather. The people at MMI have been concerned by our drop in ad revenues for a while now. Very concerned. Now, they could have just shut us down, which would have been a *disaster*. Instead they've decided to start up a Canadian edition of *Business Report,* and *Bay Street* will be folded into it. Each issue will include eight to ten pages of purely Canadian content."

Heather nodded.

"I'm sorry to say that the restructuring will involve some redundancies in our editorial staff here, and I'm especially sorry to tell you that your position has been eliminated."

"Uh-huh," she said. Not the most articulate response, but it wasn't as if Richard was really listening.

"I want you to know that I've insisted they give you a very attractive package, *very* attractive, and I'll provide a glowing reference. Absolutely. As well, MMI also offers career counseling and a variety of transition resources. Kendra in HR will be furnishing you—"

"So I'm out." Finally she'd found her voice.

"Yes. I wish I could—"

"What about the offshore banking piece? I only just started digging in."

"We've got it covered. And, well, I hate to do this, but MMI is asking that redundant staff vacate the premises as soon as possible."

"Okay. I guess I had better get on it." She stood, went to his door. "Good luck with everything," she said, not bothering to turn around.

Since she routinely sent blind copies of all her emails to her Gmail account, all she had to do was copy her contacts list, send it and a handful of story ideas she'd been developing to her private account, and erase a few hundred personal messages. Easy enough to sort out before they sent in security to frog-march her out.

"God, Heather. This sucks." Brett flopped down on his chair and let out a long, lingering, highly annoying sigh. He wasn't the one who'd been canned.

"That's okay. It's not your fault." Her voice felt weird. Robotic, if she had to describe it.

"Do you want me to get you some boxes? There's a whole pile of them already set up in the hall."

The suits had thought of everything. "Sure. But I only need one. I don't keep much stuff here."

It took her another ten minutes to pack up her things—some pictures in frames, her aloe vera plant, a handful of pens and sticky notes—and she was done. The box held before her like a shield, she said good-bye to her friends, promised she'd stay in touch, and retreated to the safety of the cab that Brett had called for her.

Not to cry. Not even to fume. She couldn't be sure about it yet, but she wasn't all that upset. A little unsure about what she'd do next; a little embarrassed, too. But her main feeling was relief.

Maybe this would give her a break. A chance to step off the hamster wheel and think about what she really wanted to do with her life. She hadn't stopped scampering on that wheel for years. From high school to university to internship to job to job, she'd always said yes to the offers she'd been given, always convinced that forward was the only way to go. She'd had her head down for more than a decade now, staring at that wheel beneath her feet, so sure she'd trip and fall if she ever looked up.

Screw it. She was going to stop, and breathe, and let herself think for a change. And she was going to take a vacation before she set foot in another office.

SHE SPENT THE afternoon napping, only waking when a text from Michelle set her phone buzzing.

MICHELLE: hey you. still up for dinner tonight? where are you anyway?

HEATHER: upstairs. came home early. long story.

MICHELLE: ok. didn't hear you. do you want to walk? reservation's for 7. tanya's meeting us there.

She didn't say anything to Michelle and Sunita on the way over. Better to wait until they'd all had at least one drink, and then she'd get it over with. By the time Tanya arrived, a solid half hour late as usual, Heather was on her second glass of sauvignon blanc and was feeling a little punchy.

"So I lost my job," she said as soon as Tanya was settled and their starters had been delivered.

"Whaaaat?" her friends chorused.

Sunita was shaking her head. "How is that even possible?"

"Corporate restructuring. I'd go into the details but it's actually pretty boring."

"Tell me they gave you a package," Michelle implored. She was an accountant and the most practical person Heather had ever met.

"They did. Three months of pay, which isn't bad. They also threw in career counseling, which, let's be honest, is a total lie. They'll probably just give me a pamphlet that describes how to write a winning résumé."

"You're not panicking, are you?" Tanya asked worriedly. "Because you really shouldn't panic."

"Of course you shouldn't," Sunita agreed. "You were the smartest person there."

"Your stories were the best thing about that magazine. Everyone knows that."

"Tanya's right. They'll be lost without you," Michelle said. "And you don't have to stay in magazines. You could try public relations. Or corporate communications—those jobs pay really well. You'd be making twice what Richard was paying you."

"And you wouldn't have to deal with his tit-talking at the office Christmas party," Sunita added. "Or his awful neck massages when you're working late."

"There is that," she agreed. And then, through a mouthful of fried calamari, she added, "I'm thinking of taking a vacation."

"That's the spirit! Where are you thinking?" Michelle asked.

England, she thought.

Until that very moment it hadn't occurred to her. Thirty seconds ago she'd been thinking of the beach, or maybe a few weeks at her parents' cottage up north.

"England," she said. "I want to see if I can find out about Nan. Remember those embroidered flowers she saved for me, and how we had no idea where they'd come from? I finally did some digging, and I know it might be wishful thinking on my part, but I think she might have worked for Norman Hartnell. I think she might have worked on the queen's wedding dress."

"Holy shit!" Tanya burst out. She owned a vintage clothing boutique, the sort of place that sold fifty-year-old designer dresses for thousands of dollars, and the expression on her face reminded Heather of a little kid at the front gates of Disneyland. Michelle and Sunita, on the other hand, looked mystified.

"Oh, come *on*," Tanya chided. "Hartnell was *the* British dress designer back in the day. His stuff wasn't what you'd call cutting edge—he was no Alexander McQueen, that's for sure—but he did design some fabulous things for the queen. Hold on a sec." With that, she pulled her smartphone out of her purse and began to type away.

"Here," she said, and handed her phone to Michelle. "This is from 1954. Just look at this dress—you can't tell me it isn't gorgeous. For that matter, look at the queen. We think of her now as this little old lady, but she was really beautiful back then. And Hartnell knew how to make clothes that really suited her."

Their main courses arrived just then, so Tanya took her phone back and they all dug in, and it was a few minutes before conversation resumed.

"So what's the plan?" Michelle asked. "Will you go to London and see if you can find out anything more about Nan?"

"Hartnell died a long time ago, but maybe you can find someone else who worked there," Tanya suggested.

"I may have already," Heather allowed. "Have you ever heard of Miriam Dassin?"

It was Sunita's turn to be astonished. "The artist? Of course I have. I love her work."

"I've got two photos of her and Nan together, and in one of them they're sitting in a workroom around embroidery frames. I couldn't find any mention of her having worked at Hartnell, but there isn't much about her personal life out there, anyway. A few interviews from the fifties, and then some short things that are tied to anniversaries of the end of the war. The fiftieth anniversary of the liberation of Ravensbrück—that kind of thing."

"Is there any way of getting in touch with her? Just to find out more about Nan?" Tanya asked.

"I tried, but she doesn't have a website or email address that I could find. I did email the gallery that used to sell her work, but they said she's retired and they can't pass on any inquiries or messages."

"Even if you can't track her down," Tanya reasoned, "it's not as if there aren't other reasons for you to visit England."

"You're right. I can still see her work at the Victoria and Albert Museum, and the queen's wedding dress is on display at Buckingham Palace this summer. I definitely don't want to miss that. And maybe see the places where Nan worked and lived? If only so I can take some pictures for my mom."

Michelle extracted a notepad and pen from her bag and wrote *Heather's Big London Adventure* across the top of the first page. "Okay. Let's make a list of everything you want to see and do. There's your flight, your hotel—"

"You have to stay at that little place in Soho that I discovered last year," Tanya insisted. "Wall-to-wall antiques and the building itself has got to be three hundred years old. The rooms all have their own bathrooms and most have a fireplace, too. I'll email you the details."

"Oooh—I'm adding it to the list," Michelle enthused. "Anything else?"

"Tons," said Tanya. "But first we need to get the waiter's attention. We're going to need another bottle of wine."

As she lay in bed that night, Heather's spirits were light, and it wasn't because she was tipsy; she'd stuck to water after her second glass of wine. Losing her job had been awful, it was true, but she refused to feel depressed about it. Her friends had been awesome, they'd helped her plan the trip of a lifetime, and now she had something to get her through the next few weeks, something exciting ahead of her, and she could figure out what she was going to do with her life when she got back. Not now, not tomorrow. Not anytime soon.

She lay in bed, Seymour at her side, his steady purr endlessly comforting, and she let her fingers sweep over the wispy warmth of Nan's blanket. Everywhere she'd lived, on every bed she'd called her own, she'd always had the crocheted blanket Nan had made for her tenth birthday.

She'd been going through a super-girly phase, so Nan had used something like ten different colors of pink wool in the granny squares and trim that ran around the border. It was pretty ratty now, and the corner where Seymour liked to nest was covered in orange fur, but if her apartment was burning down it was the first thing she'd save after her cat.

What would Nan say if she could talk to her now? What would she expect her to do?

Heather sifted through her memories, trying to conjure up some scrap of remembered wisdom from their shared past. Nothing . . . nothing . . . and then, just as sleep overtook her, the faintest whisper.

She'd been at Nan's for the day and she'd fallen off her bike and skinned her knees. Her grandmother had taken her into the kitchen, dampened a cloth, and wiped away her tears.

"This may smart a bit," Nan had said, just before she cleaned Heather's knees and dabbed on some iodine. "But you're a brave girl, aren't you? So chin up, and when we're done we'll go into the garden and you can pick some flowers and we'll make a posy for you to take home. How does that sound?"

"Okay."

"Good girl. Keep your chin up, and you can face anything."

Chapter Thirteen

Ann

August 18, 1947

*W*hen Mr. Hartnell came through the door of the workroom at precisely nine o'clock that morning, Ann just knew. She, and every other woman in the room, had been waiting for this moment for more than a month.

Everyone stood. A bubble of noise burst over the room: chair legs scraping across the floor, fugitive whispers pitched too loud, a volley of explosive sneezes from Ruthie, who always had the sniffles. And then silence. Even the ordinary sounds of traffic outside seemed to have dimmed.

Mr. Hartnell smiled, his grin stretching quite as wide as a Cheshire cat's. "I have some splendid news. The queen and Princess Elizabeth have graciously accepted my design for the princess's wedding gown. I shall also be designing gowns for the queen herself, Queen Mary, Princess Margaret Rose, and the princess's bridesmaids."

They applauded politely, mindful they were at work and not the music hall, and then Miss Duley, standing next to Mr. Hartnell on the landing, cleared her throat.

"The formal announcement will be made later today, and I shall speak with all of you in due course. As Mr. Hartnell has said, we will have a hand in the gowns for the entire wedding party. I promise that no one will be left out. In the meantime, however, we have a great deal of work to complete. Back to your places, please, and save your chatter for break."

Ann returned to the frame she'd been sharing with Miriam since the previous week. They'd been working on the bodice of the wedding gown for some society bride, a familiar mix of Alençon lace, dozens of sequins to catch the light, and just enough crystal beads and seed pearls to provide some texture. It did rather feel like something the bride's grandmother might have worn at the turn of the century, but it wasn't Ann's place to question or critique. When finished, the gown would be very beautiful, the bride's father would be poorer by several hundred guineas, and everyone who attended the wedding would agree that Mr. Hartnell had triumphed again.

Ann had only just shuffled her chair into the perfect spot when a shadow fell over her. She looked up to discover Mr. Hartnell and Miss Duley standing mere inches away.

"I beg your pardon," she said, and stood again. Miriam had been fetching some thread, but returned to wait at Ann's elbow.

"You remember Miss Hughes and Miss Dassin," Miss Duley said.

"Yes, of course," Mr. Hartnell answered. "Good morning to you both."

"Good morning, sir," Ann said. "Congratulations. It really is splendid news."

"It is, isn't it? I've come to tell you that Miss Duley has recommended you both for the samples we'll be sending to Her Majesty and the princess. What say you to that?"

She did her very best to look surprised. "Thank you ever so much. I'm honored, sir. Truly honored." She looked to Miriam, who seemed more taken aback than anything else, and tilted her head fractionally. *Say something,* she implored silently.

"Yes, of course. Thank you. I am very grateful to be chosen," Miriam added promptly.

"Her Majesty has specifically requested duchesse satin from Winterthur in Dunfermline for the gown, as well as a heavier satin for the appliqués from Lullingstone Castle. It will be several weeks before the fabrics are ready, I'm afraid."

"And the pearls are still in America," Miss Duley added.

Mr. Hartnell sighed mournfully at this reminder. "Those wretched pearls. I swear they'll be the death of me."

"I've suggested to Mr. Hartnell that we proceed with materials we have on hand. We'll do up half a dozen samples in total. Here are his designs for the motifs. Let's look at them in the light."

They followed Miss Duley to the windows, where she set out eight sketches on the wide sill, then stood aside so Mr. Hartnell might show them the particulars of his design.

"This is the gown itself, and here is the train. This is a rather impressionistic view, I'm afraid, but I will draw up a full-size pattern of where the various motifs ought to go. I need to see the entire thing in front of me."

"We can clear the floor in here tonight, sir, and put down some paper," Miss Duley suggested.

"Excellent suggestion—let's do just that. In any event," he went on, turning again to Ann, "this is generally what I have in mind for the train, which will attach to the princess's shoulders rather than her waist. Her Majesty is agreeable to a length of fifteen feet for the train."

The silhouette of the gown was familiar enough, and largely indistinguishable from several other gowns that Ann had embroidered over the past year or so. A sweetheart neckline, long fitted sleeves, full skirt. What set this gown apart, she saw instantly, was the embroidery.

The skirt was adorned with garlands of flowers and greenery, tier upon tier of them, and the same motifs appeared on the bodice and the entire length of the train. The design was perfectly symmetrical, yet there was nothing stiff or mannered about the embroidered decorations and their placement.

"It's lovely, sir," Ann said quietly.

"Thank you, Miss Hughes. I will say that it's quite my favorite of the sketches I submitted to Her Majesty and Princess Elizabeth. My initial inspiration was Botticelli and his figure of Primavera— perhaps you've seen it?"

It wasn't the time or place for Ann to admit to the deficiencies of her education, so she simply nodded.

"At any rate," he went on, "here are the most significant of the motifs. York roses in several sizes, star flowers, ears of wheat, jasmine blossoms, and smilax leaves. I think one sample with a large rose, a second with a cluster of the smaller roses, and then one each of the remaining motifs should be sufficient for our purposes. These are only the motifs that appear on the train, but I don't think we need to worry about the additional motifs from the gown itself. Not yet, at least."

"What do you think?" Miss Duley asked. "Will two or three days give you enough time?"

"I should think so," Ann said. "What were you thinking in terms of the embellishments, Mr. Hartnell? You mentioned pearls before."

"Yes. Lovely little round seed pearls at the edges of most of the appliqués, larger ones at the centers of some of the motifs, and a variety of crystals, beads, and the like."

"I'll go over everything with Miss Hughes and Miss Dassin," Miss Duley promised. "First I propose we go to the stockroom and see what Miss Louie has on hand for the backing."

Mr. Hartnell nodded. "Yes, of course. Ask for a good stiff duchesse satin for the appliqués, not too white, and a silk tulle for the backing. Failing that a silk gazar will do. But nothing too opaque."

"Yes, sir," Miss Duley said. Then she turned to Ann and Miriam, her expression uncharacteristically severe. "I'm sure you are aware of the heightened level of interest in this commission. Princess Elizabeth is very keen that no details of her gown appear in the press, and I know Mr. Hartnell would consider it a great disappointment were anyone here to betray her trust."

Ann glanced at Mr. Hartnell, whose delight had faded with the introduction of what had to be a dispiriting topic. "The news of the commission will be in the papers this evening, and you may well have friends and family asking about my designs. It feels rather ridiculous to even mention such a thing, really, since I know you've worked on important commissions before. I do hope . . ."

He looked so uncomfortable, his happiness at the great news all but extinguished, that Ann's heart went out to him. He really was such a kind man. "I do understand, and I don't mind your asking at all," she reassured him. "I won't breathe a word of it to anyone. I promise I won't."

"As do I," Miriam added.

"Thank you. Well, I suppose I ought to leave you ladies to your work. Do you need anything else from me, Miss Duley?"

"Not for the moment, sir. I'll let you know if we have any questions."

Miss Duley walked him out of the workroom, and then, after pausing to speak with Ethel and Ruthie, returned with them in her wake. "Ann and Miriam are helping me with something for the next few days, so I need you to take over work on this bodice. I know you were working on some pieces for that American department store, but they can wait. Miriam will show you what to do."

They murmured their agreement, and though they looked inquisitive they said nothing more. Nor would she, in their stead. It was clear enough that she and Miriam had been chosen to do up the samples. Mr. Hartnell always had samples made for his really important commissions, after all, and this surely ranked as the most significant work they'd done in years.

"Ann, if you'll come with me?"

The stockroom was the domain of Miss Louie, who had been with Mr. Hartnell since his earliest days as a designer, and who knew, down to the last quarter yard of Honiton lace, the entire contents of their on-hand stock. She was respected and not a little feared among the younger staff, not least because she guarded the stockroom with the single-minded intensity of a lioness.

"I hope Miss Louie's in a good mood today," Ann said as they hurried along. "Remember last week? When Ethel came back empty-handed?"

"That was Ethel's own fault. There's an art to managing our Miss L, as I've told you girls more than once. You need to *ask,* not demand. Take a moment to inquire how she is. Thank her for her time. No doubt Ethel came rushing up and didn't even bother to say good morning. Silly girl. Miss Louie has been here longer than anyone excepting Mr. H himself. She's entitled to run that stockroom as she likes, and if that means taking a few minutes to butter her up, so be it."

A wide wooden counter was set across the entrance to the stockroom, beyond which Ann could just glimpse the rows of shelving, laden with hundreds and hundreds of bolts of fabric, that lined the perimeter of the space. An enormous table stood in its center, yardsticks affixed to its edges, though Ann would wager good money that Miss Louie hadn't spared them a glance in years.

She came hurrying toward them now, a neat and efficient figure in her white coat and ruthlessly pinned-back hair.

"Good morning, Miss Duley," she said, her eyes sparkling with excitement. "Wonderful news, isn't it?"

"Simply wonderful," Miss Duley agreed. "Mr. Hartnell came by just now to tell the girls in my workroom, and to ask us to get started on some samples for HM and HRH. Of course I'm certain he showed you the designs before anyone else. What do you think?"

"Perfect. Quite, quite perfect. And it will suit the princess to a T."

"Indeed it will. He's asked us to do up half a dozen samples of the most important motifs, but I gather the Lullingstone satin isn't yet ready. Is there any chance we might prevail upon you? But only if you aren't busy with anything else. I know you're run off your feet most days."

"Don't I know it! But you've come at the perfect time. I do have some lovely duchesse satin, heavy but not too unwieldy. I'd say it's a fair match for the stuff you'll end up using. What did he say as regards color? Bright white? Or something softer?"

"Softer, I should think, so there's some contrast with the backing fabric. For that, I was thinking a really fine silk tulle. I thought we'd do up the samples as if they were for the train. It will give a better effect, don't you agree?"

"I do, indeed I do. How much will you need?"

"Say a yard and a half of the tulle? And a yard of the satin? If that's not too much to ask."

"Not at all. Let me just fetch them now."

When Miss Louie returned with the bolts of fabric, not more than a minute or two later, she first came to the counter so Miss Duley might look them over.

"What do you think? Will these do?" she asked, unrolling the satin and tulle with brisk efficiency.

"They're exactly what I had in mind. What would we do without you, Miss Louie?"

"I expect you'd all muddle along, but it's kind of you to say so."

Back at the table, Miss Louie lined up the satin with the edge of the table, whisked out a pair of gleaming shears from the depths of her coat pocket, and cut the satin, then the tulle, with the precision of a surgeon. After folding the fabric in neat squares, she returned to the counter and handed the bundle to Ann.

After a final round of thanks and well-wishes, Ann and Miss Duley returned to the workroom. Ethel and Ruthie had taken charge of the society bride's bodice, while Miriam, never one to be idle, had gathered fresh needles, spools of cotton and silk thread, and the stretcher bars and pegged side laths of an empty frame.

"Very good, Miriam," Miss Duley said approvingly. "If you could stretch the tulle for us—this piece is fifty-four inches wide, so you'll have room for three samples across, with plenty of room to finish the edges. Then thirty-six inches as far as depth, I think. Ann, if you could start by cutting out the appliqué pieces? Once you've arranged them on the backing, let me have a look."

Ann fetched half a dozen sheets of onionskin from a box on the side table, then went to a window at the far end of the room. Taking up Mr. Hartnell's sketch of the largest of the York roses, she held it against the window, overlaid it with the onionskin, and carefully traced over the petals.

She repeated the exercise for all the motifs, save the jasmine and ears of wheat, which would be created through beadwork alone. One by one, she cut out the shapes from the onionskin and set the pattern pieces on the sketch. Fearful that a whiff of air might throw them into disarray, she weighted down the wisps of paper with a handful of buttons from the odds-and-sods jar.

Moving to one of the side tables, she dusted it thoroughly and then, when she was certain it was spotless, spread out the satin. Had it been a less delicate or light-colored fabric, she'd have marked the perimeter of the pattern pieces with a prick-and-pounce method: first perforating the pattern's edges with a needle, then rubbing through a scant amount of powdered charcoal. The satin was so tightly woven, though, that the needle marks alone would be enough to guide her.

Ann set the first pattern piece on the satin, picked up the needle, its blunt end set in a cork to make it easier to hold, and began to mark the edge of the petal shape. She cut out the petal with her very best scissors, just the one piece to begin, and decided to experiment a little before she went any further.

Like most satin, it was the very devil to work with, for it managed to be slippery and quite stiff at the same time. It didn't take well to finger-pressing, but there was no way to baste under the edges without leaving marks. She would just have to turn under the edges as she went and hope they didn't fray too badly.

With that settled, she returned to the satin and cut out petals large and small, star flowers and heart-shaped smilax leaves, and as she finished each one she set it on its matching sketch. There were more than two dozen pieces when she'd finished, all needing to be appliquéd with invisible stitches onto the stretched tulle. Only then could the embroidery proper begin.

She looked at the clock; it was almost half twelve. She must have worked through morning break.

Miss Duley, noticing that Ann had paused in her work, came over to the table. "I'm sorry, my dear. I didn't notice you and Miriam hadn't gone down with the others until they were on their way back. You may have an extra quarter hour now to make up for it."

"That's all right. If I'd been desperate for a cuppa I'm sure I'd have noticed." Ann gestured to the array of satin shapes. "What do you think? I took account of the grain as I was cutting them out."

"Well done. Once you've attached them to the backing, we'll go over the placement of the beadwork. Miriam—I was just saying to Ann that you may make up your missed break with extra time at dinner."

"I do not mind. I was happy at my work."

"Then off to your dinners you go, and don't rush back," Miss Duley commanded smilingly.

Seated at her usual table in the canteen, with her usual fare of a cheese and salad sandwich failing to tempt her, Ann let the others talk over and around her. It was important to eat and drink and keep up her strength, but all she wanted at that moment was to return to her frame and begin to attach the appliqués.

"Ooh," Ruthie said as they were finishing, "you never did say how it went. Yes, Ann, I'm talking to you."

"How what went?"

"Your date with that dishy captain. Was he nice?"

"Oh, that. I didn't go."

A chorus of disappointed groans swept around the table.

"Why ever not?"

"And you never said a thing?"

"But you said you'd ring him up. I heard you tell him."

She had wanted to go, very much, but when she'd rung up the number on his card a sleepy voice had answered. A woman's voice.

"May I speak with Captain Thickett-Milne?" she'd asked once the worst of her surprise had worn off.

"Wrong number."

"I beg your pardon," she had said, but the woman had already hung up.

Ann had looked at the card, memorized the number, and dialed again with painstaking care.

"Hello? May I speak with—"

The same peevish voice had replied. "Oh, bugger off. I told you already—you've the wrong number."

She'd been too cowed to try again.

"I wasn't feeling well," she now fibbed.

"Well, now that you're feeling better you should call him back," Ruthie advised. "Otherwise someone else will snap him right up."

Ruthie was a sweet girl, but Ann couldn't bear to think about it anymore. He was probably married, or involved with someone, and that was the woman who had answered the phone. It had been stupid of her even to try.

"I'm off back to work," she told the table. "Are you ready?" she asked Miriam, and they were sitting at their frame before anyone else had returned from dinner. "So much for our extra quarter hour. But since we're here—which one would you like to do?"

"The *fleurs d'étoile*? The star flowers? But only if you—"

"No, that's fine. I think I'll start on the larger of the roses. But first let's move the frame into the corner. The light is much better there."

Miriam had set basting stitches in blue to divide the backing into six equal squares, and once Ann had washed her hands at the sink in the corner, set up her little side table with her things, and adjusted her chair just so, she cast an eagle eye over the tulle. Its grain was perfectly straight, without the slightest ripple or bump, and the fabric was as tight as a new drum.

"You've done a beautiful job on the stretching," she told her friend.

"Thank you. At Maison Rébé we were permitted no more than thirty minutes to set up our frames, but I allowed myself rather more time today. I did not wish the tulle to warp when I laced up the short sides of the frame."

With Mr. Hartnell's sketch for reference, Ann set the first of the petals on the tulle. She took a curved needle from her pincushion, the same as a surgeon might use, ran it through a scrap of chamois cloth a few times to remove any trace of tarnish, and threaded it with a double strand of silk floss so fine it was almost transparent.

Ann turned under the edge of the satin by the tiniest amount, held it in place with the index finger of her left hand, and then, bringing the needle from beneath the tulle, she caught the fabric just below the edge of the petal and pulled the thread taut.

One stitch completed.

She worked slowly, methodically, taking a half hour or more to affix each petal to the tulle. Inches away, Miriam was doing the same with the first of her star-flower shapes, and while they often liked to talk as they worked, today they were silent.

They continued on in this fashion all afternoon, and when they set down their needles at five o'clock they had attached all but a few of the appliqué pieces. Miss Duley had come by every hour or so, invariably pronouncing herself pleased with their work, and near the end of the afternoon had reminded them, more than once, to cover their work with a clean length of cambric before they left.

Supper that night had been the simplest thing Ann could devise: sardines on toast, which Miriam ate with gusto, and some tiny greengage plums that Mr. Booth had brought by. The weather was still warm and fair at eight o'clock, and the sunset promised to be a pretty one, so she and Miriam carried the kitchen chairs into the back and drank their tea and listened to the agreeable noises of children playing in the half-wild lane that ran along the end of the gardens.

"I do wonder how we'll get it all done on time," she said after a while. "The wedding is on November twentieth, but the fabric won't be ready for another week at least, if not longer. That leaves only six weeks, but really it's more like four. We can't expect the girls in the sewing room to make up the gown overnight. And did you see how many flowers are on the gown and train? Hundreds and hundreds. It took us the entire day just to make a start on a handful of them."

"Yes, but we are only two. There are twenty-four of us in the workroom. Also, you know, the work will go faster once we have done it a time or two. With each flower we will learn."

"I suppose you're right. I wanted to ask . . ."

"Yes?" Miriam asked.

"It's just that you didn't seem terribly excited. When Mr. Hartnell asked us to do up the samples. I'm not saying that to be critical. Only that I was a bit surprised."

"I know. I am sorry. I was not certain how to act. In France we have no king, and I know very little of this princess and her family. Have you ever met her?"

"Me? No. I mean, I've seen her several times, and I've curtsied as she's walked by, but I've never been introduced to her. Usually they—I mean the queen and princesses—don't come to us. Mr. Hartnell goes to them when they need something, to Buckingham Palace or Windsor Castle or wherever the king and queen are living."

"What do you think of them?" Miriam asked, and Ann was a little taken aback by her expression of disdain. "These people who live in their palaces and eat off gold plates while the rest of you queue up for your rations?"

"They're not like that. Honestly, they're not. The king and queen have ration books like the rest of us. And they might eat off gold plates, but they have to make do with the same food as everyone else."

Miriam frowned at this, still skeptical. "What of the rations for their clothing? If all is to be truly fair, as you say, then the princess will need coupons for her wedding gown, will she not?"

"I suppose she will," Ann admitted. "I wonder how they'll manage it."

"No doubt something will be done. No one will be brave enough to say no to the king."

"But they aren't like that at all. The king and queen could have left England during the war, or they could have sent the princesses to Canada, but they all stayed here. And Buckingham Palace was bombed, and the king's brother was killed. And the queen is ever so nice.

"There was one time, before the war, when she invited all the girls who'd worked on one of her gowns to come and see her in it. So we walked over to Buckingham Palace, and they let us in through a special door at the side, and we waited in this very grand hallway with paintings hung all the way to the ceiling. I remember we were so nervous we barely even breathed. And then the queen herself appeared in the gown we'd made for her, with a beautiful fur over her shoulders, and a tiara that was nothing but diamonds, hundreds of them, and besides that a necklace and bracelets and the most enormous earrings. One by one she said hello to all of us, and asked our names, and thanked us for our hard work. No one else has ever done that, in all the time I've been at Hartnell. Not a note, or a word of thanks, or anything. And she sends gifts, too—the white heather, just at the front of the border there, came from her. Balmoral heather, and it's in my garden now."

She had to stop and take a breath, and it was a bit embarrassing to realize how red-faced and strident she'd become. Miriam would think she'd lost her mind. "I'm sorry. It's just that I'm that fond of the queen. Most people are. I think that's why everyone is so excited about the wedding."

"Then I will be fond of her, too. And you are right. It is a great honor to work on the princess's gown."

"It makes me nervous just to think about it. What if it shows in my work? What if my hands get shaky, or—"

"Then do not be nervous," Miriam said.

"The whole world will be watching. How can I not?"

"The world will watch the wedding itself, yes, but not our workroom. And you must ask yourself: Is any of this beyond your capabilities? No. You are a fine embroiderer, the equal of any of my peers at Maison Rébé. You can do this. Of course you can."

It was a rare compliment from Miriam, and all the more precious as a result. "Thank you. I'm glad we're in this together."

"So am I, my friend. So am I."

Chapter Fourteen

Miriam

August 23, 1947

The longing had taken hold earlier that week at supper. Ann had made chicken, two wizened and rather tough legs, seasoning them with salt and pepper and nothing else. It had been good, if bland, and she had found herself wishing for something that tasted of more— what, exactly, she couldn't say. Only *more*.

And then, as she was falling asleep that night, the memory of Grand-Mère's Friday-night chicken had come upon her. She hadn't tasted it since her childhood, nor in all the intervening years had she ever considered making it herself. Yet her desire for the dish, once awakened, would not leave her.

The difficulty was that almost everything she required, excepting the chicken itself, was impossible to acquire in Barking. Not that it had surprised her, for one could not even buy a decent bottle of olive oil in the local shops. She'd asked Ann, but her friend had explained it was only carried by chemists. "For earache," she'd explained.

Miriam had nodded, bitten her tongue, and resolved to look further afield.

On Wednesday afternoon, Monsieur Hartnell's chief fitter, known to all as Mam'selle, had paid a visit to the embroidery workroom. Miriam had been intent on the spray of jasmine blossoms she was creating, her thoughts returning again and again to the impossibility of tracking down ingredients that were regarded as exotic rarities by the English, when the Frenchwoman's voice caught her attention. Mam'selle was deep in conversation with Miss Duley, likely over some detail of the royal ladies' gowns, and it occurred to Miriam that if anyone in London might be able to recommend a good French *épicier,* it would be Germaine Davide.

Few people made her nervous, but Mam'selle was one of them. Revered and feared in equal measure by the seamstresses whose work she governed, she was renowned for her impeccable taste, adored by her clients, and even, on occasion, deferred to by Monsieur Hartnell himself.

She waited until Mam'selle had finished speaking with Miss Duley and was about to climb the stairs that led out of the workroom. Her palms damp with nerves, her heartbeat hammering in her ears, Miriam rose from her seat and approached in as diffident a manner as she could conjure. Never would she have dared to directly approach such a personage as Mam'selle when she had been a lowly *petite main* at Maison Rébé, but she had dared many things in recent years, had she not? And this was not the sort of thing for which she might be dismissed. Of that she was almost certain.

"I beg your pardon, Mademoiselle Davide, but may I ask your advice on a small matter?"

Her hand already on the banister, Mam'selle turned to face Miriam, her bearing as imperious as an aristocrat of the ancien régime.

And then her expression softened. "You are the girl from Maison Rébé," she stated, her accent as thick as crème fraîche. "I have heard about you."

"Yes," Miriam admitted, wincing inwardly at the reminder of her effrontery in approaching Monsieur Hartnell. "My name is Miriam Dassin."

The merest smile, and then Mam'selle switched into French. *"Comment pourrais-je vous aider?"*

Miriam explained her dilemma, also in French. It was such a relief to let her mouth relax into the familiar words and cadence of her mother tongue. "I thought that you might know of a grocer, perhaps, where I might find what I need," she concluded.

Mam'selle rolled her eyes dramatically. "I love this country, but the food . . . let us speak no more of it. It is possible to find such things in South Kensington. Around the French embassy there are several provisioners, and there are one or two good shops in Soho, of course. But the prices are criminally high. Simply criminal."

"Oh. I see. I was hoping—"

"That is why you must go to my friend Marcel Normand in Shoreditch. To the east of here, not far from the market at Spitalfields. He has an *épicerie* on Brushfield Street. I cannot recall the number but the awning is striped green and white. Impossible to miss. Tell him I sent you."

Miriam had stammered out her thanks, the great lady had taken her leave, and later, after supper that evening, she had confessed all to Ann. How she wished to make a favorite family dish for supper on Saturday evening, but needed to go to Shoreditch to fetch the ingredients.

"I do not wish to neglect my share of the chores. Would you mind if I do them on Sunday instead?"

Ann hadn't minded at all. "It won't hurt to let things slide for a week or so. How about I fetch the chicken on Saturday morning, and you head into London? If I go early enough the butcher will probably still have something."

Miriam decided to keep her opinion of the butcher to herself. To voice her conviction that he was a wretch who sold meat that was fit only for dogs, and who ought to be prosecuted for his black-market dealings, would only depress them both. Instead she cautioned Ann that she ought to keep her expectations low as far as supper was concerned.

"I have never made it myself, you see, and I have no recipe. Only the memories of watching my grandmother make it many times, and of course its taste. I fear I will disappoint you."

"Oh, I doubt *that*. And you know already that I'm a poor cook. Who am I to criticize?"

On Saturday morning she took the train into London, but rather than continuing into the West End she alighted at Liverpool Station. From there it was only a short walk east to the neighborhood of Shoreditch and the ancient market of Spitalfields.

She didn't venture into the market building itself, but instead went straight to the French grocer. It was, as Mam'selle had said, impossible to miss. There was the green-and-white-striped awning, to begin with, and the name above the door.

MARCEL NORMAND GROCER & PROVISIONER

FINE FRENCH FOODS OUR SPECIALITY

She hurried inside, thinking only of finding what she needed as quickly as possible, but halted in the doorway, her senses awhirl. Garlic and herbes de Provence scented the air, and the labels on the packets and cans were all in French, and there was Marcel Normand himself, standing behind the counter, his red face and prodigious mustache instantly familiar, never mind she'd never set eyes on the man before. All of it was so comforting. She smiled at the grocer, raising a hand in greeting, and let herself wander about, her greedy eyes making a feast of everything they saw. If she'd had the money she'd have emptied the shop.

"Good afternoon," Monsieur Normand said as she finished her tour and approached his counter. *"Bonjour, mademoiselle."*

"Bonjour," she answered. Seeing how his smile widened, she continued on in French, explaining that Mademoiselle Davide had sent her, that she was in need of one hundred grams of green olives, the same amount of prunes, about twenty-five grams of fennel seed, and—although she knew it was a rarity indeed—something that might impart the flavor of fresh orange peel. With his every nod her heart lightened. He even found some dried orange zest for her, apologizing in advance for its elderly state.

"I do not think it will taste much of anything," he said after taking a sniff, "but it is better than nothing." He refused to take anything for the pinch of orange zest he'd given her, and only asked one shilling and sixpence for the other items.

She shook his hand, thanked him several times for his kindness, and tucked her purchases into her bag. Feeling in need of refreshment, she followed her nose down the street to an Italian café. It was amazing how restorative a few gulps of coffee could be. Hot, bracingly black, and pleasingly bitter, it lifted her spirits far more effectively than the insipid cups of tea so beloved by her English friends.

She paid for the coffee and took out her fare for the Tube ride home, tucking the coins in her coat pocket so she wouldn't have to dig for them later. As she did so, her fingers brushed against something. It was the business card, now rather battered, of the man she and Ann had met on their way home from the dance hall a few weeks before. Walter Kaczmarek.

Unbidden, a single thought dropped into her mind. She had liked him. Liked him despite *not* wishing to like him. There had been something compelling about the man, impossible to measure in words alone, and she realized, abruptly, that she badly wanted to see him again.

She took out her *A to Z* and searched for Fleet Street. It wasn't far away at all—a half hour's walk, if that. She stood at the counter of the café for a long while, her gaze flitting between Mr. Kaczmarek's card and the place on the map, half-hidden by her forefinger, that marked the location of his office. And then, for the first time in living memory, Miriam threw caution to the wind.

Tucking the card back in her pocket, she walked down the street to a phone box by the corner. After inserting her pennies, she dialed the number and waited for someone to answer.

"Good morning, *Picture Weekly*," a cheery voice said in her ear. And then, after a long pause, "Good morning? Hello?"

Of course. She had to press the button to deposit the coins and complete the connection. "Good morning. I would like to speak to Mr. Kacz—"

"To Kaz? Of course. May I furnish him with your name?"

"Yes, if you wish. It is Miriam Dassin."

"Please hold the line."

A few seconds, no more, and then the clatter of someone picking up a receiver. "Miss Dassin. What a pleasant surprise. May I hope you've decided to take me up on my offer of lunch?"

"Only if you are not occupied. I have been shopping nearby. At least I believe it is not far—the market of Spitalfields?"

"Then you're quite close indeed. There are some decent pubs near the market, but the food isn't what I'd call inspired. Do you like fish?"

"I do," she said, and then, cautiously, "I assume you do not speak of fish and chips."

"No, this place is several steps up from your typical chippie. Do you have a pencil to write down the address? Yes? It's called Sweetings. Thirty-nine Queen Victoria Street. The easiest route is south along Bishopsgate, then, at the point where it branches into two, stay on the right. That's Threadneedle Street. When you get to the intersection at Bank Street, continue straight ahead onto Queen Victoria Street. Sweetings will be on your left. What time suits you?"

"I have finished my errands. Any time is convenient."

"And I'm just finishing my day here, so you've caught me at the perfect time. It should take you twenty minutes to walk there. Shall we say half an hour? Just to be on the safe side?"

"Yes. Thank you."

"I'll wait outside. *À tout à l'heure,*" he finished, his accent surprisingly good.

She had walked along Bishopsgate on her way to the market, so it should be an easy matter to find it again by heading in a general southwest direction. She set off down the street, holding her bag close to her chest as she shouldered her way through the crowds. It seemed as if half of London had decided to do their weekly shopping at the market.

She turned onto a side street, walking south for a block before turning west, the sidewalks growing steadily emptier. Ahead, a group of people were emerging from a narrow lane, the men all dressed in dark suits. Some of the men wore hats. A few, she noticed, wore a *kippa*.

The sight almost stopped her in her tracks. Did they not realize it was dangerous to be seen so in public? But no. They were in England.

And this was the East End. Thousands of Jews, she had heard, lived and worked here. Had been here for hundreds of years.

Her feet carried her across the street and down the lane. It was narrow, curving, bare of shop fronts. If not for the people emerging, she would have missed the place. There was little to signify the building's purpose, and its brick façade was the same as the rest of the buildings on the lane. Except for the small, unobtrusive noticeboard to the side of the entrance.

SANDYS ROW SYNAGOGUE, it read, and below it were some words in Hebrew, as well as the days and times of services.

She slowed her pace, hoping to catch a glimpse of the interior as she passed by, but she couldn't make out anything beyond some steps and a shadowy corridor. She faltered, her limbs made clumsy by longing and regret.

How she yearned to hear, after so long, the beloved prayers and invocations. To repeat the words her grandfather had taken such pains to teach her. To belong, once again.

But she had nothing to cover her hair, and the services had finished, besides, and Mr. Kaczmarek was waiting for her, and she wasn't sure that she could bear it. To hear and see and sing would be to remember. To let the wounds be opened once more, and the bitter pain of loss consume her.

Not today. Not yet.

She walked on, blind to everything but the pavement before her, until she looked up and realized she was at the restaurant. Mr. Kaczmarek was there, waiting outside as he'd promised. Such a big man, though like most tall people he stooped a little, and his hair was so bright and fair under the midday sun. It didn't surprise her that he didn't bother with a hat.

He had a battered old canvas satchel slung over one shoulder, and his head was bent over a newspaper, which he'd folded back on itself so it didn't flap in the wind. He looked up just as she crossed the street, and the expression of delight on his face made her heart skip a beat.

It pleased her, his interest, yet it was a puzzle as well. What did this cultured, well-connected, and presumably successful man want to do with *her*? She had no education, no connections that would interest him, and she knew almost nothing of English life beyond the confines of an embroidery workroom and a council house in Essex. She was in her early twenties, while he had to be something close to forty. For all she knew, he might even be married.

It would be wise to remain on her guard. Perhaps he was the sort to befriend young women and turn their heads with compliments and gifts and the luxury of his attention. Perhaps he had only one aim in mind.

Even as the suspicion arose, she knew it to be false. If he were such a man, to begin with, would he not be better dressed? He was no lothario, not with his ink-blotched cuffs and shaggy hair and shoes that cried out for polish. He was the sort of man, she decided, who might easily forget to put on his coat when he left for work in the morning. Her father had been like that, too.

They shook hands and said hello and he ushered her inside the restaurant. To their right was a marble counter laden with platters of gleaming fish, so fresh she could smell only the sea, and then only faintly. Waiters in long aprons were moving purposefully about the space, which looked to encompass a series of rooms, none of them especially grand. Most of the restaurant's patrons were seated shoulder to shoulder at a series of high counters, though there were a few small tables scattered about.

One of the waiters hurried over to shake Mr. Kaczmarek's hand and welcome him to the restaurant.

"Lovely to see you, Kaz."

"Any tables free?"

"There's one in the far room. Do you need a menu?" the waiter asked.

"Just the one for my guest. We'll seat ourselves?"

"If you don't mind. I'll be along in a minute."

Their table was nicely secluded, at the far end of the second room, and by the time they had settled into their chairs the waiter was back with a menu for Miriam.

"Pint of the usual?" he asked Mr. Kaczmarek.

"Yes, please. What would you like, Miss Dassin? A glass of wine, perhaps? They have a very nice Sancerre."

She nodded her head, relieved he hadn't asked for her opinions on the wine, since she hadn't any worth sharing. Inspecting her menu, which was almost poetic in its simplicity, she halted when she came to the names of the fish being served. Brill? Newlyn hake? John Dory?

"I usually have whatever the waiter recommends," he said, perhaps sensing her confusion. "They'll prepare it any way you like. And the vegetables they serve are cooked with some care, which is a rarity in England. Did you want something to start? Or were you thinking of leaving some room for pudding?"

"No . . . perhaps just the fish?"

The waiter returned with their drinks just then, and when prompted by Mr. Kaczmarek he recommended the plaice. "Fresh in from Cornwall this morning."

"Very good. Shall we both have that, Miss Dassin? Grilled, I think. And an order of samphire as well."

Miriam took a sip of her wine, then another for courage, and tried to think of something to say. Mr. Kaczmarek, however, had no such difficulties. "You know what I do for a living," he began. "What is your profession?"

"I am an embroiderer," she said. Best to be honest from the start. If he were disappointed to discover she worked for a living it was best to know straightaway. "I work for Monsieur Hartnell," she added, and immediately cringed. That was a detail she might have kept to herself.

"Ah," he said. "Your employer has been in the news this week."

"Yes. I cannot say any more. I should not have told you."

"There's no need to worry. I assure you I'm not about to start fishing for a story. On my word of honor, I'm not."

"Very well. Shall you tell me of your work? Of this magazine of yours?"

"I don't own the thing, so I can't properly say it's mine. But I did found it, a little more than twelve years ago, and I've been its editor from the start. I was given, or rather lent, the money to get it off the ground. And beyond the staff's salaries and the costs of running the office and so forth, our profits get plowed back into the enterprise."

"You said, the evening we met, that it is a serious publication. That your stories are about important things."

"Much of the time, yes. But I'm not averse to lighter fare. We all need the occasional taste of cake in between our rations of National Loaf. Now more than ever."

"Why now?" she asked, though she had a good idea of what his answer would be.

"Life here is a far sight less dangerous than it was during the war. I won't dispute that. But it's also a good deal more miserable. The nation is beggared, the empire is crumbling, and we just lived through a winter where people froze to death in their own homes because there wasn't coal enough to go around. No wonder everyone is over the moon about this royal wedding."

"You know I cannot—"

"I'm not talking about what the princess is going to wear on her wedding day. But you have to admit the timing couldn't be better."

She frowned at this, surprised by his cynicism. "I know little of your king and his family, but do you really believe he arranged for his daughter to be married in order to . . . how do you say it . . . ?"

"Relieve some pressure on the government?"

"Yes."

"I don't. And from what I do know of the man, I suspect he'd much prefer if she waited a few years. She is very young, after all. I do think, however, that it's come at an opportune moment. What better way to get people's minds off the misery of their own lives than by having a national holiday?"

"A holiday? Really?"

"I doubt they'll give everyone the day off. But there will be street parties the length and breadth of this land."

"Will you have a party?"

"Me? No. I'll be busy working that day—we're doing a special edition of the magazine. But I'm sure we'll drink a toast to the happy couple at some point."

"I bought a copy of *Picture Weekly*. I thought it was very interesting. The person who chooses your photographs has an artist's eye."

"That would be me," he admitted, smiling almost shyly. "Would you like to see our latest issue? I brought it for you."

She accepted it with a smile, spread it open on the table, and began to read. There were several pages of advertisements, a long article on the hopes for a vaccine against infantile paralysis, complete with many heartrending photographs of children in iron lungs or with splinted limbs, an essay on the import-export gap by a professor of economics, a story about Britain's many species of game birds, and last of all a photo essay on a young American actress who was starring in a West End musical. She was also the cover model for the issue.

"I see what you mean. The way you must mix important things with . . ."

"A day in the life of Miss Loveday Lang, star of *Put On Your Best Blues*? I know. And I wish, sometimes, that— Ah. Here's our food."

The fish, white and delicate and perfectly cooked, was delicious, as were the accompanying vegetables. She even accepted a portion of the samphire Mr. Kaczmarek had ordered, which he explained was a form of seaweed, and, undeterred, found it not unlike a briny sort of *haricot vert*.

"So," he said, arranging his fork and knife on his empty plate. "Tell me about your work. I'm not fishing for details of the royal waistline, I promise. I'm interested in you. Why did you become an embroiderer?"

"There was no 'why.' I was fourteen, and one of my teachers thought I might have a talent for it. She told my parents, and before I knew it I was beginning my apprenticeship at Maison Lesage. From there I went to Maison Rébé."

"And during the war . . . ?"

She shook her head. "Another time. What of you? Did you remain at *Picture Weekly* during the war?"

"I did. I'm blind as a proverbial bat, so none of the services would take me. Said I was in a reserved occupation anyway, so I might as well stay put. Surprised the hell out of me. I've been a thorn in the side of the establishment, as it were, for my entire working life, so I was sure they'd want to throw me in the path of danger as quickly as possible."

"It was dangerous here, though, was it not? With the Blitz?"

"I suppose. At times it was. In the main it was just depressing. I . . ." He took off his spectacles and pinched at the bridge of his nose. "I lost someone I loved very much. She was killed in an air raid. In the summer of 1941, after the Blitz proper had ended."

It was easier to see his eyes without the barrier of his spectacles. They were a pale blue that faded to silver at the edge of his irises, and there was something about the color that put her in mind of a mid-winter sky. But there was nothing cold about his gaze.

"After Mary was killed I had a hard time. It was a long while before I . . . well . . ."

"Before you were content to face each new morning?"

"Yes."

"And after Mary? Was there anyone?"

"No," he said, his gaze meeting hers readily.

"Why did you give me your card?" she asked, emboldened by his honesty.

"I'm not precisely sure. Perhaps it was the way you reacted to your shoe being caught in the grate? You didn't fuss, or panic, or even complain. You were rather funny about it, as I recall. And I knew straight off that you'd lay me out cold if you'd thought I was a threat."

English people and their baffling idioms. "Lay you out?"

He mimed a punch to his jaw.

"Perhaps," she acceded, "but you behaved yourself."

"Of course. Whatever else I may be—and I have my share of faults—I would never stoop to harassing a woman. In any fashion."

"That I believe. I do not know why, but I do."

He smiled, and his pale eyes grew even warmer. "Then I shall endeavor not to give you any reason to change your mind."

The waiter, returning to clear their plates, asked if they wanted pudding, but Miriam shook her head. English desserts were nearly as frightful as English bread.

"Not today, thanks," Mr. Kaczmarek answered, and she suspected, from the gleam in his eye, that he had read her mind.

"I must go," Miriam said after stealing a glance at her wristwatch. "It is half-past one, and I promised Ann that I would not be late. I am making my grandmother's Friday-night chicken for our supper tonight."

"Even though it's Saturday?"

"I did not have time to stop in Shoreditch yesterday. There is a French grocer there. He sells things I could not find in Barking."

"Such as?"

"Olives. Prunes. Fennel seeds. And also some dried orange peel. I looked for fresh oranges but they are not in season."

"No, they wouldn't be. Even if they were, you wouldn't be able to buy one. They're reserved for children. For the vitamins, I suppose."

The waiter returned with the bill, which Mr. Kaczmarek barely glanced at before handing the man several bank notes and shaking his hand. And then he was helping to pull back her chair, his hand grazing the small of her back for the briefest instant, and she couldn't be sure if she welcomed or feared his touch.

It was warm outside, and far brighter than in the restaurant, and she had to shield her eyes in order to properly see his face. Noticing, he pivoted so the sun fell on his back.

"Which way are you going?" he asked.

"I need a District line train. To Barking."

"Then it couldn't be easier. The entrance to Mansion House station is just over there."

"Thank you for lunch. I had a very good time."

"I'm glad to hear it," he said, and he held out his hand so she might shake it in farewell. She did so, but then, her fingers still wrapped around his, she rose up on her tiptoes and kissed his right cheek, then his left.

"I beg your pardon," she whispered, taken aback by her boldness. "I only—"

"Thought to give me a proper good-bye? I certainly don't object. Do you have a telephone number where I might reach you?"

"Alas, no. We do not have a telephone at the house."

"I understand, but I do want to see you again. Will you promise to ring me up before long?"

"I will."

"I shall await your call, then. If only to hear how your grand-mother's Friday-night chicken turned out."

"I have never cooked it before," she confessed, "and I have no rec-ipe. Only my memories. Let me first see what my friend thinks of it. If she survives, I will make it for you. Good-bye, Mr. Kaczmarek."

"Kaz. I'm Kaz to all my friends."

She wasn't certain she wanted to call him by that name, for it didn't suit him at all, this gentle and kind and ever so intelligent man. "May I instead call you Walter? Do you mind?"

Her question brought a shy smile to his face. "Not at all. In fact, I should like it very much."

"Then *au revoir*, Walter. *À la prochaine*."

Chapter Fifteen

Heather

August 29, 2016

Two and a half weeks later Heather was on her way to England. She hadn't flown all that much, and she'd been worried she'd get antsy on the way over, but it was actually okay in the end. Only seven hours from start to finish, and by some miracle she ended up with a window seat near the front of the plane, and after a really horrible supper of some kind of ersatz stir-fry she even managed to fall asleep for a few hours.

Going through customs was easy, and with only a single carry-on suitcase she was able to head into London right away. Although it was almost a million stops from the airport into the city center, she took the Underground, since she didn't like the idea of messing about with shuttles or buses or anything that meant she had to figure out connections. From Piccadilly Circus, assuming she'd calculated correctly, it was about a ten-minute walk to her hotel, and although she got turned around when she first made it up to street level, she soon found her bearings.

London was exactly as she'd imagined. Loud and busy and there really were big black cabs and red double-decker buses zooming along the streets, and although the shops all seemed to have modern façades she only had to look up to see the older buildings hiding beneath.

After passing at least a half-dozen theaters, since her route along Shaftesbury Avenue seemed to be taking her through London's equivalent of Broadway, she turned onto Frith Street and headed north. It was much narrower, with far fewer shops, and apart from one or two cafés, most of the restaurants and nightclubs that lined the street were still shuttered.

She almost missed the hotel, since the sign was just a small brass plate next to the door. She rang the bell and someone buzzed her in, and she knew right away that Tanya had sent her to the right place.

The man at the desk, who introduced himself as Dermot, could have fallen out of the pages of *Great Expectations,* what with his little round glasses, hair growing out of his ears, and purple silk waistcoat, although when he came around the desk to show Heather to her room the illusion was ruined by his ripped jeans and running shoes. He was very friendly, though, and promised to return with some tea and refreshments as soon as she'd settled in.

"It's a service we offer for all our arriving guests. I'll bring it by in ten minutes or so."

The room was even better than she'd imagined. It had a high brass bed piled with pillows and a foofy duvet, a fireplace that she was dying to switch on even though it was boiling hot outside, and an en suite bathroom with a big clawfoot tub and no shower, just an attachment that looked like an old-fashioned phone.

Dermot brought her the tea tray, and wouldn't let her give him a tip, and said she just had to ring down once she was done and someone would fetch it. There was a small teapot with a silver strainer, which meant there was loose-leaf tea inside, a cup and saucer and spoon, and besides that milk and sugar, a little jar of honey, and a second saucer piled with round shortbread cookies that tasted of ginger. Biscuits, she reminded herself. Not cookies.

After her tea and biscuits she had a bath and washed her hair without too much trouble, and then, dressed in her nightie, her hair still wrapped in a towel, she decided a short nap would be helpful. She'd only sleep for an hour or so, just until the early afternoon, then she'd set off for a wander through the nearby streets. She'd find a quiet place to eat some dinner, come back to the hotel early, and see if anything interesting was on the TV. Then she'd make herself go to sleep early, because she had a full day of sightseeing planned.

Only it wasn't sightseeing, not really. It was detective work.

Her first stop would be Nan's old house in Barking, and if she was feeling really brave she might even knock on a door or two and ask if anyone remembered a woman named Ann Hughes who had moved away more than sixty years ago. It was a long shot, but there was no way she was leaving England without trying to find out more. After that, she'd go to Bruton Street, where the Hartnell offices had once been, and if she was lucky someone might agree to let her inside and look around. Last of all she would visit the Victoria and Albert Museum, where Miriam Dassin's *Vél d'Hiv* was on display.

The only disappointment was Buckingham Palace, since every last entrance ticket was sold out for the days she was in England. She'd checked online the same day she'd bought her plane tickets, and when that hadn't worked she'd even called the number on the website. The woman on the phone had been apologetic but unyielding. There simply were no tickets to be had.

"Normally it isn't this bad. I think everyone is eager to see Her Majesty's wedding and coronation gowns. I do apologize for any inconvenience."

But all was not lost. She could still stand outside the palace and watch the changing of the guard, and the gift shop was open to everyone. She'd promised to bring her mom a tea caddy with a picture of the queen on it, and also a Christmas ornament shaped like a corgi if they had any.

It was more than a little crazy, her coming here, since London was ridiculously expensive and there was no guarantee she'd find out anything about Nan, and she'd probably come home to an eye-watering credit-card bill and be no closer, on top of everything else, to finding a new job. It was impractical and self-indulgent and she still was a little bit nervous that Nan would be upset that Heather was prying into secrets she'd kept for almost seventy years.

Yet the box had said *For Heather*. Nan had wanted her to have the embroideries. She had kept them all those years so Heather might one day find them, and wonder, and understand there was more to her grandmother than she had ever imagined or known.

A SHARP KNOCK on the door woke her. Had Seymour knocked something off her desk again?

Another knock. "Housekeeping!"

No . . . she wasn't at home. Her bed wasn't nearly so big or comfortable. She was at the hotel, and she had slept in, and—*yikes*. It was past ten o'clock already. "Sorry! I'm not quite up."

"No worries! I'll come back later."

Up. Definitely time to get up. She could sleep when she was back in Toronto.

She stumbled to the bathroom, used the toilet, splashed cold water over her face, brushed the fur from her teeth. Dragged her hair into a twisty kind of bun, dug fresh undies from her suitcase, and put on the least creased of her cotton sundresses.

There. Nearly ready. She eyed the room-service menu; they probably weren't serving breakfast this late. And she did need to get moving.

She dropped off her key at the front desk and set off for the café around the corner. Coffee and croissant consumed, she made her way to Tottenham Court Road and its Underground station. If all went well she'd be in Barking in less than an hour.

The train moved aboveground after a while, which made the ride a little bit more interesting. At least she was getting a sense of what ordinary people had in their backyards. Scrubby grass, rickety sheds, rusty swing sets, and here and there an unruly patch of vegetables.

In the end it only took forty minutes to get to Barking. Heather followed the other passenger who'd alighted, a young mom with a stroller, out to the road, giving her a hand with the stairs. Then she pulled up the map she'd saved to her phone the night before. Right on Station Road, left on Ripple Road, straight ahead at St. Edward's Road. For some reason, 109 Morley Road hadn't shown up on the map when she'd done a search, but the road itself was there. It would be easy enough to count along until she found Nan's house.

The streets were quiet and a little dull, in a way that reminded her of parts of Toronto, only the houses were smaller and much closer together. There didn't seem to be many shops, only the occasional convenience store, and there wasn't much traffic either. That made a nice change from downtown London.

And then, at last, Morley Road. Nan's road. The house on the end was 183, and after that came 185, the numbers steadily climbing. Heather walked until the road ended, two blocks later, but there was no number 109. She retraced her steps and even checked the map again. But that was it: she'd walked along every inch of Morley Road. And she was right about the address, for it was the one Nan had written on the back of those photographs her mom had unearthed.

She looked around, trying to make sense of things, but Morley Road ended where she stood. Ahead was a group of low-rise apartment buildings and a scrubby stretch of open land. Nothing else.

Maybe she should email her mom, just to make sure the address really was correct, and if she had taken a wrong turn at some point it would be easy enough to try again. For all she knew there was another Morley Road in Barking, or even another entire town called Barking somewhere else in England. But it was early in Toronto, and she didn't much feel like standing around, and she was pretty sure, besides, that she hadn't made a mistake with the address. She might as well head back to the station.

Turning onto Ripple Road, she noticed there was a supermarket on the corner. A neighborhood-sized place. The sort of store that had regular customers and cashiers who knew the customers' names. And she found herself crossing the street and walking inside and making a beeline for the woman at the help desk. Or, rather, Customer Courtesy Centre. What was the harm in asking?

"Good morning," Heather said to the woman at the desk.

"Good morning. Lovely day, isn't it?"

"It sure is. I'm sorry to bother you, but I wonder if you can help me find an address. One hundred and nine Morley Road. I went there just now but the house numbers start at a hundred and eighty-three. I wonder if I'm doing something wrong." Heather showed her the map on her phone.

"That's Morley Road all right, and as far as I know there's only the one stretch of it. But then, I live over Dagenham way. Let me think . . . ooh. I'll ask Shirley. She grew up right around the corner." She turned away, to the intercom on the wall, and her words echoed throughout the store. "Shirley to Customer Courtesy. Shirley to Customer Courtesy, please." And then, over her shoulder, "She won't be a moment. Just has to come over from the fish counter."

An older woman came bustling up a minute later, her white coat pristine, a hairnet pulled low over her brow. She had a nice face, round and rather red, and the short walk had left her a bit out of breath.

"Here I am," she puffed. "I came as fast as I could."

"You are a love. I was thinking you might be able to help this young lady. She's come looking for an address on Morley Road, only she can't find it."

"Whereabouts on Morley Road?"

"It's number one hundred and nine," Heather said. "My grandmother used to live there. I'm visiting from Canada and I thought I'd try to find the house." She held out her phone so Shirley might look at the map she'd saved.

"Oh, right. There's your problem. See the T-junction there, where Morley ends? It used to continue on another few hundred yards. They knocked down a whole whack of houses back in the fifties, I think, or maybe it was the sixties, and they put up a new council estate. And now they're saying a block of tower flats is going up, too."

Heather's heart sank into her shoes. "So you think my nan's house was over there?"

"Sorry to say it, but I think it probably was. Are you all right?"

Heather nodded, blinking back tears. "Yes. Sorry for taking up your time."

"Not at all. Well, I'd best be back to the counter. Lovely to meet you."

Heather thanked the women and wandered out of the supermarket. There was nothing left of Nan in Barking, and those fantasies she'd had, of walking up to a neighbor's house and ringing the bell and meeting someone who had known her grandmother, were just that. Fantasies. Nan's house had vanished into dust before Heather had even been born.

She got on the next train heading back into London, hauled out her pocket-sized *Rough Guide* to London, a bon voyage gift from Suni and Michelle, and considered where to go next. She'd planned to stop by Bruton Street, where the Hartnell premises had once been, but some online digging before she'd left had told her that only the façade with his name was left; the actual business had closed in the 1970s. And she wasn't sure if she could face going there, knocking on the door of whatever business now occupied the building, and being turned away.

That left the Victoria and Albert Museum and Miriam Dassin's *Vél d'Hiv* embroideries. Fortunately the train she was on went all the way to south Kensington, and then it was just a short walk down the road to the museum, a gigantic pile of brick that looked more like the Kremlin than a treasure house of art and design.

She'd only taken a few steps inside when her attention was caught by the spectacular glass sculpture, or perhaps it was a chandelier, that was suspended from the middle of the domed rotunda. She joined the end of the nearest queue, her gaze still fixed on the mass of glowing green and yellow tendrils, and shuffled forward unthinkingly as the line advanced.

"Hello! Hello there!"

She'd reached the front. "Whoops. Was too busy looking up," she admitted to the woman at the desk. Zahra, according to her name tag.

"You and everyone else," Zahra confirmed with a grin. "It's one of the biggest Chihuly sculptures in the world. Is this your first visit to the V and A?"

"It is."

"Well, a warm welcome to you, and here's a map. Are you interested in any of our special exhibitions? There's a fee for them, but otherwise entrance to the museum is free of charge."

"Thank you. I actually came to see the *Vél d'Hiv* embroideries by Miriam Dassin. Can you point me in the right direction?"

A regretful frown replaced Zahra's smile. "I'm terribly sorry, but they were taken off exhibit last week so they could be sent over to the Tate Modern for the upcoming retrospective of her work."

No. It couldn't be possible. "I did know about the retrospective, but it doesn't start until September fifth."

"You're right, but they built in a window. Just in case the curators here or at the Tate have any concerns about the condition of the embroideries."

"Oh, right. I guess that makes sense."

"Is there anything else you might like to see?" Zahra asked. "We have a bit of everything here." With that she unfolded an illustrated map of the museum on the desktop. A list of highlights was printed along one side of the map, and one immediately caught her eye. *Explore centuries of fashion at the V&A.*

"Do you have any dresses by Norman Hartnell?" Heather asked.

"We do. I'm not sure how many are being exhibited at the moment. We rotate them off and on display for conservation reasons. Would you like me to check?"

"That's okay. I'm here already, so I might as well try to see some of the museum. Thanks again."

"No worries. Here's a copy of the map."

Heather didn't know much about the history of fashion, but the V&A's selection of clothing and footwear was an excellent introduction. She lingered for a long while in front of a case containing several examples of Christian Dior's New Look designs from the late 1940s. Compared to the clothes women had worn for most of the 1940s, all spare and squared off and looking like uniforms even when they weren't, the Dior dresses were . . . she couldn't find the words to describe how they made her feel, and she hadn't lived through a long and terrifying war. They were impractical and ridiculous and must have been uncomfortable as hell with their enormous skirts and built-in corsets, but they were undeniably beautiful.

At last she moved on, still a little dazzled, and that's when she came across the Hartnell gown. It was from 1953, an evening dress made of pale turquoise silk, and trailing over its strapless bodice and narrow skirt was unusual greenery that Heather couldn't at first identify. She took a step closer, her nose almost touching the glass case, and realized it was seaweed. Long strands of green-gold seaweed, and here and there golden seashells and coral-colored flowers, or perhaps they were anemones? It was unusual and not at all pretty, not when compared to the Dior dresses, but it was eye-catching, and the embroidery, even at a distance, was incredibly fine and ornate.

She came to the end of the fashion galleries, and after that she spent a further hour wandering around the museum. Before long, though, the beauty of the ceramics and furniture and jewelry and paintings and metalwork began to blur together. Her eyes, not to mention her brain, had had enough.

As she was leaving she passed by the information desk, wanting to thank Zahra again for her help.

"Did you enjoy your visit?"

"It was amazing. Almost too much to take in, if that makes any sense."

"I know. I've worked here for two years and I've only scratched the surface. I'm sorry again about the *Vél d'Hiv* embroideries."

"That's okay. I ought to have checked first. Maybe one day I'll get to see them."

"Are you a student of her work?" Zahra asked.

"No. I don't know much about her at all. Only that she might have been friends with my grandmother. That's why I'm here. In England, I mean. I'm trying to find out more about my nan. She died in March."

"I am sorry," Zahra said, frowning in sympathy. And then, as if she had just made up her mind, "I do know someone who is involved with the retrospective. I could speak to him. Let him know why you came to see the embroideries. I can't promise anything, but he might be able to help."

"That would be fantastic," Heather said, her spirits soaring. "Can I write out a note or anything?"

"Just your name and email address, and perhaps your mobile number, too? I'll explain the rest to Dr. Friedman. He was one of my favorite lecturers when I was an undergrad. I'm sure he'll do his best to help."

When Heather emerged from the museum, the afternoon was so beautiful and sunny that she abandoned her plan to take the Tube back to the hotel. It wasn't so very far back to Soho, only about an hour's walk according to the map on her phone, and she didn't want to risk being underground if Dr. Friedman called.

It was almost five o'clock when she arrived back at her hotel, having made a lengthy and expensive stop at Fortnum & Mason. Room service beckoned, and a hot bath, too, but first she needed a nap. It had been a long, long day.

SHE DIDN'T WAKE until almost nine o'clock, and then her first reaction was panic. What if Dr. Friedman had tried to contact her when she was asleep?

She hadn't missed any calls, but there were a pile of new emails. Two from her mom, one from Tanya with the subject line *tell me you love the hotel!*, the usual sprinkling of spam, and one from Daniel Friedman.

To: Heather Mackenzie
From: Daniel Friedman
Subject: Miriam Dassin

Dear Ms. Mackenzie,

A former student passed on the message that you are interested in speaking to me—I understand that you are Ann Hughes's granddaughter. She and Miriam Dassin were indeed friends and I should be happy to meet with you to pass on whatever information I can. Perhaps you could let me know when and where might suit you?

Regards,
Daniel Friedman

To: Daniel Friedman
From: Heather Mackenzie
Subject: Re: Miriam Dassin

Dear Dr. Friedman,

Thank you so much. I'm staying at a hotel in Soho and will be in London until Sunday morning. I can meet with you anytime before then. Just let me know a time and place and I will be there. I really do appreciate your taking the time to speak with me.

Best wishes,
Heather

To: Heather Mackenzie
From: Daniel Friedman
Subject: Re: Miriam Dassin

Dear Ms. Mackenzie,

Why don't we say tomorrow at noon at the French House on Dean Street? If that's too early just let me know. I'll send you a text message now with my mobile number so you have it. Looking forward to meeting you.

Regards,
D

Chapter Sixteen

Ann

September 4, 1947

It was raining, and she was ever so tired, and her eyes felt as if they'd been papered over with sandpaper after hours spent hunched over Princess Elizabeth's wedding gown. With the day being so gloomy, and the workroom windows newly curtained with muslin in an attempt to keep out prying eyes, it had been a miracle she'd set even one decent stitch. Everything before her had been the same color, or near enough to make no difference, and the satin and pearls and crystal beads had all blended into one amorphous milk-colored blur after a while.

At least the rain had let up a bit. With any luck she'd make it to the Tube station before her coat was soaked through, otherwise—

"Miss Hughes? Hello?"

She stopped short and looked around, an islet in the stream of people hurrying by. The rain kept getting in her eyes, but that was her fault for leaving her umbrella at home again. She wiped at her face, blinked hard, and there he was. Jeremy Thickett-Milne.

"Miss Hughes—Ann. It *is* you. I wasn't sure at first. What a lovely surprise. I was terribly disappointed when you didn't call."

"I tried. Twice. But the woman who answered said that I had the wrong number."

His mouth tightened at this. "I do apologize. I expect it was my sister. Her idea of a joke, though not a very good one. In any event, I've found you again, so all is well. Are you on your way home from work?"

"Yes. I just finished."

She was careful not to say more, for it had been drummed into them all, again and again, that they had to be wary. That's why the windows had been curtained, and why there was talk of whitewashing them, too. That's why Captain Mitchison, who managed the business side of things for Mr. Hartnell, had taken to sleeping in his office, a loaded pistol—or so Ethel insisted—at his side.

"I wonder," Jeremy said, inching a little closer, "if you might be free this evening. It is rather last minute, of course, but I find I'm not quite ready to say good-bye."

"Oh. I, ah . . ." Why couldn't she think of something to say? But her mouth refused to cooperate with her brain.

"Please tell me I'm forgiven for my awful sister. Please tell me you'll give me a second chance."

Ann felt, suddenly, as if she were face-to-face with a film star. Ordinary people were never that good-looking, yet try as she might, she couldn't discern a single flaw. His hairline wasn't receding, his nose wasn't beaky, his lips weren't thin, his chin wasn't weak. He was tall and broad-shouldered and had a flat stomach and ears that didn't stick out and the bluest eyes she had ever seen. She stared on, even though it was probably making him feel uncomfortable, and found nothing to alarm her.

Nothing, apart from the knowledge that his interest made absolutely no sense. She had nothing to offer him. Nothing. She wasn't beautiful or witty, she had scarcely a penny to her name, and she didn't have so much as a seed packet's worth of charisma to sprinkle around. So why did he persist? Why wasn't he ringing up one of his sister's glamorous friends?

"Why?" she asked.

"I beg your pardon?"

"Why me? You've heard me speak. You know I'm an ordinary girl. Common, some might say."

"I wouldn't. I don't think you're common at all."

She shook her head so vehemently that one of the clips holding back her fringe slipped free and fell on the ground. "*Please.* I know who I am, and I have never, *ever,* attracted the attention of a man like you before."

He crouched to retrieve the clip, wiped it clean on the sleeve of his coat, and gently tucked it back in her hair. "What will it take for you to believe me? I like you. I think you're very pretty. I find you interesting. Most of all, you're nice. And that makes you different, in the best possible way, from most of the women I know. That's why."

"Oh," she said, her protestations dying away.

"Dinner together. That's all." And then, his voice deepening, "I really can be very good company."

"That's what worries me," she said, and smiled for the first time since he'd approached her.

"So? Shall we be off?"

"I, well . . . I'm not dressed properly." She wore a pretty new skirt, made from the wool tartan Milly had sent, but her shoes needed a shine and there was a splotch of tea on the front of her blouse that her cardigan didn't quite cover.

"The place we're going isn't grand at all. Just a café in Soho. You'll be fine."

"What part of Soho?" She'd heard the stories about the goings-on in that part of the city. About the gangsters and burlesque shows and ladies of the night on every corner.

"It's a perfectly safe part. I mean, I wouldn't go so far as to say it's respectable, but isn't that half the fun?"

His offer was tempting. Miriam was having supper out with Mr. Kaczmarek, they'd finished the last of the leftovers from Sunday dinner, and she didn't much feel like another meal of sardines on toast.

"All right. We won't be out late, will we?"

"I'll have you on your way in an hour. Promise." Before she could think of another excuse, he looped his arm through hers and led her along the street, his umbrella carefully positioned above her head.

By the time they crossed Regent Street the rain had grown heavier, and Ann could feel her stockings squishing between her toes. "We're almost there," he said apologetically. "I ought to have flagged down a cab. Not that there's ever one to be found in weather like this."

"I'm fine," she said. "I don't mind the rain at this time of year. And it does make my garden happy."

"An avid gardener. You'd get on with my mother. What sort of plants do you like to grow?"

He was very good at keeping a conversation moving along, never interrupting, never talking over her, his questions never too pointed or intrusive. Step-by-step, minute by minute, she grew ever more comfortable in his company. Of course she knew he was setting out to charm her, and it wasn't smart to simply let him bowl her over in such a fashion. Yet she couldn't find it in her to care.

He pointed out the café not long after they rounded the corner onto Old Compton Street. "Eye-catching, isn't it?" An enormous Harlequin figure was attached to the upper floors of the building, and just below his dangling feet was a sign: CAFÉ TORINO RESTAURANT.

"What on earth . . . ?"

"I know. Odd, isn't it? I think it may be Pulcinella—the Italian version of Punch. He doesn't look very happy to be out in the rain, does he?"

Inside the café it was warm and crowded and very noisy, and the air was laden with an array of tempting aromas, and though Ann couldn't quite put a name to what she smelled, her mouth watered all the same. Some tables were punctuated by towers of empty coffee cups, while others held piles of books and hastily folded newspapers. The tables' occupants were young for the most part, younger even than Ann. Students, she realized, and they were using this place as a sort of library—but what library allowed its patrons to eat and drink and smoke and, horror of horrors, engage in torrents of noisily passionate discussion?

"Let me see if I can find us a table," Jeremy said, and he led them through the maze of diners, occasionally pausing to ask someone to inch their chair out of the way. The table he found was small and only recently vacated, and still covered with a mass of dirty dishes, but rather than call over a waiter he stacked them neatly and carried them over to the bar.

"You get settled while I deal with these. I'll see if I can find a menu while I'm at it."

There didn't seem to be any sort of rack, so Ann hung her sodden coat over the back of her chair, then sat down and tried to restore some degree of dignity to her appearance. Her hair had probably frizzed into an enormous orange nimbus by now, but she could only finger-comb it and clip it back off her face and hope the end result didn't look too slapdash. At least she had a handkerchief in her bag. She patted her face dry, bent over her bag to apply a surreptitious dab of powder to her nose, and wished in vain for lipstick. As it was forbidden at work, she never thought to carry any with her.

Jeremy had returned. "No luck on the menu, but I'm here often enough that I should be able to help. I usually have the spaghetti with meat sauce, but they serve it with the appetite of a typical undergraduate in mind. They also do vol-au-vents with chicken and peas. Not especially Italian, but it's a more manageable amount of food."

She'd never eaten spaghetti before, although she had seen more than one comic short in which confused visitors to Italian restaurants struggled with improbably long strands of pasta. Best to stay with something she could consume in a dignified fashion. "I think the vol-au-vents. Please."

"Excellent. Ah—here comes the waiter. Right. I'll have the spaghetti, and my friend will have the vol-au-vents. And some bread for the table."

"Very good, sir. Would you like anything to drink?"

"Hmm. Do you have any Sangiovese? A bottle, then. And two glasses."

That accomplished, Jeremy sat back in his chair, produced a silver cigarette case from his inside breast pocket, and offered it to Ann. "No? You don't mind if I do?"

"Not at all."

He extracted a cigarette from the case, lighted it with practiced ease, and blew a gust of smoke toward the ceiling. "There. That's better. Now, tell me—do you have a long journey home? Since you said you don't live hereabouts."

"It's not so very long. I live just outside the city proper. I grew up there. Where do you live?" she countered.

"Here in town. At my parents' house, actually. They spend most of their time in the country, you see, so otherwise it would just stand empty. Well, apart from the servants. My sister is meant to be living there, too, but I hardly see her. Either she's off on holiday somewhere or she's at some friend's place. If my parents knew the half of it they'd keel over."

"Did you—"

"Here's your wine, sir."

"Very well. No—I'll pour. Ann?"

"Only a little. Thank you. What was I going to say . . . ?"

"That this wine is awful? Because really it is. That's the one problem with these places. Can't find a decent bottle of claret to save your life. Well, unless you're at one of the froggie places around the corner."

She took a sip of the wine and it seemed fine, but what did she know? "No, it wasn't that. I was going to ask what you were doing before the war."

"Oh, this and that. I mostly flitted about. Had a thought or two as to what I'd end up doing, which rather mystified my father. To him, you see, the entire point of being a gentleman is to do nothing." He drained the last of his wine and refilled his glass. "Even before the war, I could tell those days were gone. Like it or not, if I wanted to live in a decent fashion I'd have to earn my keep."

That was heartening, she supposed. "So what would you have done? If the war hadn't got in the way?"

"I did love to travel, and I was rather good at finding my way around, learning how the locals lived, that sort of thing. I'd thought of perhaps looking into something in the diplomatic sphere. I'd come down from Cambridge a few years before, and I had a friend who'd promised he'd put a word or two in the right ears. It was all about to come together when the war . . . well, it changed any number of things, didn't it?"

"It did," she agreed. "I remember you said you were in North Africa for a while?"

"Yes, and I pray I never see a grain of sand again as long as I live. Awful place. One doesn't forget, you know. The things one sees and hears. Even the smells, for the love of God."

The food arrived, saving her from thinking of something to talk about that wouldn't make him melancholy or down another glass of wine. His spaghetti smelled wonderful, if unfamiliar, and she wished, now, that she had been a little braver when ordering her meal.

"I see how you're eyeing my dinner. Would you like to try some?"

"Oh, I wouldn't know how—"

"It's easy. Give me your fork and I'll roll it on. See? Like a little cocoon. It helps if you put a spoon underneath. No—just open your mouth. Otherwise it'll go everywhere. There. Isn't that good?"

It was a little mortifying to be fed like a child, and in public as well, but the spaghetti was good. Far better, she soon realized, than her vol-au-vents, which were soggy and strangely bland. Perhaps it was just that they suffered in comparison to the richly seasoned pasta.

"I know you can't talk about your work," she said, picking up the threads of their conversation. "It being very secret, and all that. But do you find it interesting? Can you talk about it in a general sense?"

"It *is* interesting. Absolutely. I don't know if I'll want to stay on there forever, but it keeps me occupied now. I've been able to make a few useful connections, too. You are sure that you don't mind my being so tight-lipped about it?"

"Not at all. Loads of people can't talk about their work. And sometimes it's nice, you know, to talk about other things." *Not my work,* she prayed silently.

"I agree. What shall we talk about? I know—what's the best film you saw this year? Don't think about it too long. Just say whatever comes into your head."

That was easy. *"The Ghost and Mrs. Muir."*

He grimaced comically at her confession. "Why does every woman I know love that film? I thought it was a heap of romantic piffle. Dreadful stuff."

"Well, I liked it," she said, laughing in spite of his disdain for a very fine film. "What's your favorite?"

"The Secret Life of Walter Mitty," he said promptly.

"Really? I was thinking you'd say something very serious. Or depressing."

"Have you seen it?"

"Not yet. Some of my friends have. They say it's awfully funny."

"It is. Although I do feel sorry for Mitty. Imagine having a life so dull that one resorts to fantasy as a way of remaining sane? They ought to have advertised it as a tragedy."

"Yes, but no one wants to see Danny Kaye in a sob story."

"You're right about that," he admitted, and ate the last of his spaghetti. "Are you all done with your vol-au-vents? We could see about some pudding if you like. Or perhaps some coffee?"

"No, thank you. I had better be on my way."

"I don't like the idea of your walking on your own."

"There's a cab rank on Shaftesbury Avenue. Would you mind walking me there?"

"Not one whit, but only if you first promise to have dinner with me next week." He reached across the table and set his hand atop hers, and if he noticed how short her nails were, or how rough her skin felt, he was kind enough not to comment on it. "Please?"

"I would like that," she answered, her heart racing, and it was true.

He pulled out a little gilt-edged pocket diary, its cover embossed with the monogram *JMT*, and leafed through its pages. "I'm away for a bit, but I'll be back by the twenty-first. Perhaps the twenty-fourth? It's a Wednesday. And will you let me take you somewhere smart? I don't mean a dinner-jacket-and-gown sort of smart. Just a proper restaurant with menus and bottles of claret that don't taste like bilge water. Quaglino's would be perfect. I'd take you to my club, but the ladies' dining room isn't terribly nice. And of course the food at Quag's is second to none. I could collect you—"

Quaglino's. Even she had heard of the place. "No. It would be easier for me to meet you. What time should I be there?"

"Say eight o'clock? Or is that too late?"

"No, that's fine."

He paid their bill, ignoring her when she asked if she might contribute, and walked her down to the line of waiting cabs. Turning to face him, she held out her hand so he'd have to shake it. She wasn't ready for anything more, not yet, and certainly not in public.

"I had a lovely time," he said. "You still have my card? Just in case anything comes up? If you get my sister again, please don't mind. Just ring again a bit later, and with any luck I'll be there to answer."

"I will. Thank you for supper."

She got into the car, and waited until Jeremy had shut the door and stepped away before she confessed the truth of her destination to the driver. "I only need to go to the Tube station at Tottenham Court Road. I'm sorry it's not farther."

"No trouble at all, luv."

She was home by half-past eight. Miriam walked through the door a half hour later, and rather than go up to bed they sat in the kitchen with cups of tea and discussed their respective evenings out.

"We went to a public house near Walter's office. He had to go back to work, so it was easiest to meet nearby. We had something called a Lancashire hotpot." Miriam wrinkled her nose at the memory. "I think that was the name. It tasted of nothing. I hope your supper was better."

"Yes. We went to an Italian café, and the food was good, and he was lovely. Only . . . I'm not sure what to think. Why me? I asked him, and he said all sorts of nice things, and I mostly believed him."

"You said he was a soldier in the war?"

"An officer, yes."

"Could it have changed him?" Miriam asked. "Could he have decided to change?"

"Perhaps. He did get rather upset when our conversation turned to the war. And then we started talking about films and Danny Kaye. And I did get to taste spaghetti for the first time."

They smiled at one another, and Ann sipped at her tea, and Miriam frowned over a hangnail on her thumb, then a loose thread on her sleeve, then a spot of tarnish on her teaspoon. Miriam, who never fidgeted.

"What's wrong?" Ann asked.

"Nothing. Only . . . I have an idea for something, and I am not sure how to go about it."

"Another dish of your grandmother's? That chicken you made was wonderful. I wouldn't mind if—"

"No. Nothing like that," Miriam said, her gaze focused on the empty table between them. "I want to paint a picture, only I don't know how to paint, or draw, or even properly describe what I see. But when I close my eyes it is there . . ."

"I never learned how to draw properly, but I still like to scribble in my sketchbook when I've a few minutes to spare. You can have some of the paper from it, and I've got a set of colored pencils. We could sit here and draw and listen to the Light Programme."

"Are you certain? I do not wish to waste your paper."

"It's not a waste if it's something you enjoy."

Her worries over Jeremy melting away, Ann fetched her sketchbook and pencils and the two women settled down to their pastime. Soon she was so absorbed by the gown she was imagining, a variation on Doris's wedding dress, only with short sleeves and garlands of pastel embroidery at the hem and neckline, that she was surprised to hear the familiar introduction to the news.

"I can't believe it—ten o'clock already. We ought to—"

Miriam had set down her pencil; she, too, had been working steadily for the past hour. But she hadn't drawn a gown, nor a design for embroidery, nor anything Ann might have expected.

A group of people stood around a table, their faces indistinct, though the details of the room about them were rendered with some care. A man at the head of the table held a cup, his hands raised high. The men were all wearing hats, which was strange as they were indoors.

No—not hats. Caps. Small, round caps on the crowns of their heads. She stared at the picture Miriam had created, and somewhere in the background she could still hear the news on the wireless, and then she knew. How had she not known, before?

"Is this your family?"

"I think so. I wasn't sure when I started, but . . . yes. It is them."

"They're Jewish. You're Jewish."

"Yes."

Ann tore her gaze from the picture, and she saw how Miriam was frozen in place. How the color had leached away from her friend's pretty face.

"I didn't mean to have it come out like that. I was just surprised. Really, that's all."

"I know."

"Why didn't you tell me?" Ann asked, gentling her voice.

"I couldn't. Not to begin with. I couldn't be sure."

"That I wouldn't hold it against you?"

A nod.

"But you must know by now that I would never—I mean, I honestly don't. Oh, I don't know what to say."

"That's all right," Miriam said, and perhaps it was wishful thinking on Ann's part but it did seem, just maybe, that she'd stopped holding herself quite so stiffly.

"It's only just— Oh, *no*. How many times have I fed you bacon since you moved here? Why on earth didn't you say anything? I feel *awful*."

Miriam smiled, only a little, but it was enough to dispel some of the gloom that had crept into the kitchen. "I did not mind. My parents were not religious people. We broke all the rules when I was young."

Ann looked at the picture again. "Who is the man holding the cup?"

"My grandfather. When I was little, before Grand-Mère died, we went to their house every Friday. For *le dîner de chabbat*. The Sabbath, I think you say? He is saying the blessing. *Le kiddouch*. The cup holds wine that we would share, and after that we would wash our hands and Grand-Père would break the bread, and we would each take a piece and dip it in salt. And then our Sabbath dinner would begin."

"Your grandmother's Friday-night chicken?" Ann asked.

"Yes. She made it every week."

"But didn't you make it for me on a Saturday? I don't know much about Jewish people, but I thought you aren't allowed to do things on Saturday. Like use the cooker and so on."

"I know. Grand-Mère would have been so upset with me for breaking the Sabbath. I—"

"The stories in the papers, and those dreadful newsreels? That's what happened to your family."

"Yes." Miriam's gaze was directed at the picture, but Ann felt sure she was seeing something else.

"How did you survive if they did not?"

"I hid. I . . ." Miriam shook her head, slowly, definitively, and a single tear began a lonely trail down her face.

It took every particle of strength Ann possessed to stifle the instinct to leap up and embrace her friend. "I'm sorry. I won't ask again. Only . . . if you ever feel like telling me I should love to hear about them. Your mum and dad and your nan. Your grandmother, I mean. She must have been a very good cook."

"She was. She and my mother both."

After wiping her eyes, Ann folded her handkerchief back on itself and passed it to Miriam. And then she turned her attention back to the picture of the Sabbath dinner. "What'll you do with this?" she asked after a moment. "Will you turn it into a painting? I know you said you don't know how to draw, but it's very good. It's so good I don't want to look away."

"Thank you. I was thinking I might try to make an embroidery of it. Not at all like the sort of thing we do at work. I mean as they once did long ago. For the walls of the great castles and places like that."

Of course. What better way for Miriam to express herself than through thread and fabric? "I think those were woven, but I know what you mean. Have you ever seen pictures of the Bayeux Tapestry? You could make something like that. Stitches and appliqué work on a backing. I've got yards and yards of plain linen from Milly's parcels, and it's too good to waste on dish towels."

"Thank you. That is very generous." Miriam's attention turned to Ann's own work, and the sketchbook she'd been silly enough to leave open on the table. "May I see?"

"It's nothing to look at. Just some idle thoughts."

"Do you wish to become a dressmaker like Monsieur Hartnell?"

"Heavens, no. That's just me playing about. More a case, I suppose, of what I'd ever want for myself if I won the pools and could spend money like water."

"Like water? Oh—I see. As if you have turned on a faucet."

"But it's not likely ever to happen," Ann went on, "and I'd probably last about a day in those fancy clothes without wanting my ordinary things back again. This is make-believe on my part. Nothing more."

"What would your dreams look like? If they did come true?"

"I'm not sure. Maybe a house of my own? Something the council couldn't take away from me? And a big garden with room for as many flowers as I like." It was a reasonable sort of dream, and one she actually had a prayer of fulfilling. Asking for anything more would be foolhardy.

"A family?" Miriam prompted.

"I suppose. If the right man ever comes along. In the meantime, though, I've got my work, and lovely friends like you, and a comfortable bed to sleep in at night."

"What about romance? Love?"

"That's for beautiful princesses in palaces. Not for me. Those stories are never about women like me."

Chapter Seventeen

Miriam

September 15, 1947

$\mathcal{N}$o one at Hartnell would dare say so, but Miriam was beginning to worry they wouldn't finish in time.

There. She'd admitted it.

Last week Miss Duley had announced that Princess Elizabeth would be in London for a few days at the very end of September. "Mr. Hartnell and Mam'selle are expecting to be summoned for a fitting of the wedding gown while the princess is in London. Working backward from Monday the twenty-ninth, when she returns from Balmoral, we shall need to have all the principal embroidery finished on the gown by Monday the twenty-second."

That had left them with ten working days—and now, a week on, only five days remained, and the atmosphere in the workroom was one of grimly focused determination. They all knew there was no question of not finishing in time—but what if they didn't? What would happen then? It wasn't as if they could ring up Buckingham

Palace and ask Princess Elizabeth to rearrange her calendar because the women in the embroidery workroom at Hartnell had been slow at their work.

She'd assumed, when they'd begun work on the gown, that nothing much would change. They made clothes for famous women all the time; had been making clothes for the queen for years and years. Monsieur Hartnell had been written about in magazines and newspapers, and clips of his fashion shows were often included in newsreels. But then Ruthie had come running into the cloakroom one morning, only days after they'd begun, and she'd been waving one of the morning newspapers.

"Look—just look at this. Someone's added up the number of people who'll be listening to the wedding on the wireless, plus everyone who'll see the pictures in the papers and magazines, and it's not just millions but *hundreds* of *millions* of people. Can you believe it?"

Miriam absolutely did.

For weeks now photographers had taken to lurking outside the rear doors on Bruton Place, and she and the other girls had grown accustomed to being followed as they came and went. Usually the men just shouted questions at them, but more than once—it was always when she was walking alone—she'd been offered a bribe in return for details of the gown.

"A fiver for a picture, a tenner for a look inside," the man might say, or "Throw me a bone, luv, I'll make it worth your while." She never so much as glanced at them. The only journalist in the world to whom she'd willingly talk, now, was Walter Kaczmarek—and only because he had promised never to ask her about the gown or her work at Hartnell.

It wasn't only the junior staff who were feeling the pressure, for Miss Duley was forever confiding in Ann and Miriam about one crisis or another brewing upstairs. First there was the issue of the pearls for the dress and the difficulties in fetching them from America, including their nearly being seized by customs officers when Captain Mitchison presented ten thousand pearls for inspection. "He told them they were for the princess, and those wretches *still* gave him a hard time," Miss Duley had fumed.

Then there were the awkward questions coming from the prime minister, who in Miss Duley's opinion really ought to have better things to do, about the nationality of the silkworms whose cocoons had been transformed into the fabric they were embroidering. There was concern in certain quarters that enemy silkworms from Japan might have been used. Fortunately, Monsieur Hartnell was able to confirm the silkworms were of nationalist Chinese origin, and Mr. Atlee, so reassured, turned his attention elsewhere.

Perhaps he'd been distracted by the public's anxiety over how the princess would find enough clothing coupons for her gown, and the resulting deluge of donations that women across Britain were posting to Buckingham Palace. Of course it was illegal to use someone else's coupons, so all of them had been sent back with a thank-you note from some royal secretary. Sheer stupidity, Miriam had thought, but she'd wisely said nothing to anyone at Hartnell. They all seemed charmed by the idiocy of people giving up precious coupons to send to a *princess* who lived in a *palace*. What was next—people sending their butter and sugar rations so the bride and groom might have a larger wedding cake?

She and Ann had finished the bodice last week, and the sleeves, too, and now they had only the skirt to complete. Each panel, properly stretched, was large enough to allow room for six embroiderers, three to a side, and that was where she sat, with Ann across from her and Ethel at her left.

That morning they'd all had a good laugh in the cloakroom when someone had brought in a newspaper article that claimed Monsieur Hartnell was working them around the clock. Their days were busy, and they never lingered over their breaks or dinners as they might do in quieter periods, but the latest she had worked was half-past six, and that was only to get the bodice pieces finished so the sewing workroom might have them the following morning. There simply was no point in expecting them to work all hours, for too-long days wreaked havoc on everyone's eyes and nerves and did nothing more, Miss Duley insisted, than ensure the following day's work would suffer.

Even once the skirt panels were finished, they wouldn't be able to rest, for they had to begin work on the train—all five meters of the thing. And she knew, from her experience with the sample motifs last month, that there was no rushing the work. The satin for the appliqué pieces was slippery, frayed all too readily, and couldn't be basted or pinned for fear of leaving marks. Then, once applied, each appliqué had to be decorated with an eye-watering variety of embellishments. And they had to set each stitch with the knowledge that the reverse of their work might be clearly seen by anyone, for the train was transparent, and any sort of additional backing to the reverse of the appliquéd pieces would strain the delicate tulle.

It would have to be stretched on an enormous frame, with everyone working from the center to begin, and Miriam was already dreading it. She hated working with others at her elbows, for there was always someone who bounced her knee or dragged at the frame as if she were reclaiming her share of blankets from a sleeping bedmate. Worst of all, it was impossible to empty her brain of everything but the embroidery taking shape before her when a buzz of someone else's chatter took up residence in her mind.

She much preferred to share a frame with Ann alone. Her friend was a comforting and steadying presence, and while they did talk on occasion, most of their days were spent in a companionable silence. They had time after work, after all, to sit at the kitchen table and chat about their day and draw in their sketchbooks.

Once a week at most, she stayed in London after work and had supper with Walter; but he was a busy man, and could rarely spare much time during the week, and she was anxious, too, to have some time to herself so she might think about the embroideries that had decided to colonize her thoughts.

Five large hangings, as big as she could manage, for there were five images in her mind, and waking or sleeping they never left her. She wasn't yet certain how she would begin—would she create smaller panels and join them together? Would she make single figures and appliqué them onto a larger backing, then further embellish the whole?

It would come to her eventually. For now, she was content to experiment, using the linen Ann had so kindly given her, scraps from the workroom, and her own tentative flights of imagination. It was hard, at times, to ignore the disquieting voices that told her she was fooling herself, that she would empty herself into this misguided project, and when she finished, it would be to find that no one was interested. That no one on earth, apart from her, cared to know what had happened to those she loved.

The doubt pushed at her, woke her in the middle of the night, curdled the food in her stomach. But she was stubborn, and it became easier, after a while, to ignore all else and continue on. Worrying about what would become of her work once it was finished was a waste of time, she told herself. The act of creation was what mattered.

If she were to set aside her ideas now, if she were to turn her back on them, she would be abandoning her parents and grandfather and the millions who had been vilified, betrayed, tortured, murdered, erased. It was unthinkable. It was impossible.

Some mornings she woke, and she had been dreaming of the panel all night, had been watching herself work at it, a mere bystander to the act of creation. It was a relief, come morning, to set it aside for a matter of hours, have her quiet breakfast with Ann, walk to the station, and go to work. And then, once there, to lose herself in the familiar motifs of the princess's wedding gown. Yet by the end of the day, every day, she longed to continue where she had left off the night before.

"Can I not help you with the chores?" she asked Ann one evening. Her friend was doing the mending, having insisted she was happy to do so.

"No need. The house is clean, the kitchen is tidy, the garden is weeded, and I've almost finished turning this cuff. Why shouldn't you work on your embroidery? Isn't that the mark of an artist, anyway? Someone who has an idea and can't rest until they find a way to express it?"

"I am no artist—"

"Because you aren't carving marble sculptures or painting oil portraits of politicians? Here—I want to show you something."

Ann set aside her mending, took down a teacup and matching saucer from the highest shelf on the dresser, and placed them on the table. They were painted with scenes of the countryside, with shaggy cows in the foreground and a misty look to the landscape, and the edges of both the cup and saucer were gilded.

"These belonged to my grandmother. I loved them because of the Highland cows. She would take them off the shelf and hold them so I could get a better look, and when Nan died and left the cup and saucer to me I started to wonder. I mean, I never had a thought of selling them, but I did worry they might be too valuable to keep out.

"So I took them down to the antiques shop on Ripple Road, and the fellow there looked at the pieces and said they were Royal Worcester, and they were worth something but not a king's ransom, which was a relief, since I'd have hated to tuck them away. He told me they were painted by a man called Harry Stinton. He said Harry Stinton was one of the best artists of the last hundred years. And you can't tell me the paintings on this cup and saucer aren't art, because they are."

"And you tell me this because . . . ?"

"Because I think this, what you are doing here—*this* is art."

"If that is true, then are we not all of us artists? Everyone who works for Miss Duley?"

"I don't know about that. What we do takes a lot of skill, and a lot of practice, but nearly anyone can figure it out with some training. This, though"—and here Ann touched a finger to the square of embroidery on Miriam's lap—"*this* is different. This is the sort of thing people will line up to see, and when they do it will change the way they see the world, and when they go away they won't forget it."

"I wish you would not say such things."

"Fine. Forget I said them. What does Walter think?"

"I . . . I want to tell him. But I am afraid."

"Why?"

"I have not yet told him of what happened," Miriam confessed. "Before. In France. I want to tell him, but there is so much to say. I do not know where to begin."

"You mean what happened to your family?"

"That. And after, as well."

"What do you mean? I thought you hid from the Nazis."

"I did. But it ate at me. My parents and grandfather had been taken, and I had done nothing. I wanted to act, to resist, but I was paralyzed. For so long I did nothing . . ."

"You were in mourning," Ann whispered, her voice fractured by anguish.

"I wasn't sure what to do. How to begin. But there was a woman at work, Marie-Laure, and I heard that she was involved with the resistance. One day we were alone in the atelier, and I went to sit next to her, and I whispered that my loved ones had been taken, and I wanted to do something. She said nothing. She did not even look at me."

"And?"

"And the next day, as I was washing my hands, she came over as I finished, and told me where I might meet her. I went, and she was sitting with a man. Five minutes after I had left I remembered nothing of how he looked. He had that sort of face. He asked me why I wanted to help, and I told him it was not his concern. That it would be silly of me to trust a stranger. He nodded to her, and said Marie-Laure would tell me what to do."

"And?" Ann asked again, spellbound by the tale.

"I carried messages. I would find them in my coat, in a secret pocket in the lining, and I would hide them in my room until Marie-Laure told me the address where I was to go. A café or a shop, or a certain bench in a park. From the beginning it was always the same man who met me. I never knew his real name. If we were questioned, I was to say he was my fiancé. Robert Thibault. We would meet and I would say hello and we would talk of the weather, or what I had eaten that day. Normal things. And then he would look at his watch and say he had to go. I only had to pass the letter to him, usually under the table, or I would slip it in his pocket. And then he would kiss me good-bye. It wasn't very often. Every few weeks, no more."

"You were caught, weren't you?"

"Yes. We were betrayed. Someone else must have been captured, and likely tortured. We were arrested together. They searched my room, and even though they found nothing they did not release me. They were convinced of our guilt. The next day I was sent to the prison at Fresnes, and a few weeks later, when there were enough of us to fill a truck, I was sent to Ravensbrück."

"When was this?" Ann's face had gone pale, and she had wound her fingers together in her lap. She always did that when she was upset.

Miriam smiled ruefully. "The middle of June in 1944."

"After D-Day."

"They knew what was coming. The man who questioned me certainly did. I can still see him if I close my eyes. His spectacles were so dirty, and he kept cleaning them on the cuff of his shirt, but it only made them worse. He had such dark circles under his eyes, as if he had not slept for days and days."

"I doubt he had."

"I said nothing, I admitted nothing, but still he condemned me. He insisted that one way or another I was guilty of something, most likely of being a whore. It was not quite enough to be shot, but it was more than enough for Ravensbrück."

"He didn't know you were Jewish," Ann guessed.

"No. In that, I suppose I was lucky."

"What was it like there? I've read stories, but . . ."

How to describe the indescribable? "I was young, and strong, and once they discovered I could sew I was sent to a sweatshop where we made uniforms for Nazi officers. We had an easier time of it than those in the munitions factories, or those who were made to do hard labor outside. Or those who were forced to work in the brothels. That was the worst of all. Those women never lasted more than a few weeks."

She stopped, waited until she could breathe again, until her pulse wasn't hammering quite so loudly against her ears. "They had already begun gassing women when I got there. If you were old, or sick, or if you resisted them at all, they gassed you. At the end, the guards were panicking. They rounded us up, like farm animals being sent to market, and they shot anyone who couldn't walk, and they made us march. Away from the Americans, away from the Soviets, away from anyone who might help us. My friends died around me as we marched, and in another few days I would have been dead, too."

"*Miriam.*"

"We were liberated by some Americans. A few months later I was back in Paris, in a convalescent hospital, and once I was better, or at least well enough to get out of bed, I returned to Maison Rébé, and they gave me my job back." She looked up and saw that her friend was crying. "Do not be sad. I am safe now. I am fine." She very nearly believed it, too.

Ann nodded, wiping her eyes with a handkerchief she'd pulled from her sleeve. "It is an honor to call you my friend. Really, it is, and I'm sure Walter will feel the same way."

"I know. I will tell him."

And yet. Would it change things with him? Would he be disgusted by the months she had spent hiding away, terrified, mute, inert, after her family was taken? Or would he pity her? Nothing could be worse than his pity.

She glanced at her wristwatch; ten o'clock already, and far too late to ruin another night's sleep with worries over her past and future. "It is late. Time for us to be in our beds."

"You're right." Ann took the tea things to the sink and began to rinse them out.

"What of your Jeremy?" Miriam asked, suddenly aware that she hadn't asked her friend a single question all evening. "Shall you see him again soon?"

"Next week. He's quite good company, and he always has interesting stories to tell. Places he's traveled or things that happened during the war. And he has beautiful manners, too. Never lets me pay for a thing."

"Does he know where you work?"

"No. At least I don't think he does. I haven't said anything about it, and he hasn't asked. I suppose he thinks I work in a shop or office. Not that it matters."

"Why not?"

"This isn't going anywhere. I mean, he's handsome and interesting and I've had several nice evenings with him, but it's never going to lead to anything *more*. I'd be an idiot to think otherwise. And it is fun, you know. It gives me a little peek into how the other half lives."

"'The other half'? Ah—one of your idioms. It does make sense, does it not? Although I doubt as many as half the people in this country live as well as he does. Do you remember the people at his table that night? There was no mistaking them for anything but aristocrats. They had that soft look about them."

"They did at that. Right—it's well past ten now, and we'll both be in a state tomorrow if we don't get to sleep soon."

"Are you worried? About finishing on time?" Miriam asked.

"Didn't you tell me, not even a month ago, that it was no different from any other gown? That we just had to work as we always do and we'd be fine?"

"Yes, but I had not realized how many people would care. Everyone is so anxious at work. I can tell they are."

"We've survived rushes like this before. Not even a year ago the royal family was off to South Africa for weeks and weeks, and we had to turn out dozens of gowns and outfits for the queen and princesses. They needed so much that some of the work was given over to other designers. All told, we only had a month or so to get everything done, and we managed it then with time to spare."

"How did you feel when you finished?"

"Exhausted. I could have slept for days. But I also felt so proud I thought I might burst. We'll feel like that again when we see the princess in her wedding gown. I promise we will."

Chapter Eighteen

Heather

August 31, 2016

*T*he rain made everything look so pretty. The sun was winking out from behind the clouds, conjuring rainbows from puddles and burnishing the pavement until it gleamed. If there'd been time she'd have stopped to take a picture, but she was running late already. Her little umbrella had vanished, or maybe she hadn't remembered to pack it after all, and if she paused even for a second she'd end up soaked through.

Fortunately, the French House was just around the corner from her hotel. It was impossible to miss, with a marine-blue exterior, jauntily striped awnings, and a tricolor flag above the entrance. She paused just inside, patting her face dry with a crumpled tissue and tucking her hair, now frizzing madly, behind her ears. So much for making a polished first impression.

The interior was cramped and dark, with little in the way of Gallic flair to enliven its decor. A few men stood at the bar, their conversation subdued, and most of the tables ringing the room were empty.

She glanced at their occupants: a man and a woman, their hands clasped, their conversation earnest, and just beyond them was a man on his own, not much older than her, his attention fixed on a book. *A Country Road, A Tree.* It had been ages since she'd seen someone reading a book in a bar or restaurant; most people pulled out their phones to pass the time.

"Miss Mackenzie? Heather?" The man with the book was coming toward her. "I'm Daniel Friedman."

"Oh. I'm sorry. I saw you, but I thought—I mean, I was imagining someone, um—"

"Older? Tweedier?" he asked with a disarmingly boyish grin. He was dressed casually, in worn-out jeans and an oxford-cloth button-down shirt, its sleeves rolled back untidily. A braided leather bracelet, the sort of thing you might buy on holiday, circled his left wrist, and half-hidden beneath it were a few lines of script. Whether they were a reminder scribbled in ink, or an actual tattoo, she couldn't be sure.

"You're not the slightest bit tweedy," she said honestly, and shook his outstretched hand. "It's a pleasure to meet you, Dr. Friedman."

"Daniel. Please. Why don't you give me your coat and I'll hang it next to mine?"

He took care of her coat and then came around to pull out her chair. No one, apart from her father, had ever done that for her. Maybe it was an English thing.

"I'm sorry I was late," she said, still a little unnerved by how far he differed from the middle-aged, rumpled, and somewhat nerdy stereotype she'd concocted in the hours since they'd exchanged emails.

"Now I *know* you're Canadian. I only just arrived myself, and it's raining like stink. That buys you at least a quarter hour's grace. Why don't I fetch us something from the bar, and I'll bring back a menu while I'm at it. What would you like to drink?"

"A cider, please. Any kind is fine."

He returned with a half-pint of dark beer for himself and a glass of Breton cider for Heather. "They don't serve drinks in pint measures here. Can't remember why, but it's probably for the best. Otherwise I'd be sure to fall asleep at my desk this afternoon."

Heather took a sip of her cider, which was deliciously tart, and tried to focus on the menu. Soup, salads, sandwiches . . . she couldn't decide. Not when she was sitting across the table from a man who might be able to lead her closer to Nan.

"So? What do you think?" he asked. "I'm having the charcuterie board."

"I'll have the carrot and parsnip soup. And a garden salad."

At a nod from Daniel, their waitress approached and they relayed their orders. As soon as she'd walked away, he turned his attention to Heather once more, and she waited, hoping, wondering—

"So. Ann Hughes was your grandmother."

"She was. In your email, you said that she and Miriam Dassin were friends."

"They were. According to Mimi, they were very close."

Now she really was feeling confused. "Who is Mimi?"

"I'm sorry. That's the name I call her."

"You *know* Miriam Dassin? I thought . . . I mean, I assumed you were some kind of art history professor. That you had studied her work or something."

"I do know her." He took a sip of his beer, his gaze never leaving her face. His eyes were beautiful, with glacier-blue irises that faded to silver at their perimeter. In all her life she'd never seen anyone with such unusual eyes. "She's my grandmother."

His *grandmother.* "I don't . . . I mean, I sent an email to her gallery a while ago, but they told me she was retired and they couldn't pass anything on. And she didn't seem to have a website or email address or anything like that."

"I know. I've tried to persuade her. But she's always been a rather shy, rather private person. Even with me. Even though my work, as an academic, has focused on the experiences of French Jews during and after the war."

"You never talked with her about it?"

"I have, many times. But as her grandson. Never with the idea that I'd be recording her words for posterity."

Heather's laugh rang hollow, even to her own ears. "That's more than Nan ever did with me or my mom. She never told us anything. Until I read your email last night, I'd pretty much given up hope that I'd ever learn more."

"I think—I hope—I may be able to help. There's a retrospective of my grandmother's work coming up at the Tate, and the curators asked me to write an introduction to the official catalog. She agreed to answer my questions, and we spent a day or two looking through old photos and some scrapbooks she'd kept. At one point I asked her about the genesis of the *Vél d'Hiv* embroideries, and she said she began to work on them when she was living with your grandmother. It was Ann who first encouraged Miriam to think of herself as an artist."

The idea that Nan had been friends with an acclaimed artist like Miriam Dassin, had helped her, and then had never told anyone of that friendship . . . it was almost too much to believe.

"I don't know what to say," Heather admitted. "It's a lot to take in." Her voice, embarrassingly, had gone all shaky. If she didn't pull herself together he'd be sure to notice.

"I had known, from earlier conversations with Mimi, that she'd lived with another Hartnell embroiderer when she first came to England, but the friend had emigrated to Canada and they lost touch with one another. Does that square with what you know?"

"I guess. All I know, really, is that Nan came to Canada after the war. At first she lived with Milly, her sister-in-law, but later on, I think after Milly died, she bought a little shop, and eventually a house, too."

"Your mother was born in Canada?"

"Yes, in the summer of 1948. She wasn't able to add much to what I've told you, although she did give me some photos." Heather pulled her bag onto her lap and dug out a small folder. "These aren't the best quality. Just printouts from scans that my mom sent me. This picture is Nan on her own, and this next one is her with Milly. And this one—"

"Is Mimi and Ann together."

"I also have this picture of her and Nan with some other women. Do you think they might have been at work? My mom thinks they're sitting around embroidery frames."

He nodded decisively. "They are. That woman in the corner, with the dark dress and white collar, is Miss Duley. She was the head of embroidery at Hartnell." Daniel turned over the photo. "This handwriting on the inscription—is it Ann's?"

"My mom thinks it is. I just wish I could figure out what it means. The London and date bits are easy enough. But *Waiting for HM*? Who was HM?"

"'Her Majesty.' The queen. Today we're more likely to think of her as the Queen Mum. But this was 1947, before Princess Elizabeth became queen in her own right."

Of course. "Well, duh. Now I feel stupid."

"Don't," he said, leavening the command with a smile. "It helps that I recognize the photograph. My grandmother has a copy, and she showed it to me not so long ago. They were, as the inscription says, waiting for the queen to arrive. Apparently, such visits were rare, so everyone was on pins and needles. I suppose that's why they all look so grim."

Their food arrived just then, so she put the photographs away. If there was time after lunch she'd show him the pictures of the embroidered flowers. Perhaps he might know why they'd been created, and by whom. If Miriam had embroidered the flowers, for that matter, it would only be right to return them to her. Never mind that they would probably be worth a fortune.

"When did you arrive in England?" Daniel asked.

Of course she had just taken a huge mouthful of salad. She chewed and chewed, finally managed to swallow, and then ran her tongue over her teeth to make sure they weren't painted with bits of baby spinach. "On Monday morning. I didn't do much—just walked around Soho and did my best to shake off my jet lag. Then, yesterday, I went out to Barking, where Nan used to live. I had this silly idea that someone there might remember her, but all the houses on her part of the street were torn down years and years ago."

"I'm sorry to hear of it."

"After that I went to the V and A. I wanted to see the *Vél d'Hiv* embroideries, but . . ."

"But they're en route to the Tate for Mimi's retrospective."

"Yes. It was my fault, really. I should have checked the museum's website before I went. I did get to meet Zahra, though, and without her help I wouldn't be sitting here with you now."

"There is that. So what now?"

She ate another bite of salad as she considered her response. "I'm not sure. I thought of trying to visit the Hartnell workrooms, but what's the point, really? They closed years and years ago. The building probably looks totally different inside."

"It's actually been preserved quite well. Would you like to go? The current tenants are happy to let people visit as long as they have a bit of warning."

"Really? That would be amazing." Heather was tempted to reach beneath the table and pinch her leg, hard, just to make sure she wasn't having an incredibly detailed dream.

"We can go today if you like. I'll ring them up as soon as we finish lunch."

He made it sound like it was nothing. As if he honestly didn't mind spending almost the entire day listening to a near stranger and showing her around London. If he had come to her in search of answers, would she have been so accommodating?

"Why are you going to so much trouble? And don't say you didn't have anything better to do. One of my best friends is a university professor, and she's always researching or writing or marking essays. Sunita hardly ever takes a day off."

His answering smile was understanding. "I know I said that Mimi can be reticent, and she is. All the same, she's told me most of her story, and to my knowledge she hasn't kept any great secrets in regard to her past. But you have so little of your nan. Only a few fragments, really, compared to what Mimi has shared with me. Why wouldn't I want to help you?"

With that, he rose from the table and went over to the bar. To pay for their lunch, she realized belatedly.

"Don't even think about it," he said when he returned. "I asked you to lunch. If you like, you can stand me a coffee when we're finished at Hartnell." He lifted their raincoats from the hook behind their table, folded them over his arm, and together they ventured out into the afternoon sun.

"If you don't mind standing here a minute I'll ring up the boutique. Just to make sure someone is in."

Heather waited as he talked to someone called Belinda, and she tried, not very successfully, to avoid staring at him. She'd met men who were arguably better-looking than Daniel, but they were never as interesting or nice or funny. And his *eyes*. It was hard to think straight when he was looking at her with those silver-blue eyes.

"There. That's sorted," he finally said. "The boutique manager is in and we can wander around upstairs as much as we like. You don't mind walking there, do you? It's not very far."

"I don't mind at all."

The streets were narrow, with equally modest sidewalks, and again and again Heather found herself brushing against Daniel's side as she tried to avoid other pedestrians. He didn't seem to object, and at one point, when she was about to step off the curb into oncoming traffic, he swiftly reached across her back and took hold of her in a sort of sideways hug.

"Not just yet," he cautioned. "What would I tell Mimi if I let you get run down?"

Once the way was clear he let his arm fall away, but the echo of his touch lingered, and she couldn't be sure if she welcomed or deplored the current of sensation that continued to hum so distractingly just under her skin.

He kept the conversation going as they walked, at first by recounting some of the history of Soho and its surrounding neighborhoods, and then by asking her about her flight and the hotel on Frith Street. And then, though she'd have happily kept walking for another hour, they were turning onto the ungainly assortment of old and new buildings that was Bruton Street. When they were about halfway along the block, Daniel stopped and motioned for her to look up. Just opposite, at number 26, was the main entrance for Hartnell. It was a grand sort of art deco affair, faced with dark green stone that looked a bit like marble, and both above the entrance and high on the white-painted façade the designer's surname was displayed in large capital letters.

"Where do we go in?" Heather asked, seeing how the main floor of the building was taken up by an antiques dealer. Hadn't Daniel said something about a boutique?

"One door along. Their offices stretch between the two buildings."

A tall, thin, and alarmingly chic young woman was waiting by the door of the boutique as they entered. The fair Belinda, Heather supposed, and wasn't at all surprised when Daniel was greeted as if he'd been dipped in chocolate.

"Thanks for letting me prevail upon you again, Belinda. This is my friend Heather Mackenzie. Turns out her grandmother also worked at Hartnell."

"How super. Well, you've come on a good day. Nearly everyone upstairs is on holiday, so you've got the place to yourselves. You know the way, right?"

"That I do. Thanks again."

With Heather trailing behind, Daniel set off up the stairs, along a long hallway, and into a sunny room with tall windows and improbably high ceilings. The walls and much of the trim were painted in a pretty sort of grayish green, there were mirrors hanging everywhere, and several enormous crystal chandeliers further illuminated the space.

"This was one of the salesrooms," Daniel explained. "Rather a miracle that it survived, when you think of it. So many of these buildings were stripped bare in the seventies and eighties."

"It stayed this way the whole time Mr. Hartnell was a designer?"

"It must have done. Mimi remembers that everything seemed to glitter. It reminded her of Versailles, she says."

"And what about the workrooms? I can't imagine they had chandeliers hanging from their ceilings."

"You're right about that. Let me show you—they're tucked away at the back." Heather followed him through a part of the building that had definitely not been restored, for its decor, in contrast, was little more than peeling paint and dust-laden cobwebs. Along a narrow corridor, up and down several short flights of stairs, until finally they stood before a battered metal door.

Daniel hauled it open and ushered her through. "This is it."

They were on a landing. A rickety run of steps led down to the workroom floor, which was largely obscured by stacks of folding tables and chairs and a hodgepodge of boxes. The far wall was nearly all windows, though they were so dusty they didn't let in much light. In spite of the changes, Heather recognized it as the room where Nan and Miriam had posed for the picture as they waited for the queen.

Deciding not to think about the relative safety of the steps, she hurried down and strode across the room to the windows. Pulling a tissue from her bag, she wiped clean one pane of glass so she could look out on the street below.

"This is the mews that runs parallel to Bruton Street," Daniel said, coming to stand next to her. "The big entrance was only for Hartnell and his customers. The only time Mimi ever walked through it was when she first came to London and needed a job. She was desperate, and certain she'd be turned away if she went to the staff entrance, so she pretended to be a client."

"She never came back, later on, to have clothes made?"

"No. Her work has grown in value, but my grandparents were never wealthy people."

Heather turned to look at the workroom again, then closed her eyes and tried to imagine the space as it had once been. Busy, so busy, and full of life and color and beauty. She tried to imagine Nan in the room, a Nan who had been young and pretty and full of hope. A Nan who had loved her work and was happy with her life.

What had happened? What had driven her away?

"This is the closest I've felt to her since she died," Heather whispered. "As if I open my eyes she'll be here, and she'll be ready to tell me everything." She blinked away the tears that were trying to embarrass her in front of Daniel. Nan was gone. Of course she was gone.

"I just don't understand why she never told us. It doesn't make any sense. I was close to her, really close, and so was my mom. I told Nan *everything*. And then to find out about all of this, and to know she kept it all locked away."

"Nothing?" he asked softly.

"Nothing. Not one word."

"You said she had a shop?"

"Yes. Ann's Knitting and Notions. She sold yarn and knitting needles and buttons and things. She loved to knit. Liked keeping her hands busy, she always said."

"And you never saw her do any embroidery?"

"Never. I can ask my mom, but I'm pretty sure she never did."

"Mimi might know why," he said.

Heather turned to face him, not quite willing to believe her ears. He smiled, his pale eyes warm, and she knew she hadn't mistaken him. "Would you ask her for me?"

"You can ask her yourself. I'm sorry I didn't offer to introduce you straightaway. I'm a little protective of her, for reasons that . . . well, let's just say I try to err on the side of caution."

"What made you decide I'm a safe bet?"

"It's simple. Your grandmother was kind to Mimi at a time when she badly needed a friend. Now it's my turn to do the same for you."

Chapter Nineteen

Ann

September 24, 1947

*A*nn was looking forward to her evening out with Jeremy. She was. It was only the matter of what she would wear that was keeping her awake at night.

"If we were going back to that little café in Soho it wouldn't be a problem," she confided in Miriam at the beginning of the week. "But this is Quaglino's. You can't swing a cat without hitting a debutante there. And everyone will be dressed to the nines."

"I wish I had something suitable to lend you. There is my suit from Paris, but you are dining at eight o'clock. You will need something more formal, and good shoes and gloves as well. If only we could make something."

"I did think of that, but even if I'd started right away there wouldn't have been time. Do you think I might ask Carmen? I don't know her terribly well, but she's always dressed so nicely. Perhaps she might have some ideas."

Carmen, as it turned out, was full of ideas.

"Good old Quag's. One of my boyfriends used to take me there. You're right about needing to make an effort." The model stepped back and assessed Ann's figure with a practiced eye. "You're about the same size as my sister. She has a frock that might do. I had it made up from one of Mr. Hartnell's patterns as a birthday gift for her, but she hardly ever wears it. Says it scratches."

"Scratches?" Ann asked.

"It's made from this gorgeous brocade—pale pink with bits of gold here and there. Meant for upholstery, but still light enough for a frock. I suppose it might be the *slightest* bit itchy. At any rate, I don't think she'll mind very much if you borrow it. What about shoes?"

"I have the ones my sister-in-law sent me from Canada. They're beige with closed toes."

"They'll do. Make sure your stockings aren't too dark. You'll need gloves, white ones, to your elbows at least. If they're any shorter you'll look like your granny. And you absolutely *have* to do something about your hair."

"But I don't—"

"I don't mean a permanent wave or anything like that. But you should have it washed and set. I'll ask Reggie if he can fit you in. He has a little place on New Bond Street. Such a dear and he'll make your hair look *divine*."

"How much?" Ann asked, wearily resigning herself to the expense.

"Usually he charges fifteen shillings but he'll do it for ten if I ask nicely."

"*Fifteen bob* to wash and curl my hair?"

"Not fifteen—ten. And the man's a miracle worker. You can even get your nails and makeup done if you like."

Ann had no difficulty in rejecting that proposal. "No. I can't put varnish on my nails, not when I'm working on the princess's gown. Miss Duley would just make me take it off. And I would feel strange with a full face of makeup. I'll stick with powder and lipstick. I'm sure that will be fine."

On Wednesday she changed into her borrowed frock after work, and despite being lined it was just as scratchy as she'd feared. But it was a very pretty garment, with neat cap sleeves and a full skirt that ended well below her knees. Carmen walked her over to the hairdresser's and introduced her to Reggie.

"Gorgeous hair, my love," he pronounced, and proceeded to set it in a cascade of soft waves. Carmen sat in the next chair and gossiped with Reggie while he worked, which saved Ann from the ordeal of small talk with a complete stranger, and when he was done she took over the job of applying Ann's lipstick and powder.

"And a coat of mascara, too. No, don't fuss. Your eyelashes are completely invisible without it."

Even Ann's coat didn't pass muster. "You're not going to wear that ratty old thing, are you? Take mine."

"I can't. You've already been so nice."

"Yes, but you deserve a bit of nice. Just don't lose it. Now, do you have enough for a cab?"

"I was thinking I'd walk there. It's only about ten minutes away."

Carmen rolled her eyes heavenward. "No, no, no. You can't just walk in off the street. You must take a cab. And be late—at least ten minutes. Fifteen to be safe. He needs to feel a little nervous."

"But I—"

"When you arrive, just say 'so sorry I was late' and change the subject. That's a good time to pull off your gloves. Loosen the fingertips one by one, like this, then pull the glove off in one long sweep, like so, and set it on your lap."

Although Carmen made it all look wonderfully elegant, Ann had the uncomfortable feeling that she would look like a burlesque dancer if she tried to do the same. Better, though, to simply nod and agree.

"What should I order?" she asked.

"Hmm. The menu is in French—too bad Miriam isn't here to walk you through the basics. You should just say everything looks lovely and that you can't possibly make up your mind and you'd rather he just decided for you."

"What if he orders something awful?"

"Like frog's legs? I doubt it. The strangest thing on the menu there is the oysters, but they're quite nice."

"All right," Ann said doubtfully.

"Don't worry. It will be wonderful." Carmen glanced at the clock on the wall and jumped up. "I have to run—I'm having supper with a sweet old fellow. It's a quarter to eight now. If you walk to the corner you can get a cab outside the hotel there. Take your time, though. You want to be fashionably late."

Ann arrived exactly ten minutes late, the most she could bear to delay, and was greeted by a smoothly smiling maître d'hôtel. "Good evening, madam, and welcome to Quaglino's."

"Good evening. I'm meeting—"

"Captain Thickett-Milne, yes. He did say he was expecting you. May we take your coat? Wonderful. If you will allow me to show you the way?"

The restaurant was glorious. She tried to take it all in, the flowers and the crisp white linen and sparkling crystal and silver and the even more dazzling jewelry of the guests, and she thought she might have seen Laurence Olivier sitting at one of the tables, but she didn't dare to turn her head for a second look.

Jeremy stood as she approached, took her hand and kissed it, then waited until she was settled in her chair before sitting down himself. He was dressed in a beautifully tailored suit, and to Ann's mind was easily the handsomest man in the room.

"I'm sorry I was late," she said, and resisted the urge to offer a more robust excuse.

"I only just arrived. Shall I pour you some champagne?"

"Yes, please." She almost reached for her glass, but remembered in time that she was meant to remove her gloves. Her hands were so damp with nerves that it was an effort to tug them off. So much for glamour.

She took a sip of the champagne and was a little taken aback by the taste, which reminded her of too-dark toast, and by the bubbles, which made her want to sneeze. The waiter handed her a menu and, as Carmen had warned, there was nothing she recognized apart from "sole." Did it mean the same thing in French as in English? She might easily end up with a plate of frog's legs or snails.

"Do you see anything you fancy?" Jeremy asked.

"Oh, it all looks so delicious. I'm not sure I can decide. What do you recommend?"

"The oysters are splendid here. Don't know of anyone who's ever been served a bad one. As for mains, I was thinking of the steak."

Her frock was so tight that she'd never be able to manage more than a few bites of beefsteak. "I, ah . . . I was thinking of the sole?"

"Excellent choice." He looked up and their waiter materialized at his elbow, rather as if he'd read Jeremy's mind. He took their orders and whisked away the menus, and only then did Ann realize there hadn't been any prices on hers. Better not to know, she decided.

"I believe you said you'd been away?" That seemed like a safe place to start.

"Yes, but only for a week or so. Was quite happy to come back to town, especially since I knew we'd be dining tonight. And now here we are, and you are a vision in that frock. Is it new?"

New to *her*, at least. "Yes. Do you like it?"

"Very much. The pink is quite pretty against your skin. Even more so when you flush because my compliments make you nervous. They shouldn't, you know."

The oysters arrived just then, saving her from thinking up a response. "Been ages since I had the oysters here," Jeremy said. "They really are terribly good." He squeezed an odd pair of tongs over his oysters, and she saw that they held a wedge of lemon, and then she noticed the way the edges of the oysters fluttered when they were spritzed with the juice.

She must have made some small sound, for he looked up and smiled. "Don't you love it? So fresh they're practically wriggling."

"I, ah . . . I never realized they were alive," she said faintly.

"'Course they're alive. Expect they'd taste awful if they were dead." He picked up one of the shells and tipped its contents into his mouth. She watched the muscles of his throat contract as he swallowed the oyster, and a faint sheen of perspiration broke out on her brow, and she looked down at the six oysters on her plate and thought she might topple off her chair.

Instead she did exactly as Jeremy had done. She squeezed the little lemon-filled tongs over her oysters, picked up a shell, poured the oyster and its surrounding brine into her mouth, and swallowed before she could think twice.

"Delicious," she said, and reached for her champagne.

The oyster shells had just been tidied away when Jeremy looked over her shoulder, smiled, and waved a hand in greeting. A couple approached, and he stood and said hello and chatted with them for a few minutes. The man ignored her; the woman, looking down, smiled thinly at Ann but said nothing. She was wearing a gorgeous dress of eau de nil silk with delicate bands of sequins and larger matte paillettes on the bodice. A dress that Ann had embroidered herself only a few months earlier.

"Your gown is lovely," she said unthinkingly.

Rather than thank her for the compliment, as anyone with manners would have done, the woman simply stared, her smile twisting into an odd little frown, her brow gathering into disdainful pleats. Plucking at her husband's sleeve, she whispered something in his ear and he, in turn, swiveled his head around to stare at Ann.

"We won't keep you," the man said, and he and his wife continued on their way.

"I do apologize," Jeremy said as he sat down. "George and his wife are the most frightful snobs, which is ridiculous when you consider how his family made their money."

"How?" she asked, praying that her face wasn't as red as it felt.

Jeremy leaned forward, his voice dropping to a conspiratorial whisper. "Lavatory brushes. Can you believe it? I'd have taken them to task, but my line of work requires the utmost discretion. You won't let them ruin our evening, will you?"

"Of course not."

Any further awkwardness was curtailed by the arrival of their main course. Her sole really was sole, thank goodness, and was tender and delicate, served with little roast potatoes the size of marbles and a buttery sauce that tasted almost but not quite of mint. It was the nicest thing she'd eaten in years, apart from Miriam's Friday-night chicken, of course.

No one else interrupted them, and an hour later she couldn't have said what they talked about. He did ask how her day had been, and she simply said it had been fine, for she could hardly tell him that the entire week before had been a mad rush to get the pieces of the princess's gown finished and ready for making up, or how she'd stayed late every day so as to be certain the center front panels of the skirt were perfect. Perhaps after the wedding she would be able to tell him. Surely he would understand how she had been constrained by her promises to Mr. Hartnell and Miss Duley.

They were just finishing their pudding—profiteroles for Jeremy and chocolate ice cream for her—when the maître d'hôtel approached.

"I do beg your pardon for the interruption, madam. I've had a call for Captain Thickett-Milne." Then he whispered something into Jeremy's ear before backing away.

"Is anything the matter?" she asked.

"Not at all. It's only that I'm needed back at work. I had a feeling I'd be called in."

"We were finishing anyway. I don't mind." It did seem odd for him to have received a call at the restaurant, but he did have that top secret job in Whitehall. Perhaps such things happened to men like him all the time.

"You are a brick. We'd best be on our way—I don't dare keep her waiting."

"You work for a woman?"

He shook his head, and for a moment she worried she'd angered him, but his fleeting smile put her at ease. "A slip of the tongue. Remember what they say about loose lips."

He took her arm and led her back through the restaurant, and she wished she'd looked around more when she'd had the chance. She didn't recognize any of the other diners, but she did see several Hartnell frocks, their wearers draped in furs and jewels, their faces made up like gleaming, perfect masks, and she wished, only for a moment, that she'd let Carmen cover her freckles with something more opaque than a dusting of powder.

The maître d'hôtel had her coat waiting. "I'll take it," Jeremy said, and he even did up the buttons for her. When he was finished, he bent his head to kiss her cheek, right by her ear, and his breath was ticklish and smelled faintly of the chocolate sauce from his profiteroles.

"You'll be all right to get home?" he asked as they walked out to the pavement and the cab that seemed to be waiting just for her.

"I will."

"I just realized—we haven't arranged for another evening, and now there isn't time. Will you ring me tomorrow? I'll be home by half six. Do say you will."

"I will. Thank you for a lovely evening."

"You are most welcome." He leaned in and kissed her cheek again, and then she got in the cab, and only once it had turned the corner did she ask the driver to drop her off at the nearest Underground station.

THE NEXT MORNING she was still feeling rather dreamy. Miriam had already been in bed when she'd arrived home, so they discussed the meal itself over breakfast—simply remembering the oysters was enough to put Ann off her porridge—and she shared the unsettling experience of meeting someone who was wearing a frock she'd helped to make.

Having sent the princess's gown, or rather its constituent pieces, next door to the sewing workroom the week before, they were now concentrating on the fifteen-foot train. She and Miriam were positioned at the very end of the frame, directly opposite one another, as that was where the most important elements of the design were focused.

Within five minutes of sitting down she was lost in her work, oblivious to the chatter of the other girls at the frame, and only when Miss Duley came into the workroom at half-past nine did Ann look up.

"Have you been running?" she asked, for Miss Duley's face was flushed, her hair was slipping out of its neat knot, and she was having difficulty catching her breath.

"Yes," Miss Duley gasped. "Only found out now."

Ann rushed over and took the older woman by the arm. "Come here and sit down. Take a deep breath. Good. And another. Now tell me what's wrong."

"Queen. Afternoon. *Here.*"

"The queen is coming here for a fitting?" It didn't make sense. The queen and princesses never came to Bruton Street. Mr. Hartnell and Mam'selle always went to them.

"No. To see the gown. Queen, Princess Elizabeth. Margaret, too. Queen Mary, Duchess of Gloucester." Poor Miss Duley still couldn't catch her breath.

"Just to see the gown?" Ann repeated.

"Yes. They want to visit the workrooms. But the state of this place . . . what'll we do?"

Ann didn't have to look around to know what was distressing Miss Duley. The workroom was a shambles. It was clean and orderly where it counted, which at that moment was the great, long frame that held the princess's train, but everywhere else was a disaster.

"Mr. Hartnell will have a fit if he sees it like this," Miss Duley went on. "And what will the queen say?"

"She won't see it like this. We'll tidy it now," Ann promised. "If we all work together it'll be done in no time."

"Where'll we put everything?" Miss Duley waved a hand at the stacks of empty tambour frames, messily folded lengths of fabric, overflowing boxes of trim, and unraveling spools of ribbon that had colonized the fringes of the workroom.

"We'll hide it."

"I know," Miriam said. "We will take those empty frames, the ones that are stacked in the corner, and set them up along the wall there, and then we will put whatever we must hide underneath. Then we will cover all of it with, ah . . ."

"We've those old sheets. The ones we're meant to put up if we notice anyone trying to take pictures from the opposite windows." Then another idea occurred to Ann. "Do we have the samples back again from the queen and Princess Elizabeth?"

"Yes," Miss Duley said promptly. "They're in Mr. Hartnell's office. I saw them there yesterday."

"Let's see if we can fetch them back. We can set them up on the table by the stairs, and we'll put Mr. Hartnell's sketches there, too. In case he wants to show them."

"Good. Yes, that's a splendid idea," Miss Duley said. "Thank you, Ann."

"Are you feeling better? Why don't you stay put for now? We'll take care of sorting everything out."

It only took an hour to set everything to rights, although they had to work straight through their morning break to ensure everything was tidy and clean. Just as they were finishing there was another small panic, this time over everyone's appearance. But Miss Duley, now herself again, was not to be moved. No, lipstick was not allowed under any circumstance, and no, the queen and other royal ladies would not notice what any of them were wearing.

"I can't believe I'm going to meet the queen and I'm dressed in any old thing," Ruthie complained. Ann, who was wearing her least favorite blouse and skirt under her coveralls, wisely said nothing.

"You'd look ridiculous if you were dressed up in your Sunday best," Miss Duley reasoned. "Besides, they're not coming to see us— they want to see the gown. We'll be part of the scenery, no more."

As soon as the workroom was ready for inspection, Miss Duley pulled out her box Brownie camera, which made Ann wonder if perhaps she had been hoping for a visit from the royal ladies, and had one of the girls from the sewing workroom take a photograph from the top of the steps of everyone at their places. That accomplished, there was just enough time for dinner, and for Ann to run over to the models' cloakroom to return Carmen's frock and coat.

"I promise to tell you everything later, but I have to rush back— the royals are coming."

"I heard. Good luck! And don't forget your coat."

A dropped pin would have sounded like a falling anvil in the workroom that afternoon. Ann resolved to focus only on the work before her, and did so with such success that she nearly jumped out of her skin when the telephone on Miss Duley's desk began to ring.

"Yes, Mrs. Price. Thank you. We'll be ready." Miss Duley set down the receiver and stood. "They'll be here in five minutes. Please line up in front of the frames, ladies, and mind you don't brush against them and knock off the coverings."

They all did as she suggested, and then, frowning, she beckoned Ann and Miriam to come forward. "I want you to stand at your chairs. Just in case they wish to see a demonstration."

Approaching Ann, her hands fluttering over her hair, Miss Duley asked worriedly, "How do I look?" She had added a white lace collar to her usual black dress, and her hair was in an even tighter bun than usual.

"Very nice," Ann said. "Now off you go and I'll make sure everyone is ready when the door opens."

Miss Duley vanished out the door, they took their places, and Ann slowly became aware of how nervous she was. She even had to wipe her hands on her coverall several times. The younger girls broke into giggles after a few minutes of aching silence, but a good hard glare was enough to quiet them.

At last they heard the noises of people in the corridor. The door opening, creaking on its hinges, and there were the queen and Princess Elizabeth and Queen Mary, and just behind them Princess Margaret and the Duchess of Gloucester. They stood at the landing for a long moment, and the queen looked down at all the girls with a dazzling smile.

Ann bent her knees into a curtsy, and the others followed but not quite at the same time, which made for a rather comical effect as their heads bobbed up and down at intervals. But the queen didn't notice, or rather was too polite to take notice, and instead she and the others swept down the stairs and into the workroom.

Mr. Hartnell and Miss Duley and Mam'selle followed just behind, and he showed the royal ladies the samples that Ann and Miriam had worked, and explained that the gown itself was next door in the sewing workroom.

"Having completed the principal embroidery on Your Royal Highness's gown, we are now working on the train. Miss Hughes and Miss Dassin are my two most senior embroiderers, and they have led the way in the embroidery on both the gown and the train. Would

Your Majesties and Royal Highnesses care to observe them at work for a moment or two?"

"I should like that very much," said the queen with another wonderful smile, her cornflower-blue eyes so friendly and warm, and Ann sat in her chair and picked up her needle and began to work.

"They begin by attaching the satin appliqué pieces to the tulle, after which they affix the pearls and other decorations, and all the while they must take great care to ensure that every stitch is invisible," Mr. Hartnell said in his most serious voice.

The queen and Princess Elizabeth had come to stand next to Ann, and just knowing they were so close made Ann's hands go all wobbly, but it wasn't so bad as to be noticeable. She managed to set several pearls at the center of one of the York roses before the queen nodded and said, "Thank you very much. We are so grateful for your hard work."

Ann wasn't sure if she was allowed to say anything, but it seemed rude not to respond. "Thank you, Your Majesty," she said, and out of the corner of her eye she saw both Mr. Hartnell and Miss Duley nod.

The royal ladies processed back up the stairs, and Ann and Miriam stood up, and at the landing the queen paused and turned to say good-bye to everyone. They curtsied again, still horribly out of unison, and then the door shut and their visitors were gone.

"There," Miss Duley said. "We survived. Well done, girls. Let's all sit down and catch our breath, and mind you don't start to chatter until our guests have left the premises. After that you may have your break a little early."

Ann crossed the workroom to Miss Duley, who had collapsed onto her desk chair. "What do you think?"

"I'd say they were very pleased. They never talk much, you know. Only the queen, and she always has something nice to say. It was a very good idea to have the samples brought down, by the way."

"Shall I take them back? Mr. Hartnell will probably need them again before the wedding."

"Yes, do. But make sure to avoid the royal ladies."

Ann set off for Mr. Hartnell's office, taking the long way round so as to stay out of everyone's way. It sent her through the show-room, which should have been empty, since any appointments would certainly have been canceled once the queen had announced her intention to visit.

Only it wasn't empty. Three young men were sprawled on the upholstered chairs where clients usually sat, chatting amiably with one another, and they jumped to their feet when they heard her approaching.

Jeremy was one of the men.

Desperate to set the record straight, she took a small step toward him, then another. She hadn't meant to deceive him, she wanted to say. She had been planning on—

"*No,*" he mouthed silently, his eyes wide.

"I, ah . . . I hadn't expected anyone to, ah, to be here," she stammered, and now she clutched the box of samples close to her chest. As if anything so insubstantial could shield her from what was to come. "I do apologize."

"No need," said one of the men in an airy tone. "On your way somewhere important?"

"Yes. I need to take these to Mr. Hartnell."

"Don't you want to know why we're here?" asked the third man, and she recognized him from the night she'd met Jeremy at the Astoria. The chinless Clark Gable.

"Leave her alone," Jeremy said. "Can't you see she has work to do?"

"Usually the girls love it when they find out I'm an aide to Princess Margaret."

"Chief carrier of handbags and lighter of cigarettes," said the man who'd first spoken to her. "That's what you are."

"Laugh if you like. You'd all change places with me in a heartbeat," said No Chin.

"Excuse me. I must go," she said, not that any of them were listening, and she backed out of the room. She would return the samples later. After the royal ladies were gone. After Jeremy, who had to be some sort of aide to one of them, had also gone.

There was no chance, now, that she'd see him again. He hadn't introduced her to his friends, just as he hadn't introduced her to the people at the restaurant the night before, for what man in his position would admit to knowing a girl like her? He hadn't introduced her, because he'd at last been confronted with the truth.

He might swear that it didn't matter, that times were changing and things like class and money and accents didn't matter, but he was wrong. It was wrong and unfair that they mattered, but they did. Even if, by some miracle, they could ever have managed to paper over those differences in their private life, there would always be someone who would refuse to acknowledge her in a restaurant, or who turned away when she tried to engage them in conversation, or who whispered about her just loudly enough that she heard every word.

If she were honest with herself, it was her own fault. Had she been forthright with Jeremy from the very beginning—had she told him where she worked and where she lived, and had she made certain he understood the differences between them—he would have thanked her and gone away and that would've been that.

It was her own fault, as simple as that, and fussing over it or letting herself feel sad wouldn't do a whit of good. It was a shame she wouldn't see him again, for she had truly liked him, and in a different world . . .

Enough. *Enough.* It was done, and over, and she'd forget him soon enough, because she had never been the sort of girl to sit around and lick her wounds and moan about how life was unfair.

That's what her mum had taught her. "Chin up," she'd always said when Ann had come to her in tears about something awful that had happened. A teacher had been cruel at school, her cat had run away, awful Billy from round the corner had pulled her pigtails and said no one would ever kiss her because of her ginger hair.

"Just keep your chin up, Ann, and you can face anything," Mum had said. "And don't look back, no matter what you do." Her mum had never been one for hugs or soft words, but she had been honest, and most of the time she'd been right, too.

So chin up it was, and no looking back.

Chapter Twenty

ℳiriam

October 5, 1947

*I*n recent weeks Walter had taken to sending Miriam a letter when he wished to invite her to supper, and she would then ring him from one of the telephone kiosks in the post office near Bruton Street. This week he had proposed a change to their usual plans.

"You wish to visit your friends on Sunday? And for me to accompany you?"

"Yes. They live in Kent, about an hour's drive south of the city."

"Do they know that you wish to bring me?"

"Yes. They're very keen to meet you. It's a longish drive, but it'll do us both good to breathe in some fresh air. And . . ." It wasn't like Walter to sound hesitant. As if he were nervous of saying the wrong thing. "I am rather keen, as well, for you to meet them. That's all."

She decided to ignore the way her heart had begun to flutter. "In that case I will come with you."

"Excellent. I'll come to collect you at—"

"No, you will not. If it is south of the city then you will be going far out of your way. I will meet you in London."

"Very well. Since you're determined to be sensible about it. I live near Chancery Lane station. Can you meet me there? Say at ten o'clock?"

He was waiting outside the station when she emerged on Sunday morning, and after wishing her good morning and stooping to kiss her cheek, he led her to his car. It was an alarmingly small vehicle, or perhaps it was only the case that his long legs and broad shoulders were too large for an ordinary automobile. He certainly didn't seem very comfortable once he'd shoehorned himself into the driver's seat.

"Made for Lilliputians. And this bloody thing is so underpowered I might as well have put wheels on one of the sewing machines from your work," he grumbled. "I'll apologize now for my bad language over the next hour. I loathe driving and I particularly loathe driving in London. Once we're clear of the city I'll be in a better mood."

"Why do you have a car if you hate driving?"

"I don't. This belongs to my neighbor."

"Then why did we not take the train?"

"Ordinarily we'd have done just that. But there weren't any running this morning that would get us there for midday."

Not wishing to distract him, she turned her attention to the passing view. So much of London was ugly; there was no denying it. Even the most beautiful buildings were marked by neglect, their façades stained with soot, their brasses pitted by tarnish, their paint worn ghostly thin. The strange and sad spaces between buildings, as random as fate, no longer puzzled her.

They crossed a bridge, very long and wide, the waters of the Thames roiling angrily beneath. When she leaned forward to look across him

she glimpsed the clock face on the tower in Westminster, and just beyond it the ancient abbey where the princess was to have her wedding.

"There," Walter said. "We're across the river. Not long until we're
clear of the city."

It wasn't a sudden thing. There was no sign to say they had left
London behind. The buildings thinned, a little, and after a while they
became a patchy sort of frontier, with glimpses of something calmer
and greener beyond. The road narrowed, the hedgerows grew taller
and wilder, and then they were surrounded by gently rolling hills and
golden fields set aglow by the late morning sun.

"Much better," he said. "Sorry I was a bear at first."

"It did not bother me."

"Good. How are you? Busy, I expect."

"Yes. It was a busy week. As you say."

"I expect having the queen to visit didn't help very much."

"How did you know?" she asked, a ribbon of dread gathering close
around her heart.

"I wouldn't be much of a journalist if I didn't. They were photo-
graphed leaving the premises."

Now it would happen. Now he would begin to ask his questions.

"Miriam. *Miriam.* I am not about to break my promise. Do you
hear me?"

She licked her lips and tried to swallow back the fear. "Yes," she
said. "I know you will not."

"Good. I will say I'm worried about you and your friends. The
interest in this gown alarms even me, and I'm usually unflappable.
People are so avid for details, the Americans in particular, and I've
got to wonder—"

"They offer us money. The men waiting outside the back door.
When we leave work every day they are waiting. They shout their

questions and they never move out of the way. Sometimes there are so many we have to push past them."

"Good Lord."

"All the windows have been whitewashed over. At first it was just curtains, but then the man who owns the building across the lane came to Monsieur Hartnell. He said an American newspaper had offered him a fortune if they might have his top floor until the wedding."

"You read *Picture Weekly*. You know I would never stoop to that sort of thing."

"I know you would not. I do know. But what if anyone should see us together? I worry about this, for I have only worked for Monsieur Hartnell since the spring. If I were to be seen with a famous journalist—"

"Ha," he barked, but his laugh held no humor. "That is very kind of you, but I hardly qualify."

"Very well. The editor of a famous magazine. If they were to find out, I would be finished. No one would employ me. You must know this."

"I do, though it pains me to admit it. And if you don't wish to see me again until after the dress is completed and gone, I understand. It won't be so very long, at any rate," he reasoned. Always so reasonable, this man.

He was right. It would be sensible, and safe, to do as he said, and it would only be for a month or so. Why, then, did she feel so unmoored at the thought of it?

She had only known him for two months. Added together, the hours she'd spent in his company scarcely amounted to an entire day. She couldn't properly say that she knew him, or that he knew her, and if she were never to see him again she would survive. She would survive, but another piece of her would be forever lost.

"What if we are very careful?" he asked. "No more restaurants, no more walking about in public? At least until after the wedding."

"And instead?"

"Time with friends. And you could always come to my flat. I could make you supper."

"Do you know how to cook?"

He stole a smiling glance at her. "After a fashion."

"I suppose that would work," she agreed, her heart suddenly light. And then, curious, "Who are these people we are visiting?"

"My oldest friend and his wife. Bennett and Ruby. I feel certain you will like them. And they you."

"Do you mean Ruby Sutton who writes for you?"

"Yes. I brought them together—something in which I take rather a lot of pride. They've been married for something like two years now. And they've a baby on the way."

"You have been friends with Bennett for a long time?"

"More than twenty years. We were at university together. His parents had died, mine were nearly always abroad, and Bennett began inviting me home. To this house we're about to visit. We were nearly always here for Christmas and Easter, and we also stayed with his godmother in London. Insofar as I have a family, he and Ruby are my family. My family of intention, as it were, rather than blood. But no less precious for all that."

He reached over and took her near hand in his, and as the warmth and weight and sureness of his touch crept under her skin, a little of her loneliness began to leach away. Could it be this simple? A resolution, a choice, a path forward?

"What is it like, this house? Is it very big?"

He took back his hand, but only so he might shift gears as they came to a bend in the road. "Not especially. Parts of it are truly ancient, I think as early as the fourteenth century, and over the years Bennett's ancestors added to it in a rather piecemeal fashion."

"Is it in a town?"

"Near to one. Edenbridge. Pretty little place. Ah—we're getting close now."

They turned onto a winding single-lane drive that led them up and over the crest of a hill, and there, nestled into the slope below, was a rambling old house, perched just so at the heart of an expansive garden, its beds still bright with blooms.

Walter parked the car on a raked gravel forecourt and switched off the engine. Miriam got out and stretched, though it hadn't been such a long drive after all, and saw that he was doing the same.

"Brace yourself for the welcoming committee," he said, and she was about to ask him what he meant when she heard it. Them. The din of a pack of dogs, barking and braying and howling, and they were getting louder and louder.

The front door of the house opened, and before she could react, let alone flee, five—no, six—dogs came running out, directly at them, at her. The largest was an Alsatian, with enormous paws and a head almost as big as a man's, and the noise they made was burrowing inside her skull, making her head pound, but she couldn't cover her ears. If she moved they would bite her, one after the other, and even a man as big as Kaz would not be able to stop them.

Once, long ago, she had loved dogs. She'd never had one of her own, but her parents' next-door neighbors had kept spaniels, and she had loved playing with them and brushing their silky fur. They had been such sweet animals, and she'd had such fun teaching them how to sit and fetch and shake her hand.

Before Ravensbrück she had loved dogs.

In that place of horrors, she had seen what evil men could train a dog to do. She had seen what happened to prisoners who tried to run, and so she forced herself, now, to stand perfectly still. The dogs were far less likely to attack her if she didn't move or resist in any way.

Walter had come round to her side of the car. One by one, he was introducing her to the animals. "And this one is Joey, and this shaggy fellow is Dougal—yes, yes, I *am* glad to see you. I *am*. And this one is— Miriam? My God, you're frightened of them. What an ass I am not to have noticed."

"I can't . . ." Her throat was closing in. She couldn't breathe.

"I want you to sit back down, in the car, and I'll shut the door. I'll be right back."

Walter whistled for the dogs, and they listened to him and followed, still barking, as he led them inside. He returned a moment later, his shoes crunching loudly on the gravel, and then he opened the car door and crouched low beside her.

"What did you tell your friends?" she asked worriedly. "They will be annoyed with me."

"Over being nervous around dogs? Of course not. And there are rather a lot of them."

"I do like dogs. I did, before . . ."

She told herself that Bennett's dogs were friendly animals, trained only to sit and roll over and play dead. Not to chase. Not to snarl and snap and bite at anything, or anyone, that moved. Yet her heart kept racing.

"Can you hear me, Miriam? I am here. I won't let anything happen to you. Just breathe. In and out. Slowly, now."

It felt like forever before she was able to look up. "I am so sorry. I hope—"

"Please, Miriam. Please don't apologize. Do you feel able to go inside?"

At her nod, he helped her out of the car, tucked her hand in the crook of his elbow, and led her across the forecourt to the door. "Ready?"

"Yes."

The front hall was lined with coats on hooks and boots on trays, and there was a jumble of dog leads in a wicker basket and an umbrella stand crammed with walking sticks and a lone fishing rod. Framed maps and a watercolor portrait of the house hung on the walls, while a battered Persian rug, its colors faded almost to nothing, softened the ancient flagstones underfoot.

"I'll take your coat and add it to the collection here, and we'll hang up your bag, too, so the dogs can't get at it. Right. Let's go find every-one."

The sitting room was a close cousin to the entrance hall, with fray-ing rugs and slipcovered sofas and oil paintings gone dark with age, and at the far end an enormous old fireplace, the sort that might have been used for cooking when its stones had first been fitted together.

A pretty young woman, only a few years older than Miriam, was seated in a chair drawn close by the fire. She was enormously preg-nant, her face rounded and rosy, and next to her stood a man about the same age as Kaz, his dark curling hair cut very short. He bent to kiss the woman's brow, and then, his expression sweetly solicitous, helped guide her out of the chair.

They came forward, and the man held out his hand for Miriam to shake. *"Mademoiselle Dassin. Nous vous souhaitons la bienvenue."*

She looked at Walter in surprise. Why had he not told her that his friend spoke perfect, unaccented French?

"Show-off," Walter said, and made a childish face.

"I'm merely welcoming our guest," the man said. "I'm Bennett. Delighted to meet you at last. And I do want to apologize for the dogs just now. Kaz tells me you had a bad experience when you were younger."

"Please, I—"

"All that matters to us is your comfort. And it will do them no harm to stay out of the way for a few hours. For that matter, we'll enjoy a far more civilized lunch if we don't have to shout over the barking."

The young woman now took Miriam's hands in hers. "Bennett's right. And we won't have them pestering us for table scraps either. I'm Ruby, by the way. It's just wonderful to meet you. I've been asking Kaz for weeks now."

"Thank you. I, too, am very glad to make your acquaintance."

"Lunch is almost ready, but until then I want you to sit next to me. You can have Bennett's chair, and he and Kaz can perch on the sofa."

"When is the baby expected?" Miriam asked once everyone was seated and Bennett had made sure his wife was comfortable.

"At the end of the month. It's only in the last week or so that I started feeling like a hippopotamus. I can't even tie my own shoes, and if I need to roll over in bed I have to wake up poor Bennett so he can help me."

"Good training for when the baby comes," he said, grinning at his wife. "I'm a light sleeper at the best of times."

Ruby leaned forward, as much as she was able, and fixed her attention on Miriam. "Kaz hasn't told us much of anything about you. We know you're French, but not much more than that."

"I am an embroiderer," she said. And then, though she ought to have left it at that, "I work for Norman Hartnell."

"You do? It must be so—"

"No, Ruby," Walter said. "I saw the look on your face just now. No questions about the royal wedding. Not a one."

"Oh, fine," Ruby said, and smiled at Miriam. "I wouldn't have asked. Just so you know. I'm sure you can't say anything, and it would make everything so awkward if I did ask."

"Thank you."

"All the same, I am very interested in your work. Was it difficult to learn how to embroider?"

"It was so long ago," Miriam began, and then stopped short. Only eight years, which was hardly a lifetime. Never mind that it felt like a century or more had passed. "I was fourteen when I began my apprenticeship, and I did not like it at all. Not at first. Perhaps it was the shock of being away from my family for the first time. I had . . . I do not know how to say it in English. *J'avais le mal du pays.*"

"You were homesick," Bennett said.

"Yes. There were many nights when I wept and wished to be home, to wake up in my own bed again. But of course it never came true. And I learned to like the work."

A bell clanged in the distance. "That's Cook calling us in," Ruby explained. "Her feet are getting bad, so this is easier than her walking all the way from the kitchen. Although it does make me feel like I'm a cowboy on a ranch."

The dining room was as pretty as the rest of the house, its table set with blue-and-white china, heavy silver cutlery, Battenburg lace mats instead of a cloth, and a sparkling crystal bowl massed with white chrysanthemums. They began with a soup of pureed vegetables, and then, for their main course, there were game birds braised with mushrooms and leeks. To finish, they were served a dessert that reminded her of *pain perdu,* though it was richer and sweeter.

"Bread pudding," Ruby explained. "It's Bennett's favorite. I'll bet Cook used up our entire egg ration to make it."

Miriam found the conversation difficult to follow at first, for it moved back and forth across the table, from topic to topic, and she was never quite sure which thread to pick up. It was pleasant, all the same, to listen as Walter and Bennett debated one topic after another, often interrupted by Ruby, and to marvel at the obvious affection they had for one another.

At the end of lunch, Walter and Bennett stayed on to clear the table and help Cook with the washing up. Miriam began to gather their water glasses, but was promptly deflected by Bennett.

"Guests aren't allowed to help. House rules. You can keep Ruby company in the sitting room, or you can poke around outside. I'll keep the dogs shut away."

As much as she wished to spend more time with Ruby, she also needed a few minutes to herself. "I think I would like to see the garden. Where shall I go?"

"Door's at the end of the hall. That'll take you to the kitchen garden. Things get wilder the farther you get from the house."

The garden, hemmed in on three sides by the house, was set out in symmetrical parterre beds of vegetables and herbs. Rambling roses, their faded blooms fattening into rosy hips, climbed three-sided wrought-iron trellises set in the center of each square, while espaliered fruit trees spread expansive boughs across a south-facing wall.

Miriam walked around each bed, taking stock of the flowers and herbs, and then stood in the center and let herself breathe. The sun felt so lovely on her upturned face.

She turned at the sound of footsteps. Bennett. "It is beautiful," she said.

"My mother's creation. Inspired by memories of her childhood home in Normandy."

"So that is why you have no accent."

"Maman was relentless. Always insisted on French at home. But it has served me well." He turned his head, caught her gaze, kept it. "I was in France during the war. I saw terrible things. And the memories of what I saw will never leave me."

She nodded, not quite understanding.

"I expect you saw worse," he said. "I expect that worse things were done to you."

"How?" she asked.

"A guess. I understand your reluctance to discuss your past. I do. But if ever there were a safe place to do so, this is it. I promise you that."

"I want to tell him. I do."

"There isn't a drop of hate in Kaz. None at all. As I think you know."

"He is important to me," she said. "He has become precious to me."

"I can see it. But you— Hello, Kaz. Didn't hear you come out."

"I know. The two of you were as thick as thieves." Walter had Miriam's coat over one arm. "Shall we go for a walk? Cook insists rain is on the way."

"Excellent idea," Bennett seconded. "I'd come with you, but I need to keep an eye on Ruby. Otherwise I'll return to find her at the top of a ladder or doing something else that stops my heart."

Walter led them down the hill, through a stand of beeches, and into a grassy meadow that was crisscrossed with mown pathways. They walked in silence, the sun hot upon their backs, and after a few minutes he reached out and took her hand in his.

"What were the two of you rabbiting on about?" he asked.

"France. The war."

"I thought so," he said, and his hand tightened around hers for an instant. "Earlier, when you were frightened by the dogs, you told me you'd once liked them. 'Before,' you said."

"Yes. Before I was imprisoned. Before I was sent to Ravensbrück."

"The guards there had dogs," he said, and there was something odd about his voice. He was angry, she realized, so angry that he could barely speak.

"They did." They walked on, and she knew she had to tell him the rest of it. "There is something else you must know. I am a Jew."

He squeezed her hand even tighter. He did not let go. "I thought you might be."

"How?" How was it that he was not surprised?

"I'm not much of a detective. But you did speak of your grandmother's Friday-night chicken. And there's your name. Miriam isn't a very typical name for a Catholic. Combined with your reluctance to speak of your life before the war, it seemed likely."

"Why did you not say anything?"

"I was waiting for you to tell me. I didn't want to push you. I certainly didn't wish you to feel threatened."

"And you do not care?"

"I think the better question is if I *mind*. To that I say, no, I don't mind at all. But I do care. Very much so."

"I do not understand the difference."

"Your being Jewish is a part of you. It's a part of your family and your history, and also your suffering. How can I truly know you without also knowing you are a Jew?"

He embraced her then, opening his arms so she might huddle close, one big hand cradling her head against his chest. He held her, and waited while she wept, and when her sobs had tapered into hiccups he handed her a wrinkled handkerchief.

"It's clean. I promise."

She wiped her eyes and blew her nose and then, because she still needed to be close to him, she looped her arm through his. "Do you mind if we walk some more?"

"Not at all. Perhaps . . . would you like to tell me a little of your family? Where did you grow up?"

"In Colombes, just across the river from Argenteuil. We had a little house on rue des Cerisiers. My mother's parents lived on the next street over."

"A close family, then."

"Yes." And then, after they'd walked for another minute or so, "Have you heard of the Affaire Dreyfus?"

"Of course."

"My father used to say that it had forced his parents to make a choice. They could be French, or they could be Jews. And they chose France, and I suppose my father did, too. There was hardly anything in our home that would tell you we were Jewish."

"I see."

"But my mother's parents were devout. When I was little we would have *le dîner de Chabbat* at their house every Friday, and Grand-Mère would serve her special chicken. It was my favorite thing in the world."

"Only when you were little? What happened?"

"Grand-Mère died when I was twelve. After that we had no more Sabbath dinners. And Papa had become fearful, too. We could see what was happening in Germany."

He wrapped his hands around hers, engulfing them, and she was safe enough, in that moment, to let the door to her memories open. Only a fraction, only enough to see her father's face and, written on it, the fear he had tried to hide for so long. The knowledge he had swallowed down, like poison, for her sake.

"You said, earlier, that you left home when you were fourteen. What year was that?"

"It was the spring of 1938. Even then, Papa was forever warning me to say nothing about being a Jew. And he was so worried I obeyed."

"And after the Occupation?"

"There was a census. They counted us, all the Jews in France, and marked where we lived. Papa knew it would happen, for he had a friend who worked for the police, and he came all the way into Paris to tell me. He waited for me outside my lodgings, and then he took me to a café and told me what was going to happen. He and Maman could not avoid the census, for they were known to be Jews, and there was my grandfather to think of, too. He was too frail to travel."

"And when it was your turn to be counted?"

She shook her head. "Papa gave me false papers. Dassin is a Jewish surname, so I became Marianne Dessin, with an *e*. He put as my birthplace a small town in the Auvergne. I knew a little about it, for we used to go on holiday there in the summers. Then he told me to look for new work, to leave Maison Lesage, and to hide in plain sight. It was that, or try to leave France altogether."

"Was it difficult to find a new position?"

"Not at all. I had a position at Maison Rébé within the week, and I moved to new lodgings as well, and when the census of Jews was made I was not counted. I never wore the star. I lied. I hid. And I never saw my family again."

"You *lived*," he said, wiping at his eyes with a second, equally crumpled handkerchief.

They were back at the kitchen garden. Walter guided her to a stone bench and helped her to sit. Only then did she realize she was shaking. His arm went around her shoulders, his free hand enfolded both of hers, and he waited.

She had never said the words aloud, not to anyone, not ever. She was so tired of keeping them to herself.

"Only after the war did I learn what happened to them. They were rounded up in 1942. In July. They were sent to the Vélodrome d'Hiver. It was only a few kilometers away."

"And then?" he prompted, his words a whisper against her brow. He was hunched over her now, protecting her as best he could.

"And then I am not certain. I doubt I will ever know. I think they probably were sent to Auschwitz."

"My darling. I am sorry beyond words. Oh, my darling."

"I cannot stop thinking of it. I dream of that place," she hurried on, the words tumbling from her mouth, "though I have never been. Not before the war, nor since. I dream of that *vélodrome* and the thousands who were sent there. They had to have known what would happen. Papa and Maman and Grand-Père. They must have known what would be done to them."

His arms tightened around her, so tight it was hard to breathe.

"I think about it all the time. What was it like. First in the *vélodrome,* then at the camps, and then the final journey to the east. I see it. I see them, and they are reaching through time and space to me. To *me,* so I may bear witness and tell the world the truth of it."

"Will you?" he whispered.

She had told him so much already. Surely he would understand what she wanted to do. What she meant to do. "I have an idea . . . but I need to show you. It is too difficult to describe. May we go back to the house?"

"Of course."

He waited while she fetched her bag from the hall, and then he led her into the library and watched as she took out the bundle she was never without, not for weeks now, and unfolded it upon the table.

It was a square of fabric about the size of a cloth napkin, and on it she had embroidered a woman standing alone, and she was made of many smaller pieces of fabric appliquéd to the backing, one by one, like so many layers of paint. The background was impressionistic, with scattered lines of stitching that hinted at close-set buildings, or perhaps they were faces in a crowd.

The woman was looking over her shoulder, her face in profile, and one arm was thrown back in warning. She wore a Star of David on her coat.

"Is it you?" Kaz asked.

"No. I never wore the star."

"Your mother, then."

"I think so, yes. She was so beautiful."

"This is . . . my God, Miriam. This is the work of an artist. *You* are an artist. Do you not see it? You must continue this work. Promise me you will."

"It will take a very long time," she cautioned. "This alone took me weeks. And my ideas for it are not small. I cannot imagine how I will ever finish."

"A long time, yes," he agreed. "But not forever."

Chapter Twenty-One

Heather

September 1, 2016

Heather was awake at dawn the next morning. Daniel had walked her back to the hotel after their late afternoon coffee, and after promising to talk to his grandmother, he and Heather had exchanged cheek kisses as if they were both French or, more accurately, unsure of how to behave when a handshake was too formal, a hug was too touchy-feely, and a straight-up kiss was just too much.

True to his promise, he'd called that evening.

"Mimi is keen to meet you. We thought ten o'clock tomorrow would be a good time. Her flat is on East Heath Road in Hampstead, just around the corner from the Tube. The building is called Wells Manor and the name on the buzzer is Kaczmarek. I'll email you all of that, as well as a map."

"Thank you. I know you think this is no big deal, but it really is. At least to me it is."

"You're welcome. I was also wondering if you might like to go out for dinner with me. I would've asked you earlier, but then I began to worry you might feel I was taking over your holiday."

"Not at all. If anything, you've saved it. Were you thinking to-morrow?"

"Unfortunately, I have a department meeting at six and they usu-ally drag on forever. Would Friday night suit you?"

"It would," she said, feeling very glad he couldn't see how she was bouncing around her hotel room.

"Then it's a date. We can sort out the details tomorrow—and do let me know how things go with Mimi. Ring me anytime."

HEATHER HAD LET herself get so starry-eyed over her date with Daniel that she'd forgotten to ask him what sort of gift she ought to take to his grandmother. It didn't seem right to show up at Miriam's empty-handed, but she could hardly hand over a bottle of wine at ten in the morning. Food was tricky, since Heather had no idea if Miriam had any allergies or was diabetic or simply didn't like certain things. But she had a feeling that flowers would be a safe bet.

Dermot was at the front desk when she headed out, and was able to recommend a good florist around the corner from the hotel. "Ask for one of their hand-tied posies," he advised. "I get one for my mum every Christmas and she loves them."

Armed with the posy, which looked and smelled like it had come out of Nan's garden, though its thirty-five-pound price tag would have horrified her grandmother, Heather found her way across Lon-don to Hampstead station. According to the map Daniel had sent her, she had only to walk down the hill a little before heading east to Wells Manor, one of several blocks of century-old mansion flats that overlooked Hampstead Heath.

The manor's redbrick exterior was patterned with zigzagging rows of a light-colored stone, the overall effect making the building look, rather comically, as if it were wearing an argyle sweater. An ancient intercom system was set into the wall of the vestibule, and she found the button for *Kaczmarek* without trouble; there were only sixteen apartments in the entire place.

Miriam answered right away. "Hello? Is that Heather? Do come up. I am on the top floor. I shall wait by the lift."

The inner doors unlocked with a click, and Heather walked into an entrance hall that was impressive and homey at once, with polished oak paneling, burnished brass fixtures, and a tile floor with an intricately patterned border. An elevator was straight ahead, the broad flight of the central staircase curling around it. It had a scissoring gate that passengers had to pull shut behind them, and in every movie Heather had ever seen with such an elevator, it ended up getting stuck. The stairs it was.

She was hot and sweaty and out of breath by the time she got to the top floor, and for a moment, just as she came eye to eye with Miriam for the first time, she fretted that the other woman might disapprove of her. Her sundress was wrinkled, her makeup was melting away, and her nose told her that the all-natural deodorant she'd swiped on an hour before had failed her entirely. It didn't help that Miriam was the picture of effortless French chic in a white linen tunic and slim, ankle-length trousers. Even the silk scarf she'd knotted around her neck was perfect.

"It is so nice to meet you," she said, still puffing a little, and held out the posy.

"What a lovely surprise," Miriam said, and sniffed at the flowers appreciatively. "But come here first." She gathered Heather into a fierce, heartfelt embrace, only loosening it enough so she might kiss her on both cheeks. "At last, at last. Do you know, I hardly slept last night? I was so eager to meet you. And now you are here and you look so much like Ann. The same pretty hair, and the same eyes, you know. But let us not linger here—come with me and we will have some coffee, and I will put your beautiful flowers in water."

Miriam led her into the flat, and even though they were in an apartment building it felt like a big old house, with high ceilings and a wide hallway and parquet floors the color of maple syrup. The walls were closely hung with oil paintings, brightly colored modern prints, and photographs of a gaggle of children at different ages, all of them evidently related in some fashion or another. In one picture, Miriam stood arm in arm with a tall, distinguished man with a shock of white hair and pale blue eyes—Daniel's eyes, Heather realized—and she was holding up an enameled medal in a velvet case.

"That was taken at Buckingham Palace," Miriam said. "Such a happy day."

Heather nodded, because she wasn't sure what to say, and then they were in the kitchen, and instantly she felt at home. There was an enormous French gas stove, the kind that had brass handles and enameled blue doors, and the counters were made of marble, and there was a set of copper pots hanging from a rack on one wall, and on the other was a dresser piled high with mismatched blue-and-white china. On the windowsill above the sink there were pots of herbs and a carved wooden rooster with a quizzical expression on his face.

Miriam went to a compact espresso maker on the counter next to the stove and switched it on. "My daughter bought this machine for me," she explained. "She was worried I would burn myself on my old stovetop espresso maker. It is tremendously convenient but the coffee is not, I think, quite as good. Would you like a cappuccino?"

"Yes, please."

After the espresso machine had begun to hum away, Miriam took a small china jug from a low shelf on the dresser, filled it with water, and set the posy inside. "There. So lovely." Then she turned to Heather.

"You must know that it is one of the great regrets of my life that I lost touch with your grandmother. For a time we were very close, you see. We shared a house for much of 1947, the year I came to England, but she emigrated to Canada at the end of the year. I never heard from her again."

"She just left?" Heather asked, dumbfounded yet again by another of Nan's long-ago decisions. "Even though you were friends?"

Miriam nodded, her expression bittersweet. "It was a long time ago, and in those days Canada seemed very far away. It was not unusual to fall out of touch with people, you know, and we had no Facebook or Google. And I . . ."

The espresso machine began to sputter, and Miriam turned and fussed with the buttons before retrieving the cups she'd set beneath. "Would you mind taking these through to the sitting room? I almost forgot about the biscuits. Beautiful *sablés* from my favorite patisserie."

The sitting room was large and bright, with one wall taken up entirely by three enormous bay windows. Bookshelves rose to the ceiling on either side of the fireplace, and opposite, out of reach of the sun, an embroidered panel hung from a scrolling wooden valance. It was as wide as the sofa below but half as high, and the view it depicted was a twin to the one from the sitting room's windows: a green, sloping hill woven through with walking paths and ancient woods, the sky above a clear and limitless blue. Only just seen, in the far distance, was the familiar silhouette of London's skyline.

"It is rather out-of-date," Miriam said, nodding apologetically at the embroidered panel. "When I made it forty years ago, the church spires were all I noticed. Now it is nothing but skyscrapers. Yet I still love the view. We both did, Walter and I."

"He was your husband?" Heather asked.

"Yes. For forty-eight years. He died twenty years ago. At his desk, pen in hand, exactly as he would have wished."

"I am so sorry."

"It has been a long time. And yet, even now I am surprised when I wake in the night and he is not there. I suppose I shall never get used to it."

They sat in silence for a moment, and Heather sipped at her coffee and nibbled at the edge of a cookie. How should she begin? She had so many questions—

"She never told us anything," she said abruptly, her voice a degree too loud, too sharp, for the sunny room and their tentative friendship.

But Miriam didn't seem to mind. "It does not surprise me at all," she said.

"My entire life I thought she was a shopkeeper. She sold yarn and knitting needles and buttons. Not once did she ever mention that she'd worked on the queen's wedding dress. I mean—I'm not wrong about that, am I?"

"You are not wrong. Some of the most beautiful embroidery on Princess Elizabeth's gown was your grandmother's work. She was exceptionally talented, and she was very, very kind to me when I first came to England." Miriam smiled rather tremulously. "She was my first friend here."

"I know she was upset about my grandfather and being widowed and all, but . . ." Miriam had smoothed out her expression and was examining the crumbs on her plate. "Oh, boy," Heather said. "Was she married when you knew her?"

Miriam looked her in the eye. "No."

"But she had my mom in 1948, so she must have been involved with . . ."

"She was. Briefly."

"Wow. Just . . . *wow*." Of all the things she'd expected to learn to-day, the fact that Nan had been a single mother had not been one of them. Never mind that it actually made a weird kind of sense. "Times were different then, I guess."

"They were. And such a thing was more complicated, I think, than it would be today. Perhaps we should begin by your telling me what you know. Then I will tell you what I know."

"Okay. I guess I don't actually know all that much. She only ever said that her parents had died when she was young, that her brother was killed in the Blitz, and that she came to Canada at the end of 1947. I do remember her saying the snow wasn't that much of a shock because the previous winter in England had been so bad. And that was about it. She never talked about my grandfather, not even to my mom. We just assumed he had died. And there weren't any pictures of him anywhere. I did ask her, once. She had photographs up of her parents and brother, but not my grandfather, and it made me curious."

"What did she say?"

"She just changed the subject. Not in a mean way. She just said something like, 'Let's not waste the day talking about things that happened a long time ago,' and that was that."

"Did she ever speak of her old life in England?"

Heather shook her head. "Never. The only person who knew her from before was her sister-in-law, Milly. But she died when my mom was still young."

"And of her work at Hartnell?"

"Nothing. I only started figuring things out after she died in March. My mom was going through Nan's things and she found this set of embroidered flowers, and my name was on the box. 'For Heather,' Nan had written. As soon as we saw them we knew they were something special. I brought pictures if you'd like to see."

"Yes—yes, of course. Let me fetch my spectacles."

Heather moved her chair to sit alongside Miriam's, and she set the stack of photographs on the tea table, and they looked through them together.

"Oh, yes. I remember these. I had forgotten how pretty they were."

"What were they for? Were they samples of some kind?"

"Indeed they were. We made them for the princess and the queen, to ensure they approved of the motifs. I had one of them, I believe, for there were six or eight in total, but I haven't seen it in years. I do hope I haven't lost it."

"What about the *EP* in the corner—could that be someone's initials?"

"It is. *'Elizabeth Principessa.'* For the bride."

"Did you ever meet her?"

"Yes, although it was more a case of *seeing* her. Certainly I was not introduced. She and her mother—the Queen Mum, as you would know her—came for a visit before the wedding, along with Queen Mary and some of the other royal ladies. We were all quite *bouleversées* about it, but Ann was calm. Nothing ever seemed to fluster her."

"Did you go to the wedding? When I was trying to learn about the gown, I read that some of the people who worked on it were invited to the ceremony."

"No, although I was at Buckingham Palace on the morning of the wedding. In case of any last-minute disasters with any of the gowns we had made. But your grandmother was invited to Westminster Abbey, and Miss Duley, too. The woman in charge of our workroom."

"Nan went to the royal wedding and she never told me?" Had she ever known anything about her grandmother? What, between them, had been real?

"No, *ma belle*. Do not be upset with her. Ann had her reasons for not speaking of the past, and it was a usual thing, in those days, to keep our secrets. It astonishes me, you know, the way you young people are so honest about everything. Every moment of grief or trauma or loss, laid bare for all to see on your Facebook and Twitter."

The phone, which sat on a desk a few feet away, began to ring. "I shall let the machine answer for me," Miriam said, and offered Heather the plate of *sablés*.

"*Allô*, Mimi? It's Nathalie. I feel so bad, 'cause I just looked at my calendar and I know Ava and I are supposed to go see the queen's dresses at the palace with you, but the tickets are for the same time as our exam. It's that summer course we're both taking, and I—"

"If you will excuse me," Miriam said. "The poor child will wear herself out with apologies." Heather would have offered to bring over the phone, but it was an old-fashioned one that was attached to the wall.

"Nathalie? Yes, I am here. I am having coffee with a friend. No, no. It is quite all right. I am certain I can find someone. Yes. And perhaps we can see about getting tickets again at the end of the summer? Of course. *Toi aussi, ma belle*."

Miriam set down the receiver and returned to the tea table. "I do apologize. As you heard, that was one of my granddaughters. I was supposed to take her and her best friend to the summer opening at Buckingham Palace tomorrow, but they have an exam." And then, fixing her bright eyes on Heather, "Would you like to come with me?"

"Are you sure?"

"Of course. It will give you a chance to see the gown itself, and the state rooms are certainly worth seeing. The tickets are for one o'clock in the afternoon. Does that suit you?"

She wouldn't have objected if they'd been for five o'clock in the morning. "It does."

"Wonderful. I shall ask Daniel to join us. Such a lovely boy. I shall miss him very much when he goes to America."

"America? Doesn't he live here in London?"

"He does, but he is going to New York City for a year to teach at one of their universities. I gather it is a very great honor for him to have been invited."

"I'm sure it is," Heather said dutifully.

"New York and Toronto are not very far from one another, are they?" Miriam asked, her eyes sparkling with mischief.

"They are not, but I hardly know Daniel. I wouldn't want to presume—"

"It would make me very happy if you were to become friends. That is all."

"Okay," Heather acceded. She really had only just met the man, and no matter how much she liked both him and his grandmother she wasn't about to start picking out an engagement ring.

Longing to change the subject, she returned to the problem of the tickets for Buckingham Palace. "Are you sure I can't pay you back? I tried to buy one, but they were sold out."

"Of course not. Consider it, instead, a partial repayment of the kindness your grandmother once showed me. She helped to convince me I should begin work on my embroideries, you see."

"The *Vél d'Hiv* ones?"

"Yes. She was the first person, in all my life, to tell me that I was an artist. And I never had the chance to thank her."

Chapter Twenty-Two

Ann

October 7, 1947

$\mathcal{T}$he envelope was sitting on her chair when she returned from morning break. *Miss Ann Hughes,* it read.

"The guard at the back door called up to say someone had left it for you. I needed to stretch my legs, so I popped down to fetch it," Miss Duley said. "Go ahead and have a look before you get stuck in again."

Dear Ann,

As I haven't your address I resorted to leaving this at your work—it was that or wait for you outside. I only wish to say that I am sincerely sorry for my rudeness on the day of the royal ladies' visit, and while there is no excuse for such un- gentlemanly behavior on my part, I do wish to try to make it up to you as best I can. Do say you'll dine with me as soon

as you're able—any night at all. I await your telephone call
most eagerly.

Your devoted admirer,
JTM

She read it a second time, just to be sure, and then tucked both
it and the envelope in the pocket of her coveralls. The others were
back and taking their places at the great frame that held the princess's train, and she'd only end up having to answer a hundred
questions if they noticed her goggling over the note. So she bent
her head to her work and tried to sort out just what was bothering her.

Had Jeremy hurt her when he'd pretended not to know her? He
had, but she could understand why he'd done it. It must have been
a shock to see her there, of course, and it wasn't as if she had been
entirely forthcoming with him. No wonder he'd been taken aback.

When dinner came she set off in search of a telephone box that
wasn't occupied, and found one on New Bond Street. She dialed the
number, holding her breath as it buzzed and buzzed at the other end.

"Hello, Thickett-Milne speaking. Hello? Ann? Is that you?"

"I, uh . . . it is."

"You got my note?"

"I did."

"Oh, good. I am terribly sorry about what happened. It's only that
you took me by surprise. I'd absolutely no notion you worked at
Hartnell."

"I'm sorry I never told you. Really I am. It's only that with our having the commission for the wedding we aren't supposed to talk about
work with anyone."

"I understand. And now you know about my top secret job, so we're even."

"Are you an aide to the queen?" she asked, her curiosity getting the better of her.

"To Queen Mary, yes. And that's about all I'm allowed to say. At any rate, I was hoping you might like to come to dinner."

"Are you sure? Now that you know what I do for a living?"

"I don't see why that should affect anything. Why don't I collect you after work one evening this week?"

"That would be lovely, but I can't leave any earlier than half-past six."

"Then why don't we say seven o'clock? I can wait for you at the corner of Bruton and Berkeley. Is there any particular day that suits you? How about tonight?"

"Tonight is fine," she heard herself say.

"Very well. I'll see you there at seven this evening."

Miriam and Walter were spending the evening with their friends Bennett and Ruby, whose new baby had arrived a fortnight early, so Ann told Miriam that she, too, was going out, but wouldn't be that late. She took her time in the cloakroom after work, waiting until the other girls were gone before powdering her nose, combing through her hair, and fixing a button that was threatening to come loose on her coat.

When she did walk to the end of the street, a few minutes before seven, Jeremy was already there, standing next to his car, bareheaded in the cold. "Don't you look lovely. That scarf brings out the green in your eyes." He dropped a kiss on her cheek and opened the passenger-side door for her, waiting until she was settled before closing it softly. "I was thinking we'd go somewhere quiet for supper, but first I need to collect my gloves. I can't believe I forgot them at home."

It seemed odd that he would need his gloves badly enough to return home for them, for it was warm inside the car, and presumably they wouldn't be outside for very long. But there was no point in being a pill about it.

"It's not far at all," he assured her. "Eaton Square in Belgravia. Enormous old pile but it keeps the rain off my head."

He kept the conversation going as he always did, moving from topic to topic in his smooth way, never seeming to desire or require much involvement on her part. Likely it was a skill that served him well in his work.

After about fifteen minutes he turned the car onto a side street, or perhaps it was a mews of some kind. It was lined with large doors, the sort that once had led to carriage houses but now were fitted up for expensive motorcars.

"We'll be going out again, so I won't bother putting the car away," he said. He dragged open one of the doors, just enough for them to pass through, and led her through an empty garage and, beyond it, a darkened garden. No lights were shining from the interior of the house ahead, and she tripped more than once as she followed him through the night.

They went down a short flight of steps to a door, and after fumbling for the correct key, Jeremy let them inside and switched on an overhead light.

"Hello?" he called out, but no answering voice broke the silence. "My sister must be out. Oh, well. Shall we go upstairs?"

"What about your gloves?" she asked.

"Like as not in my bedroom. Or the drawing room. No point in your staying down here—it's as cold as a tomb. I'll make a fire and you can have a drink while I rummage around. Give me your coat so I can hang it up."

He led her up a flight of stairs to street level, switching on lights as he went, and along a high-ceilinged hallway to a drawing room that was, on its own, at least as big as the entire main floor of her little house. It was decorated in the usual style of such places, with elaborate draperies, wedding-cake plaster moldings, and several centuries' worth of intimidating antiques.

"Come and sit while I deal with the fire," he said, and nodded in the direction of a pair of settees that flanked the hearth. "We'll have a drink together before I try to run down those blasted gloves."

She sat, shivering, and waited as he piled coals in the grate and set them alight. "There. That'll take the chill from the air. Would you like a sherry? Or possibly something stronger?"

"Sherry is fine," she said. The glass, when he handed it to her, was dusty. In fact, everything in the room was dusty, and the air was stale, too, and she was almost certain she could see cobwebs clinging to the top of the draperies. On the far wall, opposite the fireplace, were a pair of darkened patches.

"My mother had them sent out for cleaning," Jeremy said, noticing her interest. "The paintings that usually hang there. Said they needed a freshening up."

"Oh. I, ah . . ."

"So. Hartnell. Have you worked there for long?"

"Since I was a girl. I've never worked anywhere else."

He sat opposite her and sipped at his drink. "You must have had a lot of people asking after the princess's dress. You know there's a king's ransom to be made there."

"I don't understand," she said, although she had a terrible feeling she did.

"It's a secret, and there's nothing people love more than secrets.

Uncovering them, I mean. In the right hands, a picture of that gown is worth a lot. A fortune, even."

"Is that what this is about? The princess's gown?"

"'Course not. I mean, I *did* have an idea of what you did for a living. Saw you with Carmen that first night, didn't I? She used to go out with a friend of mine. Until he found a decent girl to marry, that is. But you never said a word about your work, or that bloody gown, and I wasn't about to go digging. I do have my pride." He gulped at his drink; it was half gone now.

She was going to be sick. "If I told you anything, even a single detail, I'd be sacked. I'd be betraying all of my friends at work."

"Have I asked? No. So let's forget about it. Do you feel like seeing some more of the house? Been in the family for ages, you know." He tipped the glass to his mouth. Emptied it.

And then he looked at her, and there was something in his eyes, or behind his eyes, somehow, that set every nerve in her body jangling with apprehension. His easy friendliness of their earlier meetings was gone, and in its stead was a sort of avid, predatory watchfulness.

"I'm not feeling all that well," she protested. "I think it might be best if I went home."

"Don't be such a wet blanket. Finish that sherry, and let me show you this house. How often does a girl like you get a peek inside a place like this?"

He'd taken her coat when they came in, but she still had her bag. The front door was only yards away. But would it be locked? And surely he didn't mean to hurt her. He'd think her mad if she suddenly ran across the room and started clawing at the front door.

"Come on," he said, and took her hand in his. He led her to the stairs, wide and carpeted, and she was surprised by how gritty the banister felt under her free hand. As if no one had wiped it down in months and months.

They reached the top of the stairs. "There's another drawing room at the very front," he explained, "and several guest rooms along the hall. At the back are my parents' bedrooms. You'll like my mother's room. She had it done up by some poncy decorator just before the war."

He hadn't let go of her hand, so she had no choice but to follow him. He opened the door, swore under his breath when the overhead light failed to come on, and went over to the mantel, still dragging her along, and switched on the lamp there.

It was hard to make out much, for the light wasn't especially strong, but she could see pink and silver everywhere: the carpet, the draperies, the upholstery on the occasional chairs and settee by the hearth. Even the bedcover was made of pink-and-silver bro-cade.

"What do you think?" he asked, and she realized he had let go of her hand. He'd gone over to the windows and was pulling back the draperies. Now was the time for her to go—just run. *Run.*

But then he was at her side again, his hand combing through her hair, and she was too frightened to move. "It's very pretty," she lied.

The room, and the house, had once been pretty, but now they felt and smelled as if they were rotting away. Armies of mice and silver-fish and woodworm were nibbling away at his house, and Jeremy didn't seem to notice or care.

"My mother hasn't been here in years. She and my father never come in from the country. They live their lives, and I live mine, and they don't care that it's all gone. That my inheritance is nothing but this moldering heap and mountains of debt. I'll never be free of it. And now I'm almost out of time."

He twisted her hair in his fingers, winding it tight, so tight she couldn't move her head. "You are very pretty, you know."

He began to kiss her, and his mouth was a little too hard against hers, his fingers pressing a fraction too tightly against the soft skin of her arm, and he didn't seem to notice, or care, that he was pulling her hair.

It was the first time he had kissed her and she didn't like anything about it. "Jeremy," she said. "Please stop."

His hand moved from her arm to her breast, kneading, pawing, and one of his fingernails scraped against the soft skin just above her brassiere. She flinched, and he laughed softly.

"Were you expecting hearts and flowers? Stupid, silly girl."

"I wasn't expecting anything. I'd like to go downstairs now."

"Why did you think I brought you here, if not for this?"

"You said you wanted to show me the house, and now I've seen it and I'd like to go home."

"Stupid, silly girl," he repeated, and he pulled at her hair so sharply that tears came to her eyes. He might do anything to her now, for they were alone in the house. She was alone and she had gone into this bedroom with him willingly, or at least that was how anyone else would see it.

He propelled her backward, one stumbling step after another, and then the back of her knees hit something. It was the bed, the *bed*, and he pushed her back, finally letting go of her hair, but only so he might pull at her skirt, higher and higher, oblivious to her slapping hands. The same fingernail that had caught at her breast before now tore one of her stockings. It laddered, splintering, and he laughed, a cold, sharp *heh* that killed the last of her hope.

"No, Jeremy! I said *no*! I'll scream," she threatened, and she pushed at his shoulders with all her strength. It made no difference.

"There's no one to hear you. My sister's staying with friends, and the daily girl doesn't come in until eight. Scream all you like." And then, his mouth hot against her ear, "I actually rather like it."

He wrenched aside the crotch of her knickers. "That's better," he said, and then he spat. She flinched, but he'd aimed the spittle at his own hand. It made no sense—why should he do such a thing?

He opened the flies on his trousers, and now he was rubbing his wet hand over his—no, *no*—and he pushed at her legs, forcing them wide, and the horror of his invasion, the tearing, wrenching brutality of it, stunned her into immobility.

What had she done for him to be so cruel? Or was this what it was simply like? Did all women have to endure such indignities? Were the love stories Milly had read aloud to her all lies?

Everything had been a lie.

He was so heavy, and his breath against her face was so rank, and everything he was doing was so painful and disgusting, and the sounds he made under his breath were just awful. Filthy words, over and over, right against her ear, and soft, whining groans that turned her stomach.

She hardly noticed when he rolled off her.

"Up you get," he said, slapping at her thigh. He sounded almost playful. "You'll want to clean yourself up. I'll see you downstairs."

How long did she stay there, her legs splayed open, her eyes hot and dry and sightless? She had to get up, she knew, and find some way out, but it was a long while before she was able to move. Even then the room spun around her and she had to fight hard not to be sick.

She noticed an open door, and beyond it the cool gleam of white tile, and somehow she managed to stand and then stumble to the bathroom. She was still wearing her shoes.

She switched on the light above the sink, and was surprised by the woman she found in the mirror. Eyes wild, face ghostly pale, hair dull and straggling and damp against her neck.

A stack of linen hand towels, impossibly fine, sat on a table next to the sink. She wet one of them with cold water, wrung it out, and wiped her face. Then her breasts, where a long, livid scratch had risen against her milky skin. And, last, between her legs. She had to rinse the towel again and again, but after a while the water no longer ran pink.

She pulled down her skirt, straightened her ruined stockings, and, after a moment's hesitation, stepped out of her torn knickers and stuffed them in the bin. Her blouse was intact, for the buttons had obediently popped through their holes when he'd tugged it open.

He was in the kitchen, and her bag was on the table. He must have taken it with him when he'd gone downstairs. He had made himself a sandwich and a cup of tea, and he didn't even look up when she came in.

"I'd like to go home," she said.

"Fine. You know the way out. I hope you didn't make a mess on my mother's bed."

"No," she said, enjoying a moment of perverse pride in her lie. There was no easy way to get blood out of silk brocade. She put on her coat, which he'd thrown over the back of a chair, and picked up her bag.

She stared at him, wondering how he could be so calm. So unaffected by what he had done to her. "Why?" she said at last.

He kept eating his sandwich, bite after bite, and when it was gone he wiped his mouth with the back of his hand and went to set the empty plate in the sink. Only then did he turn to look at her.

"You have no idea what it costs to live properly. No idea of the expectations people have, of the things I've had to force myself to do, just to keep a foot in the door."

"It was all lies."

"In the main, yes. I kept hoping you might be silly enough to tell me about that bloody gown. But not a word—not one word. And I couldn't come straight out and ask, could I? You'd have run in the other direction if I'd said a thing. I've wasted weeks on you, and I'm no further ahead than I was in August."

"So it was revenge just now?"

"That? That was me having some fun. You, too, if you'd bothered to unclench your teeth."

"You raped me."

"Did I? You came to this house with me. You walked upstairs on your own. You let me kiss you. There isn't a judge in this land who'd agree it was rape."

"But I know it was. You can try to forget, but it will never leave you. I know, and you know, that you are the farthest thing in the world from a decent man." She walked to the side door and tore it open. "I hope you drown in your debts. It's no less than you deserve."

She didn't look back. Her heart pounding out of her chest, she ran up the darkened steps, through the garden and garage, and back into the mews. She ran until she could see lights and traffic and safety ahead.

Soon she would be home. She would be home, and safe, and she'd have a hot bath and a still hotter cup of tea, and she would mend the parts of her he'd broken.

He had been a mistake. That was all. The sort of mistake she'd never be stupid enough to make again.

The sort of mistake she would take to her grave.

Chapter Twenty-Three

Miriam

November 10, 1947

Something was wrong with Ann. Miriam was certain of it. About a month ago she had fallen ill with some nameless malady, and it had left her wan and shaky, her stomach so upset that she hadn't been able to face anything more than tea and toast. Still she'd gone to work, faithful to the dictates of the great project before them, but the long days had left her flattened. It had gone on like that for weeks, and no matter how often Miriam begged her Ann would not go to the doctor.

"All I need is some sleep," she kept saying. "I'll feel better after I've had a good night's sleep."

Miriam had tried to cheer her with news of Ruby's baby, for was it not the case that everyone loved to hear about babies? She had shown her pictures of the infant, named Victoria in recognition of her parents having become engaged on VE Day, and Ann had nodded and agreed the baby was very sweet, her voice an almost inaudible monotone.

"Is anything the matter?" Miriam had asked.

"No, not at all. Please do pass on my best wishes to your friends."

At the end of October, when Princess Elizabeth had asked Monsieur Hartnell to nominate three women from his staff to attend the wedding ceremony, Ann, together with Miss Duley and Miss Holliday from sewing, had been chosen for the honor. Ann had smiled, and accepted the other women's congratulations, and had sworn she was indeed excited beyond belief, but Miriam had remained unconvinced. Her friend was unhappy, deeply so, and her melancholy only seemed to deepen as the day of the royal wedding grew near.

This past weekend, Miriam had watched Ann's every move, and when she realized, as of Sunday night, that her friend had eaten only a few crackers over the course of two days, she had made up a mug of Bovril and taken it upstairs. It was that or summon the local doctor.

"Ann, *ma belle,* will you let me come in and give you this Bovril? It smells vile but I know you like it. I am worried that you have not eaten. Will you let me come in?"

Ann had opened the door, still in her nightgown and robe, and had tried to smile. "Thank you. I'm sorry I made you worry."

"Is anything the matter?" Miriam had asked gently.

"No," Ann had said, and she'd hidden her face behind the mug of Bovril, and Miriam had known she was lying. She knew it because she would have done the same. "I do feel badly that I didn't go to church today. Since it's Remembrance Sunday."

"It is only one year. And we can observe the silence on Tuesday, on the eleventh, as we still do in France. Even if it is only the two of us in the corner of the workroom."

By Monday morning Ann seemed a little better, and Miriam began to hope she might be on the mend. She had some porridge for breakfast, and she even managed a bit of conversation as they sat on the train. How awful the weather had been and how cold it was for November, yet not once did she smile. Not once.

They were in the cloakroom with the other women, on the point of going downstairs to begin their day, when Ruthie upended everything. Digging in her bag, she extracted a newspaper and held it up so they all might see the front page. It featured a drawing of a woman in a long white gown, a veil streaming from her dark hair, a small bouquet in one of her hands. Above, in large, jet-black type, was the headline:

EXCLUSIVE TO THE EXAMINER
THE GOWN OF THE CENTURY

"Can you believe it? 'Gown of the century,' they say, and it's not even the right dress! I wonder where they got it from."

Ann had been rummaging through her own bag, oblivious to the talk around them, and now she grew still, a sudden gasp hitching in her throat. Miriam looked to her friend, but she had shut her eyes.

"Does it say anything more?" Ann asked.

"Hold on . . . here goes:

> "'Our insider source at the Mayfair premises of Norman Hartnell has provided us with this exclusive peek at Princess Elizabeth's sensational wedding gown more than a month before the rest of the world gets to see it. We can reveal that it is made of white silk and is covered with "a king's ransom" of diamonds and pearls, in the words of our top secret source. Behind the closed doors and whitewashed windows of his exclusive atelier, Mr. Hartnell has teams of seamstresses and embroiderers working around

the clock on the finery that the princess and all her family, including the queen herself, will wear to Westminster
Abbey. More news inside, including behind-the-scenes details and an estimate of how much this fairy-tale gown is
likely to cost.'"

"None of it is true," Miriam said. "How can they print such things? And this gown—it is not even close. Why do they bother?"

"Pounds, shillings, and pence," Ethel said. "Just think how many newspapers they'll sell today. Doesn't matter that Mr. Hartnell and the palace will say they've got it wrong. People will believe it until they see the princess on her big day."

They were saved from further discussion by Ethel's exclamation that it was half eight already and Miss Duley would be waiting, so they all trooped downstairs, Ann as silent as the grave, and moved to their usual places, clustered around the princess's bridal train in its long, cumbersome frame, and Miriam listened to the same whispered discussions they'd been having for weeks now. Husbands, beaux, rationing woes, gossip about film stars, and none of it was noteworthy enough to hold her attention. Not when Ann was suffering so.

She worked in silence, and she watched her friend wither before her eyes, and before long Miriam had had enough. Rather than follow the others down to the canteen at morning break, she took Ann's arm and led her to the cloakroom.

"What . . . ?"

"Come with me," Miriam hissed. "Wait until we are alone."

Once in the cloakroom, Miriam retreated to the bench in the far corner, by the masking noises of the ever-clanking radiator, and patted the spot beside her. "Come. Something is wrong, and I insist you tell me what it is."

She waited, and waited, and at last Ann came to join her.

"The sketch of the wedding gown in the newspaper," Ann whispered. "It's mine."

"How is that possible? I know you would never—"

"It was stolen from my sketchbook, the blue one I sometimes carry around in my bag. I checked earlier and there's a page missing. I think it was cut out of the book."

"You are certain of this?"

"Yes. I mean, I could look again. But I know it's not there."

Suddenly Miriam remembered the night she and Ann had sat at the kitchen table and shared glimpses of their work with one another. Her drawing of Grand-Père offering the *kiddouch* blessing, and Ann's drawing of a bridal gown. "Is it the dress you showed me? Doris's dress?" It had been hard to see the picture in the newspaper from across the room, but thinking on it, now, she did recognize the sketch. It was indeed Ann's work.

"Yes."

"I understand that you are upset it was stolen, but why are you so worried? What is there to connect you to it?"

"My handwriting. 'Fit for a princess,' I wrote at the bottom, and I added in little details, too. About how there was a secret good-luck motif for the bride. Miss Duley will know. As soon as she takes a good look at that newspaper she'll know."

"Surely she will understand."

"I'm awful at drawing figures. Getting the proportions right and so on. So I traced one of Mr. Hartnell's sketches from his last collection. Just the arms and head. But it will look as if I was trying to pass off his work as my own. What was I thinking?"

"You say the drawing was cut from your sketchbook. Who might have taken it? Who even knew you had such a thing in your bag?"

"I showed the sketch to Doris. It was meant to be her dress, after all. We were in the canteen at dinner, with everyone sitting around the table. But I— Oh, God, no. *No*."

"What is it?" Miriam asked, thoroughly rattled.

"I know who did it," Ann muttered, her voice thick with suppressed tears. "Jeremy."

"Why? Why would he do such a thing?"

"He said information about the gown would be worth a king's ransom in the right hands. He was so angry. He'd thought a few evenings out would soften me up, and I'd tell him everything he wanted to know, or I'd let something slip. But I never said a thing, and he . . ."

"What did he do?"

Ann covered her face with her hands. "Nothing. Nothing."

"When did he take the drawing?" Miriam pressed. "Could it have been the night you last saw him?"

"It must have been. I was . . . I was in the other room. For a while. And he was alone with my bag, and I think he looked through it then. I don't know why, though, because he knew I don't have any money. I don't have anything worth taking."

"Had he known about your sketchbook?"

Ann shook her head, wiped at her eyes. "No. At least I don't think he did. Oh, Miriam. He must have thought he'd won the pools. A sketchbook full of designs, and a grand wedding dress right at the end. With a label just in case it wasn't clear. 'Fit for a princess.' I'm going to be sick."

"Put your head between your knees," Miriam directed her. "Yes. Breathe deeply. You are not going to be sick, and you did not do anything wrong. It is not the correct gown, to begin with. If anything, this will make things better for all of us. The journalists will think they have uncovered the secret. They will leave us all alone."

"I have to tell Miss Duley and Mr. Hartnell. I have to tell them what happened."

Did Ann not possess a single gram of self-preservation? To admit the truth of it, blameless though she was, would be madness. But that was an argument for another day.

"Wait until we know more. After work, I shall go to see Walter. He will be able to help. I am certain he will help."

"What can he do?" Ann whispered wretchedly.

"To begin with, he can confirm that this Jeremy, *cet espèce de con*, is the thief. Now, tell me everything you remember about him."

THERE WASN'T TIME, in what was left of the day, for Miriam to run out and find a telephone box and ring Walter at his office. He worked late most evenings, though, and she did have the telephone number for his flat. One way or another she would find him.

He'd taken her to his office once before, so she knew the way—a good thing, too, since the door to the *Picture Weekly* premises was tucked away on a side street.

The receptionist remembered Miriam from her previous visit. "Miss Dassin. What a pleasant surprise."

"Is he in?" She would apologize later for her abrupt manner.

"He is—no need to wait. Just go along down the hall. If you don't find him in his office, come back and I'll help you."

He was at his desk, hunched low over a sheaf of typewritten pages, and even from the doorway she could see how he'd marked them up with slashes and notations in red pencil.

"Walter," she said, and he looked up, startled from his thoughts.

"Miriam," he said, smiling. And then, "Something is wrong."

"Yes. I am sorry to bother you here, but I need your help."

He came round his desk, shut the door, and cleared a mountain of books from two battered chairs. "Sit down, next to me here, and tell me what is the matter."

"I know you had nothing to do with it. I must say this at the start. I want you to know this, and that I have not come to accuse you of anything."

"The gown," he said. "On the front page of *The Examiner*."

"Yes," she acknowledged. "Although it is not the real gown. It is not even close."

"So why the concern?"

"The drawing was stolen from Ann. Her handwriting is on it."

"Bloody hell."

"She believes it was taken by a man she was seeing. They had dinner about a month ago and at one point he was alone with her bag for some time. He cut the drawing from her sketchbook then."

"Does she have any proof?"

Miriam shook her head. "None at all."

"Could one of your colleagues at—"

"No. It would have been easier to make their own drawing. And they—we—are all loyal to Monsieur Hartnell. None of us would do such a thing."

"Of course. What does he look like? The thief? Have you ever met him?"

"Only the once. It was the same night you and I met. He came up to Ann at the Astoria and asked her to dance. He was very handsome. Tall and fair and beautifully dressed."

Kaz pulled a notebook from his coat pocket and, balancing it on his knee, began to take notes. "His name?"

"Jeremy Thickett-Milne."

"Age?"

"I think about thirty? Ann was not certain."

"Anything else?"

"She told me he was an officer in the war. A guard of some kind?"

"With a Guards regiment? Yes? Any idea which one? No matter. And did Ann say what he does for a living? Assuming that he works, of course."

"Oh—I ought to have said. He is an aide to Queen Mary. So I suppose that makes him very important."

"Not necessarily. Young, ex-Guards, tall and good-looking . . . more likely there for decoration. Think of him as a footman with a better line in small talk." He closed the notebook, capped his pen, and rubbed at his eyes. "That'll do for now. Let me ask around—discreetly, I promise—and I'll meet you and Ann later. Shall I come out to your house? Say around ten o'clock? It may take a few hours."

"I do not wish to inconvenience you," she protested. "Barking is very far."

"Nonsense. I'll try to be with you by ten, but don't fret if I'm late."

"Thank you."

"I should tell you that the editor of *The Examiner* is an old enemy of mine. I gave Nigel the sack some years ago and he hasn't forgiven me. It won't be as simple as my just ringing him up."

"Then what will you do?"

"Nigel runs that rag on a shoestring. He wouldn't have been able to offer much by payment for the drawing, and that makes me think your thief likely went elsewhere first. I'll ring up some friends and find out if he approached any of them."

"So I should go home and wait?"

"Yes. Tell Miss Hughes not to panic. It may help her to know that Hartnell was already planning to reveal the design to the press on the thirteenth. Ruby received her invitation at the beginning of October. I wouldn't be surprised if that's what prompted the theft of Ann's drawing. After then, you see, it won't be worth a penny."

"Will everyone see the design then?"

"Not everyone. Only a handful of writers from the broadsheets and weekly magazines. And there'll be an embargo until the wedding day."

"I do not know this word. Embargo?"

"A restriction. We agree not to describe the dress or print any photographs of the design until November twentieth. In principle, it means we can have our write-ups ready for the day of the wedding."

"What of those who break this embargo?"

"They never get a return invitation. That's incentive enough."

WALTER KNOCKED ON their door at half-past ten that night. It had been raining, and in lieu of a mackintosh or coat he had thought only to wrap a long and moth-eaten scarf around his neck.

"Did you walk all the way from the station?" she asked worriedly, though he didn't seem especially rain-sodden.

"I borrowed Bennett's car."

"Come through to the back with me. Even if you are not wet, you must be cold. I will make you some tea."

She led him to the kitchen, and he greeted Ann with a gentle handshake and an apology for his lateness. Miriam took his jacket, just so she might hang it on the drying rack before the sitting room fire, and he looked so handsome in his shirtsleeves and ink-stained tweed vest, and his expression was so kind and understanding, that her heart cracked a little at the sight of him.

"I do have some answers for you," he began. "It's all pretty much as you suspected. This Thickett-Milne started shopping around your drawing last month. Not under his real name. He rang up a friend of mine around a fortnight ago. Told him he had details of the princess's wedding gown and insisted they meet at the bar of a hotel up in Bayswater. He appeared to be wearing a false mustache, if you can believe it."

"Did he have the drawing with him then?" Ann asked.

"Yes. Insisted it was from Hartnell himself. Asked for five thousand pounds."

"Five thousand pounds?" Miriam echoed. "He must be mad."

"Not mad," Ann said flatly. "Desperate."

"And desperate men do awful things," Walter agreed. "My friend just laughed in his face. Told Milne he'd have better luck with the Americans. Of course he didn't, otherwise he wouldn't have ended up at *The Examiner.* I'd be surprised if Nigel—he's the editor there— was able to scrape together even a hundred pounds."

"Why was no one interested?" Miriam asked. "I thought the entire world was hoping to see the gown before the wedding."

"The handwriting on the sketch gave it away. Totally different to Hartnell's. Everyone knew it was a fake. And with the preview of the gown so soon, why take the risk?"

Ann's eyes were closed, her fists clenched, her face stark with agony. Miriam looked to Walter and, understanding, he nodded.

"I had best head back into London. I'll leave you with a copy of my card, and of course Miriam knows how to find me. If there is anything else I can do, please let me know."

Back in the front vestibule, Walter shrugged on his jacket and knotted his scarf around his neck once more. "I meant what I said before. If there is anything I can do to help, call me straightaway. Do you promise?"

"I do."

"Very well. I'll say good night." He bent his head, set a fleeting kiss upon her cheek, and retreated into the night.

Ann had not moved. Her hands were folded on her lap, and she was staring, her expression unfathomable, at the cooling mug of tea that Walter had left untouched.

"I'll be sacked," she whispered. "I know it."

"You do not know any such thing. Monsieur Hartnell is a good man. A fair man. He gave me a position even after I forced myself into his office without permission or an invitation. I am certain that he will understand."

"And if he doesn't?" Ann's voice was so flat, so devoid of hope.

"Imagine the worst thing that can happen to you. Are you thinking of it? Now tell me. What is it? What would ruin your life?"

"I . . . I can't talk of it. I can't." Ann shook her head and covered her face with her hands, and in that moment Miriam knew. It was all she could do not to run into the night with a knife in her hand, find the wicked man who had brutalized her friend, and thrust its blade into his black heart.

"You do not have to say any more, *ma belle*. I will not ask it of you. But I wish you to know that not so long ago I, too, believed my life was over. That my dreams were dead and buried, along with those I loved, and the most I could expect from the days left to me was to endure. But I do not believe that now. I have hope."

"How?"

"Because of you, and Walter, and the other friends I have made here. You have changed everything for me. I will not say that anything is possible, for we both know the world is too broken for such a thing, and there are people like this Jeremy who will try to stand in your way. But you have many friends. This you must know. And you are not alone."

"But—"

"But you are young and intelligent and kind and strong. Too strong to let him win. And that is what will happen if you allow him to ruin your life."

Ann nodded, and wiped her eyes, and then she took Miriam's hand in hers and held it tight.

"What now?"

"I will go with you tomorrow. If you wish to see Monsieur Hartnell I will stand at your side, and I will fight for you if it comes to that. And if, as you fear, the worst should happen? I will still be at your side."

WATCHING ANN TELL Miss Duley of her betrayal was exceedingly painful. Miriam knew her friend would survive, and perhaps one day be happy again, but she would never forget the humiliation visited upon her by Jeremy Thickett-Milne.

"I am so sorry," Ann said when she had finished recounting the entire sorry tale. "I should never have gone out with him. I know that now."

"How could you have known? Oh, my dear girl."

"I swear I never said a thing about the gown. I never even told him I worked here."

"I believe you. Now, this drawing of yours—who was it for again?"

"It was for Doris. I'd had some ideas for how she might make over her mum's wedding dress, and I did up a sketch for her as a keepsake. I liked it so well I made a version of it for myself in my book. My good sketchbook."

"Only for your private use? Not because you had a thought of setting up shop on your own?" Miss Duley pressed.

"Me? *No.* I'd never do that. It was just a way of passing the time.

And it's not as if they're very good. Set next to one of Mr. Hartnell's drawings, it's as plain as day that he's the artist, not me."

Miss Duley sighed, swiped a hand over her eyes, and then she went to the mirror and smoothed back her hair. "I suppose we had better tell Mr. Hartnell, if only to reassure him there's no spy in our midst."

"Don't you believe me?" Ann asked, an edge of panic creeping into her voice.

"Of course I do. But now that you've told me we have to tell him, too. Let's get it over with."

Miss Duley called up to Mrs. Price, just to make sure he was in his office and alone, and then they set off, as gloomy as if they'd been herded into the back of a tumbrel.

He was in a cheerful mood, fortunately, but then again he nearly always seemed to be in good spirits. "Come in, Miss Duley, ladies. Do sit down. Is anything the matter?"

"Yes and no, sir. We've come about the article in *The Examiner* yesterday."

"Dreadful rag. Useful for lining a rubbish bin but not much more."

"I agree, sir. The thing is, Miss Hughes came to me just now, and she has a . . . well, a story to tell about how the drawing ended up in that paper, and I'm hoping you'll hear her out."

Monsieur Hartnell had begun to frown. "Very well. Do go on, Miss Hughes."

Every particle of color had drained away from Ann's face, and her hands, which she held tightly clasped in her lap, were shaking. "The drawing was stolen from me, from a sketchbook I sometimes carry in my handbag. I draw things I'd like to make for myself, or for friends, if I had all the time in the world and could afford really lovely materials. I'd drawn a wedding dress for Doris a while back.

Just some ideas I'd had on how to make over her mum's old dress so it looked new and fit her properly. One version stayed in my book and the other went to Doris. Only, well, I'm not very good at people's faces or hands, so I'd traced those parts from one of your drawings. Just to get the proportions right. And I wrote 'fit for a princess' at the bottom, only I don't know why, now, that I did that. I think I must have been feeling a bit silly and romantic that day."

"So you are saying that someone stole a drawing that you had created for your own personal use, and having taken it from you then sold it to a newspaper under the pretext of it being a copy of my design?"

"Yes, sir. I'm so sorry."

"I appreciate your honesty very much, Miss Hughes, but I fail to see why you are so worried. There isn't a person in England who believes it to be an actual sketch of the princess's wedding gown. If the editor of *The Examiner* paid more than a fiver for it, he's a bigger fool than I'd imagined. I'm certainly not going to chastise you for playing an inadvertent role in its publication."

"But the queen . . . Princess Elizabeth . . ." Ann faltered. "Won't they be upset? What if they think someone here went to the press?"

"I doubt either of them even noticed. Even if they did, they're used to people printing lies about them. I suppose it goes along with the job." He paused to light a cigarette and then, his nerves suitably soothed, he directed his attention at Ann once again. "You didn't say how the drawing was stolen. It wasn't someone from here, was it?"

"No, sir," said Miss Duley, her face reddening in indignation. "Certainly not."

"It was a man I was seeing," Ann explained. "I met him just before you were awarded the commission for the gown. He thought he could get me to tell him something about the design, but I knew not to say anything, not even to admit I worked here. And then, about a month ago, he took me out and . . ."

"That is when he took the drawing," Miriam intervened, for the last of Ann's composure was melting away. "That is when he stole it from her."

"My goodness. What a dreadful experience for you. I had no idea a journalist would stoop to such villainous behavior," Monsieur Hartnell said, his brow creased in a sympathetic frown.

"No, sir," Miriam said. "He was not a journalist. Only a man with debts to pay."

"I see. In any event, I can assure you that it did us no harm. No one from the palace has breathed a word to me on the matter, and if ever they do I can quite confidently swear that the scoundrel responsible has nothing to do with us."

"You see?" Miss Duley said, and reached over to hug Ann's hunched shoulders. "She was that worried, sir. Was all but certain you'd give her the sack."

"For that? Heavens, no. Miss Hughes, you are one of my best embroiderers. I'd be a fool to let you go."

Miriam smiled at his compliment for her friend, and resolved to remind Ann of it later. No doubt she would need to be reassured often in the coming days.

"If that's all, sir?" Miss Duley asked.

"Not quite. There was a small notation on the printed version of your drawing, Miss Hughes, which mentioned a 'good-luck' motif. In the article they speculated it was a four-leafed clover. Is that the case?"

"No, sir. It was a sprig of white heather. Just like the pots of heather the queen brought us all from Balmoral. I read somewhere that it brings good luck, so I added it to Doris's dress."

"Hmm. I'm trying to picture it, but all I can see are tiny white flowers. Like a spikier version of lily of the valley. Not a very charming sort of blossom."

"It can look that way, but the trick is in making the flowers tiny enough, and arranging them just so on the stems."

"I like it. Yes, I do. A secret motif on the gown, something that no one apart from the four of us, and the princess, will know about. Would you make me up a sample? Nothing too large—say two inches square at the most? If you can make it look like an actual sprig of white heather, we'll find a place for it on the train. What do you think, Miss Duley?"

"I think it's a splendid idea. How long do you think it will take to do up a sample, Ann?"

"An hour or two? Maybe a bit more? I'm thinking of seed pearls for the blossoms and rocaille beads for the stems."

"Perfect. See, Miss Hughes? There's a silver lining to every cloud, and you've found one for us with your splendid idea. Now go work your magic on that sample."

The three of them thanked him, and Miss Duley and Ann took their leave, but Miriam turned back at the door. It was the work of a moment to provide Monsieur Hartnell with one last detail regarding the theft of her friend's drawing.

"His name is Jeremy Thickett-Milne. That is the swine who betrayed my friend."

Chapter Twenty-Four

Heather

September 2, 2016

*H*eather would never forget her afternoon at Buckingham Palace with Miriam and Daniel. They passed through something like twenty state rooms on their tour, each one bigger and richer and grander than the last. They took their time because Miriam, though steady on her feet, didn't walk very fast. She was also full of interesting anecdotes about the times she and Walter had been invited to dinners there, and of course the occasion twenty-five years earlier when she had been made a dame.

"Do you remember what the queen said to you?" Heather asked excitedly.

"Would you believe I do not? I was terribly nervous, so it all went by in a blur. I do remember how very blue her eyes were, and also how very enormous the diamonds were in her brooch. One of them was as big as an egg yolk."

They were in the White Drawing Room when Miriam turned to her with a mischievous smile.

"So? What do you think?"

"Is it wrong to think it's a bit much? I mean, everything is really beautiful, but it's all so overwhelming."

"I do not disagree. But this is not meant to be a home. At least, not this part of the palace. This is the queen's place of business, I suppose you could say. I imagine their private homes—Balmoral, for instance—are much less formal."

"The sort of places where a corgi wouldn't get in trouble for jumping on the furniture?"

"Precisely."

Before long they had arrived at the beginning of the *Fashioning a Reign* exhibition, and though Heather was keen to go straight to the queen's wedding gown, she didn't feel comfortable in rushing Miriam along. By the time they reached the ballroom, where the wedding and coronation gowns were on display, as well as the most spectacular of the queen's many formal gowns, Heather's heart was racing in anticipation.

Of course there were a ton of people just planted in front of the glass case that held the wedding gown and train, and despite the barrage of death glares Heather aimed at their backs, they took their sweet time in moving on. When a space finally did open up, Daniel caught Heather's eye. Together they moved forward and installed themselves directly in front of the display case, leaving ample room between them for Miriam.

Heather was surprised, now that she was able to see the gown, to find that it had been arranged on a slanted backdrop, the folds of its skirts propped up by invisible supports. The train, too, had been laid flat, with the nearest part of it only inches away from the edge of the case.

"Did you and Nan do all of that?" she asked.

"Oh, no. We were responsible for the bodice and sleeves, but for the embroidery of the skirt panels there were four of us, and the train itself had six or eight embroiderers. Perhaps more—my memory is not as clear as it ought to be. What do you think of it all?"

"I think it's amazing. I'm a little overwhelmed, to be honest." The gown was so close that she could make out even the smallest details, many of them already familiar from her careful study of Nan's embroidered samples. "Which is your favorite part?" she asked Miriam.

"That is a very good question, and one I have not been asked before. I suppose it would be the heather."

"Like Scottish heather?"

"Yes. It was Ann's idea. Two small sprigs of white heather, and no one apart from us, Mr. Hartnell, and Miss Duley knew about them. If you count up from the bottom center of the train, they are just between the fourth and fifth of the central roses. Can you see them? Yes? She added them at the very last, and I doubt that anyone else in the world knows of their significance. I am not sure if even the queen herself knows they are there."

They remained in the ballroom for close to another hour, spending long minutes in front of nearly every other gown, and by the time they came to the exit Heather was ready to fall over. Daniel seemed to feel the same way, for he directed them to the refreshment tent, found them a table with a terrific view of the lawn and gardens, and promised to return with something delicious. "I can't promise they'll have decent coffee, Mimi, but they might run to a glass of champagne."

At this Miriam brightened visibly. "Wouldn't that be a treat?"

Unfortunately, there was no champagne to be had, but Daniel did buy coffee for himself and Miriam, a tea for Heather, and plates of éclairs and scones for them to share.

"I can't believe I'm sitting in the private gardens at Buckingham Palace having a cup of tea. And with *you*, Miriam. I'm not sure if Nan believed in heaven, but if she could see us now I bet she'd be happy."

"I am certain of it, *ma belle*. Now, I must ask before I forget — are you coming to the reception on Sunday evening? I told Daniel that he must invite you."

"I told you, Mimi—Heather is going home that morning."

"Of course. Yes, you did tell me. Such a shame."

"I could change my flight home," Heather said impulsively, and only after the words were out did she decide she absolutely would change her flight. It would probably cost a bomb, and she would have the mother of all credit-card bills next month, but she was going to do it. "I'll sort it out as soon as I get back to the hotel."

They set off for a walk through the gardens as soon as Miriam had finished her coffee, and although Heather would have loved to visit the gift shop, it was clear the older woman was running out of steam. Daniel flagged down a taxi as soon as they passed through the exit gates, one of the big black ones that seemed to have room for about ten people inside, and they set off for Hampstead.

"Are you sure?" Daniel whispered in her ear after a few minutes had passed. "About your flight, I mean."

"Of course I'm sure. I'll probably only have to pay a change fee. It really isn't a big deal."

"If you say so. I will warn you that most of the guests at the reception will be members of my family. Cousins galore, and Mimi is insisting that everyone bring their children. It'll be a miracle if the reception ends without some sort of alarm being triggered."

They saw Miriam upstairs, and after ensuring she was comfortable in her chair, Daniel prepared her a coffee, steadfastly ignoring his grandmother's insistence that he overlook the canister marked *décaféiné.*

"It's decaf or nothing, Mimi," he insisted. "Otherwise you'll be up half the night."

Heather approached Miriam so she might say good night and have her cheeks kissed, promising again that she would change her flight home, and then she retreated to the far side of the room so Daniel might speak to Miriam. He crouched beside her, and he let her fuss with his hair, smoothing it off his brow, and the look of love on his face was enough to crack Heather's heart in two.

"*Si t'as besoin de quoi que ce soit, tu dois m'appeler,*" he said. "*Tu connais mon numéro.*" Call me if you need anything. You know my number.

"*Oui, oui. Et maintenant, je veux que tu ailles dîner avec Heather. Ton intelligence va l'épater—*" Yes, yes. Now go and take Heather to dinner. Wow her with your intelligence—

"*Ça suffit, Mimi—*" Enough, Mimi—

"*—et ton charme.*" —and your charm.

"*Tu sais que je t'aime. Même si tu me gênes devant Heather.*" You know I love you. Even though you're embarrassing me in front of Heather.

Heather tried not to listen, but they weren't lowering their voices, and short of walking out the door or putting her fingers in her ears there wasn't much she could do. All the same, she had to tell him that she'd heard and understood. She waited until they were outside and walking up the hill to the Tube station, having agreed on the way downstairs that a cab would take forever that late in the afternoon.

"I guess I should tell you that my stereotypical Canadian-ness extends to speaking French. I'd have said something, but I didn't want to intrude."

"You weren't intruding. I just hope you didn't mind being talked about as if you weren't there. Normally I'd have switched to English, but when she gets tired she prefers French."

"I didn't mind at all. And I do find you charming and intelligent. Just so you know."

"I'll file that away for future reference. Before we go much farther, though, where would you like to eat? Are you in the mood for anything in particular?"

"Anything at all."

"I've a place in mind. Italian food, hasn't changed in years, and not so very far from your hotel."

It was hard to talk much on the Tube, which was packed tight for rush hour. Daniel took hold of her hand as he led them from one train to another, and in far less time than she'd have thought possible they were emerging into the early evening sunshine.

"Where are we?" she asked, blinking in the golden light.

"A bit south of Clerkenwell. That's where we'll find the Victory Café."

Had Heather been on her own, she'd never have found the restaurant; and had she happened to walk by, she'd probably have dismissed it out of hand. The sign was faded and hard to read, the front window was steamy and disguised the interior, and the menu, posted outside, was handwritten and of a haiku-like simplicity. But the smells drifting out the door were divine.

Daniel ushered them inside and, waving a hello to someone at the back, led them to the only unoccupied table.

"What do you think?" he asked.

"It's perfect. Much more my kind of place than one of those trendy fusion spots where everything is layered in little piles, and they put a dot of foam on the plate and insist it's one of the vegetables."

"I'd never dream of doing such a thing to you," he said, grinning. "Now let's decide on what we're eating. I'm starving."

It wasn't a first date, of course it wasn't, but it felt like one, and Heather's nerves insisted on thrumming with excitement the whole time they were ordering their meal and deciding on a bottle of wine. The impulse only deepened when he rolled back his sleeves and she caught sight of the tattoo on his wrist.

"When I first saw it, I thought you'd written a note to yourself," she said. "Your to-do list, maybe."

"Milk, eggs, bread? There's an idea."

He flattened his arm upon the table so she could see the lines of script that ran parallel to the tendons of his inner wrist.

I would have poured my spirit without stint.
But not through wounds; not on the cess of war.
Foreheads of men have bled where no wounds were.

"It's familiar, somehow . . ."

"Wilfred Owen. From one of his long poems. 'Strange Meeting.' You might have read it in school."

"Is that your handwriting?"

He shook his head. "Owen's. Taken from the manuscript of the poem. Mine is illegible."

"I like it," she said. "You don't regret it, do you?"

"Not precisely. The sentiment is the same, but I doubt I'd choose to immortalize it in the same way today. I was nineteen when I got it, which is about the same age as many of my students."

"What do they think of it?"

"When they notice they're usually gobsmacked. At least one per term is brave enough to ask me about it."

"What do you say?"

"I tell them my grandmother's family had tattoos forced upon them before they were murdered at Auschwitz, but I was able to choose the one I wear. I tell them it reminds me why I teach the history of the world wars."

"Did you always want to be a history professor?" she asked.

"Not at first. I wanted to follow in my grandfather's footsteps. He was a journalist, a rather famous one, at least in this country, and I idolized him."

"What changed your mind?"

"The summer I was eighteen, just before I went up to Oxford, he took me out to lunch, and at some point we began to talk about what I'd been studying and what interested me and so forth. The same conversation we'd been having for years, but that day it felt rather more serious. More momentous, I suppose. He told me that he'd read history as an undergraduate, and while he'd been very happy with the direction his professional life had taken, he did regret that he hadn't become a historian. He felt it would have helped him to better understand the war he had lived through and written about. And then he died a few weeks later, and if there'd been room on my arms I'd have tattoos of every word he said that day."

"But instead you picked the poetry."

"I did. And I can't say I regret it."

"So you became a historian because of your grandfather."

"Yes, but also because of Mimi and the murder of her family. My family. I've been studying and writing about the Holocaust in France for close to twenty years, and even if I keep on for another century I'll still have questions to ask. I'll still be searching for answers."

"Isn't it depressing?"

"At times, yes, but that's true of a lot of jobs. And I only live with the shadow of what happened, whereas Mimi's entire life has been marked by it. Scarred, if I'm honest. So I cannot bring myself to turn away."

Their food arrived, and their talk turned to lighter, softer, easier things. Daniel's students and the courses he was teaching. Heather's little apartment, her cat, her friends. Places they'd been on vacation and dream destinations they aspired to visit. Nothing to make the food in her mouth grow tasteless, or the wine she swallowed turn to vinegar. Nothing to make her worry about what was to come when she went home to Toronto and what she would do with her life.

They cleared their plates and Daniel refilled their glasses, and the silence between them was comfortable, and for the first time in her life she didn't mind that a man was staring at her, since she was doing exactly the same to him.

"You," he said finally. "I can tell you're a journalist because you keep asking me questions. But I want to know more about you."

"I'm game. Ask away."

"Did you always want to be a journalist?"

She shook her head. "Historian."

"Really?" He was leaning across the table now, his plate pushed aside, his arms folded in front of him. His wrist and its compelling lines of script were so close to her hand.

"Really. It was my favorite subject in school, and university, too. But I didn't want to teach, and my marks weren't high enough for graduate school. So I did a postgraduate diploma in journalism. I found a job right away, and that was ten years ago, and in all that time I never really took a moment to stop and ask myself if I loved my work. Until a few weeks ago, that is."

"What happened?"

"I was made redundant, and I probably should have jumped into a job search right away. That would have been the smart thing to do. But I felt like I had to come here first."

"To find your nan. And now? What will you do when you return home?"

She was leaning forward, and their heads were all but touching. They were whispering to one another.

"I have no idea," she admitted. "I hope that doesn't sound pathetic."

"Not at all."

"I know I can keep the wolf from the door. I can pick up work as a copywriter, or I can go the public relations route. Except I can't stand the idea of writing puff pieces that I don't care about. I want to write stories that interest me. Stories that keep me up half the night because I can't turn off my brain. Does that ever happen to you?"

"All the time."

"I want that, too."

"Then do it. Tell me, now—what would you write about if you could choose any topic at all? Don't think—just say it."

"I'd write about the gown. Nan and Miriam. What it was like to work at Hartnell and create a wedding dress for a princess. How it felt to make such beautiful things and never be acknowledged in any way. I remember thinking that after William and Kate's wedding. Everyone was talking about her dress and the designer and I don't think I saw a single article on the people who made it. How hard they must have worked on that dress, and how they couldn't breathe a word to anyone, not even their best friends."

"If I were a magazine editor I'd be interested."

"It needs a hook, though. I wish I were brave enough to ask Miriam. No editor in the world would turn down an interview with her."

"Why don't you ask?" he suggested. As if it would be no big deal.

"You told me she hates to talk about herself. I don't want to upset her."

"It won't. She avoids publicity because she tends to attract the attention of hatemongers, to use a polite term for an especially loathsome group of people. That's why she has no email address or website, and that's why everyone who knows her is so evasive."

"Oh, God. I feel like an idiot for not thinking of that before."

"If you hadn't included your grandmother's name in the message you left with my former student, I probably wouldn't have emailed you back. God knows I get enough of that shit in my own in-box because of my own work. But compared to the vitriol that's been aimed at Mimi over the years? It's nothing."

"I'm sure it's awful."

"I'm sorry. I'm ruining our dinner. Once I get started, though—"

"Talk about it as much as you like. I'm happy to listen."

"Another time, maybe."

"Sure. Maybe when you're in New York? Miriam was telling me all about it."

He looked down and began to fiddle with the stem of his wineglass. "I expect she made it sound as if they've decided to award me the inaugural Nobel Prize for history."

"More or less. When do you leave?"

"In a fortnight." His eyes caught hers, and she was surprised by how apprehensive he seemed. "Perhaps I might come up to Toronto for a visit? Or you could visit me there?"

"I would love that. I haven't been to New York in years."

"Good," he said, and his accompanying grin made her heart do a little somersault. "But back to the subject at hand—your interviewing Mimi."

"You make it sound so certain. You're sure she won't be upset?"

"I'm sure. I can't guarantee she'll agree to speak with you on the record, but she won't be angry if you ask. That I can promise."

They had zabaglione and strawberries for dessert, and then he walked her back to the hotel. A longish walk, he warned her, but she didn't care. It meant more time in his company. As they were crossing Tottenham Court Road he took hold of her hand, correctly sensing that she was about to walk into traffic yet again, but even after they were safely across the street he held on, and they continued like that, hand in hand, block after block.

He came into the hotel lobby with her and waited as she fetched her key, and then, since Dermot was at the desk, she led Daniel down the hall and around the corner to the bottom of the stairs.

"Sorry," she explained. "It's just that I didn't feel like saying good night in front of an audience."

"I feel the same way," he whispered, tucking a strand of hair behind her ear. And then he kissed her, his mouth fitting just so against hers, and it made her wonder if there was anything that Daniel Friedman didn't do well.

"I meant what I said earlier," he said, his words a whisper across her brow. "I want you to come and see me in New York. Or you can invite me to Toronto. Either way, I want to continue this conversation."

"So do I."

"What are you doing tomorrow?"

"Sightseeing?" She hadn't meant for it to come out as a question.

"Would you like to meet up in the afternoon? Let me show you around a little more?"

Heather nodded, not trusting her voice.

"Good. I'll come by at two o'clock. *Fais des beaux rêves.*"

Chapter Twenty-Five

Ann

November 19, 1947

The gown was complete.

It had come back to the embroidery workroom a week before, after it had gone to the palace and back for one last fitting, and Ann and Miriam had been given the task of re-embroidering the seams where they had been affected by such small changes as the seamstresses had made. It stood now on its mannequin in the sewing workroom next door, and everyone who worked at Hartnell had been filing past it all morning. Their expressions of mingled awe and pride only confirmed what Ann had known since she'd set her first stitch upon the gown weeks before: it was a triumph.

"Did you ever wonder if we'd manage it?" she asked Miss Duley.

"No. I knew you and the other girls would do us proud. That reminds me—did you remember to leave the edge of that last petal unstitched?"

"I did," Ann said, smiling, for she knew what Miss Duley had in mind.

"Good. Ruthie? Ethel? Will one of you go down the hall and fetch the girls from the second workroom? We don't have much time to spare, so tell them to leave off whatever they're doing and hurry along."

When everyone had assembled and fallen quiet, Miss Duley went to stand by the end of the train, still in its great frame although it had been complete since the night before. "Everyone here has worked her fingers to the bone over these past weeks. Everyone. And while only a few had a hand in making Her Royal Highness's gown and train, you should all feel you can take credit for the great task we're about to complete. That is why I asked Ann to leave one petal on the train unfinished. I want everyone who did not work on the gown or train to wash your hands, and when you are done queue up behind Ann. Very good. She will show you where to set your stitch—just one, as there are a fair number of you, and it's only a small bit of petal that needs fixing to the tulle."

One after the other they washed their hands and came forward and sat in the chair next to Ann, and she showed them the petal of the largest York rose at the bottom of the train. One after the other they set their single stitch, then ceded their place to the next woman in line. When they were done, Ann placed the final stitch, added two invisible anchoring stitches beneath the petal, and snipped the thread.

"There," Miss Duley said. "That's done, and if anyone ever asks if you worked on Princess Elizabeth's wedding gown or train, you can say in all honesty that you did. Thank you, my dears."

Now came the delicate task of removing the train from its frame. First they loosened the pegs that held it taut, just enough to make it possible to unpick the tacking stitches that held the tulle in place, then Ann and Miriam, working from the bottom and along opposite sides, set the edges of the train free. The raw edge of the tulle had been whipstitched with minute, near-invisible stitches before being stretched in the frame, and the tacking stitches had been set only a thread's width away. If all went well, the train would come free without a single telltale mark on its gossamer fabric. Ruthie and Ethel followed behind, gathering the train as bridesmaids might do, keeping it well clear of the floor.

On the far side of the workroom an immaculate cloth had been set out, and on top of it were sheets and sheets of the finest snow-white tissue paper. The four women now brought the train over and spread it upon the tissue, adjusting and straightening until not a crease or bump remained. Then they layered more tissue on top and began the work of folding it away for its journey to Buckingham Palace.

Ann hadn't expected it to be such a bittersweet moment. She would see the dress again in a matter of hours, but her part in its creation was over. This was the last time she would touch the flowers she had sewn, and the last time she would be close enough to see the tiny sprigs of white heather, tucked below one of the York roses at the bottom of the train, which were her gift to the princess.

While they had been packing the train, the women next door had been packing the gown, and Ann and Miriam now carried their folded and tissue-wrapped bundle to the sewing workroom. The gown, cushioned all round with poufs of tissue, had been nestled in an enormous box, fully six feet long and monogrammed with Mr. Hartnell's initials. They set the train carefully atop the gown, and then they closed the box and tied its lid in place with loops of gleaming satin ribbon.

"There," Ann said, and she stood back so the two footmen who usually greeted guests at the front door might carry the princess's wedding finery to the waiting delivery lorry.

It was a moment of triumph for them all, and for Ann, especially, since so much of the important work had been entrusted to her care. She knew it, and she knew she ought to be bouncing with excitement like the other girls, so she made a brave show of it in the end, smiling and laughing and congratulating her friends on a job well done.

ACCORDING TO THE pass that had come along with her invitation, Ann had to be at Westminster Abbey no later than ten forty-five on the morning of the wedding. To that she planned to add at least another hour, for she dared not risk getting caught in the crowds. Unlike most of the other guests, she would be traveling via Underground and would have no liveried driver to chauffeur her up to the door.

She'd slept fretfully, stirring at the slightest noise and taking forever to settle again, and her worries had chased her from one dream to the next. The nausea she felt upon waking further compounded her misery, and at breakfast she was only able to nibble at some plain crackers.

She had to accept the truth. She was two weeks overdue, she was tired all the time, and she turned green at the sight of foods she'd always loved. She was pregnant, and no matter how long she thought about it and turned over the possibilities in her mind, she could imagine only one way forward. There was only one path to take, she knew, and it was going to break her heart.

Miriam had come downstairs at seven o'clock, her excitement over the coming day palpable, and it had been no easy thing to convince her friend that all was well and she had just slept poorly. "I was too excited to sleep," she'd explained, and she had resolved, then, to pack away her troubles for the day.

Ann wore the best of her work dresses, its charcoal gray the least festive color she could imagine, but it would be covered entirely by the coat Carmen had lent her. Made of a gorgeous dark blue wool with a calf-length skirt and wide lapels that wrapped around her shoulders like a shawl, it was the perfect match to the hat that Jessie in millinery had let her borrow: a black felt oval trimmed with a pouf of ostrich fluff, a spiral of wired black ribbon, and the tip of one perfect peacock feather.

Earlier in the week Miss Duley had told Miriam that she would be going to the palace with Mr. Hartnell on the morning of the wedding, together with Mam'selle and the senior fitters, in case any emergency should arise that required the aid of an embroiderer. "You're to meet them at his office at nine o'clock sharp on Thursday morning, then you'll drive over together."

As soon as Ann and Miriam were dressed they went to Mr. Booth from next door and asked him to take their picture, a memento of the day, and then, the sun scarcely up, they set off for the royal wedding. They took the same train into London, with Miriam changing at Charing Cross and Ann continuing on to Westminster. They had decided it would be too difficult to try to meet up afterward, so would return home separately.

The crowds were just as bad as Ann had feared, six deep in some places, but the wedding didn't start for another two hours. She had plenty of time, and really all she had to do was cross the street and make her way to the abbey's western door.

The day was cold and gray and the skies looked as if they might open at any moment, but nothing could dampen the good cheer of the crowds. Some people had been waiting all night, equipped with lawn chairs and blankets and baskets packed with sandwiches and flasks of tea, and many were sporting paper crowns or ancient top hats. The mood reminded her of VE Day, when she and Milly had come into London and waded through the crowds on the Mall to try to catch a glimpse of the king and queen and Mr. Churchill waving from the balcony. They'd stayed out all night, cheering and clapping and singing until their voices frayed to nothing, and just thinking of it now was almost too much to bear. She had been so full of hope that day.

Again and again she came to barriers and had to dig in her handbag for her invitation and pass, and each time she worried the unthinkable would happen and she'd be turned away. But the policemen on duty all beckoned her through with a smile and some cheery remark, and one of them, old enough to have been on duty since the king and queen themselves had been married, asked her to pass on his best wishes to the princess.

"I don't think I'm likely to get very close to her, but I'll do my best," she promised.

In the end she had to walk farther west than she needed before doubling back, but before too long she was rounding the end of the abbey and the great west door was in sight. For some reason it had been covered over with a temporary entrance painted white and red and gold, its interior softened with white draperies, and the effect, unfortunately, had a sort of ersatz wartime feel that was quite at odds with the splendor of the great church itself.

Ann was only one of a river of guests who were arriving, most of them in stately limousines, and she hung back until a group of dignitaries bristling with medals and sashes and jeweled orders had been ushered in. Only then did she step forward, her invitation and pass in hand.

"Good morning, madam, and welcome." An older man in full dress uniform, his chest shingled with medals, had come up to greet her. "I'm Major Ruislip, one of the gentlemen ushers. May I see your pass for a moment? Thank you very much. Here it is back again, and here, too, is a copy of the order of service. If I may walk you to your seat?"

She followed him in, so intimidated by his magnificent appearance that she dared not say a word, and instead tried to absorb everything her eyes were showing her. The stark slab of the Tomb of the Unknown Warrior, the banks of reeded pillars reaching heavenward, the delicate stone traceries that reminded her of lace, and everywhere the magical, jeweled light of the abbey's ancient windows. There weren't any flowers that she could see, and the chairs were quite ordinary bentwood ones. In that sense, she supposed, it was a true austerity wedding. Not that a building as beautiful as Westminster Abbey needed to be covered in flowers and bunting to make it presentable, of course.

They hadn't gone far, only a third of the way along the nave, when Major Ruislip halted at a narrow aisle between the rows of chairs. Miss Duley and Miss Holliday were seated in the second-to-last row. Upon seeing Ann, Miss Duley raised her hand in a diffident wave.

"Here we are, Miss Hughes. You are seated just to the right of your colleagues. I do hope you enjoy the ceremony."

The difficult part was over. She was at the abbey and she had found her friends. She could breathe again.

"I see we got here on the early side," she said, looking at the empty chairs around them.

"In half an hour it'll be a different story," Miss Duley said. "Can you imagine showing up after the queen? Horrors. What time is it now? I was in such a fluster to leave that I forgot my watch on the dresser."

"It's a quarter past ten, so we've a little over an hour to go." Ann looked around, then lowered her voice to make sure they weren't overheard. "I haven't had anything to drink since last night. I was that worried I might need the loo partway through."

"Fair enough, but mind you have a cup of tea as soon as you get home, else you'll end up with a headache. You know you will."

Ann paged through the order of service, and though she recognized a few hymns, most of the music was unfamiliar. "I wonder if we're meant to sing along," she mused.

"No idea. Better wait until we hear if others are joining in," Miss Holliday suggested.

The seats around them had almost all been filled, and the people being shown in by the gentlemen ushers were looking progressively grander. The women's gowns were floor length, their furs were ever more lush and exotic, and the volume of jewels they wore was truly startling.

A great fanfare of trumpets sounded at a quarter past eleven, and everyone stood, but try as she might Ann was unable to see past the people in front, all of whom were built like stevedores.

"It's the queen," the tallest of the men whispered. "It won't be long now."

They sat down, and waited, and listened to the organ music, and Ann read her order of service again, and another ten minutes or so inched past. Then came the bells, ringing clear and bright, and before their chimes had faded a second fanfare rang out, again from the unseen trumpets. The congregation stood once more, and a hush fell over the abbey and its congregation of two thousand souls. Ann didn't so much as breathe.

"*Praise, my soul, the king of heaven,*" the choir began to sing, and Ann knew, from the order of service she'd now memorized, that the processional had begun. She stood on her tiptoes, straining to see past the giants blocking her view, and was rewarded with the briefest flash of glittering white.

That was it, that was all she was going to see of the bride until the ceremony came to an end, and still her heart thrilled to it. No one at their end of the abbey could see or hear much, for that matter, and it was rather strange to sit so quietly and strain to hear what was happening at the high altar.

It startled her, a little, when everyone got to their feet again, but then the organ began to play the opening bars of the national anthem and they all sang, a choir of thousands of voices, and it sent shivers up her spine to know the subject of the anthem, the king himself, was listening.

Another hymn followed; Ann consulted her order of service and saw that the bride and groom had gone to sign the register. Yet another fanfare, and then, at last, the joyful chords of Mendelssohn's "Wedding March." On and on it continued, measure after measure, and just as it was beginning to wear on her nerves she spied flashes of gold and red passing by. It was not Princess Elizabeth and Prince Philip but the assembled clergy, the Archbishop of Canterbury included, and all the choristers as well.

"I'm going to crouch down," Ann whispered in Miss Duley's ear. "It's that or stand on my chair."

The last of the choirboys passed by, and behind them another man in clerical robes carrying a golden cross, and outside the cheers were growing louder and louder. To her left, she saw, people's heads were bobbing up and down, and it made her think of the day of the royal visit to the workroom and the way they'd never quite managed to sort out their curtsies.

A gleam of white—the princess—and when everyone else strained high to see the bride Ann bent her knees a little. She saw the flowers she had embroidered on the lustrous satin of the gown, she saw the hundreds of blossoms she had appliquéd to the train, and she was wonderstruck at the magical way its crystals and pearls glittered and gleamed in the harsh glow of the electric lights. Again came the singing bells far overhead, and meeting them a swell of joyful voices as the princess and her husband emerged from the abbey, and Ann was grateful in that moment, grateful down to her toes. She had seen the princess in her gown, the gown she had helped to make, and her heart was full with the delight of it.

"My heavens," Miss Duley said. "Wasn't that splendid? Of course we'll have to wait for the newsreels to see more."

They waited and waited, and at last the stream of departing guests began to thin. "Shall we try to make our way out?" she asked, and when Miss Duley and Miss Holliday both nodded she followed them out into the central aisle and then to the door, but first she stopped to turn for one final look. It was something to remember, she told herself. No matter what happened in the years to come, she would never let herself forget this day.

"Well," she said to the other women. "That was something, wasn't it? Where are you off to now?"

"I'm going home," Miss Holliday said. "My sister's been listening on the wireless, and she'll be keen as mustard to hear all the details."

"And I'm going to a party in the parish hall at my church," Miss Duley said. "At last I can tell everyone what I've been up to all these months. My friends all suspected but they knew better than to ask. I'm looking forward to setting a few things straight, I must say. Working us around the clock, my eye! As if Mr. Hartnell would insist on such a thing."

"I'll see you at work tomorrow?" Ann asked. It was only Thursday, after all, and they'd a mountain of orders waiting for them.

"You will, but if you feel like having a lie-in you go right ahead. You've worked yourself half to death over these past weeks, and it hasn't escaped my notice how tired you've been. If you want the day off I won't say a thing, and if anyone takes any notice I'll go straight to Mr. Hartnell."

"I'm fine, Miss Duley. Go and enjoy your party, and I'll see you tomorrow."

Chapter Twenty-Six

Miriam

November 20, 1947

Miriam arrived at Bruton Street at precisely nine o'clock, as instructed, and went straight upstairs to Mr. Hartnell's office. She had with her a small kit of supplies she'd assembled the day before, for there didn't seem much point in going to the palace without any means of actually effecting repairs. Ann had lent her a lidded wicker sewing basket, a smaller version of the one that sat in the sitting room and held their mending, and it was just big enough to hold everything Miriam might need: curved and straight needles, spools of thread, examples of each kind of pearl, bead, and crystal used on the gown and train, and two pairs of scissors.

Mr. Hartnell was there already, as were Mademoiselle Davide, Miss Yvonne, the princess's personal *vendeuse*, and Betty from the sewing workroom; like Miriam, she had been asked to come to the palace in case of a last-minute disaster. Before five minutes had passed they were joined by two additional fitters, and though Miriam recognized the women by sight she couldn't recollect their names.

"Good morning, ladies. Is everyone ready? In that case we ought to be on our way." They followed Monsieur Hartnell downstairs and out through the front entrance, where two enormous black cars were waiting. He, Mam'selle, and Miss Yvonne got into the first car, leaving the rest of them to squash into the second, and as soon as the doors were shut they were off. There was no risk of being caught up in traffic, since theirs were practically the only vehicles heading in the direction of the palace, so it took only a few minutes to skirt the edges of Green Park and come around onto Buckingham Palace Road.

Monsieur Hartnell's car turned into a gateway, pausing as it crossed the pavement, but when the guards peered in and saw its occupants, they waved both cars through onto the raked gravel forecourt. Seconds later they drew to a halt in front of a rather grand entrance.

"This is the servants' entrance?" Miriam marveled.

One of the fitters shook her head. "Usually we go in through the Privy Purse Door on the north side. This is the Ambassadors Entrance. I guess they thought it would be easier because of all the crowds out front. Makes me feel rather a star, though."

A man in uniform came forward and shook Mr. Hartnell's hand. "Good morning, Mr. Hartnell. Ladies."

"Good morning. Shame about the gloomy weather. Shall we see ourselves in? I'm sure you're run off your feet."

Mr. Hartnell led them up a set of low stairs and along an unremarkable corridor to a lift, and though it was rather small they all managed to squeeze inside. It stopped after one floor, at which point the two fitters got out.

"Go straight along to Her Majesty's apartments," Mr. Hartnell told them, "and please let her know I shall be along once I'm certain all is well with the bride."

The lift doors shut and they went up another floor. This time everyone got out, and Mr. Hartnell led them along another corridor, this one red-carpeted and high-ceilinged and decorated with gilt-framed mirrors and oil paintings and glass-fronted cabinets filled with mysterious treasures.

A door near the end opened as they approached, and a plainly dressed woman in her early forties came out to greet them.

"Miss MacDonald," Monsieur Hartnell said, shaking her hand. "How are you today?"

"Very well," she said, smiling brightly. "Good morning to all of you, and do come in."

Miriam was at the very tail end of their little procession, and it was only chance that had her glancing at the door as they passed through. *HRH The Princess Elizabeth* was engraved on a shining brass plaque. So these were the princess's private rooms—that would be something to tell Ann about later.

They now stood in a sitting room, and something about it reminded her of the house in Edenbridge where Bennett and Ruby lived. Not the room itself, for it was enormous and rather cold, but rather its furnishings, which were comfortable and homey and not especially grand. A small wicker dog basket, rather battered and worn, sat next to the sofa, but fortunately its occupant was elsewhere. It wouldn't do for her to shrink back in fear from the princess's own dog.

"How is Her Royal Highness this morning?" Monsieur Hartnell asked.

"She is very well, thank you, and ready to get dressed. If Mam'selle and Miss Yvonne could come with me we'll get started."

"Of course, Miss MacDonald, of course. I'll remain here until

I'm needed." And then, as if only just remembering, "I've brought Miss Dassin and Miss Pearce from my embroidery and sewing workrooms. In case any emergency repairs are required. Would you like them to remain here, or might they be of help elsewhere?"

"Perhaps they could help with the bridesmaids?" Miss MacDonald suggested. "There's only the six of them, as Princess Margaret and Princess Alexandra have their own dressers." She turned to face Miriam and Betty. "Will you be all right finding your way? It isn't far—back to the lift and down one floor, then turn left and go around the corner to the first of the guest suites. They're bound to be making a fair amount of noise."

"Yes, ma'am," Betty said, nodding.

"Go straight on in and ask for Flora. If you run into the king or queen along the way, don't panic. Simply move to the side of the corridor and let them pass. Don't say anything, but it's fine to smile. Especially today."

"Go on," Monsieur Hartnell added, "and I'll come by once the ladies have finished dressing."

It was a bit disappointing not to see the princess at close quarters, and especially not to see her in the wedding gown itself, but Miriam could hardly blame her for preferring to have people she knew well in attendance on her wedding day. And it did mean that she would get to see a little more of this English palace that so few English people ever had the chance to visit.

As soon as she and Betty stepped out of the lift they knew exactly where they were meant to go, for the sounds of happy conversation and laughter were impossible to miss. They knocked at the door and went in, and it was a relief to find the room beyond was filled with young women and not King George in his shirtsleeves.

"Hello there," Betty said. "We're with Mr. Hartnell. Miss Mac-

Donald asked us to come along and see if we might help. She said to ask for Flora."

A young woman came bustling forward and shook their hands. "I'm Flora. The hairdresser just finished and we're more or less ready to get the ladies into their gowns. Have you any experience as dressers?"

They both shook their heads. "I am an embroiderer," Miriam explained, "and Betty is a seamstress. We are here in case any repairs need to be made to the gowns."

"Oh, right. Well, Lady Mary Cambridge does need some help with her gown. Make sure it goes over her head, since she might catch a foot or tear it if she tries to step into it. Make sure that everything needing doing up is done up, and whatever you do, don't force anything. I think she may have on some makeup, so have a care for that. If you get stuck, give me a shout. I'll be roaming about."

As she spoke she led them across the room, bypassing several of the bridesmaids and their dressers, until they were standing in front of a tall, dark-haired, and very pretty young woman who seemed, at least to Miriam's eyes, a little unsure of herself. Perhaps she was nervous about the day ahead.

"Lady Mary, I have some girls from Hartnell to help you dress," Flora said before hastening away.

"How lovely," Lady Mary said, her expression brightening. "There wasn't room in the car for my girl and"—here she dropped her voice to a conspiratorial whisper—"I was going to be stuck with Pamela's girl. The poor thing is all thumbs. The maid, I mean, not Pamela. And this isn't the sort of frock one puts on by oneself, is it?"

"No, Lady Mary," Miriam said, which seemed an awkward way to address the woman. Was she supposed to call her Miss? Ma'am? Madam? It was all so confusing.

"Where is the gown, my lady?" Betty asked.

"Hmm. I'm not so sure. Perhaps you might ask the girl who brought you over? She seems to be in the know."

"Yes, my lady," Betty said, and hurried away.

"So you're from Hartnell? What do you do there?"

Miriam had fully expected to stand in silence until Betty returned with Lady Mary's gown, so it took a few moments for her to produce an answer. "I am an embroiderer."

"You made all those gorgeous flowers and stars and so forth?"

"Some of them. I did not work on your gown, however. Only the bride's. Although the motifs are similar."

"They're jolly lovely. My father has been teasing me that we'll just hold on to this frock and use it when I get married. 'No sense in wasting hundreds of guineas on something new if you've already got one that'll do perfectly well,' he keeps saying. Silly old dear."

It seemed imprudent to agree, so Miriam smiled and tried to think of a safely anodyne response. Fortunately, Betty chose that moment to return, the gown draped over her outstretched arms like a bejeweled cloud.

Lady Mary shrugged off her dressing gown, beneath which she wore a strapless brassiere and floor-length petticoat, and stood, shivering, as Betty unfastened the back of the gown. Only then did Miriam remember Flora's warning about makeup. Lady Mary had on some lipstick, and possibly some rouge as well.

"I am sorry, Lady Mary, but I am nervous of marking the gown. Perhaps if we were to place a handkerchief over your face? It will also prevent your coiffure from being disturbed."

"That is a good idea. Do you have a clean hanky?"

Ann had tucked one into Miriam's pocket that morning, explaining that weddings made people cry and it would be sensible to have

one on hand. She had privately thought there was no chance whatso-
ever of her crying at the wedding of a complete stranger, but now she
was glad of Ann's sentimental gesture.

"I do, Lady Mary. I promise it is clean. Could I trouble you to hold
it in place?"

It made for a rather comic moment, with poor Lady Mary standing half-naked with a handkerchief over her face, and so tall that
Miriam and Betty both had to stand on tiptoe to lift the gown over
her upstretched arm and head, but they managed to get it more or
less where it ought to be without incident.

Miriam whisked away the handkerchief, gently brushing back a
few strands of hair that had come forward to tickle at Lady Mary's
face, and then she and Betty began the painstaking work of fastening
their charge into her gown. It took many long minutes to do up the
endless rows of hooks and eyes, and Miriam had to pause more than
once to dry her perspiring fingers.

"*Et voilà*," she said when at last they were done, and then she took
another minute to fan out the attached tulle stole over Lady Mary's
graceful shoulders.

The hairdresser stopped by to set a silver-colored wreath of ar-
tificial orange blossoms and ears of wheat upon Lady Mary's head,
and then they helped her into her shoes, and someone else came by
with face powder and lipstick, and then yet another person handed
Miriam a pair of long white kid gloves, so thin they weighed almost
nothing, and it took several minutes to draw them up Lady Mary's
arms and fasten the tiny pearl buttons at her wrists.

At last they were done. Miriam stepped back, trying and failing
to find any fault in the gown or any other aspect of Lady Mary's ensemble.

"How do I look?"

"You look perfect," Miriam said honestly. *"Ravissante."*

The bouquets had arrived, lush cascades of white orchids, lilies, and other hothouse flowers that had no business being in bloom so late in the year. All about them the other bridesmaids were laughing and twirling around, and one or two were complaining about how scratchy the tulle stoles were against their skin, and Miriam wouldn't have changed places with any of them for all the money in the world. To willingly expose oneself to the eyes of millions, with all the attendant possibilities for disaster if one were to trip or drop something or faint, and to have every aspect of one's appearance discussed and dissected by unsympathetic critics, was something she could never imagine facing, let alone enjoying.

There was a knock on the door, and when Flora went to answer it she ushered in Monsieur Hartnell, who went from bridesmaid to bridesmaid, giving each his full attention, and he was so charming and friendly that he had them all laughing gaily by the time he'd completed his inspection.

He came to stand with Miriam and Betty, taking out a handkerchief to dab at his brow, and his smile was tight when they asked him if anything was the matter.

"Not with the gown, no," he said, "but as the hairdresser was fitting the tiara on the princess the frame snapped in two. They've called for the jeweler, and the queen did remind Princess Elizabeth that they can certainly unearth a replacement, but she is set on that particular tiara. So *that* part of the morning has been rather exciting."

"My goodness," Betty said.

"And they've just now sent someone over to St. James's Palace to retrieve the pearls she was planning on wearing. Apparently they're still on display with the rest of the wedding gifts. God only knows if they'll appear in time."

"But the gown—"

"The gown itself is perfection, and the queen is also delighted with her ensemble and that of Princess Margaret. Has all gone well here? Any need for repairs?"

"No, sir," Miriam said. "None at all."

"Good, good. Well, I'd better go upstairs to say farewell to the princess, and see if those pearls have shown up."

Mr. Hartnell slipped away, and then Flora was hailing the bridesmaids, for it was a quarter to eleven already. How had an entire hour gone by?

"My ladies, if everyone is ready you do need to be downstairs in the Grand Hall very shortly. Do you have your wraps? Yes? Please follow the footman who is waiting in the corridor."

Then they were gone, a flock of glittering swans, and when Miriam turned to survey the room she was appalled to see what a shambles it had become. She bent to collect Lady Mary's dressing gown, but stopped short at Flora's voice.

"Don't worry about that. Come along to see the princess before she leaves. We need to hurry, though."

Flora led them downstairs and along yet another sumptuously gilded corridor, and then they entered the grandest space Miriam had yet seen. "The Marble Hall," Flora explained as they hastened along. True to its name, the space was lined with shining marble columns and decorated with a museum's worth of monumental oil paintings and classical sculptures. Servants were lined up on either side, their excited whispers sweeping back and forth, all of them waiting to see the princess in her wedding finery.

"They'll be coming down the Grand Staircase in a minute," Flora explained, "and once they go into the Grand Hall we'll be able to see them through the colonnade. Oh—I think they've arrived."

Miriam hadn't expected that the princess would look so beautiful, but she did, her smile wide and engaging, her lovely eyes radiant with happiness. The king was holding her arm, and the queen had appeared, and fluttering around them were the bridesmaids, their ranks bolstered by Princess Margaret and a much younger girl who couldn't have been more than ten or eleven years old. Princess Alexandra, she supposed. There were two little boys in kilts and lace-trimmed shirts, both of them looking as if they were plotting some kind of mischief, and her heart nearly stopped when one of them came very close to stomping on the delicate train.

But then the queen and Princess Margaret and the bridesmaids and the little boys were summoned to their carriages, which left the king and Princess Elizabeth standing alone in the middle of the hall, and as they looked at one another, his expression so tender and adoring, Miriam felt a pang of guilt to be intruding on such a private moment. She shut her eyes for an instant, and when she opened them again the princess and her father were walking away, arm in arm, to their waiting carriage.

"Well, now we can breathe," Flora said in an ordinary voice, and around them everyone else was talking and exchanging smiles of relief and looking at their wristwatches. Miriam and Betty followed her upstairs, and they spent a few minutes helping to tidy the room where they'd spent the past hour. Only when the crowd outside let out an earthshaking roar did it occur to Miriam to go to the nearest window.

She hadn't realized it before, but they were at the front of the palace. The view was incomparable, for she could see all the way up the broad avenue before them, and along either side of it were masses of people, thousands upon thousands, and every last one of them was cheering.

"What can you see?" Betty asked.

"There is a carriage, about halfway along the avenue, with many men on horseback, too. The crowds are very deep on either side of— What do you call it?"

"The Mall," Betty said, coming forward to stand by Miriam. "I was out there on VE Day. The king and queen stood on the balcony, and the princesses, and Mr. Churchill, too. I was so far back I could hardly see, but my friends lifted me up on their shoulders and we had a pair of binoculars. I could just see them, little specks they were, and I was so happy. In all my life I've never felt so happy as I was that day."

They stood and watched the carriage disappear from sight, and then they gathered their things, including the sewing basket that Miriam hadn't once opened, and followed Flora downstairs to the side entrance. Monsieur Hartnell and the others arrived only a minute or two later, and Miriam was relieved to see that he was in far better spirits than he'd been earlier.

"Miss Dassin and Miss Pearce—the rest of our happy band. Shall we be off?"

"Isn't Miss Yvonne coming with us?" Betty asked.

"She'll stay until after the photographs have been taken," Monsieur Hartnell explained. "Fortunately, the rest of us are free to spend the rest of the day as we please, and I plan on going straight home to bed."

"May I leave on my own? By foot?" Miriam asked him.

"Hoping to join in the festivities? By all means. Tell the bobby at the gate that you were here with me. And thank you again for your splendid work."

In moments she was walking down Buckingham Palace Road, only rather than melt into the crowd, as Monsieur Hartnell had assumed, she made her way south, against the current of merrymaking well-wishers surging toward the palace and the burgeoning crowds. It was rather touching, the way everyone seemed so avid for a glimpse of the royal family on their distant balcony, and it was sobering, too, to imagine how the princess would feel when she stood before the multitude in a few hours and thanked them with her smile and a wave of her hand. How did she not find it unendurable?

It was raining again, and Victoria Station was just ahead, so she ran inside, hoping she'd be able to find the entrance to its Underground stop without going back into the rain. She'd never had cause to use the stop before, nor the rail station above—

No. The night she had come to England, her train had arrived at Victoria. Not even ten months distant, though her memories since then encompassed something like a lifetime. So much had changed over those months.

On the far side of the arrivals hall, a group of people were gathered around a newsagent's kiosk. She approached, indulging her curiosity, for it was only a few minutes past eleven thirty. Ann would still be at the abbey for some time.

A portable wireless, the size of a large hatbox, had been set up on the counter of the kiosk. The people were listening to someone speak, a man with a deep, sonorous voice, but he was not a newsreader, for there was something in the cadence of his words that made her think of poetry. She inched ever closer, straining to make out the words. It was a prayer, not poetry. The group of people were listening to the royal wedding.

The prayer ended, and another man began to speak, and then she was surprised to hear the softer voice of a young woman. The princess herself, making her promises in a clear, high voice. Around Miriam, the other listeners smiled, and some even wiped tears from their eyes. It was rather moving, she decided, if not quite enough to bring her to tears, and she was tempted to remain and listen until the end.

Ann had said the entire ceremony would be broadcast again that evening, however, and she much preferred to listen to it with her friend at her side, if only so she might have the unfamiliar parts of the wedding service explained to her. So she stepped back and continued to the Underground entrance a few yards away, and in another forty-five minutes she was home.

She was shivering by the time she walked through the door, for the rain had been falling hard enough to soak through her coat. After exchanging her good suit for her warmest skirt and jumper, she built a small fire in the sitting room hearth, which quickly took the chill out of the air, and filled the kettle with fresh water. Ann would certainly want a cup of tea when she returned.

She was still setting out the tea things when the front door opened.

"Miriam? Are you there?"

"I am. I had not thought you would be home so early."

"Me neither. I thought I'd have to fight my way through the crowds, but everyone outside the abbey charged off in the direction of the palace. The Tube was practically empty."

"You should change. I will put the kettle on to boil."

When Ann came downstairs again, she wore her nightgown, robe, and slippers. "I know, I know. It's not even one o'clock. But I'm that tired. Seemed like the easiest thing to put on." With that, she flopped down on the sofa and let out a long and rather tremulous sigh.

"Are you hungry? There is not much in the larder, but we have some bread, and a tin of sardines, too."

Ann shut her eyes and let her head rest against the back of the sofa.

"Maybe just some tea. Now, tell me all about the palace. Were you upstairs in the private apartments?"

"Yes, but I only saw the princess's sitting room. After that Betty and I went to help with the bridesmaids. We did see Princess Elizabeth before she left."

"How did she look in the gown?"

"Beautiful," Miriam said honestly. "Beautiful, and very happy, too."

"They'll be coming out on the balcony soon. Do you want to switch on the wireless?"

At first, all Miriam could make out was a thrum of voices and cheering and the occasional car horn, but then, after a minute or two, a melody emerged from the din. The great crowd was singing, a choir of hundreds of thousands, and had she still been inside the palace she would have been deafened by it.

"'All the Nice Girls Love a Sailor,'" Ann guessed. "I can't imagine Queen Mary'll approve of *that*."

There was an even greater roar from the crowd, so loud it drowned out the song, and at that moment the BBC announcer began to speak.

"The doors are opening, and here is Her Royal Highness the bride, and the Duke of Edinburgh is at her side. They are standing alone on the balcony and receiving a tremendous ovation from the crowd. Listen to them now—just listen to the crowd as they cheer. And now we have the whole family group before us, on this famous balcony, and the princess is waving. This is what we'll all remember. This is the picture of the day that we shall all remember."

"That's all we'll see of them until they leave for their honeymoon," Ann said after another minute or two. "Do you want to turn it down a bit?"

Miriam lowered the volume on the wireless and sat in the armchair that was usually Ann's favorite spot. "You must tell me about the abbey. Did you sit with Miss Duley and Miss Holliday?"

"Yes. We were right near the back, and there were people in front of us, so we couldn't see much. The music was lovely, though."

"We will listen to it later. Did you not say it would be on the wireless this evening? In the meantime we should have something to eat. I will prepare some sardines on toast."

"I, ah . . . I think I had better wait. I'm feeling a bit off my feed."

"What is wrong?" Miriam asked, noticing how pale her friend had become.

"I feel a little light-headed. That's all. I only need a minute."

The kettle was singing, so Miriam returned to the kitchen, filled the teapot, and left it to brew. Then she found a clean dish towel and dampened it with cold water. Returning to the sitting room, she folded it in quarters and set it on Ann's perspiring forehead.

"*Voici.* This should help."

"I don't know what's come over me," Ann fretted. "I ought to have eaten something earlier."

Miriam was about to reassure her friend that she simply needed a cup of tea or a bite of toast, and then she would feel better and all would be well. And yet . . .

Ann had been feeling unwell for several weeks. Often in the morning, and not always when she was hungry. It never lasted for very long, and after nibbling on a plain cracker or a piece of dry toast, she always said she felt better. She had been tired, too, so tired that she had been going to bed at eight o'clock or even earlier, and she had even complained, more than once, that she was exhausted. Ann, who never complained about anything. Ann, who—

Of course. How had she not realized, long before now, that Ann's missed breakfast had little to do with her white face and trembling hands, and her exhaustion had nothing to do with their endless hours at work on the gown?

She sat beside her friend on the sofa and gathered Ann's hands in her own. "Are you going to tell me?" she asked, her voice gentled to the merest whisper. "Because you know, do you not? At the very least, you suspect it."

"I am. I . . . I was going to tell you."

"I know."

"I can't stay here. People will talk. I want my baby to have a good life, but here, he or she will forever be Ann Hughes's bastard. I'm sure it's the same in France."

"It is."

"I'll go to Canada. To Milly. In Canada no one needs to know. I can be a widow and no one will ever question me about how . . . how . . ."

Ann squeezed her eyes ever tighter, but she wasn't able to hold back the tears that rained down her ashen face. "Oh, Miriam. This is my home. This is all I know. I can't bear to leave it all behind."

"You can bear it. You will."

"I'm running away."

"You are not. You are beginning again, that is all. As I did when I came to England."

"So is distance the cure? To simply take myself to the opposite side of the world?"

"It will help. It helped me, and I did not go so very far. But time is also important. Time will help you to heal, and it will wash away some of the memories that trouble you."

"I don't think I can ever forget."

"No," Miriam admitted. "You will not. But the weight of it is not so much after a while. Perhaps it is the case that you grow stronger? For you will. I promise you will."

"And until then?"

"You endure. You have done it before, have you not? When your brother was killed?"

Ann nodded, her movements slow and pained. "Yes," she whispered. "You're right. I have done it before." Straightening herself, she wiped at her eyes with the tea towel. "What now? What do I do next?"

"First, I think, you wait a little. To be absolutely certain of the baby. Once you are sure, you write to your Milly and ask for her help. You tell Miss Duley you are moving to Canada to be with your family there. You sell what you can. You take what you cannot bear to leave behind. You say your farewells. And you never look back."

Chapter Twenty-Seven

Heather

September 4, 2016

*E*xcited as she was to have been invited to Miriam's reception, the question of what to wear had concerned Heather, who hadn't anything more formal than a sundress in her suitcase. When her panic level could still be classified as low grade she'd texted Tanya, who had promptly replied with the name and address of a boutique in Soho and firm instructions on what to do once she got there.

Ask for Micheline. Tell her about the event. Buy what she tells you to buy. Stop freaking out. Have fun. xoxo

She'd followed Tanya's advice to the letter, and had emerged with a black dress in some kind of silky fabric that made her feel like a movie star when she put it on, a pair of heels that were a solid two inches higher than her usual shoes but looked sensational, and a necklace that reminded her of chain mail but was actually a kind of crocheted silver lace.

Daniel picked her up at a quarter to six, and he looked just as good in a suit and tie as he did in jeans. They took a taxi to the Tate Modern, and the driver, after some consultation with Daniel, took the long way round so they wouldn't get caught up in traffic. At some point they crossed a bridge, and the traffic seemed to ease a bit, and then the driver was pulling to a stop at the side of an enormous brick building that looked more like a warehouse or factory than a museum.

She let her gaze roam from the building's exterior to the crowds of people still milling around outside, and that's when she noticed the gigantic banners hanging from the largest of the museum's facing walls.

MIRIAM DASSIN
COLLECTED WORKS
UNTIL 31 DECEMBER

They walked around the perimeter of the building until they reached the entrance for the Boiler House wing, and even though the museum was about to close they were waved inside after Daniel showed them his invitation. Although Miriam's artworks were being shown on the third-floor exhibition space, the reception itself was two floors up, in the members' bar.

The reception had only begun a few minutes before, but already there were at least a hundred people milling around. Waiters were circulating with plates of hors d'oeuvres and bottles of champagne for anyone who needed a top-up, and a handful of children had been installed at a table loaded with art supplies and bowls of baby carrots and mini pretzels.

"My brother's children," Daniel explained. "Along with two strays I don't recognize. The little girl is his youngest, Hannah, and a particular favorite of Mimi's."

"For someone who is so private, your grandmother has a lot of friends."

"She does," he agreed, "but they respect her reticence, and the Tate people have accepted this is the most they'll get from her. She's allowing them to take some photographs, but she's asked them not to film her remarks."

"She's giving a speech?"

He collected two glasses of champagne from a passing waiter and handed one to Heather. "She said she would, but I'll check in on her later. I can always offer up a round of thanks if she's feeling shy. Right—brace yourself. Here comes my family. You might want to drink your champagne while you still have a chance."

In a matter of minutes she was introduced to Sarah, Daniel's mother, a younger and somewhat sterner version of Miriam; Nathan, his father, who seemed to be enjoying his son's discomfort at being the momentary center of attention; Ben and Lauren, his brother and sister-in-law; David and Isaac, his mother's younger brothers; and assorted spouses and cousins and family friends who were honorary aunts and uncles. "The lines between friend and family are always a bit blurry in my mind," Daniel whispered in her ear.

It seemed that someone, presumably Daniel, had told his parents and siblings about Nan and her connection to Miriam, and apart from condolences on her grandmother's death and the standard sort of inquiries about her trip and hotel, they didn't bombard her with too many questions. She likely had Daniel to thank for that, too.

They probably noticed that he'd been holding her hand when they walked in, and that he looked to her every few minutes, no matter where in the room she was, as if he was making sure she was fine and not trapped in a tedious conversation, but they were too nice to say anything about it.

Daniel took her outside to the terrace, which had incredible views of St. Paul's Cathedral and the Thames, and that's where they found Miriam. She was talking with a pair of young women, and Daniel greeted one of them with a quick hug before making introductions.

"Heather, this is my cousin Nathalie and her friend Ava. It was their badly timed exam that meant you and I were able to visit the palace the other day."

Miriam was wearing a beautiful coat that was embroidered with interweaving ribbons of every color imaginable, and it was either something she had made herself or some kind of couture marvel from Paris. Heather kissed her on both cheeks, and she listened to Nathalie and Ava talk of their summer course at university, and it was hard, at times, to keep her attention on Daniel's cousin and her friend because the view across the river was so distracting.

After ten or fifteen minutes had passed, someone from the museum sidled up to Miriam and asked if she was still interested in addressing her guests. She nodded, and Daniel smiled at his grandmother and took her arm to escort her inside.

Miriam accepted a microphone from the museum employee and went to stand, alone, in the middle of the room, and by then everyone, even the children, had fallen silent.

"Good evening. I will not take long, for it is no secret that I much prefer to express myself through my work alone. It is also the case that an excess of silence may be interpreted as rudeness or ingratitude, and so I wish to tell you that I am very grateful for your friendship and love, and that I am deeply honored to have my work displayed here, in one of the world's greatest museums of art."

Miriam thanked those who had put together the exhibition, and she acknowledged her children and their families, and then she paused, her eyes shining.

"I have earnestly tried to never play favorites among my offspring, but if you will allow me, just this once, to single one of them out for special praise, I shall do so now. My grandson Daniel Friedman is the reason I stand before you now. No, my dear boy, do not shake your head. I shall praise you whether you like it or not.

"My Daniel is a seeker of truth, a historian, and in that regard he follows in the footsteps of my beloved Walter. He had to convince me to be interviewed, and I will admit it took some time for him to prevail"—at this everyone present began to laugh—"and then, once I had been persuaded, he held my hand as I spoke of long-lost friends and relatives. As I remembered."

Miriam dabbed at her eyes with a handkerchief she pulled from her sleeve and waited for the applause to end, and then she beckoned Heather forward.

"Yes, yes—you, *ma belle*. Come and stand next to me." She took hold of Heather's hand. "This is my friend Heather Mackenzie. Many years ago her grandmother, Ann Hughes, was also my friend. When I first came to England, in that dark winter of 1947, I knew no one. I had no friends here. So Ann decided to become my first friend. She befriended me, and she gave me a place to live, and when I first began to dream of the *Vél d'Hiv* embroideries she encouraged me. She believed I was an artist before I dared to believe it myself. She was a true friend, and it is a very great regret to me that we were separated, and that is why I wish to thank you, Heather, for coming to find me, and for standing at my side tonight. My heart is full."

With that, Miriam handed the microphone back to the waiting museum employee, and she held out her arms so that little Hannah, who had been waiting impatiently, could run up and give her an enormous hug. Heather inched away, pleading the need for a glass of water to one well-wisher, then asking the location of the ladies' room from another, and without too much trouble she was able to escape.

"Excuse me," she asked a passing waiter. "What's the best way to get to the exhibition? Can I take those stairs?"

"Certainly. Two floors down and then follow the signs."

She hurried down to the third floor, urgency lending her speed, and walked straight to the gallery, at the very far end of the exhibition space, which held the *Vél d'Hiv* embroideries. It was darkened, quiet, and empty, apart from a single guard standing sentinel in the far corner.

Five embroidered panels ringed the room, each about six feet across and nine feet high. Lights were trained on the artworks, leaving the rest of the gallery in shadow, and apart from several introductory paragraphs on a printed stand, and a single line of text to the left of each embroidery, the surrounding walls were blank.

Heather moved to the first of the panels, *Un dîner de Chabbat*. A Sabbath dinner. A group of people, a family, stood around a table laden with food, and the oldest of the men held high a silver cup. The colors of the embroidery were extraordinarily vibrant, as if it had been illuminated from within, and the delicately rendered faces were beautiful in their joy.

On to the second work, *Le Rassemblement*. The roundup. Some of the people from the first panel were being pushed down a narrow street, rifles at their backs. Their tormentors were in uniform, though they looked more like police officers than soldiers, and several wore the noxious emblems of Nazi Germany on their jackets and hats. At either side of the embroidery passersby looked on, men and women and children alike, their faces blank.

A figure at the center of the panel caught, and held, her attention. It was a woman from the Sabbath dinner, and she was turning back, reaching for someone, or perhaps she was warning them. The entire panel, Heather suddenly realized, was devoid of color, or rather so bleached of color, set against the first of the embroideries, that it appeared monochrome. The world had been reduced to brown and gray, black and white, and only the stark, sullen yellow of the Stars of David, neatly affixed to the family's coats, broke free of the deadened palette.

Then *Le Vélodrome d'Hiver*, the third panel. The setting was a twisted blob of an arena, its bleachers and field obscured by the huddled figures of hundreds, perhaps even thousands of people. Those at the back were silhouettes, hardly more, but the people in the foreground were minutely detailed. In her every line of stitching, every subtle change of color, Miriam Dassin had captured their weariness, their hunger, their fear.

Again Heather recognized the figures at the center of the panel: the elderly man, the woman, and a second man, taller than the others, his eyes dark with sorrow. He was embracing his loved ones, bending protectively over them. It was all that had been left to him.

Le Voyage à l'est. The journey east. A train arched across the fourth tapestry, its farthest carriages all but unseen in the gloom, only the train wasn't made up of passenger carriages but cattle cars, their slatted wooden sides as weathered and barren as the empty landscape through which they moved. Heather could see nothing of the cars' interiors, nothing that confirmed there were living, feeling, suffering people within, but she knew they were there. She knew it down to her bones.

And then to *Au-delà*. Beyond. This, the final panel, was drenched with color, its vivid hues so startling after the monochrome of its predecessors that Heather found herself blinking in surprise. In the foreground of the panel was an archway, its crumbling stones blanketed with a tangle of roses in full, bounteous, exuberant bloom, and beyond was the family, walking hand in hand, their faces upturned in wonderment. Surrounding them was a garden, and it reminded her of Nan's flower beds with their old-fashioned flowers, only this garden was larger and wilder, its every petal, leaf, and branch a work of glorious perfection.

There was a bench in the middle of the gallery, and Heather now sat and stared at the embroideries, one after the other, turning and turning. It was impossible to look away.

"Have you found her yet?" It was Miriam. How had she known Heather would come here?

"I wasn't looking for anyone. I just came down to see the embroideries."

"What do you think?"

"I feel like I could stare at them for days, and even then I'd still be trying to figure them out," Heather said, wincing inwardly at her feeble response. People had written entire books about these embroideries, and that was her answer?

But Miriam only nodded. As if she approved of Heather's response. "Thank you. Just now I asked about Ann. I wanted to know if you had found her. She is there in the first panel, you know."

"Really? But how . . . ?"

Heather approached *Un dîner de Chabbat,* and she searched the faces, one after the other. "Is that her? The woman at the back? I can't believe I didn't notice before."

"Well, you never knew Ann when she was that age."

"I suppose. And I always forget that she had red hair. It was white by the time I came along."

"I placed her among my family, along with some other friends. They became my family after my own was taken from me."

Heather stared and marveled and tried, unsuccessfully, to smother an unexpected wave of sadness. "I so wish Nan had known. She'd have pretended to be embarrassed, but secretly she'd have loved it. I know she would."

"I agree. Come back and sit down, my dear. I have something to tell you, and I also have something to give you. We haven't much time before everyone else barges in and fills the air with their chatter."

"Is it all right if I ask you something first? Actually two some-things. Otherwise I think I'll lose my nerve."

"Go on."

"I was wondering, first of all, if you remember the name of the man Nan was seeing. The man who I think was probably my grand-father."

There was a long pause. "Jeremy," Miriam said at last, her voice edged with disdain. "I cannot recall his last name."

"What did he look like?" *Not like Mom,* Heather prayed. *Not like me.*

"I only met him the once, but I remember that he was tall, with fair hair. Blue eyes. But there was something too . . . how should I put it? Too smooth about him. Too easy."

"Did she love him?"

"In the beginning, I think, she may have been infatuated with him. She may even have thought she loved him. But that did not last. Not after . . ."

"After what?"

Miriam's expression became unsure. Hesitant. "He hurt her, and the pain of it went very deep."

"It must have been so upsetting." To think of Nan being hurt, even though it had happened so long ago, tore at her heart. Never mind it had happened decades and decades ago and Nan was dead and, very likely, that Jeremy asshole, too. Heather still ached for her grandmother.

"It was, but your nan was a strong woman. Never did I know her to feel sorry for herself. Never."

"Is that why she left? Because she was pregnant with my mom?"

"Yes. She could think of no other way to protect her child. It was considered a shameful thing, in those days, to be an unwed mother, and she could not bear the thought of her child suffering in any way. So she left for Canada, and she never looked back. We said good-bye, and I never saw or heard from her again."

"Didn't it hurt your feelings? She was your best friend, wasn't she?"

"She was, but I knew it was for the best. At least, that is how it seemed at the time."

"Did you never wish to see her again?"

"Oh, yes. I missed her terribly. But the years passed so quickly, and after a while I could not imagine how we should begin again. I expect she felt the same way."

"Okay," Heather said, though none of it really seemed okay to her, not least because she was almost totally certain that Miriam had told her only part of the story. How, exactly, had that Jeremy guy hurt Nan? Had he hurt her feelings—broken her heart? Or had Miriam been speaking in a literal sense? Just thinking about it was enough to turn her stomach.

"What of your second question? Your second 'something,' as you put it?"

"Oh, right. It's a long story but I'll try to boil it down to the essentials. I was talking with Daniel about my job, which I actually lost not so long ago, and how I wanted to try something new."

"You are a journalist, are you not? Just like my Walter."

"I'm not sure I'd ever dare to compare myself to someone like him. But thank you for even suggesting it."

"Are you still a journalist?"

"I am, I guess. I lost my job at the magazine, and that got me thinking about what I really want to do. How I want to write about things that actually matter to me. So I told Daniel I wanted to write about the work Nan did at Hartnell, and what it was like to be an embroiderer and to work on the queen's wedding dress. Only I can't ask Nan about it, and I haven't been able to find anyone else who was there, except, um . . ."

"Me."

"Yes. I know you don't give interviews, and I respect that, I do. Only I'm not sure how to write it without you."

Miriam set her hands atop Heather's, and the cool weight of them was like a drink of water on a humid July day. "Of course I will help you. That is what I was going to say."

"Did Daniel tell you already?"

"Yes. I think he was hoping to ensure I would not refuse you. Such a dear boy."

"And you're fine with talking about your time at Hartnell? You've never discussed it publicly before."

"Would you believe that I did? Only a few times, in interviews when I was just beginning to become known, but none of the people asking questions—none of the men, I should say—seemed to care. The better story, in their eyes, was that I had appeared out of no-where, a sort of phoenix rising from the ashes of the war. And so my having trained and worked as an embroiderer for many years was at odds with their description of my overnight success. In any case, I stopped giving interviews after that."

"Despite being married to a journalist like Walter Kaczmarek?"

"Despite that. We agreed that it wouldn't be right for him, or his magazine, to run stories about me, and the only journalists I knew and trusted were the people who worked for him."

"Didn't you ever want to tell your side of the story?"

"But I did. It is there for anyone to see—there in my work."

They sat in silence for a moment, and just as Heather was beginning to feel a little steadier and calmer, another worry descended upon her.

"Do you think Nan would mind? I won't go into anything about her personal life. About that awful Jeremy or having to leave England. But would she be okay with my writing about the two of you and how you were friends? How you worked on the gown together?"

"She put your name on the box with the embroideries, did she not? She saved them all those years, and she left them for you to find, and if she had truly wished to shut the door on her time at Hartnell I believe she would have destroyed them long ago."

"But she didn't."

"She did not, and you were the one who saw the ray of light peeking through, and you were the one to open the door. It is past time that she, along with all of us who made the gown, be recognized for our work. And I will help you do it."

"Thank you." Relief clogged Heather's throat, and something that felt like joy, too, at the chance to learn more of Nan and her life and the work she had done.

Miriam patted Heather's arm, and then she reached for her handbag. "I also have something for you. Do you remember the sprigs of white heather that Ann had the idea of adding to the train? This is the sample she made up for Monsieur Hartnell. I wish for you to have it."

As she was talking, Miriam pulled a small parcel from her bag and gave it to Heather. Inside, beneath several layers of tissue paper, was a square of silk about the size of a cocktail napkin, and embroidered upon it was a sprig of heather. The same kind of heather that Nan had always grown in her garden.

"I remember the day she told Monsieur Hartnell about her idea for the heather," Miriam said fondly. "She was inspired, she said, by a pot of white heather that the queen had given her. The present queen's mother, that is. I believe Ann brought it with her when she emigrated to Canada."

"She did. It was all over her garden, and when she sold the house my mom and I kept some of it."

"It lives on?" Miriam asked wonderingly, tears in her eyes.

"It does. Maybe I could send you some? Only I have a feeling I'd be breaking about a hundred laws."

"It is no matter. To know it is there—oh, Heather. That alone is enough."

Chapter Twenty-Eight

Ann

December 3, 1947

*A*nn did as Miriam had suggested, and visited her doctor to ensure she really was pregnant. She had been a patient of Dr. Lovell her entire life. He had cared for her parents in their final illnesses, he had comforted her and Milly when Frank had been killed, and she hoped he would understand and have some sympathy for her predicament.

She was wrong.

"What would your mother say if she could witness your shame? This is what comes of getting ideas above your station. I always knew it would do you no good to work at such a place." That, and variations of the same, were all he had to say, and after a solid ten minutes of listening to his verbal abuse she walked out of his examining room, her heart pounding but her head held high.

She went straight to the post office, for she'd stayed up half the night before writing her letter to Milly, and the only reason she hadn't sent it off already was the slim hope she'd had, until fifteen minutes ago, that she might not be pregnant. So much for hope.

She'd paid extra for an airmail form, and she'd written out what she would say to Milly ahead of time on a plain sheet of paper to ensure it would all fit. Not that there was much to say at this point.

Dear Milly,

I hope this finds you well and that you aren't yet frozen solid by the Canadian winter. This will come as a surprise but I have decided to emigrate. As you know I have some small savings but will need somewhere to stay when I arrive. Do you think your brothers will object to having me if I pay my way? I will explain all when I see you but I am well and happy and certain I am doing the right thing.

With love from your friend and sister,
Ann

A week had gone by, and then another, and Ann had begun to fear that she would never hear back from Milly. She wasn't showing, nothing close to it yet, but the waistbands of her skirts were getting tight. Before too long, anyone who knew her well would notice, and then they would *know.*

Milly's telegram was delivered three weeks to the day after Ann had posted the fragile airmail slip to Canada. It was Christmas Eve, and she and Miriam were waiting for Walter, who was to drive them out to his friends' house in Edenbridge.

There was a knock at the door, and Ann heard the sound of something being pushed through the letter box, so of course she went running in the hopes that something had finally arrived from Canada.

It had. The telegram was in an envelope, and her hands were so unsteady that she tore the form inside almost in half as she pulled it free.

DEAR ANN SORRY FOR DELAY YOUR LETTER
LANDED YESTERDAY. YES TO EVERYTHING.
COME SOONEST. GO VIA HALIFAX THEN TRAIN
TO TORONTO. WIRE ME DETAILS ONCE PASSAGE
BOOKED. WAITING WITH OPEN ARMS. LOVE
MILLY

"What does it say?" Miriam asked, her anxiety palpable.

"Yes. Milly says yes."

A knock sounded, likely Walter come to collect them, yet still Miriam hovered. "Are you all right?"

This was not something to cry over. This was good news, and on Christmas Eve besides. She looked up, met Miriam's questioning gaze, and tried to smile. "I'm fine. It's only that I'd been worried she might say no. Or that she'd want to have me, but couldn't manage it."

"I think your Milly would do a great deal to help you. And her letters make Canada sound like a wonderful place. Cold, yes, but with many consolations."

There was just enough time, on their drive to the house in Edenbridge, for Walter to explain to Miriam, with Ann's help, some of the rituals of a traditional English Christmas. Caroling and wassailing and paper hats, the king's message on the wireless, the tree with its paper chains and treasured ornaments, and the spectacle of the pudding, already sodden with brandy, being set afire with even more spirits.

She and Miriam were given a room to share, and she spent ages holding baby Victoria, and in the morning there were stockings laden with little gifts that Ruby had painstakingly amassed for everyone, even Ann. And there were moments when she forgot to be sad and was able to let herself be buoyed along by the others' happiness. Only for an instant, but it was enough. It would have to be enough.

ON DECEMBER 29 SHE booked her passage to Canada, all but emptying her modest savings account in the process. On December 30 she told Miss Duley.

Ann waited until the end of the day, after everyone had left for home, and then she sat the other woman down and told her that she was emigrating to Canada. Not as baldly as that, of course, for she tried to couch it in terms that would make it rather less of a shock. She explained that she missed her sister-in-law very much. She said she wished to see more of the world. She claimed to believe that Canada was the sort of place where a hardworking young woman like herself might better herself.

Miss Duley didn't believe a word of it. "The truth, Ann. This has something to do with that young man, doesn't it?"

"Please, Miss Duley. *Please.*"

"I don't blame you one bit for leaving, my dear. Only I will miss you. I hope you know that."

"I do. I love it here. I always have, and I don't want to go. I truly don't. But everyone here knows I'm not married. All the other girls. Mr. Hartnell, too. I can't bear the thought of everyone knowing, and thinking the worst of me. I just can't."

"Could you go away? Have the baby and give it up? There are so many families who'd be grateful—"

"I would, only I want this baby. I never saw myself getting married, you know, not really, but I did want to be a mum. Now I have the chance."

"I see, and I don't disagree. But why go so far away? Why the other end of the world?"

"He doesn't know, and I don't want him to find out. Not ever. He might try to take the baby from me. Don't you see? I can't take that chance."

"Oh, you needn't worry about *him*. Mr. Hartnell did confide in me, not so very long ago, that he had put a word in the ear of someone at the palace, just a quiet word, and naturally the wretch was given the sack straightaway. It then came out that he'd run up a number of debts. Very large, I gather, and when they came to light he did a midnight flit."

"He . . . he did what?" Ann asked, not quite able to believe her own ears.

"He vanished. Made for somewhere in the Far East? Or perhaps it was Australia."

"How did Mr. Hartnell know who he was? I never told him."

"Nor did I. I don't suppose it matters, does it? The scoundrel is gone, and is in no position to be a threat to you ever again. Surely that must be a relief. Now—tell me when you are leaving. I know Mr. Hartnell will be very sad to hear of it."

"My ship leaves on January fifth," she answered, though saying it out loud didn't make it feel any more real. Not until the coast of England had faded from view would it truly feel real to her.

"Then you'll just miss him. He won't be back from the south of France for another week after that. Oh, well. I'll write you a splendid reference, of course, which will certainly carry some weight with the Canadians. Presumably they have one or two decent dressmakers there."

"Thank you, Miss Duley. I've never said so before, but I'm very grateful for all you taught me."

"And I'm every bit as grateful for your many years of hard work. I'm also rather concerned that if we continue on in this vein we'll both end up in a puddle of tears. So why don't you let me treat you to supper at Lyons? Only a small token of my esteem, but no less sincere for all that."

ANN WAS ABLE to put a few more pounds in her savings account by selling the wireless and some of the better pieces of furniture, and as she'd always been a tidy and frugal sort of person she hadn't much in the way of smaller things to pack. Photographs of her parents and brother, her nan's Royal Worcester cup and saucer, the rose-patterned china that had been her mum's.

The sketchbook would not be coming to Canada. She had only used up a third of the pages; these she ripped out and burned in a small but satisfying bonfire in her garden. The rest of it, still perfectly serviceable, she left on a shelf in the pantry for the next tenants of her house to find. There would be children, like as not, and they could use it for their schoolwork.

It took much longer for her to decide on what to do with the samples of embroidery Mr. Hartnell had given her. After the shock of seeing Jeremy on the day of the royal ladies' visit, she'd taken the box of samples back to the embroidery workroom and promptly forgotten about them. It was only after the wedding, when Miss Duley had insisted on a long-overdue tidying up of the room, that Ann had remembered the samples.

"I can't believe I forgot to take them back, Miss Duley. I'm so sorry."

"No need. And besides, Mr. Hartnell wants for you and Miriam to keep a few each of the ones you worked. A memento of the day, he told me."

In the end Ann had chosen three—the single York rose, the star flowers, and the ears of wheat—and when Miriam had hesitated, Ann had encouraged her to keep the smaller sample of white heather. "For good luck," she had explained.

Now she sat on the floor of her empty sitting room, the samples in her lap, and tried to decide what she wanted to do with them. Not what she *ought* to do, which was to quietly return them to Mr. Hartnell or pass them on to Miriam. Certainly she wouldn't destroy them as she'd done her sketchbook. It had been tainted by Jeremy, but the samples held no such poisonous associations for her. She had been happy when she had made them. She had been so full of hope.

One day, far in the future, she would give the samples to her son or daughter, or even a beloved grandchild, and by then she would know what to say. One day, if she were very lucky, there might be someone who would understand.

Ann packed the embroideries among her other precious things, and that was the last difficult decision she had to make. All that remained, now, was the queen's heather from Balmoral. She would dig it up tomorrow, and she would coddle it all the way across the ocean to Canada, and there, come spring, the white heather would be the first thing she planted in her garden.

It had been hard to say good-bye to Miss Duley and her friends from work, hard to turn the key in the door of her little house and walk away, hard to visit her parents' and Frank's graves for the last time. But hardest of all was her farewell to Miriam.

Ann tried to remain composed when Miriam and Walter took her to Euston Station. Miriam was fretful, asking her to check that she had her train ticket to Liverpool and her steamship ticket to Halifax, and of course her passport, and that her purse was tucked safely into the inside pocket of her coat, and eventually Ann hugged her tight and told her she must stop worrying.

"You know I'll land on my feet, just the same as you did when you first came here. You know I will, so you aren't to fuss."

"Very well," Miriam agreed. "Only—"

"I will be fine. But I want you to promise one thing in return. You must keep working on your embroideries. No matter how long they take, and no matter what else happens in your life, you must *never* abandon them. Do you promise? It's that important to me."

"I know it is. I swear I will never set them aside."

A whistle sounded, and Walter came forward, clearly reluctant to interrupt, but mindful of the need for Ann to board her train.

"Miriam, my dear. Ann must go or she'll miss her train." He bent down to kiss Ann's cheek. "Good-bye, Ann, and good luck."

"Thank you, Walter." She'd never dared to call him by his first name before. "You will take care of my friend?"

"I will."

There was so much more she wished to say, but she was out of time, and what would it change? Miriam knew already. She had to know this was their farewell.

"*Adieu*, Ann. *Adieu, ma chère amie.*"

They embraced, one last, heartfelt hug, and she fixed the memory of it deep in her heart. She stepped away from her friend. She turned around, and she made herself walk, one deliberate step after another, all the way to the far end of the platform, to the open door of the third-class carriages, and to the new life that awaited her half a world away.

She had cut the final thread. She did not look back.

Chapter Twenty-Nine

Miriam

March 3, 1948

Miriam finished work at half-past five, another quiet day in a succession of quiet weeks at Hartnell. Rather than take the bus or Underground, she walked to Walter's flat, glad of a chance to stretch her legs and make the most of a mild and clear evening. Winter was over, or inching near to being over, and only that morning she'd seen snowdrops in the gardens at Bloomsbury Square. Flowers were blooming once more, and spring had come again.

She hadn't thought to ask Walter what they would have for supper. They could go out to one of their usual haunts, but part of her fancied the idea of staying in, never mind that she would need to work some magic to transform his bachelor's provisions into something edible. The other night his pantry had yielded nothing more promising than a can of baked beans and half a loaf of that ghastly brown bread everyone hated but had long since resigned themselves to eating. So she'd turned to him and raised a single, questioning eyebrow, and he'd put on his coat and taken her to eat at the Blue Lion around the corner.

In recent weeks his flat had become her favorite place in the world. She loved its high ceilings and tall windows with no view to speak of, its walls blanketed with overflowing bookshelves and, where they left off, dozens of paintings and prints and photographs he had collected over the years, none very valuable but all significant to him in some way. Most of all, she loved Walter's flat because it was so close to her own, new home.

When Ann had decided to emigrate, there had been no question of Miriam staying on in the council house, not least because she didn't relish being evicted when, inevitably, the council realized only one woman—and a foreigner at that—was living in a house meant for a family of five or more. She had told Ann that she would be fine and she'd never been truly worried, but she had been anxious. None of the other women at work needed a flatmate, and the prospect of moving to a boardinghouse again was distinctly unappealing. Even after almost a year her memories of those dispiriting weeks in Ealing had not faded.

Walter had been just as concerned, and for a while she'd lived in fear of his suggesting she come to live with him in true bohemian style, or even that he might propose they get married and solve the problem in that fashion.

Instead he had come out to the house in Barking and, over a cup of tea in the kitchen, surrounded by packing crates, he had made a confession.

"I got to talking with Ruby the other day. She's worried about their flat, for she and Bennett are thinking of living in Edenbridge fulltime until the baby gets a bit older. She's been losing sleep worrying about what will become of the place when they're away, she told me.

Mice in the pantry and silverfish in the linen cupboard, and burglars noticing the lights are off and ransacking the place. That sort of thing.

"I asked if she and Bennett had considered getting a lodger to stay in the spare room and keep an eye on the flat while they were away. She admitted it had occurred to her but she'd been too tired to do anything about it.

"So I then asked if she might consider having you to stay, and I reminded her that Ann was emigrating to Canada, which means you need somewhere to live."

"Oh, Walter—"

"Hear me out. She was delighted. I wish you could have heard her reaction. And Bennett is in full accord."

"Are you sure they aren't trying to please you?"

"Quite sure. You would be helping them, and although I doubt they intend to ask you for anything by way of rent, you might be able to induce them to accept a token amount. But only if you truly feel it's necessary."

"But why should they do such a thing for me?"

Her question appeared to baffle him. "Why shouldn't they? That's what friends do for one another. I do know that if you refuse their offer and move into some grubby boardinghouse it won't be a week before Ruby lands at your front door with baby Victoria in her arms, and she'll be begging you to move into their flat. You could also lodge with Bennett's godmother in south Kensington, as Ruby once did, but it's all the way on the other side of London. And I'm not certain I wish for you to be so far away."

"Far away?"

"From my flat. It's the next street over from Ruby and Bennett's. Just so you know."

He wasn't giving her any room to think, let alone form a coherent objection to his plans. "Where shall I go when they return? I cannot live there once they are back in London."

"That's a worry we'll save for another day. Until then, you'll have a roof over your head and friends nearby."

That had been a little more than two months ago, and in the weeks that followed Miriam's evenings had fallen into a pleasant sort of pattern. On the nights Walter wasn't working, she would go to his flat for supper, and when he was busy or she was tired, or when she wished to work on her embroideries or have some time to herself, she remained at Ruby and Bennett's flat for the evening. She had yet to spend the night with him, and he had yet to ask her.

She knocked softly at his door, for it wasn't her home, after all, and it would be rude to simply barge in. It was unlocked, as usual, and as soon as she entered she was struck by the wonderful smells coming from his kitchen. Without even bothering to wipe her feet she hurried down the hall to investigate.

The kitchen door was open. He had his back to her, his sleeves rolled to his elbows, and was preoccupied with the contents of the frying pan before him. Garlic and shallots, she guessed from the smell, and he was cooking them in the fat from a heap of browned chicken pieces that now sat on a plate by the cooker.

He peered at a note he'd tacked to the cupboard door next to the cooker, then uncorked a bottle of vermouth, added a splash to the pan, and jumped back when the drippings hissed at him. She stood at the kitchen door and watched him cook and let her heart grow full at the sight.

"Walter," she said.

He turned his head a little, just so she could see he was smiling. "Hello, there."

"Will you turn off the cooker? Just for a moment."

He did so, and then he turned around to face her properly. She took the spoon from his hand, set it on the counter, and hugged him close.

"How?" she asked wonderingly.

"I've watched you make it often enough." His arms came around her, returning her embrace. "I even remembered your wishing for vermouth that one time, and how it would make the entire dish taste better."

"That is why you had all those questions for me. I thought you were simply being a journalist."

"I was. But I was also learning."

"Why tonight? Why not wait for Friday? I usually make it on Friday."

"I know, but today is March third."

"And?" she asked, puzzled.

"You told me once that you came to England on March third. That's a year ago today. I thought we ought to mark the occasion in some way." And then, his voice a little uncertain, "What do you think?"

"It looks and smells wonderful. Where did you get the olives and—"

"Prunes and fennel seeds? From Marcel Normand in Shoreditch. He even sold me an orange. It was a little dried out, so he decided to bend the rules."

Looking around him, she spied a small bottle next to the cooker. "Is that olive oil?"

"It is. According to Monsieur Normand, the stuff from the chemist's is fit only for the greasing of motorcar engines."

"Do you need any help?"

"Not in here. I've come this far—I want to see if I can turn out something worth eating. But would you mind setting the table? Just push all the papers and books down to the far end. There's no rhyme or reason to them. Oh—and there's one more thing."

She tilted her head back, curious about what he meant, and he bent down and kissed her until she was deliciously dizzy.

After supper they did the washing up together, and then they sat on his big, comfortable sofa, drank the black coffee he had made in his little espresso pot, and they told each other of their respective days. It was getting late, and she would ask him to walk her home before too long, but it had become their habit to listen to Walter's favorite pieces of music on his gramophone after supper. He had strong opinions about music, and some of the pieces he played were not at all to her taste, but one concerto had been echoing through her mind for days.

"The music with the cello—you played it several times last week. What was the name of the composer? You told me but I have forgotten."

"Edward Elgar."

He found the record, set the needle arm onto the spinning disc, and a swell of music filled the room. The melody was plaintive and swooning, the chords insistent, haunting, mournful. Miriam held her breath, waiting for her favorite part, a rising thread of sound so anguished and expressive that tears always sprang to her eyes.

Normally she was able to blink them back, but now they overflowed, cascading down her cheeks, and though she knew she ought to wipe them away, she did nothing. This time she wept and let him see. She could hide nothing from him.

A heartbeat later he was kneeling before her, so tall that it put them eye to eye. He touched his brow to hers.

"Don't cry," he whispered. "Please. I can't bear it."

"I never meant for this to happen. Any of it. But there you were in the street, rescuing my shoe. Rescuing me."

"No," he said. "You rescued yourself. Never forget it."

"I was so sure I would be alone. That it would be easier, better, after what I had lost. It comforted me to know it."

"Why? Solitary confinement is the worst sort of imprisonment. Nothing is worse than being alone, my darling. Nothing."

"I—"

"You survived. Do you think yourself unworthy of it? I fear that you do."

"I didn't—"

"Did you collaborate with the Nazis? Of course you did not. Did you take up with a German, and make use of his weakness for your protection? I don't believe for one second that you did, but even if you had I would not condemn you. We all found ways of surviving the war, and the enemy who sought to kill you was a far more determined and pitiless foe than the enemy I faced at a distance."

"Please do not make me think of it, not now. Not tonight."

"I won't," he said, and he bent his head in contrition. "Only believe me when I say I am glad beyond measure that you survived. Every selfish particle of me is glad, because without you I would have been alone, too. I won't pretend to have suffered as you did, but when Mary was killed I thought I might die from the grief of it."

"Do you miss her?"

"Of course I do," he said, and now he looked up and met her gaze steadily, his pale eyes shining with emotion. "She was my friend, and my lover, for many years. But I don't see her when I look at you. I don't long for her when I'm with you."

He pulled off his spectacles, tossing them on the table, and took her face in his hands, cradling it ever so gently. And then he touched his mouth to hers, deepening the kiss by degrees, and she leaned forward, almost tipping off her perch on the sofa, so eager was she to reciprocate.

He pulled away, only far enough to scatter kisses across her cheek, and then to whisper in her ear. "You are the woman I want, the woman I desire, and I will wait for you as long as you need. For years, if it comes to that."

"You do not need to wait," she said, and if she was trembling it was only out of happiness and excitement and more than a little apprehension. But she was safe with this man, and sure of his intentions, and she wanted this intimacy with him more than she'd ever wanted anything in her life.

He sat back on his heels, his breathing a little ragged, and looked her in the eye. "I love you. I need you to know that."

"And I love you," she told him. "I do."

"Then will you be with me now, and tomorrow, and the days after that? Is that something you can give me?"

"I will," she promised. "And now, if you are ready, I should like for you to kiss me again."

Epilogue

Ann

March 21, 1997

*I*t had been years since Ann had gone to downtown Toronto on her own, and she was more than a little nervous of getting lost on the way to the gallery, but it wasn't enough to deter her, nor did she want to ask her daughter to come along. This was something she needed to do on her own.

It was a Friday afternoon, the day of the week when she usually took care of the sort of errands that couldn't be done on the weekend. Visits to the bank, medical appointments, that sort of thing. Today, though, she took the subway all the way downtown, and then, instead of getting on a streetcar, she decided to walk. Her route took her through the heart of Chinatown, which had always been one of her favorite parts of the city, but she didn't have time to stop. Not today.

She soldiered on, and just as she was beginning to feel a little tired she caught sight of the banners.

MIRIAM DASSIN
VÉL D'HIV
ART GALLERY OF ONTARIO
SPRING 1997

She couldn't remember, now, how she'd learned that the embroideries would be exhibited in Canada. Most likely she'd heard it on the news. Their coming to Toronto was nothing short of a miracle, for she'd wanted to see them for years and years, and it had been hard to wait out the crowds. She hoped the gallery wouldn't be jam-packed today.

Ann paid her entrance fee, politely declined the suggestion that she become a member, and made a beeline for the gallery where Miriam's embroideries awaited her. According to the pamphlet she'd been given, the exhibition was set up as three separate spaces. First was the historical context for the embroideries; this she bypassed, for she already knew more about Miriam than any potted history could tell her.

The second space was set up like a small theater, with a short film that repeated every ten minutes. This, too, held little interest for her, particularly since Miriam herself had not been interviewed.

She was rushing, she knew she was, but she could come back to all of this later, after she had seen the embroideries. She walked on, drawn to the final room, and found herself before the first panel. *Un dîner de Chabbat,* the one Miriam had first imagined while sitting at Ann's kitchen table fifty years before.

Ann had seen pictures, of course, but nothing could have prepared her for the actual thing, so vivid and vibrant that the people it depicted seemed more real, somehow, than any of the strangers who surrounded her. She stood and stared, and suddenly she realized that she was staring at her own face. Her younger self, no more than twenty-five, her hair the color of marmalade, her skin unlined.

She lost track of how long she stood there, her heart alternately seized by joy and grief. Her friend had thought of her long after they had been parted. Miriam had not forgotten her.

She circled the room, admiring the other panels for long minutes, and when she was done she returned to *Un dîner de Chabbat,* and only after every detail of it was fixed in her mind did she step back and away.

What would she say to Miriam, if ever she had the chance to speak with her again?

She would tell her friend that she had been happy. Her daughter was happy, too, and was married to a good man, and she had a daughter of her own.

She would tell Miriam about Heather, her only grandchild, and the light of her life. A single smile from that child was worth more than everything Ann had left behind, and she had never, not once in all the years since, ever had cause to regret what she had done.

So little remained of her life before Canada. A few pieces of her mother's rose-patterned china, the cup and saucer from her nan, a handful of photographs, the heather in her garden. The embroidery samples, still packed away, unseen and unloved. She had never shown them to her daughter, for they would have provoked questions she couldn't, even now, even after half a century, bear to answer.

She would leave them to Heather. As soon as she got home, she would take the box down from the top shelf of her linen cupboard, she would look through the samples one last time, she would let herself remember, and then she would put them away for good. Only this time the box would have a label. *For Heather.*

Outside the sun was shining and the air smelled like spring, even in the middle of the city. It was a beautiful day, the first day of spring, and soon the Balmoral heather would be in bloom.

She had a family who loved her, and she had made something of herself. She had survived. She had been happy. She was happy, now, in this sunshine, on this spring day, with the surprise and delight of Miriam's embroideries a delectable secret to savor and cherish.

It was enough.

Miriam

October 2, 2016

Nearly everything was ready for dinner. With the help of Rosie, her home help who came in every morning, Miriam had polished her silver and rubbed the dust from her best wineglasses, and they had spread her best cloth upon the table. The cloth she had embroidered for the first Rosh Hashanah she and Walter had celebrated together. There were stains here and there, and her children often said she should hand it over to a museum to be cleaned and preserved for posterity, but in this she ignored them.

Most days she tried not to dwell on how much she missed him. She thought of Walter constantly, and when she was alone in the flat, she often spoke to him as if he were still at her side, listening as attentively as he had always done. Their life together had been good, and long, and she was very nearly certain she would see his face again.

Sometimes, in the early morning, in the long, quiet minutes between her dreams and the day, she let herself imagine that moment. He would be waiting for her, his shoulders stooping a little, his hair bright against the sun, and his cold, pale eyes would be ever so warm for her. And she would reach out to him—

But today was not a day for sadness. It was the beginning of the new year, and soon her children and grandchildren would be arriving for dinner, all of them including Daniel, who had come home for the holidays though he'd moved to New York City only two weeks before. It had been selfish of her to insist, but it was, she felt, her prerogative as matriarch.

Her guests would bring most of the food, excepting of course Grand-Mère's Friday-night chicken, which Rosie had helped her make the day before. It wasn't the most traditional dish to serve at Rosh Hashanah, but the prunes were sweet, as were the memories it evoked, and it was Hannah's favorite.

Hannah was the youngest of her great-grandchildren, and she was little enough to still want hugs and kisses and cuddles in Walter's big old Morris chair by the sitting room windows. When Hannah arrived they would sit in the Walter chair, as the child liked to call it, and they would speak in French together, and Miriam would tell her about Rosh Hashanah when she, Mimi, had been a little girl long, long ago.

Yesterday she had taken down one of her favorite embroideries from her bedroom wall and wrapped it in layers of tissue, for she was sending it back to America with Daniel, with instructions that he give it to Heather when she visited him in New York. Miriam had held it back from the retrospective, for reasons she hadn't understood at the time. She had assumed, then, that she couldn't bear to be parted from it, but in that she'd been wrong. Now she knew that she had been waiting for Heather.

"Mimi! Mimi! Where are you?" came Hannah's piping voice from the front hall.

"Here I am! And what is this you have for me?"

"Uncle Daniel and I looked for peonies, because those are your favorite, but the man in the flower shop didn't have any. So we brought you some dahlias. I hope you aren't disappointed."

"Not at all, and they are very lovely. Come with me now and we will put them in water. Then we will sit together in the Walter chair, if you like, and I will tell you some stories."

Heather

October 14, 2016

*H*er flight from Toronto had arrived early, and the train ride in from Newark had been easier than she'd hoped, and her hotel in Manhattan's West Village was just around the corner from Washington Square and had a main-floor lounge with Django Reinhardt playing softly in the background and twenty different wines by the glass on the menu, and even though Daniel wasn't supposed to show up for another half hour, she'd made sure to sit where she could see the front door. She was thinking about a glass of white wine, even though it was barely five o'clock, and had gone so far as to snag a menu from a nearby table, when some impulse made her look up.

Daniel stood in the doorway, a solid twenty minutes before she'd hoped to see him there, and he looked tired and serious, and for a moment she wondered if she'd made a mistake in coming to visit.

Maybe it would have been better to stick to texts and emails for a little longer.

He turned, as if he'd somehow divined what she'd been thinking, and for a moment she forgot to breathe as he stared at her. And then he smiled, crossed the room, and kissed her until they were both a little breathless.

"Hello," he said. "You made it."

"Hello. I did."

He shrugged out of his coat, dumped it and his messenger bag on the far end of the banquette where she was perched, and sat next to her, just as she'd hoped he would.

"What do you think? I've stayed here myself a few times."

"I love it. Teeny tiny rooms, but that's New York, right? And this common area is amazing."

"It is, although later on it'll be overrun by NYU students. God knows I didn't have the money to pay fifteen bucks for a glass of wine when I was an undergraduate."

"Me neither. Although I do feel like splurging on a glass of something. I got some good news just before I left."

"The story about your nan and Mimi?"

"Yes." She looked around, a little nervous of being overheard. "It isn't official, but I sold it."

"You did? That's fantastic. Was it to the same place we talked about? The one that despite its title has absolutely no connection to William Makepeace Thackeray?"

"Ha ha. Yes. That one."

"Then we definitely need to celebrate. But first I have to give you something." He opened his bag and retrieved a flat box about ten inches square. "Here you are."

"What is it?"

"A gift from Mimi. She was nervous about putting it in the post."

"Why? Is it delicate?"

"Yes, and also rather valuable. I put my laptop in the overhead bin on the way home, but *this* I held in my lap."

"You know what it is?"

"I do. Go on."

Inside, under half a dozen sheets of tissue paper, was a framed embroidery of a wreath of flowers: antique roses, the spidery apricot blossoms of a honeysuckle, tiny sprigs of lavender and lilac, and three sumptuously perfect peonies, their petals as ripe as berries. Wedged into one corner was a small notecard, the handwriting bold and almost calligraphic.

October 1, 2016

Ma chère Heather,

I embroidered this wreath in 1949 when I was pregnant with my daughter, Daniel's mother, and the flowers were inspired by my own mother's garden, a place long vanished but ever dear to me. Its creation brought me great happiness, and no small measure of peace, and I hope that whenever you see it you will be reminded of my love for your grandmother, the joy she brought to my life and yours, and the friendship I now extend to you, ma belle.

With my affectionate good wishes,
Miriam

Acknowledgments

My greatest debt of thanks must go to Mrs. Betty Foster, one of Norman Hartnell's seamstresses, who graciously agreed to be interviewed about her memories of working at Hartnell and her involvement in the creation of Princess Elizabeth's wedding gown. Without Mrs. Foster, I would have struggled to finish this book, and I am deeply grateful to her.

I would also like to thank Juliet Ferry and Jessica Jane Pile of the renowned bespoke hand embroidery studio Hand & Lock for helping me to understand the mechanics of the work done by my characters. My day at Hand & Lock was a delightful experience and I am very grateful to both of them for their enthusiastic support. Thanks to Natalie Woolman and Eleanor Scoones of Oxford Film and Television, who put me in touch with Betty Foster and shared some of their knowledge of the royal wedding, as well as the staff at The Royal Collection for early assistance with my research. I would also like to thank Dr. Carolyn Harris of the University of Toronto's School of Continuing Studies for reading over passages concerning the royal family, and Chrystel Turcotte for her advice regarding my usage of colloquial French.

In the course of researching *The Gown*, I relied upon the collections of a number of libraries, archives, and museums. I would specifically like to acknowledge the Bodleian Library at the University of Oxford, the British Newspaper Archive, the Mass-Observation Archive at the University of Sussex, the Museum of London, the National Archives (UK), the National Art Library, the Victoria and Albert Museum, the Royal Ontario Museum, and the Toronto Public Library.

To my literary agent, Kevan Lyon, and her colleagues at the Marsal Lyon Literary Agency, in particular Patricia Nelson, I once again extend my heartfelt thanks. I would also like to thank my personal publicist, Kathleen Carter, for her inspired and creative support.

I am profoundly grateful to my editor, Tessa Woodward, for understanding what I wanted to do with this book long before I had figured it out, and for guiding me with such sensitivity and certainty. I am so fortunate to have her (and her keen appreciation of all things royal) at my side.

I am also very grateful to Elle Keck in editorial, as well as my HarperCollins publicists Camille Collins, Jessica Lyons, Melissa Nowakowski, and Irina Pintea for supporting me so ably.

I want to thank the amazing team at William Morrow, in particular Samantha Hagerbaumer, Jennifer Hart, Martin Karlow, Julia Meltzer, Carla Parker, Shelby Peak, Alison Smith, Diahann Sturge, Serena Wang, Molly Waxman, and Amelia Wood. Thanks to the producers at HarperAudio for once again creating a beautiful audiobook. I'm also very grateful to the incredible sales staff in the U.S., Canada, and the international division, as well as the wonderful people at HarperCollins Canada, among them Leo Macdonald, Sandra Leff, Cory Beatty, Colleen Simpson, Shannon Parsons, Suman Seewat, and Kaitlyn Vincent.

Closer to home, I'd like to thank my friends for their love and support: Amutha, Ana, Clara, Denise, Erin, Jane D, Jane E, Jen, Kelly F, Kelly W, Liz, Margie, Mary, Mary Ellen, Michela, and Rena.

I would not have survived the race to the finish without the counsel and group texts from my band of sisters, aka the Coven: Karma Brown, Kerry Clare, Chantel Guertin, Kate Hilton, Elizabeth Renzetti, Marissa Stapley, and Kathleen Tucker. My sincere thanks as well to fellow authors and friends Janie Chang, Megan Crane, Karen Lord, and Kate Quinn for their sage advice and unflagging support.

My loving thanks to all my family, in particular my sister Kate and my children, Matthew and Daniela, for all they did to support and encourage me when I was buried in the world of *The Gown*. Most of all I want to thank my husband, Claudio, whose loving and steadfast heart is the inspiration for all of my heroes. (Now just go out and get that Wilfred Owen tattoo, okay?)

About the author

About the book

Insights,
Interviews
& More . . .

Read on . . .

Meet Jennifer Robson

Natalie Brown/ Tangerine Photo

JENNIFER ROBSON is the *USA Today* and #1 *Globe & Mail* (Toronto) bestselling author of five novels, among them *Somewhere in France* and *Goodnight from London*. She holds a doctorate in British economic and social history from Saint Antony's College, University of Oxford. She lives in Toronto, Canada, with her husband and children. ∾

Closed Doors and
Open Windows

I wish I could say that the premise for *The Gown*
came upon me in true "eureka!" fashion, but the
reality is a little more prosaic. It was the summer
of 2016, I was having lunch with my editor and
literary agent, and we were brainstorming ideas
for my next book. After agreeing that I ought
to write something set in Britain after World
War II, we'd begun to flounder. I'd floated a few
suggestions, none of them terribly compelling,
and was starting to feel a bit desperate. So I
posed the question: What felt important to the
people who lived through that time? What was
significant and memorable *then*? And that's
when I remembered one event, late in 1947, that
had transfixed the entire world: the wedding of
Princess Elizabeth to Lieutenant Philip
Mountbatten.

Nothing could have stood in greater
contrast to those draining, dispiriting, and
miserable postwar years than the glittering
and bejeweled spectacle of a royal wedding.
The great celebrations of VE Day and VJ Day
were over and the hard work of rebuilding
the world had begun, but Britain's economy
remained in a calamitous state after years
of ruinously expensive warfare. Not only did
austerity measures such as rationing remain
in place, but in a number of respects they also
became even more stringent. For many people,
life seemed to be getting worse, not better.

That is the world I set out to explore when I
began work on *The Gown*. What would it have
been like to live through those lean, hard years?
And what did the royal wedding mean to the
people of the time—was it indeed "a flash of
color on the hard road [they had] to travel," as
Winston Churchill famously said? Or was it a ▶

3

bitter and unwelcome reminder of how little they had and how much they had lost?

From the start, I didn't want to tell my story from the point of view of Princess Elizabeth or anyone in her inner circle. Not because I feel the princess—Queen Elizabeth II as we now know her—is in any way uninteresting, but rather because I believe her true character is a mystery to anyone beyond her close family and friends. The queen has never given an interview and never will, her thoughts and opinions on most subjects are largely opaque, and the woman we *think* we know is, I believe, largely a projection of our individual feelings and beliefs. Here I want to be clear: I am fascinated by the queen and her family, but no amount of research will ever allow me to know them; and if I cannot truly know and understand them, I feel it is better to remain at a distance.

But back to my lunch and the brainstorming session, because I still needed a hook for my story—even more so once I'd discounted the possibility of telling it from the point of view of the bride or anyone in her inner circle. And that's when two words popped into my head: *the gown*.

A few seconds later, we were admiring pictures of the royal wedding on my phone, and I had the central question on which my story would turn: who made Princess Elizabeth's wedding gown? I knew it had been designed by Norman Hartnell; what I wanted to know, rather, was who *constructed* it. Who were the women who created the dazzling embroidery that embellished the gown, and what were their stories?

As a writer and a historian, I'm uncomfortable with the idea of sacrificing historical authenticity for dramatic tension, and that's why my first four books have as their protagonists entirely fictional characters. While the same is true of *The Gown*—Ann, Miriam, and Heather are entirely products of my imagination—its cast also includes a number of real-life figures, among them people who were known to have worked at Hartnell, but whose personal stories were never recorded and are now all but impossible to accurately recount.

This uncomfortable truth dawned on me not long after I began work on *The Gown*: I would have to fictionalize the stories of real people, as well as insert fictional characters into a setting populated by known and recognizable figures. I would also have to take some liberties with minor aspects of recorded history, if only to make the story I was telling more comprehensible.

Germaine Davide, for instance, the formidable Frenchwoman employed by Hartnell as his chief fitter and known to everyone in the workrooms as Mam'selle, was mentioned by name in any number of sources, among them Hartnell's memoirs, but she wrote no memoir herself and gave no interviews, and details of her personal life, at a remove of more than half a century, are now impossible to unearth. The same is true of Edith Duley, who was known to have been a senior figure in the embroidery workrooms: I came across her name in several newspaper articles, and I believe she is the woman described as the "head of embroidery" in a photograph that appeared in a *Picture Post* article in the autumn of 1947, but that is all. In his memoir *Silver and Gold*, Hartnell also mentions a woman named Flora Ballard, but she proved even more elusive, and so for the purposes of narrative clarity I elected to streamline the number of women in supervisory roles in the workroom. To that end, Miss Duley is not only a composite of several people, but also a fictional character in every respect apart from her name and the barest details of her physical appearance.

Even more daunting, for me, was the mystery of the embroiderers themselves. Dozens of articles were written about the creation of Princess Elizabeth's wedding gown—nearly every British magazine and newspaper ran one or more in the latter half of 1947—but no one, it seems, thought to interview a single embroiderer.

If anyone from Hartnell were to read *The Gown*, they might reasonably protest that they don't recognize any of my characters: not Mr. Hartnell, not Mam'selle or Miss Duley or Miss Holliday, and certainly not Ann or Miriam. In this I hope I may be forgiven, not only for conjuring their characters from the ether, but also in attaching real names to largely fictional creations. Only one person, within the walls of Hartnell, is true to life: Betty from the sewing workroom.

Betty Foster, née Pearce, was one of four seamstresses who worked on the wedding gown, and it was only by the purest stroke of good fortune that I met her at all. For months I had attempted, with diminishing success, to get in touch with anyone who had worked at Hartnell in the 1940s, and although many decades had passed I was hopeful that I might yet find someone who could tell me about life in the workrooms.

I had tried, and failed, to gain access to Sir Norman Hartnell's personal papers and archive, which are held privately. I had contacted the curators at the Royal Collection, with the hopes that they would be able to put me in touch with one or more of the women who had once worked at Hartnell, but they were unable to help me.

With those doors firmly closed, I consoled myself with a trip to London to see the wedding gown itself, which was on display at ▶

Closed Doors and Open Windows (*continued*)

Buckingham Palace as part of the *Fashioning a Reign* exhibition. I also wandered around Bruton Street and Bruton Place (though I was never brave enough to knock on the door and ask to go inside), and I searched online and in person at every library and museum with holdings related to Norman Hartnell and the royal wedding of 1947.

I was gathering ever more information, but it still felt incomplete, for I was never able to find more than the barest scraps of information about the women who sewed and embroidered the wedding gown. A few photographs, some maddeningly vague details in Hartnell's published memoirs—that was all. With barely more than a year until the first draft of my book was due, I was still bumping up against closed doors.

I wasn't willing to give up, however, so I asked myself: if I can't speak to those who worked for Hartnell, or read their stories, or even unearth basic details such as the shape of an ordinary day in the workrooms, can I speak to someone who does similar work *today*? And that's how I ended up at Hand & Lock, London's oldest and most prestigious bespoke hand embroidery atelier, on another trip to England in early 2017. I wanted to know how it felt to sit in front of an embroidery frame for hours on end, to take those first stitches on an immaculate piece of silk, to feel my eyes blur and my neck ache after hours of concentration on that same piece of silk and the motifs I had been tasked with creating.

The day I spent at Hand & Lock happened to coincide with the visit of a documentary film crew, part of the team who were working on *A Very Royal Wedding*, and as I chatted with their producers I mentioned how difficult it had been to research my book, and how much I would have loved to speak to someone who had worked at Hartnell at the time. To my astonishment, they offered to put me in touch with Betty Foster.

The next day I went to meet Mrs. Foster, and I listened to her stories of life at Hartnell, and the memories she shared with me made all the difference to how I approached the story I was writing. She opened a window into the heart and soul of Hartnell, and I am deeply grateful for her insights. It was she who told me how Miss Holliday kindly allowed all the women in the sewing workrooms to add a stitch to the gown, and thereby say they had worked on the princess's finery; and it was Mrs. Foster who described the royal ladies' visit to the workrooms and the unpracticed curtsies she and her friends offered their guests. She told me about the workroom interiors, Mr. Hartnell's kindness, and Mam'selle's impenetrable accent, as well as dozens of other details that brought my story to life. With Mrs. Foster's permission, I later added her to *The Gown* as a character, and so it is Betty herself who accompanies Miriam to the palace on the wedding day.

Here I need to make one last confession: on the wedding day itself, Mrs. Foster actually was outside, just by the gates of Buckingham Palace, having been given a special ticket to stand in a roped-off area with many of her friends from Hartnell. It was with her permission that I instead put her inside the palace on November 20, 1947, and let her look out along the Mall, with Miriam at her side, as the carriages with the royal party left for Westminster Abbey that morning. I feel she deserved no less.

As with my other novels, in *The Gown* I have attempted to describe the past—not the far-distant past, but a vanished and largely unfamiliar world all the same—with authenticity and accuracy. I accept that I have made mistakes, and that those errors are my fault and responsibility alone. Yet I hope, in the end, that you will read this story in the spirit in which it was written, which is one of respect, reverence, and above all profound gratitude for those whose sacrificed and lost so much during those terrible years of war.

An Interview with Betty Foster

Jennifer Robson

In February 2017 I had the good fortune to interview Mrs. Betty Foster, one of the four seamstresses who helped to create Princess Elizabeth's wedding gown in 1947. The following passages are only a brief sample of our hours-long conversation, which took place at her home in the south of England; transcribed in its entirety, my interview with Mrs. Foster stretches to dozens of pages.

Q: When did you begin work at Hartnell?

A: It was 1942, during the war but after the Blitz, although there was still a blackout and some air raids going on. I'd turned fourteen in May and finished school, and in August I started at Hartnell. I think I was the last apprentice to go into this workroom, because all the others after me came from the college. Miss Holliday, who trained me, she preferred apprentices, because when they went to college they were taught a certain way, weren't they? Whereas I didn't know anything. I knew nothing about dressmaking. I wanted to be a dress designer! And I ended up with Miss Holliday, who was Mr. Hartnell's senior seamstress. She'd been with him forever.

Q: Can you describe an ordinary working day at Hartnell?

A: I'd go in early, because if you got the train before seven it was cheaper. So I'd get to Hartnell's quite early, about eight o'clock, and we didn't start until half past eight. So I used to go to the Lyons Corner House nearby— there used to be one near the station on Bond Street—and I'd go in there and have a cup of tea and a bun. And then I'd make my way down to Bruton Place. That's where we went in—through the mews behind Bruton Street. We'd work through the morning, with a half-hour break at some point, although often it wasn't even that, and we had a very short lunch, too. And then we left at five. There was a canteen downstairs, so that's where we'd eat.

Q: How did you find out you'd be working on Princess Elizabeth's wedding dress?

A: Mr. Hartnell came to our table, Miss Holliday's table, with the sketch that the princess had chosen, and that's when he asked if Miss Holliday would make the dress. Would you believe she was hesitant? She made all the important dresses for him, and she was the oldest of his seamstresses, and had been there the longest. But she did hesitate, because it was such a big responsibility. And we said, "Oh, please, Miss Holliday!" So she gave in, but she made us promise to behave ourselves!

Q: Were you nervous when you worked on the gown?

A: Would you believe I wasn't? We didn't have much time but I don't remember feeling rushed. Of course we were used to having film stars ordering dresses for premieres and things like that, and often at the last minute. But I don't remember being a bundle of nerves. We always made the queen's dresses—the queen mum, you know—and we were used to working on important things.

Q: Can you tell me a bit about how the dress was made?

A: The princess had two fittings with a toile before the dress was embroidered, and then the pieces were sent to the embroidery room, and only then did it come back to the workroom where it was all put together. Before it was made up I had the task of making the buttons. I sewed all twenty-two buttonholes on the back and I also made the ▶

sleeves. Because I'd never made a buttonhole before, I had to practice on scrap bits of fabric. Only then was I allowed to work on the already meticulously embroidered dress. I remember sitting at my table and Miss Holliday telling all the other girls that no one was allowed to talk to me whilst I was practicing. After the dress had its final fitting, the seams were re-embroidered, because they couldn't do the embroidery until it had been properly fitted. That's when the embroiderers went back over the seams and filled in the empty spaces. I remember, too, how when everything was done, Miss Holliday let the other girls do a stitch or two, just so they could say they had worked on the wedding dress. And then, just before it was delivered to Buckingham Palace, we all got to see it, and the bridesmaids' dresses, too, because we hadn't seen them before—they'd been made up in another of the workrooms.

Q: What was Mr. Hartnell like?

A: You know, he wasn't at all proud or snobbish. He was really lovely, a friendly, friendly man. Just a wonderful person.

Q: Did you ever meet the queen?

A: Not then, although I was one of the guests at her Diamond Wedding celebration at Westminster Abbey. After she was married, we made up some clothes for her. I think she was going on a tour somewhere. We had to check to make sure they fitted properly, so I got to go to the Palace. Mam'selle—Germaine Davide, who was Mr. Hartnell's chief fitter— and Miss Holliday and I got in a taxi, and when we got to the palace we just went through the gates, because I think the policeman recognized Mam'selle. I remember we went in through the basement, where the kitchens are, and it was very cold and not very nice. There was a lift at the end, and we went upstairs. It was just us—we didn't see any servants. And we walked along this beautiful corridor, with all sorts of displays and cabinets and settees, and we walked past all the different apartments for different members of the royal family. And we got to her door and there was a plaque that said "Her Royal Highness Princess Elizabeth." Mam'selle knocked on the door and said, "Coo-ee," and we went in. Mam'selle went on ahead and left me and Miss Holliday in the dressing room, I suppose it was. And I looked out the window and I could see all the cars going down the Mall. And you know, when I've stood outside the palace since then I always look up and wonder which of those windows I looked out of that day.

Q: And did you meet Princess Elizabeth that day?

A: I didn't! The clothes all fit, so we didn't have to do any alterations. I did get to meet the Queen Mum once. It was during the war and we'd made her a beautiful gown, and the queen said, "Would the girls who worked on my dress like to see me wearing it?" I was chosen, and Miss Holliday, and somebody from the embroidery room. Miss Yvonne, the queen's saleslady, she introduced me. She said, "This is Betty, who helped to make your beautiful dress," and the queen said, "Oh, thank you so much. I do love it when they sparkle!" She was so lovely, and friendly, and standing on the other side were all the servants, seeing her already dressed. There was a big banquet at the palace that night, and the king was there, too.

Q: Can you tell me about the time the royal ladies visited when you were working on Princess Elizabeth's wedding gown?

A: Oh, yes. They wanted to see where the dress was being made, and when we learned they were coming we practiced our curtseys. I remember how they walked through the doors and we all did our curtseys, except we all bobbled up and down at different times. Mr. Hartnell brought the group over to our table, and he said, this is where the dress is being made, and then he explained how some Americans had hired the flat opposite—to see if they could get a glimpse of the wedding dress—and when he said that to Queen Mary, and explained how we'd had to cover the windows, she said, "What a bore!" in that very deep voice of hers.

Q: What do you think of the gown?

A: I thought it was beautiful. And you know, really, the embroidery made it. It absolutely made the dress. No one else could do embroidery like that, and it was so lovely. So romantic—like something out of a fairy tale. That's how I remember it. ↝

Grand-Mère's
Friday-Night Chicken

My mother made a version of this in the 1970s; I have updated it with ingredients that are readily available today, if not necessarily to cooks of 1947. This is the dish that came to mind when I tried to think of something that Miriam would have made, and though it is far from authentic in its origins, it is delicious and relatively easy to make.

Serves 4

1 medium orange
½ teaspoon fennel seeds
8 chicken thighs, skin-on and bone-in, about 3½ to 4 pounds
Salt and pepper
2 tablespoons extra-virgin olive oil
1 cup prunes, pitted and halved (quarter if especially large)
1 cup green olives, pitted
½ cup dry white wine or dry (white) vermouth

1. Position a rack in the center of the oven and heat the oven to 400°F.

2. Using a vegetable peeler, zest the orange in long strips; aim for 8 strips of zest with no white showing. Once zest is removed, halve the orange and juice. You'll need 2 tablespoons juice in total; set aside zest and juice. Crush the fennel seeds in a mortar and pestle or with the flat bottom of a drinking glass. Set aside.

3. Trim excess fat and skin from chicken thighs. Pat the chicken dry and season generously with salt and pepper. Heat the olive oil in a 12-inch oven-safe skillet, ideally cast iron, over medium-high heat. (See below if you don't have an oven-safe skillet.) Add the chicken to the skillet (in batches, if necessary) skin side down and cook until skin is well browned, 6 to 8 minutes.

4. Tilt the skillet and spoon off all but one tablespoon of the fat. Turn the chicken skin side up, sprinkle the prunes, olives, and fennel seeds around and over the pieces, and tuck the strips of orange zest in where you can. Pour the orange juice and wine over everything and sprinkle with an additional ½ teaspoon pepper. (If you don't have an oven-safe skillet, transfer the browned chicken to a casserole

dish, pour off excess fat, scrape remaining drippings into casserole dish, and proceed with remaining ingredients.)

5. Transfer the skillet or casserole dish to the oven and roast until cooked through (chicken should have an internal temperature of 165°F), 25 to 30 minutes. Remove from the oven and let stand for 5 minutes. Serve with fresh bread and a green salad. ∾

Reading Group Guide

1. How would you have reacted to the news of the royal wedding in 1947? Would you have been happy for a diversion from the depressing realities of postwar life? Or would you have been annoyed that so much attention and resources were being focused on one day when so many were struggling to simply survive?

2. How do you think you would have coped with the difficulties of the postwar period? Would you have carried on with your "chin up," as Ann does? Would you have danced away your cares, like some of her younger colleagues at Hartnell? Or would you have been bitter that, even after sacrificing so much, everyday life remained so hard and cheerless?

3. If you could snap your fingers and become a princess, with all of the duties and obligations and relentless attention that such a position entails, would you do it?

4. Why do you think Ann made a clean break with her past? Why did she never attempt to contact Miriam? Would you have done the same?

5. Can you close your eyes and picture Miriam's *Vél d'Hiv* embroideries? What do they look like to you?

6. If you had a chance to stand in Ann's shoes, would you tell your daughter or granddaughter the truth about your life?

7. Was Heather right to persevere in uncovering the secrets of Ann's past?

8. Do you think it's possible to accurately depict the life of a public figure who is still alive? And what do you think it must be like to be that public figure, and to know that strangers are reading about or watching the story of your life? Would it upset you, or would you find it entertaining to see what novelists and filmmakers get wrong— and what they get right?

9. Daniel has lines from a poem by Wilfred Owen tattooed on his arm. What poem or quote would appear in *your* tattoo (or on a T-shirt if you'd rather not make such a permanent gesture)?

10. What is your favorite iconic wedding gown—it doesn't have to have been worn by a royal bride—and why? ॐ

Suggestions for Further Reading

For reasons of space, the following bibliography is by necessity an incomplete record of the sources I consulted when researching *The Gown*. Not all of the books cited below are still in print, but most should be readily available to anyone with access to a good public library.

Benaim, Laurence, and Florence Müller.
    Dior: The New Look Revolution
Davies, Jennifer. *The Wartime Kitchen and
    Garden*
Evans, Paul, and Peter Doyle. *The 1940s Home*
Garfield, Simon. *Our Hidden Lives:
    The Remarkable Diaries of Post-War Britain*
Hartnell, Norman. *Silver and Gold*
Helm, Sarah. *If This Is a Woman:
    Inside Ravensbrück: Hitler's Concentration
    Camp for Women*
Judt, Tony. *Postwar: A History of Europe
    Since 1945*
Kelly, Angela. *Dressing the Queen: The Jubilee
    Wardrobe*
Last, Nella. *Nella Last's Peace: The Post-War
    Diaries of Housewife, 49*
Marrus, Michael, and Robert O. Paxton.
    Vichy France and the Jews
Palmer, Alexandra. *Dior*
Pick, Michael. *Be Dazzled!: Norman Hartnell,
    Sixty Years of Glamour and Fashion*
Pile, Jessica Jane. *Fashion Embroidery:
    Embroidery Techniques and Inspiration
    for Haute-Couture Clothing*
Rhodes, Margaret. *The Final Curtsey:
    A Royal Memoir by the Queen's Cousin*
*The Royal School of Needlework Book of
    Embroidery: A Guide to Essential Stitches,
    Techniques and Projects* ▶

Suggestions for Further Reading *(continued)*

Sebba, Anne. *Les Parisiennes: How the Women of Paris Lived, Loved, and Died Under Nazi Occupation*
Smith, Sally Bedell. *Elizabeth the Queen: The Life of a Modern Monarch*
Williams, Kate. *Young Elizabeth: The Making of the Queen*

Links to online sources related to the royal wedding, among them British Pathé newsreel footage, documentaries, audio recordings of BBC radio coverage, and websites associated with the Royal Collection and Hand & Lock, may be found at my website: www.jennifer-robson.com ᔐ

Discover great authors, exclusive offers, and more at hc.com.